A. McPartlin

Below the Big Blue Sky

ZAFFRE

First published in Great Britain in 2020 by
ZAFFRE
80–81 Wimpole St, London W1G 9RE

A CIP catalogue record for this book is
available from the British Library.

Hardback ISBN: 978–1–83877–078–5
Trade Paperback ISBN: 978–1–83877–079–2

Also available as an ebook

1 3 5 7 9 10 8 6 4 2

Typeset by IDSUK (Data Connection) Ltd
Printed and bound in Great Britain by Clays Ltd, Elcograf S.p.A.

MIX
Paper from
responsible sources
FSC® C018072

Zaffre is an imprint of Bonnier Books UK
www.bonnierbooks.co.uk

In Memory of Catherine 'Terry' McPartlin

Born 15th October 1935
Died 22nd March 2016

We loved ya, Terry

Prologue

OUTSIDE THE BIRDS WERE singing. Inside the small, over-crowded, slightly pungent hospice bedroom Molly Hayes was holding her daughter's hand in hers. Light streamed through the window opposite, warming Molly's face and hurting her tired eyes. Despite ever-encroaching exhaustion she remained awake, eyes wide open and staring at her once-beautiful child now an unrecognisable, bloated, wretched being, battling to breathe. Scattered around her and sleeping on chairs were the rest of Molly's family. Her husband, Jack, sitting upright, hands clasped, his chin resting on his chest and head occasionally bobbing like a comatose man on a train. His low, rolling snores providing the soundtrack to Rabbit's departure from earth. Molly's son Davey rested against the wall, his sister Grace using his shoulder as a pointed pillow. Their breathing in contrast to their dying baby sister's, slow and steady. Rabbit's best friend Marjorie lay on the floor, her rolled-up jacket between her head and a cold hard tile. She made very little sound, maybe even none at all.

Molly maintained a calm facade. She knew death was imminent. She was one hundred per cent aware that any second now, Rabbit would leave and never return. *I love ya, Rabbit. I love ya. I love ya so much. Your mammy loves ya.* Then out of nowhere Rabbit found that last burst of strength and gripped Molly's hand, frightening the living shite out of her. She levitated off the chair. 'Frigging fuckersticks,' she mumbled under her breath and, her hand on her heart, she briefly considered whether or not her youngest was trying to take her with her. When her heart resumed its normal rhythm she steadied herself and leaned in towards her dying daughter. 'Rabbit?' she whispered. 'Are you still with me, love?'

'Have to catch the van, Ma,' Rabbit said, and Molly felt her soul shatter. *This is it*. Her eyes filled, nose blocked, ears buzzed, throat burned. 'Safe trip, Rabbit,' she said. One moment later, her child's grip loosened and she was gone. Molly sat in silence; she didn't cry out or scream or even whisper to her family to wake up. She didn't press the buzzer to alert the nurses or move to the hallway to tell the first passerby. Instead she sat perfectly still. Outside on the windowsill a bird twittered. Inside and just underneath that window, the heater hummed. A spider tootled across the window before jumping onto the wall. Molly sat up straight, her head and spine perfectly aligned, caressing her daughter's head. At the tender age of forty, Rabbit Hayes was dead. Molly's youngest and bravest child was dead. Her legs didn't move, not even a muscle. She returned to holding Rabbit's hand, waiting for it to cool and stiffen. The clock on the wall read 5.23 a.m. when Rabbit spoke of getting into the van. She repeated *5.23* over and over in her head. It was important to remember the time of death and the date. The twenty-eighth of April 2014. Oh, and the weather. She knew the weather would be important to Rabbit. It was warm and bright but the sun was accompanied by an almost imperceptible, hazy rain.

2

Davey was the first to wake. He sensed immediately that Rabbit was gone. He sat up slowly and stared at his rigid mother.

'Ma,' he whispered urgently. 'Ma, look at me, Ma.'

But Molly was somewhere else. He nudged Grace, who woke with a start. 'I'm up, just sort the lunches,' she half shouted before absent-mindedly rubbing dribble from her chin and blinking to calibrate her blurred vision. Then it dawned on her, *shit, I'm not home. This is no ordinary day.* Rabbit's corpse came into sharp focus. *Oh no.*

'She's gone,' Davey said, and Grace was on her feet and immediately crying.

'Oh no, Rabbit!' It was strange because she couldn't quite believe or accept it, even though Rabbit had been riddled with cancer and was dying for days. It seemed impossible. There was stone where there had been a person – more than a person, her sister and friend. 'Oh no,' she cried and struggled to swallow wave after wave of newly formed snot. Rabbit's best friend in the world, Marjorie, sat up leaning against the wall, her back straight and hot tears pouring from her wide eyes. Jack came round slowly. He heard of his daughter's death before he saw it. He stood up, straightened his clothes and walked over to his wife. He placed his hand on her shoulder. She was so still and quiet, possibly the most still and quiet she had been in his fifty years of knowing and loving her. He then moved in and took Rabbit in his arms.

'Jesus, Da, don't move her,' Grace squealed.

He held her tight and kissed her ear. 'There's no pain now,' he said, tears flowing freely. 'At least not for you, my baby girl.'

He reached out for Molly's hand; she grabbed it.

'I can't lose you too, Molly,' he said, holding onto Rabbit. 'Don't you leave me now,' he warned, and Molly nodded.

'On condition you stop rubbing snot on her fuckin' corpse, Jack,' Molly said, and he pulled back.

'You're right of course, love.' He let Rabbit go. Molly smoothed down Rabbit's crumpled, rumpled clothes.

'You won't leave me too, Molly?' he insisted. It was preying on his mind, as his wife had been hospitalised following heart trouble that occurred while visiting Rabbit in the hospice two days previously. The only reason she wasn't in a hospital bed herself was because she needed to be by her daughter's side.

'How could I? You'd be lost without me,' she said, and she gave him a smile and a wink to let him know that despite a dead child and a dodgy ticker, she wasn't going anywhere. But looking back, mentally and emotionally, she was already gone.

Part One

D-Day

Chapter One

Davey

A TRAUMATISED DAVEY LEFT THE hospice an hour after his sister died and got in the car and drove to her home. Davey had abandoned singer-songwriter Casey's American tour nine days earlier when the call came that Rabbit was being transferred to a hospice. He knew instantly it was the end, unlike his insane parents, who tried to find a cure and/or miracle up until the last second. Casey supported him abandoning the tour. Davey was more than her drummer: they'd been close friends for too many years to count. She assured him she would be fine and that his drum tech knew the set inside out.

'Don't get too used to him,' he'd said.

'No chance,' she'd said. It was comforting because nine days ago his job as Casey's drummer was all he had. Davey had a strong support network in Nashville; it was half the reason he'd fought his family and begged his sister for the chance to raise her twelve-year-old daughter. It wasn't his plan or intention to put himself forward as guardian, but over the course of the eight long days and nights watching his sister die, and being party to the arguments as to who was fit to care for Juliet – also known to those who loved her most as Bunny – he thought, why not me? His parents Jack and Molly were too old. His sister Grace had four boys already packed into a tiny house. Why not the guy with more money than sense, no wife, no kids and a hole in his life to fill? Anyway the child picked him. They'd always had a special, close relationship, conducted from afar. She knew he had room for her in his home and heart; what she didn't know was how impulsive, selfish, clueless and messed-up he was. In her final days Rabbit agreed to Davey caring for her daughter. The rest of the family were up in arms but she was steadfast. 'Just love her, Davey, that's all anyone really needs.' Of course the cancer had gone into her brain by then. *What was I thinking? What was she thinking? Even with brain cancer our Rabbit was smarter than that. Oh God, they're all right, I am a gobshite! What have I done?*

He walked through the door, unshaven, hungry but too sick and sad to eat. He needed to shower and to change out of clothes that smelled of antiseptic and death. On the way to the bathroom he realised that his GPS seemed a little off when he walked into a wall. Then he was standing fully dressed in front of a thundering shower, the steam rising overhead. He stayed there for a while just staring at the water pounding the tiles and under it for even longer, drowning a little physically and emotionally.

When he emerged, soaked through and more miserable than refreshed, he looked in the mirror. He was wearing his pain, having aged ten years in nine days. Aged forty-four, he was still handsome, like a pampered musician should be, but he was weary now.

He dreaded telling Juliet of her mother's passing. He didn't wake her. As long as she slept her mother was still alive.

When dressed, Davey's heavy legs walked him down the stairs and into the kitchen. He just sat in silence until he heard the sounds of her feet hitting the floor above him, the patter as she made her way to the bathroom, the door closing and opening, her feet on the stairs, that creak in the second-last step. He felt his back and neck stiffen. His chair was facing the kitchen door. The child walked in wearing pyjamas with red stars on them; her long brown hair, freshly brushed and loose, fell down her back. She looked so like her mother at her age except for the horn-rimmed glasses and eyepatch Rabbit had worn for so many years. She stared at her clean but dishevelled uncle, biting back emotion.

'Oh,' she whispered.

'I'm so sorry, Bunny.' He stood and she automatically stepped back.

'OK,' she said, and she crossed her arms, hugging herself. 'It's OK.'

He moved to hug her but she shrank back – she didn't want to be touched. He got the message instantly.

'I'm here,' he said, and he meant it. She nodded. 'I know.'

She sat at the table remaining silent and she didn't cry. She picked at a boiled egg and after a few minutes she asked to be excused.

'Of course, Bunny,' he said. 'Of course.'

She pushed her chair away from the table. 'Don't call me Bunny. Rabbit's gone. I'm not her bunny anymore.' Her voice was raspy and laced with pain.

He put his head in his hands, fighting a migraine. Juliet walked up the stairs, taking two steps at a time, went into her mother's room, wrapped herself in her duvet and fell asleep hugging her pillow until late afternoon. And Davey? Well, he just sat on the chair in his dead sister's kitchen wondering what the hell he was going to do.

'You're going to make mistakes and I don't care about any of that as long as you make her feel loved,' Rabbit said in his head.

'I love you,' Davey roared up the stairs.

Oh Rabbit, what the fuck have we done?

Chapter Two

Grace

GRACE PUT HER KEY in the door and opened it to find her husband and four boys gathered on the stairs, just waiting for her. She'd phoned ahead from the car.

'She's dead,' was all she could bring herself to say.

Lenny moved towards her and took her in his arms. 'I'm so sorry, Gracie.'

'Thanks,' she said.

'Sorry, Ma,' said her eldest son, Stephen, eighteen-year-old, college-going and possibly failing.

Lenny stepped aside to allow Stephen to hug his mother.

Next came sixteen-year-old Bernard. 'I love ya, Ma,' he said. Bernard was a sports nut who lived on the pitch and loved his mammy loudly and proudly. If he noticed the other kids laughing at him it didn't bother him. Bernard was what his granny Molly called a dote.

'I know you do, son. I love you too,' she said.

Fourteen-year-old Ryan stood behind his brother; he didn't hug his mother, he just took in her appearance. 'You look like shite, Ma.' He wasn't being cruel, he was calling it like it was. Ryan was Grace's problem child, in that he had a leanings towards criminality. He'd robbed his school friends' mobile

11

phones, sold them to a Chinese-run phone shop in a back-street alley in town. He took the money he'd made and played on the stock market. The kid turned out to be a financial genius, so when he was eventually caught he could afford to pay all the kids back enough money for new mobile phones and made an apology tour around the school, using his auntie Rabbit's cancer as a reason for his errant behaviour. *The little bollocks.* He got away with it, but Grace was watching him like a hawk.

'I can run you a bath?' he asked, but she shook her head.

'No thanks, son. I'm so tired I think I'd drown.'

Lenny disappeared into the kitchen. She could hear him boiling the kettle and cooking up a storm.

'Was she scared, Ma?' Bernard asked.

'No, love.'

'How do ya know?' Ryan said.

'I just do.'

Nine-year-old Jeff, Grace's youngest son, was sitting on the stairs, wearing a way too snug-fitting tracksuit.

Grace sat down beside him. 'You all right, son?'

'I should have said goodbye,' he said. He was referring to the night all the kids had lined up to say goodbye to a semi-comatose Rabbit. Jeffrey was so freaked he'd bottled it.

'You were there, and that's enough.'

'I'm a baby,' he said.

'No, you're not.'

'Ryan says I am.'

'Ryan, don't call your brother a baby.'

'For the record I called him a fat, crying Buddha baby,' Ryan said, and Grace was too exhausted to fight him.

'Don't mind him, Jeff, you're doing great.'

'I've lost four pounds, Ma,' Jeffrey said.

'I'm proud of you, son.'

When the doctor described her youngest son as obese and pre-diabetic it had been a massive shock. How did she let that happen? And pre-diabetic? The child hadn't even made it to double digits. She'd hated herself. *I did this and I will undo it.* Jeffrey's life changed that day, and since then he'd been exercising, drinking water, living on greens and hating every second of it but trying his absolute best, mostly because of an abject fear of losing his legs. Grace wasn't a subtle woman.

'Do you want to be sick like your auntie Rabbit?' she'd asked when he refused to eat his lettuce.

'She has cancer, Ma.'

'Diabetes is worse.'

'What? No way. Nothing's worse than cancer.'

'Tell me that when you're walking around on two stumps.'

Jeffrey whinged about his new diet regime but he was both terrified and committed. *Four pounds down, Rabbit.*

Grace was always and ever a wild beauty, voluptuous and pretty as a picture, but she had a propensity towards putting on weight and had been watching her waistline since she could remember. Rabbit had been so tall and slim. She could eat anything. Grace used to say she was the lucky one, but that was before the cancer. She sat on the stairs hugging her youngest son. Ryan tried to push past them.

'Out of the way, fatso.'

Grace stood up to let him pass. 'Just stop, Ryan, please.'

As soon as she turned her back Ryan gave Jeffrey the finger.

'Don't give your brother the finger,' Lenny said, emerging from the kitchen.

Grace helped her youngest son to his feet. 'Anything else on your mind, love?'

'Yeah.'

'What?'

'I'm frigging starving.'

'Eggs for breakfast,' Lenny said.

'I'm going to have a lie-down,' she said.

'Yeah, you go to bed, love. I'll wake you in a couple of hours.' Lenny kissed her cheek. She looked into his kind eyes and brushed a hair from his handsome face before he whispered 'I love you' and turned to follow his hungry son.

'Eggs are gross,' Jeffrey shouted as he made his way to the kitchen.

'Eggs are protein,' she responded.

She noticed a stack of unopened post which had piled up over the previous week. She mindlessly flicked through it as she walked up the stairs: bills mostly, a catalogue from a holiday company she'd used once ten years ago, and then as she opened the door to her bedroom a small white envelope fell to the floor. With scribbled handwriting and no corporate stamp, it looked like a card. She opened it, expecting to see an invite of some sort or maybe a mass card from a neighbour who'd heard Rabbit was dying. *Dead. She's dead now.* She'd closed her bedroom door before she realised it was from St James's Hospital where she'd had her BRCA gene test a few weeks before. Her heart and pulse gathered pace, banging like a drum in her neck and wrists. Her palms sweaty, her knees weak, eyes suddenly unfocused, the words seemed to float off the

14

page. She was positive for the BRCA2 gene. The actual gene identifying under BRCA2 was written and presented as a long serial number. *Is that the same number that killed Rabbit?* The letter went on to say that she was on the high-risk register and advised her to make an appointment with a counsellor. Her knees slowly gave way and she allowed herself to sink to the floor where she curled up into a ball, hugged herself tightly and cried her heart out.

Grace had dithered about taking the test since her sister's diagnosis four years previously. She'd spoken to her mother about whether or not it was a good idea. Of course Molly didn't want to talk about it and thought it was a terrible idea. 'You look for trouble, you find trouble.'

'But Rabbit has cancer, Ma.'

'I don't have cancer. I'm in my seventies. Rabbit was just unlucky.'

'Rabbit has the gene.'

'Because she's fucking unlucky.'

'Yeah, but where did it come from?' Grace asked. 'Do you think cancer stopped Nanna Mulvey's heart?'

'Don't be ridiculous, cancer doesn't give you a heart attack.'

'What if she had it and she didn't know?'

'Cancer is hard to miss, love.'

'What did her sister die of?' Grace asked. Molly couldn't remember – she'd died before Molly was born and Molly's mother didn't like to talk about her.

'What age was she when she died?'

'I don't know, twenty-something,' Molly said.

'Crap. Maybe it was cancer.'

'I think it was polio.'

'Is that the one with the iron lung?'

'That's TB – your great-uncle Maurice had that, although it's possible she had a touch of TB too, it was bleedin' rampant back then.'

'So polio and a touch of TB killed her?'

'Who knows, love? If she was anything like my mother it was misery that did it in the end.'

'Right,' Grace said. 'No cancer on your side, then?'

'No cancer,' Molly said.

'What about Da's, Ma?'

Molly turned away and made her way to the sink to make noise, clanging pans and splashing water. Grace would not be deterred.

'Ma?' She picked up a towel, ready to receive a clean pan.

'They didn't use the word, no one really talked about any-thing back then, especially not sickness and death, and your da was only a child when his mother died,' Molly said.

'Cancer?' Grace said.

'His father wouldn't say, so we can only surmise.'

Grace's heart sank. 'What age was she?'

'Early thirties, I think,' Molly said.

'So there is cancer in the family.'

'We can't be sure. Besides, you're older than both of them when they were diagnosed.'

'It doesn't work like that, Ma!'

'Well, your da doesn't have cancer, does he?'

'No, Ma, he doesn't but that's not the point!'

'You don't have the gene, Grace, and I don't want to hear mention of it again.'

And that was the end of the conversation. Grace pushed it to the back of her mind where it resided, chipping away at her little by little as the cancer ate away at her sister, but when it became clear that Rabbit was incurable Grace decided to go for it. She said nothing to no one, thought it better to keep it to herself. If the result proved negative there would be no reason to mention it. The waiting list was long. It took over a year to get the appointment; when it finally came through the door she reconsidered even attending but in the end, and after six weeks of mental torment, Grace felt she had no option but to take the test. It took all her courage to walk through that door. She tried to self-soothe. It was probably going to be fine.

Except now it wasn't fine. Rabbit was dead and she had the gene. She was perimenopausal and she had the gene. She had four boys, the youngest only nine, and she had the gene. She had done none of the things she'd planned on doing, like fly a plane or climb a mountain or even work in a job she was passionate about, and she had the bloody, fudging, flipping gene. She lay on her bedroom floor for two hours, terrorised. She heard Lenny walk up the stairs so she dragged herself to her feet and hid in the bathroom, running water, washing her tear-stained face.

Lenny popped his head around the door.

'Did you sleep, love?' he asked.

'Yeah,' she lied. He turned her around to look at her. He felt her forehead.

'Ryan's right, you look like shite.'

I have the gene.

'I hope you're not coming down with anything.'

I have the gene.

'My sister just died.' *I have the gene.*

'I know, love,' he said, and he took her in his arms and hugged her close.

I have the gene.

'Why don't I make you something to eat?'

I have the gene. 'Thanks, Lenny.'

'You're probably starving.'

'No, I'm grand.'

I have the gene.

He kissed her cheek. 'I know it's bleak but everything's going to be fine.'

'I know,' she lied.

Except I have the gene.

Chapter Three

Marjorie

MARJORIE HUGGED HERSELF AND tried to prevent shivering while sitting on the cold concrete ground. She felt numb and sick and sore. She ached from head to toe and wondered if her pain came even close to the suffering her best friend had endured during her four-year cancer battle. *How did she do it? How did she keep going? I can barely breathe.* She couldn't stomach anything; even water seemed to choke and burn her. A woman passed her and did a double take.

'Are you all right, love? Did you have an accident?'

'No.'

'Are you sure? You look like you've taken a beating.'

'No.'

The woman walked on and Marjorie pulled out a small mirror from her bag. *SWEET JESUS!* Usually pretty, lovely, tidy, dainty, blonde, curly, doll-faced Marjorie Shaw's hair was flat on one side from having slept on her jacket on the floor. Her mascara was halfway down her face; despite being waterproof, and maybe because of it, it appeared as black balls of residue resting on her cheeks. Her eye shadow was rubbed away and her eyelids were red and sore. She'd bitten her lip, so that part of it was swollen and a slightly off-purple colour.

Her usually pristine clothes looked slept-in and crumpled. She had a coffee stain on her white collar, and she smelled of sweat and something sour.

She didn't know why she'd come here. She'd just left the hospice and saw a bus with a familiar number on it. She got on and rode it to her mother's house. It made no sense; Vera Shaw was the last woman on earth to offer anyone comfort but there she was, staring at her mother's perfectly manicured gardens and her imposing red-brick Victorian house. It looked dark inside, but that house always seemed dark. Her mother's car was parked outside. She was in. Maybe she'd even noticed Marjorie had been sitting on cold concrete across the road for half an hour. Her mother wouldn't appreciate seeing her in this state. She'd have something cruel to say about it. *What the hell am I doing here?* The last time they spoke it had ended in an argument. Marjorie made a difficult courtesy call to her mother to let her know that her ex-husband Neil was having a baby with a woman called Debbie.

'Well, that's what you get for sleeping with that Davey Hayes fool – your husband having your baby with another woman.'

'It's not my baby, Mother.'

'Now it never will be.'

She had slept with her best friend's brother while married to Neil. They ended up together in her marital bed when he was home two years previously on holiday. They had a long and complicated history. She lost her virginity to Davey Hayes; she'd loved him since they were both kids. It was never going to go anywhere. If she hadn't been so unhappy with her husband she wouldn't have risked her marriage, but she did and he caught her, threw her out and now she lived alone in a rented apartment. Davey apologised for blowing up her life before he skipped back to America to live out his ridiculous touring rock and roll life. She forgave him, not just because he was Rabbit's brother but because it was Davey. The Hayeses were her family and Molly Hayes the mother she'd never had. She would always forgive Davey.

'And that bloody fool doesn't want you – tainted goods,' Vera said, before following up with a pious, 'You reap what you sow.'

'Who are you to judge me?' Marjorie asked.

'I'm your mother.'

'You're a cold-hearted bitch whose vagina I was unlucky enough to slide out of.' After years of her mother's taunts Marjorie had snapped and screamed the insult. It was the first time she'd said anything remotely like that to her mother, but Rabbit was dying and she was angry and hurt.

'If only you *had* slid out, Marjorie, my life would have been very, very different,' Vera said, and hung up. Marjorie had been a difficult birth and Vera's arduous labour had ended in a symphysiotomy, a barbaric method of cutting a child out of a woman's vagina that left Vera Shaw with lifelong pain and discomfort. If it didn't drive her husband away, it certainly contributed to his leaving. After years of living a lie, five days' working abroad and weekends locked in his bedroom at home, Marjorie's father admitted he had another family in the UK, two boys and a girl. He left that night. Marjorie was sixteen. Her mother never mentioned her father's name again and Marjorie never sought him or his offspring out. Her relationship with her cold, bitter, angry mother had been trying from the start. *I must be insane.* She stood up and brushed herself down, and as she hailed a taxi she could have sworn she saw her mother's lace curtain twitch.

In her apartment, she melted into a bath and vacated her own mind for a while, lying still in warm water before holding her breath and sliding under. *Rabbit, are you there?*

I'm here.

I miss you already.

Well if you don't breathe in the next few seconds you won't be missing me for long.

She lasted two minutes before she began struggling for air. She emerged with a splash, a gulp and a gurgle, the cold air bristling her skin and a pain in her heart so sharp it felt as though she was being skewered. *I want to see you! I want to touch you! Rabbit?* The pain remained, even after washing her teeth, when her mouth was clean and her hair restored to its soft, bouncy self. Even when her body was cleansed of stale air and all trace of death had been vigorously scrubbed from every pore, her sore eyes and lips moisturised and protected – even then the hurt persisted. She knew what it was; she knew it was the agony of loss, so she found a little comfort in her discomfort. Searing pain made her feel closer to Rabbit somehow. She wiped the steam from the mirror, revealing a woman who looked like someone else. She felt like someone else, too. Marjorie without Rabbit was someone else.

'Who are you now, Marjorie Shaw?' she asked.

Her reflection had no answer.

Chapter Four

Jack

JACK WAS SEVENTY-SEVEN at the time of his youngest daughter's death. He'd lived a long and happy life up to that point. It had its share of loss and worry and sometimes even fear, but he had made enough good choices to be able to look back with pride and good humour.

In the immediate aftermath of Rabbit's death, Jack slipped out and into the corridor before anyone else. She was gone, and he couldn't stand to be in the room that took her for one second longer. He sat in the hospital garden, on a damp bench, the same one he'd sat on the day before when she was alive. *How extraordinary*, he thought. He remembered Rabbit's birth in a car sales garage forecourt, with his wife screaming and the salesman threatening to throw up his lunch, Jack at the business end, panicked and telling everyone to calm down and calling to the head that was crowning in his wife's nethers: 'Come on, little one, the world is waiting.' One moment she wasn't there, the next – and so suddenly and unbelievably – she was in his arms, screaming blue murder, eyes screwed shut and fists balled ready to take it all on. She did take it on. By God, she took it on. Then that morning she had fought her last fight; one moment she was here and the next she was

23

gone. Her birth so joyful, her death so sorrowful, yet both so natural. Rabbit had stepped into his life and filled it with light before stepping out.

Daddy loves you, Rabbit. Daddy will miss you every day till I join you somewhere, or if you're right and there's no life after death, I'll join you in the abyss. My Rabbit.

When Jack was sad, he preferred to be alone. It wasn't hiding, as everyone always knew where he was; he was just unavailable. An invisible sign appeared: 'GONE TO LUNCH'. At least that's how Molly would put it.

'Where's me da?' one of the kids would ask.

'Gone to lunch,' she'd say.

'What's up with him now?'

'Ah, who knows, but leave the auld fella to it.'

He always found a project to keep people at bay when he was gone to lunch. He'd read a book or categorise his old albums; he'd tear down a wall or build a shed. In said shed he'd build replica ships in glass bottles or paint clay sculptures – anything to be alone.

When he and Molly returned home, she took off her shoes and sat at the kitchen table thumbing the huge stack of folders they had filled with possible drug trials that would accept Rabbit. It was folly. Rabbit's consultant made shit of every one. 'They'll take your money and her last comfort. She's dying,' he'd said. Now she was gone and the files were still piled high on the Hayeses' kitchen table. Jack couldn't watch his wife sit and stare into the middle distance anymore. He mentioned Rabbit's childhood photographs as an excuse to sneak off to the attic. He pulled down the ladder, turned on the attic light, riffled through boxes and found something unexpected: his own diaries from the forties right up to the mid-nineties when he'd just stopped writing, he couldn't remember why. There they all were, year after year. Rabbit would be there, amongst those pages. In his diaries, Rabbit lived. He picked one of the boxes and sat down on the beanbag before opening it and reading to himself. *There you are, love.*

Hiya, Da.

I'm reading about when you were four and you barked like a dog every time the postman knocked on the door. Do you remember?

He used to shove the letters in my mouth, rub me head and call me Rover, he heard her say.

That's right, love, he chuckled to himself.

By 3.30 that morning Jack Hayes was officially gone to lunch.

Chapter Five

Juliet

JULIET GOT OUT OF her mother's bed at 3 p.m. Davey was sleeping by then, overcome by exhaustion. She got dressed and snuck outside. She didn't want to alert him to the fact that she was up and about. He would only want to feed her, rub her, hug her or talk to her. She didn't want food or comfort; she just wanted to move for a bit. She walked down the street and her twelve-year-old friend and neighbour, Kyle, must have been watching from his window because he was cycling by her side within seconds.

'I heard,' he said.

Juliet kept walking.

'I'm sorry.'

'What are you sorry for, you didn't kill her.'

'No, but it's crap so I'm sorry.'

'Thanks.'

'So what now?'

'I move to America with Davey.'

He stopped dead on the bike. 'Wha—?' he shouted.

'I'm going to be living with Davey.'

'Ah no,' he said.

'That's what's happening, Kyle.'

'Ah but—'

'But what? Did you think I was going to be staying here, living across the road from you, and everything would stay the same?'

'No, but—'

'No. Nothing's going to be same. My ma is dead. My life here is over.'

'Jaysus, that's intense,' he said.

'Yeah, it is.' A tear escaped and ran down her face. It was real: her mother was gone and she was moving to America with the uncle she adored but really didn't know. She had cleaved to him over the last days of her mother's life. He was available to her. He helped her. He was kind and gave her time when her grandparents were off chasing miracles and Grace was halving herself between Rabbit and her four boys. She didn't want to be any trouble. Her grandmother was suffering with her heart. Grace was already so stretched, and Rabbit needed peace of mind. So it made sense to pair up with Davey. He wanted her. She didn't want to let him down. She didn't want to let anyone down. But that was then, when her mother needed reassurance. Now her mother was gone, and in the cold light of day, going to a strange land with a relative stranger terrified her.

She sat on a neighbour's wall. Kyle sat on his bike in front of her.

'I'm really gonna miss ya, Juliet.'

'Me too,' she said.

'I think I might love ya.' He blushed ruby red.

'We're kids, Kyle,' she said with a flash of her granny's patented disdain.

'I know.'

'I can't be dealing with this.' She got up and walked back towards the house.

'Yeah, sorry,' he said, 'my bad.'

She walked indoors, crept up the stairs and back into her mother's bedroom. She looked out the window and Kyle was still on his bike outside her house.

Weirdo, she thought, but despite her whole world being turned upside down and inside out, despite her pain and confusion, her fear and anger, a tiny smile crept across her lips as she looked up into the big blue sky. She pictured her ma lying on the grass, sunglasses on, staring into the sky. In her head she stood beside her.

What ya doin', Ma?

Enjoying the view.

Juliet looked around the small garden with its patchy grass, dodgy fence and her broken-down playhouse. *What view?*

Some people live in fancy houses by the sea but we all share the sky, Bunny. Isn't it beautiful? Juliet lay down beside her ma and looked up at all that blue . . . She exhaled and felt warm.

Yeah, Ma, she said, and then the picture faded and she was standing alone and cold again. She slid under her mother's covers and put herself back to bed. She hugged her mother's pillow and inhaled its scent. *You're still here, Ma, you're in the hospice and I'm going to visit this evening. I'll paint your nails and rub cream into your head and tell you what Kyle said, and you'll say, 'I told ya so. How could he not love you? Everyone loves you.' Maybe later Francie or Jay Byrne will call in and make us all laugh, or Granny will say*

28

something inappropriate. We'll lie together in the bed and share a sandwich, you'll pretend to eat it and I'll pretend I believe you and we'll snuggle. I'll tell you that I love you and you'll breathe me in. I'm just a little tired now. I'm going to take a nap and I'll see you later, OK Ma? I'll see you later.

By the time Juliet finally fell asleep, her mother's pillow was soaked through.

Chapter Six

Molly

THAT EVENING THE ADULTS convened at the funeral home and met the funeral director, Vincent Farren, a heavyset man in his sixties with a black Elvis-style wig, a pink pudgy face and blood-red lips. Beside Vincent stood a huge man-child with a similar pudgy face and dark hair but, in contrast to the older man, a thin top lip sprinkled with bumfluff. They were both dressed in identical suits complete with silk waistcoats. Molly was a little rotund herself, but she kept her short hair a respectable cool blonde and wore clothes suitable for her age and size. She kept herself well, not like these two jokers. She found it hard to look away from them. *They belong in the circus.* She'd picked the funeral home because of its close proximity to the house. She briefly wondered if she should have shopped around.

'Our deepest sympathy,' Vincent said.

Bollocks, Molly thought, *you couldn't give a shite. Show me the money. Isn't that right, Rabbit?* But Rabbit didn't reply. Rabbit was gone.

'Thanks.'

'Please sit down,' he said, and he directed Molly, Jack, Davey and Grace to red velvet-cushioned chairs. He dragged one over, placed it directly in front of them and sat.

'Tea, coffee, water?' Vincent asked. All of them shook their heads.

'Are you sure? Edmund can make anything you want, within reason – we're currently out of yak's milk.' He laughed a little and nodded to himself after he made this remark, clearly his way of lightening the mood. *My child is dead and you're about as funny as a fart in a car.*

No one laughed. Vincent cleared his throat.

'Right then, let's talk about Rabbit's wishes,' Vincent said. The man-child with the light bumfluff moustache stood behind Vincent, watching over him like a member of the secret service. Molly looked from Vincent to the man-child and back to Vincent.

'Let's make something clear, Vincent. This will be about what I want. You know why?' And she wasn't just talking to Vincent, she was talking to her family.

'I'm Rabbit's mother and mothers know best.'

'Ma, Rabbit—'

'Don't start, Grace.'

She made it clear to all that she was making all the decisions and in some cases (where it mattered) they would be contrary to what Rabbit wanted. Grace mumbled something about her mother being a frigging Nazi. Davey stayed quiet.

'As nice as this place is I don't want her parked in here,' she said.

'Laid out is the term we use, Mrs Hayes,' Vincent said.

'Whatever, we want her home.'

'That can be arranged.'

'And I want an open coffin – we'll find space for her in the dining room.'

Jack didn't argue. Molly knew he'd be happy to have his youngest under his roof one last time. He nodded his support for his wife's plan and took a moment to dry his red-rimmed eyes.

'An open coffin in the dining room!' Grace said, aghast.

Molly turned on her. 'Well I'm hardly going to put her in the bleedin' shed, am I?'

'She'd hate that, and where would she even fit?' Davey interjected, but Molly was way ahead of them. She had worked out everything.

'We'll move the dining table by the window. We'll put Rabbit against the wall.'

'But every nosy auld one will be looking in on her,' Grace said.

'That's what curtains are for, Grace,' Molly said.

Grace turned to Davey. 'Say something.'

'Or we could just put the lid on the coffin like normal people, Ma.'

'Don't be cheeky, Davey,' Molly said.

'I'm a grown man,' he mumbled, but he didn't have the heart to argue with her. He did mention his concern that seeing Rabbit laid out, cold as marble in the dining room, would be distressing for Juliet.

'Never mind Jeffrey!' Grace said. 'He's already having nightmares that his aunt is the fucking Marshmallow Man from *Ghostbusters*.' She turned to Vincent. 'Excuse my language, Vincent, but my sister was very puffy towards the end.'

'Excused and understood,' he said, nodding his head sympathetically. Silent Ed just stood there rubbing his non-existent moustache.

'She'll be fine. It'll be good for Juliet to see her mammy one last time,' Molly said to Davey.

'And what about Jeff?' Grace asked.

'Grace, Jeff isn't scared of Rabbit, he just likes giant marsh-mallows.'

'Don't make me kill you, old woman,' Grace said, in a tone that suggested she meant it.

'Now, Grace, don't threaten your mammy,' Jack said.

Vincent decided it was time to shift gears. 'Would you like to see Rabbit?' he asked.

'Oh yes,' Molly said, but the rest of the Hayes clan remained silent. He brought them to a side room and closed the door. In the centre lay Rabbit in a temporary coffin. He and Silent Ed moved in unison and lifted the lid slowly and carefully, revealing Rabbit's face poking through a blue satin sheet.

'Bloody hell,' Grace almost screamed, 'she looks like the Virgin Mary!'

'We're just waiting on her clothes,' Vincent said apologetically.

'If the Virgin Mary was a tart.' Molly turned to Vincent. 'Jaysus, Vincent, go a little lighter on the make-up, will you, love?'

'Certainly.'

'Besides the heavy make-up, she's lovely, isn't she, Grace? Isn't she lovely?'

Grace grimaced. She wasn't lovely. She was a Virgin Mary geisha.

'She didn't really wear make-up, Ma,' Grace said.

'Well, that's because she had flawless skin and perfect cheek-bones,' said Molly. 'Now her skin is buggered and her bones are a distant memory so she'll need some make-up, just not the full Alice Cooper.'

Vincent nodded. 'Of course, good note.'

Silent Ed stifled something approaching a giggle. Vincent gave him a filthy look. Vincent sought clarification on their coffin choice but Molly was exhausted, Jack was tearful and Grace and Davey were sullen. It wasn't a good time to make any more decisions.

'We'll get back to you on that in the morning, Vincent,' Molly said.

'Of course, it's been a long day. The wake is being scheduled for tomorrow evening?'

'That's right.'

'Would you like me to engage a priest or do you have some-one local?'

'We do – Father Frank,' Molly said.

'It's not a religious service, Ma,' Grace said through gritted teeth.

'Didn't say it was, Grace. I just said we had someone local.'

'No religion, Ma,' Davey warned. Rabbit had been an atheist since she was a child despite her mother's many attempts to bring her into the Church. '*Sorry, Ma, it's bollocks, but if you're into it, good for you,*' she said more times than Molly could count, but Molly had the last word now.

'Fuck off, kids,' Molly said, before turning to Vincent and Silent Ed. 'That's that, then, we'll see you tomorrow.'

Molly and Jack returned to a still, cold house. As Molly turned on the heat she heard her husband's footsteps on the staircase and turned around in time to see him disappear into the attic. *Gone to lunch. Sure what else would you do, Jack?*

Molly went to bed alone, stared at the ceiling a while, her eyes burning. *Are you there, Rabbit? Give me a sign, please, love, nothing big, something small like your gran did – she used to leave me signs all the time, remember? Anything at all will do* . . . But no sign came, and finally Molly's burning eyes sealed shut.

Part Two

The Wake

Chapter Seven

Molly

MOLLY WOKE ON THE morning of the wake at 6 a.m. to blue skies and the contrail of a transatlantic jet curling, swirling and dissipating in the high winds. She thought about her daughter. *Send me a sign.* It was the thirtieth day in April and the sky was bright but angry. Below the leaves fluttered and the daffodils leaned a hard left, straining but so far remaining unbroken. One of Molly's pots rolled around on the ground and broke. *Is that a sign? Fuck it anyway, me favourite pot.* Jack was pretending to sleep. She knew he couldn't bear for the day to start, not yet, he wasn't ready; she let him lie.

She ate half a slice of toast and drank two cups of tea. She put on her coat and picked up the broken pot and binned it on her way out. She arrived at Grace's by 7 a.m. She didn't go in. She couldn't face Lenny and the kids. She beeped the horn. Grace appeared after a minute or two and waved. She went back indoors and Molly sat listening to the radio while Grace finished whatever it was she was doing. A woman was crying because she was losing her home to the bank. Molly switched station. A man was crying because he'd lost his entire pension and life savings in the crash. Molly switched station. Madonna's

'Like A Virgin' was playing and Molly gave up and turned the radio off. Grace arrived to the car shortly after that.

'About time,' Molly said.

'Sorry, Ma, I just can't seem to get my act together.'

Molly nodded and placed her hand on her oldest daughter's. 'It's hard.'

'Yeah.' Grace filled up. It was more efficient for both of them to ignore Grace's grief. Grace began the process of shoving it back down by grabbing a cereal bar from her bag and eating it whole. Molly drove on.

When Molly and Grace arrived at Rabbit's house, Davey was in the kitchen eating eggs but Juliet was still in her mother's bed.

'She's been there since yesterday,' Davey said.

'Has she eaten?' Grace asked.

'A little, yesterday.'

'Right then,' Molly said, 'I'll sort it.' She walked up the stairs and entered the room. Juliet, like her granda, was pretending to be asleep.

'I know you're awake, little lady,' Molly said. 'Don't kid a kidder.'

Juliet opened her eyes. Molly took her shoes off and got on the bed; Juliet automatically cuddled into her gran.

'This is the worst of it.'

'Isn't it all bad from here on in?' Juliet asked.

'Yeah, but at least you don't have to make small talk and serve sandwiches,' Molly said.

'Gran?'

'Yes, Bunny.'

'I feel so sad I want to die,' Juliet said in a small, fragile voice.

'Don't say that, love.' Molly's eyes filled and tears fell. She kissed her granddaughter on her head. 'Please, please, don't ever say that, but I know how you feel.'

Juliet agreed to get out of bed and shower and change. Molly decided it would be best if she stayed in her house that night, and asked Grace if she'd lend her Ryan and Bernard for the night. 'She needs to be with kids her own age,' Molly argued, and Davey and Grace conceded it was a better idea than leaving her to contemplate dying in her dead mother's bed.

Molly and Grace stood in front of Rabbit's wardrobe to examine each and every item. Mostly it was filled with jeans of all colours and styles and V-neck T-shirts with band names emblazoned across them interspersed with the odd skirt and jacket, a navy bridesmaid's dress and one knitted knee-length dress with a polo neck.

'What about the bridesmaid's dress?' Grace said.

'She's not going to a wedding. Besides, she hated that bridesmaid's dress,' Molly said, and sat on the bed with her head in her hands.

'I'm amazed she wore it.' Grace sat beside her mother and put her arm around her.

'She would have worn a brown paper bag if Marjorie asked her to,' Molly said, raising her eyes to stare into the wardrobe that looked more like that of a sixteen-year-old rocker than a forty-year-old mother of one.

'The polo neck will just emphasise how bloated her face is,' Molly said.

'We could buy something?'

'Like what?'

'I don't know, maybe a dress with a V-neck or a nice blouse and pants.'

'She'd hate that,' Molly said. 'She was always very particular about what she wore, even when she was a baby. I caught her putting her hand in her nappy and smearing shite on a pink top with a princess on it when she was two years old. "Message received," said I, and that was the last time she had any dealings with pink or princesses. Do you remember?'

'I do, Ma.'

'She was so wilful,' Molly lamented.

'I wonder where she got that from,' Grace said sarcastically and Molly chuckled a little.

'Well, she didn't lick it off the stones, did she, love?'

'No, Ma, she didn't.'

'Has she sent you a sign, Gracie?'

'No, Ma . . .'

'Oh . . .'

'But she talks to me.'

Molly bit her lip hard and clenched her jaw so tight her teeth hurt. *Talk to me, love, please, talk to your mammy*, but dead Rabbit had no time for her ma.

They stared at the wardrobe, found wanting, for another second or two.

'What about the beautiful silk nightdress that Marjorie brought her from Rome?' Grace said.

'You can't put her in lingerie!'

'Why not, she's asleep, isn't she?' Grace said. 'Besides, it's expensive and it looks like a dress.'

'Cop on,' Molly said.

'No one will know but us. It's probably the best thing Rabbit ever owned.' It dawned on Grace that Rabbit hadn't even had a chance to wear it.

'Cop on,' Molly repeated. 'We might have to buy something.'

Grace welled up. 'She'd hate that.'

Molly knew her daughter was right; it was all too much and it was still early.

'We don't need to make that decision now. Let's just get her home. I just want her home,' Molly said, her voice quieter. She patted Grace's back. Grace wiped her eyes and nose and nodded, OK.

Grace practically ran out of Rabbit's house; she didn't stop to take in the rooms that screamed Rabbit's presence. Molly did, though. She dallied in the hallway and placed her hand on the old photograph of the Hayes family, taken in the eighties when the world forgot taste and the Irish had only a passing acquaintance with hair products. Twelve-year-old Rabbit stared back at her with two long ponytails either side of her head, an eyepatch and thick glasses. *Where are you now, Rabbit Hayes?*

Grace waited in the car while Molly scheduled the day's events with Davey. As soon as Molly got in she put her foot down and reversed at the speed of light out of Rabbit's driveway, nearly killing Kyle, who dived off his bike to escape Molly's urgent-verging-on-dangerous driving. Grace screamed. Molly slammed on the brakes. Kyle disappeared behind the car.

'Oh God, what have I done?'

'Oh God, what have you done?' Grace shouted, staring in the wing mirror, terrified to move.

43

'I just fuckin' asked that, Grace,' Molly shouted in panic. Her nerves were now completely gone. Kyle rebounded and waved at the women. Molly rested her head on the steering wheel. 'Thank Jesus.'

He picked up his bike and walked around to the window. Molly pulled it down.

'Are you all right, son?' she enquired, filled with remorse. He held up his other hand. It was bleeding. 'Oh God,' she said.

'Ah don't worry, Mrs Hayes, I've had way worse.'

'Are you sure, love?'

'Yeah. I shattered me knee on the track two years ago, it's still mangled. This is nothing and me bike's fine, so that's all that matters.'

She nodded. 'I'm really sorry.'

'Me too.' His face blushed a little. 'About Rabbit, it's really sad.' Tears built in his eyes. 'I've never known anyone who . . .' he trailed off. His nose ran a little. He rubbed it with his sleeve. Grace grabbed a tissue out of her handbag and shoved it out the window and towards the bleeding boy. 'Here, Silversleeve, use a tissue.' Kids wiping snot on sleeves was a real bugbear of Grace's, and with four boys at home, crusty clothing had been a feature of her life for too many years.

'Sorry,' Kyle said. Grace fished a small bar of chocolate out of her handbag and handed it to him. 'Here, have that.'

He took it. 'Thanks.'

'And we're sorry again,' Grace said.

'No big deal,' he said. 'Sorry again too.'

Molly rolled up the window and continued reversing, slowly and steadily, until she was in a position to move off.

As she did so, he shouted: 'She was lovely, Rabbit was . . . She was . . .'

Molly turned on the radio, drowning Kyle out. She couldn't bear to hear anyone say anything nice about Rabbit. It was just too painful and so desperately unfair. Some government lackey was on the airwaves promoting charging people for their water. 'Over my dead body,' Molly mumbled.

'Ma.'

'What?'

'Over my dead body, really?'

'Sorry, love,' Molly said.

The rest of the journey was completed in silence.

Chapter Eight

Davey

DAVEY ARRIVED AT HIS mother's house with Juliet in tow just after 10 a.m. His nephews Bernard and Ryan were already there. Ryan nodded to Davey, who nodded back. Bernard gave Davey an unexpected bear hug. 'Love ya, Uncle Davey.'

'Love you too, Bernard,' Davey said awkwardly. He often wondered if the child was a little soft in the head.

Ryan raised his eyes and mouthed the word 'thick'. Davey hid his smile.

Davey was worried; as the morning passed Juliet's sadness seemed to increase with every passing second. 'Do you think she's sick?' he asked Molly. 'She looks sick.'

Molly examined her granddaughter. She was cool and clammy, her face pale and her pupils the size of saucers.

'Shock,' Molly said.

The child was in such a state of shock that Molly insisted on giving her a Valium, two milligrams, the lowest dose that Molly had left over from a knee injury a year beforehand.

'I don't know, Ma,' Davey said. He wasn't too thrilled at the idea of drugging the child.

Molly was adamant. 'I do know. The child needs a little something to calm her nerves.'

Maybe she was right, except that two milligrams turned out to be ten, because the old woman wasn't wearing her reading glasses at the time she dispensed the medication. 'It will relax you, love,' she'd promised the traumatised child.

'I'm all right, Gran,' Juliet lied.

'No, Bunny, you're not. None of us are.'

'Don't call me Bunny.'

'I'll try but I can't guarantee it,' she said, before leaving Juliet to stare into the middle distance, under the care of her cousins, who were busy wrestling for the remote control in the sitting room.

Molly asked Davey to bring a cup of tea to his da in the attic.

'Gone to lunch?' he said, and she nodded.

'Do you even know what he's doing up there?'

'Don't care, love, I have too much going on down here.'

Davey climbed into the attic to spend a little time with his father. Jack was in the corner, under a hanging light bulb and sitting on an old beanbag, surrounded by boxes. He was reading from an old notebook.

'What are ya up to, Da?' Davey asked.

'Ah, you know yourself, son.' Jack took the cup of tea from him.

Davey didn't know but he didn't push it.

'Did Mammy get something nice for Rabbit to wear?'

'Don't mention the war,' Davey said.

'Right.'

'How are you, Davey?' Jack asked.

'Scared,' Davey admitted.

'You'd be a fool not to be,' Jack said, then he returned to reading. Their conversation was done.

47

When he returned downstairs Ryan was waiting for him.

'I think Gran's broken Juliet,' Ryan said. 'She didn't even move when the remote control whizzed past her ear.'

Davey went into the sitting room to take stock of a silent, wide-eyed and very still Juliet.

'She's stoned off her face,' Davey grumbled, clicking his fingers in front of Juliet's face.

He walked into the kitchen to where his mother and Grace were buttering bread.

'Don't give her another one of those pills,' he said, and Molly turned to face him.

'I'll do as I see fit, Davey,' Molly said. 'She's my grandchild.'

'And I'm her guardian, Ma.'

'Rabbit wasn't in her right mind when she asked you to care for that child.'

'Ma . . .' Grace began in a warning tone.

'We all know it's madness, Grace. Davey's going to take Juliet to America with him? Really? He's going to care for her? He can't even take care of himself. Look at him.' She walked into the kitchen with Davey following and turned to point at his lower half. 'A man in his forties walking around in ripped jeans. It's a bleedin' disgrace.'

Davey had had enough of his mother's abuse. 'She picked me, Ma. Not you. Live with it.'

'She was ill. Too ill.'

'Don't, Ma,' Grace warned, but Davey knew she was right. Juliet belonged in Ireland with Molly and her granda or Grace, Lenny and their four boys. They all wanted Juliet. Davey knew that if Molly hadn't just suffered a cardiac event she would have pushed harder for Juliet. And yes, Grace and

Lenny were tight on space but with some financial assistance they could have built an extension, and in the meantime Stephen and Grace had bought a beat-up old caravan for Stephen to sleep in. It was parked outside their house, for God's sake. But Davey made a life-changing decision in haste and Rabbit rewarded him by handing him her twelve-year-old child! She could not have been in her right mind.

I'm in my forties. I live on a bus and date women half my age. My only long-term commitment is a twenty-five-year-subscription to Rolling Stone *magazine. Oh Rabbit, they're right about me. I'm a useless bastard. What now?*

Calm down, Davey, you can do this, he heard Rabbit say.

I don't know, Rabbit.

I know.

Davey was a grown man, shaking and on the verge of tears.

Molly registered Davey's pain. She regulated her breath.

'Sorry, son, I didn't mean that. I'm out of my mind.' She walked over to him and hugged him.

He hugged her back. 'I miss her too, Ma.'

'I can feel your heart beating in your chest,' she said. 'You're alive. I'm alive. Let's be kind to one another, Davey.'

'OK, Ma.'

'You see you were always kind, and Juliet Hayes needs kind,' she said, and he knew deep down that Molly Hayes believed that her granddaughter needed a lot more than kind. 'And ripped jeans suit you, son,' she added by way of an apology.

He chuckled to himself. 'Thanks, Ma.'

His smile quickly faded when he walked out into the hall and found Juliet with her head stuck between two bars of the staircase, wide-eyed and vacant.

'Ma!' he shouted. Molly appeared, knife in hand.

'God Almighty, boys, if you can't keep her with you put a bloody lead on her,' she shouted to Bernard and Ryan in the sitting room.

I can't do this, he thought. *I promised Rabbit I'd take care of Juliet, and within two days the child is a fucking zombie.*

Molly moved towards the staircase and spoke slowly and carefully to her granddaughter's face. 'You're a little lost in your head and probably better off, love.' She leaned down between the bars and gave Juliet a kiss on the forehead. 'I'm here,' she whispered. 'I'm always here, do you hear me? I've got ya, love,' she said, before shouting, 'Ryan, get me the butter.'

Juliet blinked. Stoned or not, it seemed to be the only form of communication she could commit to. Davey just stared on, feeling like a failure.

Chapter Nine

Grace

In the week leading up to her death, Rabbit had stated she wanted a basket coffin as opposed to wood.

'Why?' Molly had questioned her daughter in the hospice.

'Because it's sustainable.'

'The basket is?'

'Yeah.'

'And the wood isn't?'

Rabbit thought about that. *Oh yeah.* If she hadn't been dying she would have come up with an argument, but her brain was foggy on account of it being ravaged by cancer. 'Well, it's cheaper.'

'So you want me and your daddy to scrimp on your coffin? Is that what you want?'

'The baskets are perfectly suitable.'

'They are,' Molly said, and Rabbit grinned. 'Perfectly suitable to carry eggs and fucking ham.' Rabbit's grin faded.

Rabbit turned to Grace for assistance.

'Please, Grace, it's what I want.'

Grace promised she'd make Molly purchase the basket. Even as she made the promise she worried about failing her baby sister.

'Don't let me down,' Rabbit said.

'Scout's honour,' Grace replied, making the Vulcan salute.

It was still morning when Grace and Molly arrived at the mortuary. Grace made a conscious decision to park her own troubles and focus on Rabbit's wake and funeral. The gene would be there when she was ready to deal with it. She buried her anxieties deep. *Think about Rabbit. Only Rabbit. So you have the gene, you don't have cancer, you are not dying, get on with it.*

It's OK, Grace.

Shut up, Rabbit.

'Let me handle this, love,' Molly said as they walked through the door.

'No chance,' Grace said, and Molly gave her a look and a smile that suggested 'Game on.' *Oh God.*

Vincent and Silent Ed were waiting. Vincent was disappointed to see they had not arrived with clothes.

'We're still negotiating,' Molly said.

'We're bringing Rabbit home at five,' Vincent reminded her.

'So we've got time on our hands.'

'Not a lot.'

But Molly was already making her way towards a solid mahogany box with brass details. 'That's the one,' she said, pointing to it.

'No way, Ma, she wanted the basket.'

Molly ran her hand along its edge. 'Mind your own business, Grace.'

'You have good taste – she's top of the range,' Vincent said. Silent Ed remained silent.

'That's not what Rabbit asked for, Ma,' Grace said, dragging her mother towards the basket option.

'Is Rabbit here?' Molly asked, pretending to look around the room. 'Let's ask her again, will we? Rabbit? Rabbit? Are you sure about that basket, love? It has a green hue off it and not a nice green either, one of those greens that you cough up when you're fighting an infection,' she shouted to the ceiling.

Vincent pretended to pick lint off his suit. Silent Ed rubbed his nondescript moustache.

'Oh no, wait a minute, the dead don't have an opinion,' Molly said. Vincent wasn't sure what to do. He took a step back.

'She wanted a basket, Ma,' Grace said.

'No, Grace, she wanted to live.' Because she was choked up, Molly bit her bottom lip, and in taking a moment to gather herself she focused on the basket in front of her, touching it, really feeling it, and all the while with a disgusted look on her face. 'A basket, Grace?'

'Well, it was good enough for Moses,' Vincent said in a light-hearted tone.

'Moses was abandoned by his own in a river,' Molly said in disgust.

'To save his life,' Vincent said with great authority.

'Will this ugly greenish basket save my Rabbit?' Molly asked.

'No,' Vincent said, and he slunk back beside Silent Ed.

Grace turned on Molly. 'You promised.'

'All she wanted to do was save us money, Grace, and all I want to do is spend every penny we have to honour her.'

Grace's mother had a filthy mouth, a fiery temper, a steel core and a huge heart, and she knew how to win an argument.

Grace hugged her. 'OK, Ma, I give up.' Molly squeezed Grace hard and kissed her cheek. Grace looked up at the ceiling. 'Sorry, Rabbit, I tried.'

Molly turned to Vincent. 'I'm sorry, Vincent, sometimes I can be a real arsehole but I mean well.' She raised her arms to heaven. 'And I am what I am, so please bear with me.'

Vincent nodded. 'It's a difficult time.'

Grace followed her mother across the room and stood by her side.

'It's a lovely coffin, Ma,' Grace said, *exactly what I'd like. Jesus, Grace, stop it. You go looking for trouble, you find it. Balls. Stop. Get your act together. This isn't about you.*

Yeah, Grace, this isn't about you. Besides, brown is not your colour . . . Her sister's voice rang inside her head.

I'm warning you, Rabbit.

'We'll take it,' Grace said.

'Very good choice,' Vincent said.

'What's a very bad choice?' Molly asked.

'Excuse me?'

'You said, very good choice. What's a bad one?'

Vincent looked like he was about to cry.

'It's the basket, isn't it?' she said.

'There's no bad choice.'

She patted Vincent on the shoulder. 'It's a good thing you're in the funeral business, love, because you'd starve to death before you'd sell a fridge-freezer.' She walked out, leaving a miffed Vincent in her wake.

In the car on the way home, Grace turned to face her mother.

'Ma, do you ever get scared?'

'I'm scared all the time, Grace.'

'How come you never show it?'

'What's the point when it only upsets everyone else?'

Grace thought about that for a while. 'I'm scared all the time, too,' Grace said, and Molly nodded sympathetically.

'Our secret.'

'Our secret,' Grace agreed.

'Now, let's talk doves,' Molly said. 'Daisy Quirk released some at her Joseph's graveside, and aside from the one that panicked and slapped itself against a bus shelter it went off great.'

'Ma, with the greatest respect, fuck off.'

'Fair enough.'

They didn't speak for a time, but as Molly pulled into the car space she turned to her daughter. 'No one ever knows what lies ahead. All we can do is hope for the best.'

Grace said nothing but she nodded. Molly sighed and groaned as she lifted herself out of the seat.

I have the gene, Ma.

Chapter Ten

Marjorie

MARJORIE TOOK OVER ON sandwich duty as soon as she arrived to the Hayes household, bailing an increasingly frustrated Davey out. He was angry he'd been left to faff around with sandwiches while his mother and sister made the real decisions. 'And they can't even do that,' he said. 'Rabbit's still in the godawful blue silk yoke.'

She made him a cup of coffee and told him to sit down. He was excused from slapping ham on bread, his heart clearly not being in it. Marjorie on the other hand would do anything to avoid thinking, and assembling sandwiches was as good a distraction as anything.

'Can I ask?'

He answered with a quizzical look.

'When are you going home?' she said, and she couldn't look at him.

'Soon,' he said.

She nodded. 'Just like that.'

'It's not just like anything. America is my home, my life is there.'

'And Juliet?'

'Her life is with me now.' He didn't sound convinced. He couldn't look her in the eye.

56

When she had put cling film on a fifth plate stacked with sandwiches she sat down opposite him. He just stared past her, lost in his own world, filled with pain, loss and worries.

'We've both made a lot of mistakes, haven't we?'

'Please, don't do this, Marj. I'm on the edge here.' He looked like he might cry at any moment.

'We're arseholes,' she said, 'but Rabbit, she wasn't one. She chose you so I'm backing you.'

'Why?' he whispered. 'Why did she choose me?'

Marjorie gritted her teeth. 'Don't do this.'

'Do what?'

'Don't start second-guessing yourself.'

'I just want to know.'

Marjorie sighed a heavy sigh. Davey waited for her to speak. She remained silent. It made Davey anxious; maybe she couldn't think why. Then she spoke slowly and deliberately.

'She picked you because she idolised you, don't you know that, Davey?'

'That was Johnny – I was just the bloke standing beside him.' Davey pictured Johnny Faye, his best friend, the exotic, genius singer-songwriter that flew so close to the sun but died an early and terrible death. Johnny Faye was a real rock star with the soul of a poet and a lion's heart. Rabbit fell in love with him before she knew what love was. He was four years older, and yet she was always his little pal. He saw who she was and what she was capable of before anyone else. He named her. 'She's not a Mia, she's a Rabbit,' he said one day.

'I like that,' she said, and everyone else liked it too and that was it. He was right; she was born to be Rabbit. Back then, to Davey she was just his annoying baby sister but Johnny saw her potential. When she was fourteen years old he made her the band's sound engineer, much to Davey's disgust. 'She's shite,' he'd said.

'They're all shite,' Johnny pointed out, 'but only Rabbit's free.'

Davey had been jealous of their connection until Johnny got sick with multiple sclerosis, then she was the only one who could handle his moods and his needs. Without Rabbit, the band wouldn't have lasted as long as it did. Without her, Davey would never have tasted the possibility of success. Johnny lasted long enough to give Davey the drive to succeed no matter what or where. By the time Rabbit was old enough to be with Johnny he was pretty disabled. They had a moment, though. A shining moment where they were a couple in love, until Johnny did the decent thing and pushed her away before it all fell to shit. He didn't want Rabbit to watch him rot and die, and a part of her never got over that. Even as she lay dying, Davey overheard her twice arguing with her dead ex-boyfriend and the love of her life. The first time it was about Juliet. 'Well, Johnny Faye, if you hadn't pushed me away you could have been Juliet's father, not some random Aussie backpacker I didn't know, but then again, either way she doesn't have a dad. My poor Bunny.' She felt low for much of that day.

The second time it was over religion. Johnny was a believer; it was a real bone of contention between them.

'You're in the ground, Johnny, so if I'm joining you I'll join you there and you can stop singing . . . Sexy bastard.' She'd chuckled to herself. He pretended he hadn't heard her and that he'd just come into the room. She smiled for the rest of that evening despite her pain and anxiety. Marjorie was wrong: she didn't idolise her brother, she idolised Johnny Faye.

Are you together now? Rabbit? Did Rabbit Hayes and Johnny Faye finally get a happy ending?

Wouldn't you like to know . . . her heard her say.

I would.

'Yeah, she idolised him but she idolised you first,' Marjorie said, and Davey's eyes began to leak.

'You were always good enough for her so, as hard as it is, and it is really hard, I'm backing you.'

He knew how much Juliet meant to her. He knew she loved her like she was her own. He knew she wasn't just losing Rabbit – she was losing both of them. He looked up at her with tears staining his face.

'What if she was wrong?'

'She wasn't,' she said, and she started buttering the next round of bread.

Chapter Eleven

Juliet

ONCE HER HEAD WAS safely removed from the banisters, Juliet was put sitting on the sofa between Bernard and Ryan, who were busy playing a game on some kind of device. They were non-verbal, but the noise of guns and explosions that came from the screen were intense and the flashes hurt Juliet's sore eyes. A long time passed while the boys played on, battling scary-looking combat soldiers and kicking unfriendly ass. Nothing really registered – maybe some colours, splashes of red, grey and white lights. Nothing really made sense: it was just moving, shooting, bombing, shooting, moving, and every now and then the boys would fist-bump. She closed her eyes just to rest them while still sitting up. She couldn't talk; the drugs had rendered her dumb. She couldn't think clearly either; everything was fuzzy and kind of surreal. Her tongue felt big in her mouth. Her skin prickled and burned. Her neck felt heavy, her face like rubber and the air around her felt dense like water. She just remained still as the boys played on and on.

Marjorie entered the room at some point.

'Boys, move,' she said, and Ryan and Bernard moved to the floor without missing a shot. Marjorie sat beside Juliet, took her in her arms, and as Juliet sank into her chest she sighed with relief, closed her eyes and was asleep in seconds.

Chapter Twelve

Jack

J ACK SPENT THE MORNING in the attic. By lunchtime he'd found his diaries from the years 1954 to 1968. He was missing '69 and '70, but he located '71 to '84. He was still searching out '84 to '87, the key Kitchen Sink years, when Davey and his best friends – singer Johnny Faye, guitar player Francie, bass player Jay and Louis on keyboards – spent every waking moment they could in his garage rehearsing their music. Rabbit had lived in that garage; she loved the music but she loved the effortlessly cool Johnny Faye more. It made him smile – Davey always trying to get rid of his little sister and Johnny Faye always welcoming her back in. He wrote a lot about those years and the tragedy of it all, and how proud he was of both his son and daughter during those difficult times. Johnny and Rabbit's relationship defied time and place. He died aged twenty-six, and Rabbit lasted eighteen years on earth without him. *Ya did good, love.*

Thanks, Da.

Johnny and Rabbit were alive in Jack's diaries. There he had recorded the rise and fall of the band and Johnny and Rabbit's tragic love story. They were special years, magical even, just before he got sick and everything was possible. *We had it all back then*, he thought. *The whole world in our hands.* He always knew it, he always loved his little girl with every bit of him, but he wondered if he really comprehended how special she really was until her cancer and slow death allowed him to step back from the everyday and examine her as a whole being, and her life in its entirety. *My Rabbit*.

He was still emptying boxes and sorting piles of paper when his phone rang. He answered instantly when he saw Rabbit's editor Derek was on the end of the line. Rabbit had worked on profiles and lifestyle features under Derek for ten years. It was he who suggested she blog about her cancer, in the early days before anyone even considered a terminal diagnosis. As soon as she'd found a big enough audience, her blogs turned into articles and her cancer diary was born. The volume of letters she received from fellow cancer sufferers and survivors astonished them both. Rabbit had found herself a whole new community and her loss would reverberate.

'Derek?'

'Jack, I'm ringing to offer my sincere condolences.'

'Thanks, Derek, that means a lot. I know Rabbit had such respect for you.'

'And I for her. With that in mind, Jack, and I hope it's not too early for me to bring this up, but Rabbit passed on all of her work for the book a few days ago.'

'Oh,' Jack said, 'I wasn't aware.'

'Her blogs were so popular, Jack.'

'Yes, yes, she had quite a following.'

'The next step was a book. You know I promised I'd make that happen.'

'Right.'

'It's in good shape. I have some work to do, structuring the story of Rabbit's life around the cancer blogs, but I'm working on it.'

'Thank you, Derek, that means the world.'

'It's a love story really, Jack.'

'I don't follow.'

'Ultimately it's not really about cancer, it's about a girl who loved a boy. It's about a warm, vibrant family and endearing, enduring friendships. It's about joy, Jack.'

Jack burst into tears and fell back onto the beanbag. He sobbed and blew his nose and Derek remained silent on the line.

'Thank you for saying that, Derek,' Jack said eventually when his tear ducts ran empty.

'It's a pleasure to be a part of it. As executor of Rabbit's estate you will have to sign any deal we make with publishers.'

'Yes, yes. It will be an honour.'

'Nothing's guaranteed – of course there is interest because of the popularity of her weekly blogs, but it's a long road ahead.'

'I understand. Whatever you can do.'

'Either way, it's a beautiful story, Jack, a beautiful life.'

'Please, don't start me off again.'

'I'm afraid I can't make the wake this evening but I will see you at the funeral.'

'Thanks again, Derek.'

Jack hung up. He was all cried out, exhausted by it and having not really eaten in a week, all reserves had finally been depleted, which was an issue seeing as he was arse-deep in a snug beanbag with no energy to fight his way out. After wrestling it for what seemed like an eternity he was forced to call out for help.

'Hello? Hello there? It's Jack . . . It's Daddy . . . Up here . . . In the attic . . . Stuck . . . Anyone?'

Molly's head popped up through the hatch.

'There you are, Molls,' he said as she surveyed the situation.

'Stuck in the beanbag.'

He nodded.

'Right,' she said, and she disappeared. He could hear her voice echo around the house.

'Davey, head up to the attic and sort your da out, will ya, love?'

'What's wrong with him?'

'He's like an upturned fuckin' turtle,' she said by way of explanation. Jack just leaned back into his beanbag shell and waited. *It's about joy*, he thought, and smiled. *That will do me.*

Chapter Thirteen

Marjorie

MARJORIE LEFT JULIET SLEEPING on the sofa. Upstairs she could hear Davey heaving his dad from the beanbag.

'One, two, three, pull.'

'Oh, oh, oh, my back – watch my back, son.'

Molly was on the landing, looking upwards through the open attic door, hands on hips and shaking her head.

'Be careful, Davey, we don't have time for him and his bad back.'

'Doing my best, Ma.'

Marjorie stood beside Molly.

'What can I do?'

'Nothing, you've done enough,' she said, referring to the twenty-five thousand sandwiches piled high in the Hayes kitchen.

'What about Rabbit's clothes?'

'I've sent Grace out to buy something.'

'No,' Marjorie said, shaking her head and resting her hands on her hips.

'Excuse me?'

'No, Molly. Sorry. No way.' It was unusual for Marjorie to stand up to Molly in such a way; normally they were on the same page. Marjorie was nervous and the last thing she wanted to do was be disrespectful to Molly, the woman who'd pretty much raised her, and especially during this terrible time, but if you don't stand for something you stand for nothing – at least that's what Molly Hayes always said. Molly waited for Marjorie to find her words.

'You know what to dress her in, you just don't want to.'

Molly sucked her cheeks in and bit on them hard; chewing on the inside of her own face was something Molly did when she was in a tough spot.

'You're referring to AC/DC,' Molly said through clenched teeth.

Marjorie nodded. 'AC/DC.'

'And you have something specific in mind?' Molly said.

'*Highway to Hell* tour, 1979.'

'So you want my dead child to wear an AC/DC *Highway to Hell* tour T-shirt into her grave?'

'It's not about what you or I want,' Marjorie said, undaunted.

'Well, why did she ask me to pick her clothes, then?' Molly was losing the battle even in her own head.

'Because she knew ultimately you'd do the right thing,' Marjorie said.

'And what's that?'

Marjorie smiled. 'You'd come and talk to me.'

Molly leaned on the wall and knocked her head against it three times just as Davey counted his father down. 'One, two, three, pull.'

'Come on, son, put some welly into it,' Jack said from above.

'You're like a baby elephant, Da.'

Molly slowly removed the key to Rabbit's house from her pocket and handed it to Marjorie just as Francie Byrne walked in through the back door as though he owned the place. Francie had spent most of his youth in and out of that house, rehearsing in the garage. The Hayes household was home to many back then.

'Fine,' Molly said.

Marjorie smiled.

Francie appeared at the bottom of the stairs and looked upwards. 'What are we doin'?'

'You're coming with me,' Marjorie said.

'All right, but no touching.' He winked at Molly. 'You hanging in there, Mrs H?' he asked.

'Just about, Francie.'

'Where's DB?' he said, because in the past, and before Davey had grown into himself, his close friends and bandmates christened him Dead Bird due to his oversized nose and skinny body. It had been shortened to DB over the years.

'I'm up here – me da's wedged himself in a bleedin' beanbag,' Davey said from the attic.

'Any chance of a hand, Francie, I think my back's in spasm,' Jack said.

'Everything changes. Everything stays the same,' Francie said. 'Give us a minute, Marjorie.'

Francie Byrne and his twin Jay had been honorary members of the Hayes family since Davey joined their band aged twelve. They had been through hell and back together. Francie and Jay were as devastated by Rabbit's loss as the family and Marjorie were, but Francie understood his job description and that was to keep everyone going – smiling and even laughing if possible – and there was no one better to do so.

After ably assisting Davey in the removal of his father from the clutches of a soft beanbag, Francie drove his van like a man with a death wish. Marjorie said nothing but gripped the seat like her life depended on it. To pass the time he filled Marjorie in on the progress of the young fella who had lost his hand in a samurai sword incident on the factory floor earlier in the week.

'Playacting . . . We haven't seen the fucker who wielded it since – he ran off crying and now he's on the sick with PTSD.'

'How's the guy who lost the hand?'

'Aka The Claw – you know Sheila B's young one?'

'Sandra?'

'That's right, she put the hand in a towel surrounded by ice and they reattached it. So far, so good.'

'Do you ever see Sheila B?' Marjorie asked.

'Nah, keep clear, although word is she's fresh out of the nut house.'

'She'll probably come to the funeral.'

'That's all we need – my missus facing off my mad ex. I'll have to pick up some Kevlar to wear to this fuckin' funeral.'

Marjorie remembered Francie and Sheila B's crazy relationship during the band's heyday. Sheila was nuts but she was funny and always nice to the younger, shy Marjorie.

He drove on and after a few incidents in which he screamed orders at people in other cars who could not possibly hear him, 'Green, green, it doesn't go any fucking greener.' BEEEEEEEEEPPPPPPPP. 'What are ya waiting on, a bleedin' invitation?' BEEEEEEEEEPPPPPPPP.

After giving the fingers to a vanload of travellers who dared cut him off, mounting a kerb and driving on the path to overtake a man on his left-hand side and frightening the life out of him before rolling down the window and shouting, 'You shouldn't be on the road!' he relaxed into the drive.

'So anyway, you and Davey?' he said.

Marjorie groaned. 'There is no me and Davey.'

'Ah, keep on lying to yourself if you want, no skin off my back.'

'I'm not lying to myself. We've had sex a few times over the years, that's it.' She was lying. They had kissed in the grounds of the hospice as her best friend lay dying. *What the hell is wrong with us?*

'All right,' he said, in a really patronising way.

'Don't say it like you know better than me.'

'But I do know better than you. I am Francie Byrne and Francie Byrne sees all.'

She wasn't in the mood. 'Fine, whatever.'

In the house, Francie made himself a coffee while Marjorie picked out the T-shirt, one of the five pairs of tight black jeans Rabbit owned, her black lacy bra and knickers, and two old crew wristbands with 'Kitchen Sink' and 'The Sound' written on them. She didn't stay long in her friend's room; it was too upsetting to be surrounded by everything that was Rabbit's. She took a moment to inhale her perfume, but if she stopped any longer she knew she'd collapse. *Keep going, get through – come on, Marjorie.*

She burst into tears on the stairs. *Damn it.* She did her best to collect herself. She could hear Francie fiddle with the radio in the kitchen. Her knees gave way and so she sat on Rabbit's staircase and hugged her T-shirt. Just for a minute. Just until her eyes and nose ran dry.

When she made her way into her friend's kitchen, Francie looked at the clothes in Marjorie's hand and placed his arm around her. 'When I die, I want you to dress me.'

Marjorie smiled. Francie chugged down the coffee.

'Where to next, boss?' he asked.

'The funeral home.'

'Let's do this,' he said.

Marjorie followed Francie to the van. Kyle appeared out of nowhere.

'Juliet at her gran's?' he asked.

'Yeah.'

'She OK?'

'No,' Marjorie said.

'Tell her Kyle said hi – no, tell her sorry. No, tell her hi and—'

Francie leaned out of the window, 'Hey Romeo, do one.'

'Oh, yeah, grand,' he said, and he stepped out of the way.

'Just say—' he shouted as they drove off.

Francie took a phone call from work in the car while Marjorie went into the funeral home and handed over the clothes to Vincent and Silent Ed. Vincent seemed confused as he unfolded the T-shirt.

'You're sure?'

'Positive.'

'And Mrs Hayes?'

'She's signed off.'

'Right then, lovely, we'll get to work, then.'

'Can I see her?'

'We really have very little time.'

70

'Just for a minute, please.'

Vincent nodded. 'Give me a second.' He walked into a small room. Silent Ed stood silently. Francie arrived in.

'How we doing?' he asked.

'I'm just going to see her,' she said, and she was shaking.

'Do you want company?'

'No. Do you mind?'

He wrapped his arms around her. 'Not at all.' He turned to Silent Ed, looked him up and down. 'Hey, kid? You ever wanna get laid, lose the dodgy ronnie,' he said, referring to the young man's attempt to grow hair over his top lip.

Silent Ed instinctively rubbed his practically non-existent moustache. 'Trust me,' he said. Vincent appeared and ushered Marjorie into the room.

It was dark, lit only by candles. The blue satin that had previously surrounded Rabbit was gone; a sheet covered her to her collar bone, and her hands were placed outside it, straight and by her sides. Her bald head was shaved and smooth. Vincent had removed the heavy make-up and what was left behind was lighter, with a little Kardashian-style sculpting. She looked like herself.

'There ya are,' Marjorie said, and tears stung her eyes. She took Rabbit's hand in hers. 'Just wanted a little time, just us. So I got you sorted, and I don't want to throw bouquets at myself but it's perfect. So there's a few things we need to talk about. Firstly I'm pissed you never encouraged me to make more friends. You're it and that's your fault. Who could compare to the mighty Rabbit Hayes? Certainly not the bank dweebs I've spent a lifetime working with and yes, I know you told me to leave the bank years ago but fuck you anyway, Rabbit. Now that's out of the way. What's next? So how's your ma? Well, she's hanging in there, Jack's gone to lunch but you knew he'd find a way to disappear. He'll be back. And Grace? Well, she's doing her best. Davey's being Davey, silently freaking out, but he'll be OK. Juliet? How's Juliet, I hear ya ask. Well, she's not good, Rabbit. She's in so much pain and I'd do anything to take it away but I can't, no one can, even your mother – who's drugged her, by the way. The child is out of her mind, getting her head stuck between banisters and talking about feelings having colours. I'm going to do my best to help. I just don't know how long I have with her.'

Tears burned holes in her face. She wiped the mucus emanating from her nose at an alarming force and rate with the back of her hand. 'Me? I'm fine, you know me. So clearly not fine, but you know – fine. It's only day two and I already hate this world without you, so that's brilliant. Hey, fun fact, I sat across the road from my mother's house for an hour yesterday like a psycho, that's new. What else?'

Vincent knocked on the door, a light rap.

'Shit, I have to go, Vincent needs to get you dressed. That's an image I could do without – silver lining, you're dead so you don't have to endure that. He's an odd one, and his sidekick . . . poor kid, the good news is Francie gave him a key style tip ten seconds after meeting him. He's here, he's outside, he's being brilliant.'

Another gentle rap, 'Jesus, Vincent's not messing around. Have to go, amigo.' She sniffed hard, really hoovering up any residual nose flow. She kissed her friend's cold face. 'You really are a bitch for leaving me.'

She let go of her hand. Vincent pushed the door open, pointing to his watch.

'We really have to get moving.'

'Sorry,' she said, and walked outside to be greeted by Silent Ed flexing his minuscule muscles for Francie.

'You couldn't beat snow off a rope with them.' He handed him a card. 'Come see us in the boxing club, we'll knock you into shape in less than six months.' Silent Ed took the card.

'Don't rock up with that ronnie, the lads would make shite of you,' he said, pointing to the bumfluff moustache. Silent Ed covered it with his hand and nodded vigorously. Marjorie followed Francie to the car.

Once inside he handed her a tissue from his glove box. She wiped her face dry and for a moment his happy-go-lucky mask slipped. 'I wish this was over,' he said quietly and started the engine.

Chapter Fourteen

Grace

WHILE GRACE AND DAVEY spent a portion of the afternoon moving the dining room furniture around to accommodate Rabbit, Molly was tending to Jack and his dodgy back. In her absence her children were charged with working out exactly where best to place Rabbit to keep her bathed in light but far enough away from the window to avoid unwanted prying eyes.

'She'd hate an open coffin,' Davey complained bitterly.

'I know,' Grace said.

'And people staring at her.'

'I know.'

'We could just grab her and run,' Davey said.

Grace ignored him.

'Or I could get Francie to grab a glue gun from the van, glue around the sides and slam it shut.'

'You could close it shut with a boulder and Ma would find a way to open it,' she said.

'It's not right,' Davey said.

'Except that as long as that coffin is open, Rabbit's still with us.'

Davey got it instantly and relented. He cleared his throat. 'Makes sense,' he said.

74

Grace shoved an entire triangle-shaped sandwich into her mouth in an attempt to fill the gnawing void growing inside her. They didn't talk about a closed coffin again.

The body arrived at the Hayes household at exactly 5 p.m. that day. The neighbours came out of their homes just as the hearse pulled up. They stood in their gardens and made signs of the cross as the two men in suits rolled Rabbit onto the road. Force-of-Nature Molly stood on the front step flanked by her family: Jack to her left wearing his back brace and crying like a baby; Deer-Caught-in-Headlights Davey beside a deeply sad Grace, his hand clasping hers, the way he did when they were kids and she walked him to school. Grace's boys – Stephen, Bernard, Ryan and Jeffrey – stood behind them. Marjorie sat with Juliet on the stairs. The child was still zonked, staring at the wall.

Grace watched her little sister being wheeled up the drive-way in a brown box while the whole neighbourhood stood in their gardens, heads bowed in solidarity and quietly thanking God it wasn't one of theirs. It was incredibly difficult for her. *I have the gene.* She didn't let it show. She buried it deep. The funeral directors stalled by the gate and Grace was suddenly transported back to the 1980s and a sixteen-year-old Johnny Faye in his ripped jeans, long leather jacket and soft curly hair was sitting on the wall in front of her. She saw twelve-year-old gawky Rabbit with her long ponytails, her big thick-framed glasses and her eyepatch, there to correct a lazy eye. She was crying. He had his arm around her. She was crying because back then, aged eighteen, Grace was voluptuous, with wild red hair and a pretty face, and Rabbit was jealous. 'No one will be as beautiful as you, Rabbit,' he told her. He was right. Rabbit was something special her whole life, even with big thick-framed glasses and a dodgy eye. Grace by contrast only felt special for a very short period of time. Silent Ed tripped on a crack in the pavement, bringing Grace back into the present. Vincent gave him a dirty look. He cast his eyes downwards. Everyone parted to let them enter. No one really knew where to stand. Molly directed the coffin as though it were traffic.

'Come this way. No. A little to the left. No. My left. No. Sorry. Right. A little to the right. Stop.' She stood back.

When Rabbit was positioned in the room, Vincent took the lid off the coffin. Everyone stood back and automatically blessed themselves. Quietly the two men exited the room, leaving the bereaved to grieve. Molly stood over her youngest, dressed in her own clothes, light make-up and her favourite, perfectly coiffed, blonde wig. She looked exactly like herself.

'There you are, love.' Overcome, Molly needed a chair. Davey ran into the kitchen and placed one under his mum's bum. 'Perfect,' she said, then she turned to Marjorie. 'Who loves ya, Marjorie?'

'Molly does,' Marjorie said. Molly reached out for Marjorie's hand and kissed it and held it close.

'Just perfect,' she mumbled, and it was a minute or two before she let Marjorie's hand go. Grace felt sick with grief but she stood there, head swimming, heart sinking.

When it was time for the kids to see the body, Juliet arrived accompanied by Ryan. Bernard, Stephen and Jeffrey lagged behind.

'She rocks,' Ryan said. Juliet stood frozen, arms planted by her sides, wide-eyed and open-mouthed.

Davey put his hands on Juliet's shoulders. She leaned back on him and stared at her mother for what seemed like the longest time, then she nodded to herself and Ryan whispered to Grace. 'What's she nodding at?' Grace didn't know and wondered if it had something to do with the drugs. She shrugged. They all waited for Juliet to absorb the scene.

'I just want to go home,' she said.

'I have to stay here for the wake, and we can't leave you alone,' Davey said.

'I'll stay with her,' Ryan said.

Davey looked to Grace for permission. Grace knelt down on the floor and looked up at her niece. 'Are you sure, Bunny?'

'Don't call me Bunny.'

Grace looked from Juliet to Davey.

'Rabbit's gone, she doesn't want to be Bunny anymore,' he said by way of explanation.

'Oh.' She held onto her niece's hands. 'It's your choice.'

'I want to go home.'

'OK.' She looked to Davey and nodded. 'It's OK.'

Ryan shrugged. 'See, it's fine.'

'Lenny's on the way, he can drop them off before the wake starts.'

Davey scrambled for money in his pockets. He handed Ryan a fifty-euro note. 'Get pizza, and I want my change.'

'Score,' Ryan said, before placing his hands on Juliet's shoulders and steering her back into the sitting room.

Davey's phone rang as he entered the kitchen.

'Francie?' He listened and his face paled a little. 'You're joking.'

He listened again before saying thanks and hanging up.

'What's that about?' Grace said.

'Rabbit's death is all over the radio.'

Marjorie had been minding her own business and washing dishes up to this point. She stopped and turned around.

'It came from a tweet from a family account,' Davey said.

Molly entered the kitchen and looked to Davey and Marjorie. 'What's this?'

'Whose account?' Grace said.

'Ryan's.'

Grace felt her knees go weak for the second time in two days. 'Oh Jesus.'

'What did he do?' She needed a chair or she risked sinking onto the ground and into a ball.

'Davey?' Molly said.

Davey found the tweet on his phone and read it out. '"Atheist and journalist Rabbit Hayes died today."'

'Ah, why did he have to say she's an atheist?' Molly asked, sounding annoyed.

'And?' Grace said.

'There's a hashtag.'

'What's a hashtag?' Molly asked.

'Well, it's more of a punchline, really,' Davey said.

'A punchline?' Molly's voice rose an octave.

He cleared his throat and read the tweet out loud. '"Atheist and journalist Rabbit Hayes died today #AllDressedUpNo-whereToGo."'

For a moment Grace thought she might vomit. 'Sweet suffering Jesus.'

'And it's trending.'

'What does trending mean?' Molly asked.

Lenny walked in carrying a box of wine and four bags of shopping. He knew instantly there was a problem. Molly Hayes looked like she was going to explode, but it was the look on his wife's face that terrified him.

'What's up?' he said, placing the boxes on the kitchen table and the bags on the ground.

'You better get your son out of here now.' Grace's blood boiled and her breathing intensified. She was in full-on raging bull mode.

'Red alert,' he called out, 'red alert,' Lenny didn't even have to ask which one. 'Ryan,' he shouted, 'get to the car, son.'

Ryan walked into the room and Grace turned on him.

'All dressed up and nowhere to go!' she screamed.

'Run, Ryan. I haven't a clue what's going on, but run,' Lenny said. Ryan grabbed his coat and ran. Lenny kissed his wife, 'Calm down, calm down, OK, love? Marjorie, get her a drink, something strong.' He ran out to Ryan, who was waiting in the car. Davey got Juliet and handed her off to Lenny, who was sitting with the engine running. Grace took herself out to the backyard, opened her dad's shed and took an old chipped hurley stick that was lying by the door and just started whacking the large plastic recycling bins. Marjorie sidled next to Molly, watching from the open window.

'Should we do something?'

'Nah, she'll tire herself out.'

'She's done this before?'

'Before the recycling bins we used to keep an old washer-dryer there, just so she had something substantial to clobber.'

'Oh! I always wondered about that.'

They talked about her as though she couldn't hear them. She didn't care. She needed to pound something. She needed to obliterate it. It took Grace ten minutes of hardcore bin bashing, a blistered hand, a stiff whiskey and a talk with a visiting Father Frank to calm down. She was spent – emotionally, physically, psychologically – and the wake hadn't even begun.

Chapter Fifteen

Jack

FATHER FRANK ARRIVED HALF an hour before the crowd, and after he'd talked Grace off a cliff, he shook Jack's hand. 'I'm just paying my respects the same as anyone else.'

'It was good of you to come,' Jack said.

'You'll have a word with Molly,' Father Frank said, 'she's asking for a rosary.'

'I'll talk to her, Father, but to be fair, one wouldn't hurt.'

Father Frank shook his head. 'Rabbit had such strong opposing views.'

'Rabbit is gone,' Jack said quietly.

Father Frank sighed. 'Of course, I'd be happy to lead a rosary.'

'Thank you, Father,' Jack said. They walked together to see Rabbit.

'*Highway to Hell*,' Father Frank said with a raised eyebrow and a creeping smile.

'She would have loved that,' Jack said.

'It's her all right.'

Molly insisted that Father Frank try some sandwiches and, because he was driving, as much tea as Marjorie could pour into him. She went off to check on Grace, who was having a wash and changing her clothes following her garden meltdown. Davey hovered, unsure where to put himself, and eventually just melted away into another room. The two men sat face to face beside Rabbit, laid out with hands crossed, and instead of rosary beads holding an 'access all areas' laminate in her hands.

Father Frank nodded over to the pass. 'Nice touch.'

'All Marjorie,' Jack said. 'She brought our girl back to us.'

'She certainly did.'

'I want to talk to you about when she's gone.'

'I don't follow.'

'I'd like to keep her, at least a part of her, with me.'

'Well, the funeral directors handle the ashes, Jack.'

'Oh yes, I understand that, but I was wondering about it spiritually, how would that sit with you, some of my girl in an urn, maybe, in the Glasnevin Cemetery wall or the memorial garden, a piece of her here with her mammy and me, some for Juliet, Davey and Grace.'

'The body is just the host, Jack.'

'So it's fine, then?'

'Fine by me.'

Jack smiled. 'Well, that's good, but I'm thinking more about what God would say, if he's around at all.'

'Your faith is waning too, Jack?' Father Frank said, in a tone that suggested he was disheartened.

'Oh no, my faith has been up and down for a lifetime. Don't worry, I'm enlisted.'

'I'd say God will be fine with whatever way you choose to honour Rabbit.'

'OK, lovely, they can put people in all kinds of things now – jewellery, stones, pots – they can even do ash collages. Or maybe that's just for pets.' He stood up, slowly and painfully, holding his back, and shook Father Frank's hand.

'Back issues, Jack?'

'Beanbag trouble, Father,' he said.

If Father Frank had no idea what the old man was talking about, he pretended to. 'Fair enough.'

'You've been a good friend to Molly and me for many years,' Jack said, moving over to the coffin to gaze upon his child. 'You've put up with a lot.'

Father Frank stood beside him. 'From Molly or Rabbit?'

'Both,' Jack said, and the two men smiled. Molly had cursed poor Father Frank out of it many a time, and they'd shared many a ferocious debate, but he had huge time for a woman who was both charitable and formidable.

'I consider Molly a dear friend.'

Jack patted his back.

'As for Rabbit, you do know Molly snuck me into the hospice room to give her the last rites?'

'Oh I do,' he said. 'She had Marjorie and Grace in on it with her.'

'The woman was in a semi-coma.'

'She was.'

'And she still managed to rise out of her sleep and yell boo at me! God Almighty,' he said, blessing himself, 'I thought my end had come.'

Jack chuckled a little. 'She always loved a joke.'

'Especially at God's expense.'

Jack's smiled faded. 'Looks like he had the last laugh.'

Father Frank was mortified. 'I didn't mean anything by it.'

'I know that. You put up with a lot from my daughter over the years, especially when Johnny was ill.'

'Johnny died believing in God and heaven, Jack, he believed one day he'd see Rabbit again. I like to think that day has come.'

'Oh the things they'd say to one another.'

'Johnny Faye would love to be able to say I told you so,' Father Frank said.

'And Rabbit Hayes would give him that just to be in his arms one more time.'

The two men stood over Rabbit, nodding.

'How would you feel about a slice of Pauline's coffee cake?'

'From across the road?'

'The very one.'

'That's legendary.'

'It is,' Jack said. 'Better get in before the crowd.'

After that, and as the ladies of the house dressed and made themselves up and Davey Hayes disappeared into an episode of *Murder, She Wrote*, Father Frank and Jack Hayes chowed down on Pauline's famous coffee cake.

Chapter Sixteen

Molly

MOLLY HAD BEEN TALKING to God all day. As people started coming through the door, she asked him to give her strength. *Dear God, help me out. Do that and I'll pop ten euro in the poor box.* They arrived in their droves just after six. The room reached capacity within minutes of the first visitor's arrival. It was chaotic. *Dear God, keep me on my feet and I won't say the word fuck for the rest of the day.* She stayed busy, serving sandwiches, tea, coffee, red wine, white wine and whiskey, and sherry for the elderly.

She'd had a quick team talk fifteen minutes beforehand.

'Grace and Marjorie, you're on sandwich and cake duty. Jack's on spirits. Lenny white and red wine and Davey, tea and coffee.'

Davey put up his hand. 'Can I be on wine?'

Dear God, give me patience. I'll give you an extra prayer before bedtime.

'Fine, don't drink it all. I'll take orders.'

Grace took a moment to pull Jeffrey aside to remind him that she had eyes like a hawk and she'd be watching him. 'Two sandwiches is your limit, and no cake.'

'Ah, Ma!'

'Fine, one slice of cake – a thin slice, don't make me come after you.' He knew she wasn't in the humour for messing; he'd heard she'd taken the hurley to the bins.

Stephen wanted to help. 'What can I do, Gran?' he said.

'Just be your sweet self, love.'

'And me, Gran?' Bernard said.

'That goes double for you, sunshine.'

'I'll wash up,' Stephen said.

'I'll dry.'

'Thank you, boys.' *Dear God, mind those boys or I will come after you.*

People queued to see Rabbit and to pay their respects. Once they did so, they were greeted by a member of the Hayes family offering them food and beverages and it seemed to work – there was time for kind words and heartfelt condolences, a story or two about the good old days. No one mentioned the tweet, but Molly was in no doubt that they'd all read about it or heard it. It hung over her like a cloud but she kept busy tending to the needs of others, just as she liked it.

She spent a lot of time repeating the words tea, coffee, wine, a little nip surely? Or you have to try Pauline's coffee cake, until Pauline herself called a halt to her gallop.

'I'm taking over.'

'I'm fine.'

'This is not a restaurant and you are no waitress. Relax a bit, talk to people.'

Molly didn't really want to talk to people, but her best friend wasn't taking no for an answer so she abided.

'Fine, then, Monica Leary wants an egg mayo sandwich, a coffee and a nip of whiskey on the side.'

'Does she now?' Pauline said. 'I hope it keeps fine for her.'

Without something to do, Molly just took a moment to repose.

'It could have been worse,' a stranger said to her, a man in his early sixties.

'Excuse me?'

'My Tracy died in a three-car pile-up.'

Dear God, take these murderous thoughts away before I dishonour you in the worst way.

'How is that worse?' she asked through gritted teeth.

'Well, you couldn't have laid her out in the dining room,' he said sincerely.

'Do I know you?'

'No,' he said, 'I saw the news #AllDressedUpNowhereToGo and I only live half a mile away.'

'So you know no one here?'

'I know Father Frank.'

'Right,' she said, and she turned to face the assembled crowd. 'Ah, just a quick word from management.'

Everyone became silent and waited for the mother of the deceased to say something profound. *Dear God, forgive me for what I'm about to say.*

'Anyone who's here just 'cause of the news #GetTheFuckOut.'

As nearly everyone in the room knew Molly Hayes well, the room exploded with laughter; even Grace managed to break a smile, although she was still steaming. The ice was well and truly broken and suddenly people were nattering.

'Rabbit Hayes on the news,' Pauline said. 'And the lovely things they said about her as a journalist and blogger.'

Grace was still upset. 'Ryan shouldn't have done it.'

'Still, did you see how many retweets? Over three thousand. It's mad!' Justin from down the road said.

'I will speak to him, love,' Lenny said, addressing his wife's concern.

'I heard it on the radio,' Jack's oldest friend Gerry said. 'I don't understand social media. I can't get my head around it – a young boy can communicate with the entire country from his bedroom! It's mad.'

'Not just the country,' Bernard explained. There's a few retweets in Germany, France and the UK.'

'Bananas,' Gerry said.

Grace felt heartsick. 'I just don't understand why Ryan would do that.'

'He was just showing off,' Stephen said.

'Well 3,044 retweets – no, wait, 3,045 retweets is cool,' Bernard said, looking at his phone.

'It's not cool, Bernard, it's sickening,' Grace said. 'And your brother is . . .'

'. . . trying to make us laugh,' Molly said.

'Well he's doing a very poor job of it,' Grace said.

'Rabbit would laugh,' Molly said.

Marjorie nodded. 'She's right.'

'But it's not funny, Ma.' Tears brimmed in Grace's eyes.

Molly put her arm around her eldest daughter. 'I know, love.' She kissed her head as tears spilled down Grace's face.

'She's not a punchline,' she said, crying into Molly's chest. *Dear God, help me. Please help me.* Everyone else in the room became quiet, Grace's rawness reminding them that the people serving them drink and food were heartbroken.

All of Davey's old bandmates – Francie, Jay, Louis and Kev – were standing together with their wives. Jay pushed forward, raised his glass and addressed the crowd. Francie followed suit, and within seconds the entire room were holding up their glasses and waiting in silence.

'To Rabbit Hayes, you were loved and we will miss you whether you are here, there or nowhere,' Jay said. Rabbit had not just been their sound engineer, she was their mascot and bouncer given half a chance. It was heartfelt and Jay was choked up.

'Hear, hear!' Francie said, and everyone drank to Rabbit's memory and the room once again became noisy with chatter and buzz.

When the majority had cleared out and only the core friends and family were left, about thirty in number, the lads pulled out their guitars, Louis played the piano and Davey played on his dad's old bodhrán. Jack's friend Gerry went to his car and brought in his accordion. 'Brought it just in case,' he said as he passed Molly, holding it high. Francie's missus Lorraine had a good voice and Francie could hold a tune. So could Jay and Kev, and even Grace joined in once she had enough whiskey in her. They sang songs about freedom, love and loss. They sang about war and hope and despair. Then Louis hit a familiar key and all the other players stopped playing and he played the love song Johnny wrote for Rabbit so many years ago, and with Lorraine singing her heart out there was barely a dry eye in the house. Molly just sat with her hands in her lap and she didn't cry or sing along, she just breathed in and out and in her head she repeated the words *Dear God, dear God, dear God, dear God . . .* she couldn't think of anything else to say.

Father Frank got up to leave and in that moment she felt a little desperate. *Dear God . . . Dear God . . . Dear God . . .* 'One decade of the rosary before you go, Father,' Molly asked. He looked around at Rabbit, the musicians, friends and family.

'This is what she wanted, Molly. Not me or God.'

'You're right, Frank, but Rabbit's gone. I'm asking you to pray for us, the people she left behind.'

He sighed and pulled off his scarf. 'You should have gone into politics, Molly.' She looked around at the others assembled in the room.

'Just one decade.'

Jack piped up from the corner he shared with Gerry and his accordion. 'Maybe just one.'

'I'm in,' Marjorie said, and shrugged off Davey's dirty look.

'So we're actually doing this? Praying over Rabbit's dead body.'

'The irony's not lost, son,' Molly said, before kneeling on the ground. Grace, Jack and Marjorie followed suit, then the rest of the party, leaving Davey standing by his stone-faced sister's side. Father Frank made the sign of the cross and everyone followed.

'In the name of the Father, the Son and the Holy Spirit,' she said aloud, finishing the sign of the cross. *Here we go. Just relax, Molly, just breathe in and out and everything will be fine.* Father Frank started to rattle off the Apostles' Creed: 'I believe in God the Father, creator of heaven and earth, and in Jesus Christ.'

'I believe in God the Father . . .' Molly said, but then she stopped. *But do I? How many times do you have to knock before you have to admit there's nobody home? And the Catholic Church? Do I really believe in them and their message? Now?*

After everything they've done? Every sin they've committed? Every lie they've told? Every obstruction of justice? Why would those men and women indulge in corruption if they really believed in the all-seeing God the Father, the creator of heaven and earth?

As the others prayed she remained silent and still, looking over to where her son was standing by his dead sister, shielding her from the Catholics. *It's a scam, Ma,* Rabbit had said so many times before. *Catholic Corp. – it's just about the money. You know that. Deep down you know that.* She hadn't listened. *I'll listen now. Talk to me, Rabbit? Tell me I'm an old fool? Where are you, love?* But Rabbit didn't say a word. She was gone and it felt like she'd taken hope and the promise of eternity with her. *Sorry.*

She listened as Father Frank said the words 'the forgiveness of sins, the resurrection of the body and the life everlasting', and looking at her dead daughter and hearing them rattled off in such a meaningless way sparked a profound realisation: Molly Hayes didn't believe a word of it. When Rabbit died, emptiness crept inside of Molly, and in that void no God could reside. *You were right, love, it's all a fucking scam.* As Father Frank led the rosary and those gathered uttered the words to the Our Father and the Hail Mary, a deeply sad Molly Hayes said a short prayer of her own. *Dear God, I'm done.*

Chapter Seventeen

Davey

IT WAS AFTER TEN at night. Everyone else had gone, but Marjorie had insisted on staying on until every last dish was washed, dried and put away. She spotted the bus pulling into the terminal, which was only across the road.

'Time to go,' she said.

'Get a taxi,' Davey said.

'I can see the bus stop from here.'

'Don't get on a bus, not now. It's late.'

'I'm fine, Davey.'

She grabbed her coat and said her goodbyes to Molly, who was sitting next to Rabbit, one hand placed on Rabbit's cold head, the other hugging a cup of hot tea. Jack was asleep. Grace hugged her.

'Thank you.' Her gratitude was heartfelt. They women sank into one another, long enough for Davey to grab his coat and wallet.

'Where are you going?'

'The bus.'

'Davey!'

'Just let him,' Grace said. 'He'd follow you into a collapsing mine if it meant getting out of here.'

Davey shrugged his shoulders. His sister was right. It was bad enough looking down on Rabbit's corpse in a house full of people during daylight hours, but with just the Hayeses and in darkness, well . . . that was just . . . wrong.

They sat together at the back of a half-empty bus, the heat from the engine blowing through a grid warming the backs of their legs and slowly rising upwards.

'Like the good old days,' Davey said, looking out at the night sky. The combination of the moving bus, the passing lights, the warm air circulating around his nether regions and the whiskey was having a hypnotic effect on his overloaded, burdened, tired mind.

'You're slurring.'

'I'm sorry.'

'This isn't you trying to get laid, is it, Davey?'

He laughed. 'I couldn't think of anything worse right now.'

She smiled. 'Me neither.'

'I thought death was supposed to make people horny.'

'Maybe it's impending death,' she said. He thought about that; maybe she was right. They did share that awkward kiss outside the hospice . . .

'Hmmm, well, the way I feel right now, I may never have sex again,' he said.

'Yeah, well, you're a parent now – apparently it has a massive effect on libido.'

'How did that happen again?' He smiled but that smile didn't reach his eyes. He was scared, really scared. *What have I done? What have I done? What have I done?*

Marjorie's ringing phone interrupted the beginnings of what could have been a mild panic attack; she lifted it out of her

93

handbag and the word 'mother' appeared on the screen. She dropped it back in her bag as fast as if it were a hot potato.

'You're not going to speak to her,' Davey said.

'She didn't even come to the wake.' Marjorie spat each word out in anger. 'Rabbit was the only real friend I ever had. Molly Hayes took care of me. I spent more time in your house than I did in my own and it suited her. She lives down the bloody road. The least she could have done is paid her respects.'

'You know what she's like.'

'I do, that's the problem.'

'And Rabbit wasn't your only real friend.'

'Don't start, Davey.'

'I'm your friend.'

'I spoke to Rabbit on the phone every day. When's the last time I spoke to you?'

'Just now, yesterday, the day before.'

'On the phone.'

'I don't really do phone calls.'

'Yeah well, if we were friends you probably would have made an exception when my husband found out we'd slept together. Or maybe on the day he booted me out of my own house. Or when the separation agreement was signed. Or that first night I spent alone in a one-bed apartment—'

'OK, I get it,' he said. He couldn't stand to hear a laundry list of his selfishness and inadequacies. Not now.

'Or maybe when Rabbit's diagnosis moved to terminal, the worst day of my life.'

'I'm so sorry, Marjorie.' He meant it. 'I'm sorry for everything.' And maybe it was the moving bus, the passing lights, the warm air around his nethers and the whiskey, but tears spilled from his eyes. He wiped them away with the back of his hand. His nose started to run; Marjorie pulled a tissue from her bag.

'I'm going to be a better friend,' he said, wiping his nose and, when he'd pulled himself together, 'I'll call once a week.' He could hear Rabbit laughing.

'Yeah, right,' Marjorie said, and he put his arm around her shoulder and she snuggled in, and maybe it was the moving bus, the passing lights, the warm air circulating around his nether regions and the whiskey, but he knew that no matter what, he would keep that promise.

You better, Rabbit in his head said.

Chapter Eighteen

Juliet

Moments, minutes and hours blurred together. Time jumped and swayed, and some even disappeared into a black hole. Still, Juliet remembered snatches of time, quite clearly. When she saw her dead mother laid out in a box in her grandparents' dining room it was a shock. Despite the clothes and make-up, she didn't look like herself at all; rather instead like a shop window mannequin dressed as Rabbit Hayes, or a waxwork that was supposed to look like Rabbit Hayes but without expression or signs of life – it just wasn't quite right. In fact, if she was featured in a waxworks museum, Juliet would have asked for her money back. Her mother's lips were so thin and slightly yellow under the pale pink lipstick. Her expression was grim. She didn't care that her mother didn't look very pretty. She was used to that. Sickness often stole her beauty, only for it to return in flashes, when she smiled, or winked, or felt a little better; when she wore something pretty and her wig was on straight. When she was alive she was still beautiful, but now all beauty was gone. She was staring at a withering husk. She didn't speak – Davey was watching – instead she just called out to her ma in her head: *Go*, she said, and she heard Rabbit say the words from the end of their all-time favourite movie, *Thelma &*

Louise, *'You sure?'* and she nodded to herself *'Yeah . . . yeah.'* She turned to her uncle.

'I want to go home.'

In the car on the way home, Lenny was fuming with Ryan because of his tweet. He said nothing. They drove in absolute silence but Juliet mused that if it were a cartoon, there would be steam coming off Lenny and his cheeks would burn vibrant red. She knew Lenny thought things were bad enough without arguing over whether or not it was appropriate to announce her mother's death adding the #AllDressedUpNowhereToGo. Initially she didn't get it, but then her heart was broken, her brain felt heavy, her thoughts were fuzzy and she was confused, lost and every part of her ached. She sat in the back of the car thinking about it for a while and when she worked it out she started to smile. *That's something my ma would have said.*

Lenny left Ryan and Juliet alone in the house. 'What do you want to do?' Ryan asked as his father drove out of the driveway.

'Nothing.' It was something Juliet had said often but had never really meant it before. She wanted nothing. She couldn't think about eating, drinking, walking, talking, moving, sitting, pooing, peeing – even sleeping seemed like a big ask. She just stood paralysed in the centre of the kitchen.

'Cool. I'll be in the sitting room watching TV,' Ryan said. He walked into the other room, allowing her some alone time.

She realised she was standing exactly in the spot where her mother's leg had snapped in two beneath her just over two weeks previously. The blood had remained on the floor for over a week because they had left in an ambulance and Juliet wasn't allowed to return home other than to collect her things. She cleaned it up when her ma was in the hospice and Davey had dropped her over for some clothes. He'd waited in the car, having a snooze, listening to the radio. She'd walked in on a pool of sticky, congealed, smelly blood. She'd mopped it up the best she could. He'd walked in on her. He was shocked and upset. It was graphic. Davey didn't have a strong stomach, not like Juliet. She could handle anything except maybe death. Death had thrown her. She scanned the floor for any sign of her mother's blood – nothing. It was clean. She wondered if she had one of those blue lights from *CSI* or *Bones*, would it appear as a giant black spider? Then she saw it, a little speckle on the white skirting board. She moved towards it, got down on the ground and got really close. *Is it?* She touched it gently so that she wouldn't rub it off. A tiny remnant remained on her finger. She tried to smell it. *No smell.* She stared again at what was left – it wasn't a bright red, it was ruby, closer to black.

'What are you doing?' Ryan asked from the doorway.

'Looking at Ma's blood.'

He moved forward, standing over her. He bent down.

'Where?'

'There,' she said, pointing to the spot.

'Are you sure that's not just dirt?'

'No,' she admitted. 'But I think it's blood.'

'Do you want me to clean it?' he asked.

'No.'

'What do you want to do, Juliet?'

'I want to mark it.'

'Not sure where this is going,' he said.

She stood up, pulled a marker out of the drawer and then circled the blood and added an arrow with the word 'Ma' written in a second bubble.

'Are you all right?' Ryan asked, and he was worried – she could tell because he wasn't acting like a smart-arse.

'I'm fine,' she said, and in her bid to escape further questioning, she promptly walked into a door.

Part Three

The Funeral

Chapter Nineteen

Grace

GRACE WALKED INTO THE kitchen at 6 a.m. Molly was already making tea and Davey was in the shower. She could hear her father pottering in the attic. She stretched her tired back and rolled her stiff neck, leaned over the coffin and gave her baby sister a kiss.

'I've got to go home, see you later,' she said, then she said goodbye to her ma and got in her car and drove home.

The house was unusually still. Bernard had slept in his gran's spare room. Ryan was still with Juliet in Rabbit's. Good thing too, because even a decent night's sleep had not helped to diminish the rage that burned inside her when her thoughts moved in Ryan's direction. She checked on Jeffrey. He was sound asleep in his room. She turned off his night light. *Getting a bit old for that, buddy*. She checked Stephen's room. It was empty. She wasn't worried. He was probably with a girl or sleeping it off on a friend's floor. *You're young. Live a little – in fact, live a lot. Wish I had*. Lenny was snoring; his was a gentle snore, like a cute pug puppy. He was at peace. She didn't want to disturb him.

She stripped off in the bathroom and got into the shower. As she washed she looked down at herself, particularly her breasts, which, to be fair, looking down were hard to miss. She'd always liked her breasts. They were perfectly round, the nipple centred, and even though they'd dropped after four kids, they held a good shape; they were still impressive, and if she was honest a source of great pride. *What now?* she thought. Just cut them off? She couldn't imagine it. It was just too drastic – after all, her breasts were such a part of who she was. *Knockers Hayes.* That's what the boys had called her, back in the day. They were the first thing her husband noticed about her on the day they met in that cafeteria in the bank. Her breasts, her hair, her eyes, her smile, in that order – he said she was a knockout. Knockers the knockout, that was Grace Hayes before children. After her children she was still a good-looking woman – maybe her curves weren't in exactly the same places, and some were more exaggerated than others, but she still had those knockers, which by then had been a five-star restaurant for her kids and a private playground for her husband for many long years. She owed her breasts a lot. *What now?*

Rabbit's identity lay in her strength and vitality. Her gobby one-liners, her star-crossed love and, of course, her talent. Anything that kid put her mind to she could achieve. When Johnny bought a ticket for Rabbit to go to America, to leave him behind and start a new life, she resisted. She wanted to be with him forever but he would not be moved. He was so determined to free her. So she went and she did everything he asked of her. She lived, survived and thrived. Rabbit returned from America a journalist, and she was a good one, at least in Grace's humble opinion, but then what did boring banker Grace know about anything?

Rabbit was more than a sister, mother, friend – she was Rabbit Hayes. Grace was what? Some kids called her a MILF once. When she discovered it meant Mom I'd Like to Fuck, it made her feel sick. Now it was the only thing she could think of – MILF! *Is that what I am? Is that all I am? Just something pretty to look at?* If Rabbit was still alive, and if Grace had confided her fears, she would have told her she was so much more than that: she was smart and funny and loving and kind. She would remind her of her eye for detail and the fact that she could fix almost anything. That she was a beloved mother of four boys, a supportive wife and a successful homemaker. Grace was the natural heir to Molly's crown, and that was no mean feat. She was the one every member of the family confided in and relied on. She had helped Rabbit care for her own daughter long before she was ever sick. She enabled Rabbit to soar and was always there when she needed a place to land. Grace, like her ma, got the job done – any job – nothing was beyond her. Grace was important. Rabbit would have told her all of that and more, but Rabbit was gone. Grace was left alone with her own troubled mind. *What now?* She didn't even think about her ovaries at that point. She wasn't even sure they'd have to go. Maybe not, but if they did, she didn't care so much about what was inside, she was done with motherhood, she could handle that – at least she thought she could – but her breasts . . . *Knockers Hayes.*

She didn't hear Lenny step into the bathroom. There was too much steam to see clearly and she was crying. She felt the cold air as he opened the shower door, then the hair on his legs brush against her, his hands on her hips and his breath on her neck.

'I missed you,' he said.

'Lenny?'

'Yeah,' he said, and kissed her neck.

'What's your favourite thing about me?'

'What?'

'You heard.'

'Is this a trap?' he said, and he stopped kissing her neck.

'No.'

'It feels like a trap.' After being married for what felt like 208 years, Lenny could sense a trap a mile away.

'What's your favourite thing about me?'

'Everything. I love everything except your stupid questions.'

'My breasts?'

'Love 'em,' he said, and he grinned like a kid and found them and filled his hands.

'What if they were gone?' she said.

'Don't mess,' he said, suddenly serious.

'I'm not messing. I'm asking.'

'Well, that would make me really very fucking sad,' he said.

'Me too,' she whispered.

'But they're not gone, they're right here. Happy days,' he said. She turned to face him – an awkward turn, the shower wasn't big enough for major manoeuvring.

'I have the gene,' she said, and as soon as she saw his face fall she berated herself for saying anything at all. It was Rabbit's day. *You promised yourself you'd wait. Stupid Grace.* Lenny let her go. He stood, awkward and frozen to the spot.

'I'm sorry,' she said.

'You got tested?' he said, and she nodded.

'When?'

'A while ago.'

'Why?'

'Because I don't want my family fighting over my kids and what to do with them when I'm dead.'

'Well they have me,' he said.

'You think that's enough?'

'No, of course not.'

He stepped out of the shower, grabbed a towel and sat at the side of the bath. He was shaking.

'You have the gene?' he said, looking up at her, and she nodded. 'But you don't have cancer?'

'No.'

'But you have the gene?'

'Yes.'

'What now?' he asked, and she burst into tears. *What now?*

Later, in the car, they didn't really speak. Lenny put the radio on and they listened to the morning DJs on 2FM make jokes and banter. Lenny even laughed once or twice. 'You can't beat Bernard O'Shea,' he said, chuckling.

'Yeah, he's gas,' Grace said half heartedly, having not heard one word that had come out of Bernard O'Shea's mouth. Lenny drove. Grace looked out the window at the world passing by, everyone doing their own thing. She wondered what pain and suffering the woman who was hunched over and dragging her shopping trolley had endured throughout her life. She was making her way slowly and steadily through the streets of Dublin in a pair of brown shoes, one taller than the other. A hunch and fucked-up shoes were probably the very least of her problems, and yet there she was, pulling her trolley, keeping going. She looked at the young girl with striking painted eyebrows, wearing half nothing and with her skin covered in goosebumps, scrolling through her phone with ridiculously long nails while waiting for a bus. What loss and desperation had she experienced in life so far? She turned around to face her husband, who was crying.

'Lenny?'

'Sorry.'

'It's OK.'

'Can't believe she's gone,' he said.

'Me neither.'

'I can't believe you have the gene.'

'Me neither.'

'Oh fuck, Grace. Oh fuck.'

'It's going to be OK,' she promised. 'I'll make it OK.'

He wiped the tears away from his face with the back of his hand just as Bernard O'Shea burst into a funny little ditty. He changed the channel to Newstalk. They were debating domestic water charges. 'No,' he said, and he turned the radio off.

The house was alive with activity. Molly was cooking breakfast and feeding Bernard. Dressed in a pressed suit, he looked handsome. It was so unusual to see Bernard out of a tracksuit.

'Hey, Sporty Spice,' Lenny said to his son, 'looking good.' Bernard laughed because he liked it when his da called him Sporty Spice – Bernard was odd like that. He stopped eating breakfast long enough to give his ma a hug.

'Where's Stephen?'

'He arrived here half an hour ago with some young one. I sent him home to get Jeff.'

'OMG we forgot about Jeff,' Grace said to Lenny, and took her phone out to see she'd missed eight calls. She held it up. 'It was on silent!'

'Don't worry about it, Stephen had forgotten his tie anyway.'

'Right,' she said. She turned to her mother. 'All right, Ma?'

'Sausage?' Molly asked.

'Yeah, go on,' she said.

'Your da's moved into the attic, and I'll tell you something, if he gets caught up in that fucking beanbag again I'll . . .' She walked into the hallway and shouted up the stairs, aiming her voice at the hatch. 'Put on a suit, old man. Don't have me go up there, I'm warnin' ya.' She walked back to Grace, then as though she'd just remembered something she turned on her heel and walked back under the hole in the ceiling. 'You can go to lunch when your daughter is buried. Not one second before that, do hear me, Jack?' She waited for a second before stamping her foot. He peered out of the ceiling. 'I hear ya, Molly. I hear ya,' he said, making his way down the steps. 'The angels in heaven can hear you.'

'Well if that's the case you can tell them they can—'

'Molls, enough of that now,' he said. Jack didn't mind salty language, but telling angels to eff off was beyond the pale.

'Fine,' she said. She walked back into the kitchen as Grace was plating up sausages and toast for Lenny and herself.

'Where's Davey?'

'He dropped off Juliet and Ryan over an hour ago and disappeared.'

The hackles on Grace's neck rose. 'Ryan's here.'

Lenny stood up. 'Calm down, Grace.'

'I'm calm,' she said. Then she stood up and brushed herself down and walked out of the room. Ryan was on the sofa in the sitting room alone and in silence. She sat in the armchair opposite him, afraid of what she might be capable of if she got too close.

'Why?' she asked. 'Don't say because Rabbit would find it funny.'

'What if that's the reason?' he said.

'It's not good enough.'

'Why?'

'Because Rabbit is gone and making a bloody joke of it is disrespectful,' Grace said, and her voice shook in anger and sadness.

'I just wanted to make her proud.'

'What do you mean?'

'My job was to make her laugh, to say the things no one else would say.'

Grace sighed a deep sigh that came from her very core.

'Your job?'

'Yeah, my job, you know – since she got sick. Juliet took care of her medicines, you took her to her appointments, Gran fed her, Granda brought her little presents. I said inappropriate things that made her laugh.'

'Come here,' she said, and Ryan seemed unsure.

'Come here,' she said, and she stood up. Ryan walked up to his ma with his hands up. She took him in her arms and hugged him. He wasn't as comfortable with hugging as his older brother Bernard.

'You're hard work, Ryan, but you're worth it,' she said.

'Thanks, Ma,' he said, and he removed himself. 'So while the going is good I have something to tell you.'

Grace deflated. 'What?'

'Juliet has a black eye.'

'What did you do?' she said with alarm.

'Nothing.' His hands were up again. 'I know it sounds like a domestic abuse poster but she walked into a door. I swear.'

'God Almighty,' she said, and she walked into the hall in time to see Juliet appear with a swollen and black eye. She was holding a packet of frozen peas to its side.

'I think it's a little late for peas, Juliet,' she said.

'I know but it feels good.' She hugged her and kissed the top of her head, then she took her niece by the hand and brought her into the kitchen, pointing to her face.

'This is what happens when you give kids benzos, Ma.'

'Lesson learned, but to be fair she slept like a top, didn't you, love?' Molly said, before putting a large plate of freshly cooked sausages in the middle of the table.

'Yes, Gran,' Juliet said.

After that, Molly, Juliet, Ryan, Bernard, Lenny and Grace ate sausage sandwiches and drank tea together. Grace ordered everyone to shovel them in as quickly as possible so that there would be no temptation for Jeffrey.

'What's he supposed to eat, Grace?' Juliet asked. Grace took a breakfast bar out of her handbag and placed it on the table.

'Poor Jeffrey,' the black-eyed Juliet said, and everyone nodded. 'Still, I'd rather be fat than an orphan,' she said, and Ryan burst out laughing. Molly raised an eyebrow and when her granddaughter's lips curled into a smile, she winked. 'There's my girl,' she said as Grace stabbed her fork in the last sausage and shoved it in her mouth.

Later, upstairs in her parents' box room, Grace applied make-up to Juliet's face to cover the bruise.

'You want a little eye shadow?' she asked. Juliet hunched her shoulders. She didn't care. *Just like your ma.* She tried to encourage her to wear a pretty dress but she was more comfortable in jeans and a T-shirt. 'If Ma's wearing AC/DC, I am too.'

'Fair enough,' Grace said, brushing Juliet's long brown hair the way she'd brushed her mother's so many years ago.

'You can tell me anything, you know,' Grace said to her niece.

'I know.'

'I wish I could change things,' Grace said. *I have the gene.*

'Me too.'

'Aside from your mammy being alive, would you change anything else?' Grace asked.

'Like what?'

'Like where you want to live?'

'No.'

'America is a long way away,' Grace said.

'I know.'

'And Stephen and I bought that caravan, it's parked outside the house.' *Oh but wait, I have the gene.*

'I know, Gran says it looks disgraceful.'

'Well isn't that nice of her?'

'Stephen was really going to move into a caravan so I could take his room?' Juliet asked.

'Yep.'

She smiled. 'What are you going to do with it now?'

'Sell it, I suppose.'

'Or you could go to Wexford on your holidays,' Juliet said. 'Ma loved Wexford.'

'Maybe you could come.'

'Can't, I'll be with Davey in America.'

And I don't know where I'll be. I have the gene.

Grace left it at that. The child had made up her mind. Rabbit had made up her mind, but everything inside her screamed *THIS IS ALL WRONG*. She finished brushing Juliet's hair.

'I love you, Juliet,' she said.

'Love you too, Grace,' Juliet said, and her eyes filled with tears, which threatened to streak her make-up.

'Can I go now?' she asked, and Grace nodded, and Juliet jumped to her feet and made her way downstairs. Bernard and Ryan were back in front of the TV.

'What are you doing?' Ryan asked Juliet, as Grace passed the room and met her mother standing aimlessly in the hallway.

'Waiting for Davey,' she said. The child was staring out the window.

'He's been on the missing list all morning,' Molly said, and Grace's heart threatened to break. *Where the hell are you, Davey?*

Chapter Twenty

Davey

DAVEY WOKE WITH A head full of questions and a heart full of ache. He needed to escape – just to breathe, to think, to plan, to plot, to work out what was the best thing to do. He got into his mother's car, intending to drive to Dollymount Strand, but the car had other plans. He found himself driving towards the graveyard. He parked up and started walking. He hadn't been there in years. He wasn't even sure which way to go; he thought it might be a left at the end of the long path and then another long walk before taking another right, and then he wasn't sure. When he finally came upon Johnny's grave he sat in the dirt as the rain came tumbling down.

'Hey man, sorry it's been so long, but then again you left us so . . .' He tried to joke but his heart wasn't in it. He really felt like a drink, any drink, by the neck and covered by a paper bag. That seemed appropriate. 'So Rabbit died, the day before yesterday. You seen her?' He leaned against the cold head-stone. 'If you see her, tell her . . . No . . . Ask her what the fuck was she thinking, giving her kid to me? I know I asked but I'm a selfish asshole. She was the adult, you know that, you remember, even when we were kids, four years younger and she was still the boss.' He looked around; he was alone. 'You believed, Johnny, you thought you were going somewhere and that this wasn't the end. Did you? Did you go somewhere? Can you hear me? Give me a sign, please. Tell me I'm not alone in this.' He didn't expect a sign, not really.

'Mwahaha!' A booming, distorted but familiar voice said from behind him.

'JESUS! FUCK!' He slammed his head against the headstone. Francie popped up from behind the gravestone, laughing. 'You're so easy . . .'

'What are you doing here?' he said, rubbing the bruise that was quickly growing on the back of his head.

'Same as you,' he said, and he sat down next to him.

'What did you hear?' he said.

'You being a dope,' Francie said, and he placed his hand on the stone. 'You'll be happy to hear he's grown into his nose but he's still the same fucking eejit he was back in the day.' He patted the stone and turned to face Davey. 'Johnny says stop being a dick.'

'I'm scared.'

'Of course you are.'

'I can't mess this up.'

'You can, and sometimes you will and sometimes you won't.'

'I don't handle change well.'

'Your life changes every day.'

'My view changes. My life stays the same.'

Francie thought about this. 'You should put that in a cracker.'

'What if I let her down?'

'I'll punch you till your dead,' Francie said.

115

'So I won't do that, then,' Davey said.

'Exactly.' He stood up. 'Come on, I'm fucking soaking.'

Davey struggled to his feet. 'I'm not ready to go home yet.'

'Good thing we're going somewhere else, then, isn't it?'

They ran through the graveyard, jumping over graves and any other obstacle in their path and towards Francie's van.

Davey had been MIA for three hours. In the van he took his phone out of his pocket – four missed calls. There were still two hours to go before Rabbit's service.

'We have time,' Francie said, driving down a familiar road. Davey didn't have to ask where they were going. He knew exactly where.

Francie parked outside Johnny Faye's house. They sat in the car for a few minutes before knocking on the door, taking in the street, the little terrace of houses built in brown brick with white window ledges, although one was painted a horrid yellow. Two houses either side of it had white plaster statuettes of the Lady on the Rock in each of the four picture windows.

'It's still the same,' Davey marvelled, 'even the ladies on the rocks! Remember Johnny used to say that they were a sign of something?'

'Yeah, a brothel or a drugs den.'

'Ethel in number 24 has been blind since birth and teaches piano. So, thinking back, it's unlikely,' Davey said.

'Brendan's an ex-priest and was a milkman for forty years,' Francie said.

'Maybe he sold drugs on his milk round,' Davey said.

'He's also a pioneer and served communion at mass, so he's definitely a dealer – never trust a communion-serving non-drinker. Now that I think of it, he probably works for Ethel.'

Davey chuckled a little. Francie took off his seat belt and got out of the car. 'You coming?' he said. Davey followed.

He rang the bell and Mrs Faye came to the door. She smiled and then cried when she saw them.

'I'm so sorry for your loss,' she said.

'Thanks, Mrs Faye,' he said.

'Ah, will you stop calling me Mrs Faye,' she said, hugging them both. She insisted they came in and offered them tea.

'Can't – it feels too weird to call you Karen,' Davey said.

'How's your mammy?' she asked.

'She's OK.'

'Of course she's not, she's devastated. I hope it doesn't kill her,' she said with a straight face.

Davey wasn't sure how to respond. 'Thanks,' he said eventually. They refused tea.

'OK if we hike up to Johnny's room, Mrs F?' Francie said.

She nodded. 'Of course it is, Francie love,' she said, 'makes sense.' She handed him the key to Johnny's door and he walked up the stairs, two at a time, with Davey following.

'And no interfering with each other up there,' she shouted up the stairs. 'Still straight, Mrs F, but if I ever get curious it won't be with this ugly fucker,' Francie said, and she laughed.

'True for you. Sorry, Davey, for laughing, but sure if you haven't a sense of humour you've got nothing,' she said, and she disappeared back into her kitchen.

He unlocked the door and Davey followed him into a room where time stood still. It was 1989 and those final days before Johnny was taken to a hospice for respite. Back then he knew deep down he'd never return to the house that couldn't cater for his increasing needs and to a mother of strong mind and weak back. He knew before anyone that change was going to come. Song lyrics were splashed across his bedroom wall; they must have taken him hours to scribble down. Davey could see the shake in his hands in the lettering. He could feel the heartbreak still hanging in the air. Black marker bled onto the white wall. He could picture Johnny on his navy and white striped duvet, listening to the tapes that were piled on the wooden floor and against the wall beside an old ghetto blaster with two tape decks. There were two large posters, one of Kitchen Sink with Johnny front and centre, a strong and convincing lead singer, surrounded by Francie, Jay, Louis and Davey all smiling, happy, excited, naïve. The other one was Davey's second band with Johnny, the one they formed when they already knew he was sick: The Sound. The line-up was the same, except by now Kev had replaced Louis. Johnny was still at the front but he seemed removed, apart, untouchable, and there was an inherent sadness in his eyes. No one smiled in that photo. To young girls back then it may have seemed sexy, but to grown men it was heartbreaking. The joy was gone. Francie stood by the window. Davey moved towards Johnny's locker. It still held personal items – a brush, some hair mousse and a medal on a chain – but Davey was staring at the photo stuck to Johnny's cracked old mirror. It was of Johnny and Rabbit, arm in arm, both grinning madly. She had grown up by then, her long sleek brown hair was highlighted, her glasses were gone, she was lithe and effortlessly pretty. He was his handsome self. *The way they were.* He touched the photo ever so gently, afraid to damage such a precious relic.

'This place hasn't changed a bit. Feels like he's just out, gone to the shop and he'll be back any minute. He'll walk through that door and ask us what the fuck we're doing here,' Davey said before joining his friend at the window. Behind the terraced houses was a high old grey wall with bits of green glass sticking out of the concrete. Davey could visualise his friend running along the wall in tight jeans, leather jacket, big hobnail boots and always wearing some kind of hat. Balance wasn't an issue back then – he was like a cat, stopping to stand behind the Byrnes' place.

'I can see him calling to me and Jay: "Let's go, come on". Stamping his feet on the broken glass and my ma shouting, "Get down, ya fool, before you fucking impale yourself".'

Davey nodded and chuckled at the memory.

'He never did. He'd just laugh and run the length of that wall, passing twelve houses and gardens, saying hello as he did,' he said, and Davey could hear the emotion in his voice.

'There ya are, Johnny, you playing any gigs lately?' Francie said in a high voice, imitating an auld one.

'Ah yeah, Mrs T, we're in the Baggot, come and see us,' Davey said, joining in.

'Ah now, I'm too old for all that but I'll tell my Tina, she loves ya, Johnny,' Francie said, and he sniffed. 'All the girls loved Johnny, but he only ever loved one girl.'

Davey nodded, craning his neck to follow the length of wall to its end. 'He'd run the full length of that wall and jump down and unlock the bike he'd attached to the lamp post in the laneway, and he'd wait for you to make your way to him on bikes, the long way round.'

'Yeah, well, the Byrne brothers didn't do walls. If I wanted to be an acrobat I'd have joined a circus,' Francie said.

'Johnny used to say you wouldn't need to be an acrobat to join the circus, the state of ya,' Davey said.

Francie chuckled to himself. 'He had a point.'

Davey could hear and see his dead friend as clearly as if he was in front of him. Everything was the same: the high grey-speckled wall, the green bottle glass sticking out, the old garage, even the cloudy sky. All that was missing was Johnny.

There was a candle half burned in the old wrought iron fire-place, and on its mantelpiece rested a King James Bible and a small brass statue of Jesus carrying his cross. There was an old beaten-up leather chair in the corner and two guitars on a stand next to it. Davey sat down on the chair, picked up a guitar and played a few chords. Francie lay on Johnny's bed and closed his eyes before reciting the words written above him on the wall.

> *Dear God, you have forsaken me, a boy who loved*
> *unconditionally.*
> *The pious say you hear my cry but are you there, Lord,*
> *as I die?*
> *You made it so this dreamer's dreams would end as they*
> *began,*
> *This lucky boy, unlucky man,*
> *A blinding light, a buzzing ceiling fan, a thumb to grip,*
> *A man undone but no longer sick.*

Davey turned to look at the writing scrawled on the wall above the small black fireplace. Francie knew it all off by heart. He

120

recited the words that Davey could see, the slanted, unsteady, unsure penmanship.

Dear God, I'll be again
With her, my love, my safest place.
Her devil's tongue, her angel face,
A broken heart will heal in death, a man in love cannot
*   regret.*

Mrs Faye walked through the open door with a tray of cupcakes.

'They're not songs, you know, they're prayers,' she said.

'Davey, have a cupcake.' She picked it up and put it in his hand before he could say no. 'Eat it,' she said before throwing one to Francie, who reached up and caught it. 'Feet off the bed,' she said, and he shot up and took a bite.

'There's so much sadness in this world,' she said, and the men nodded. She looked at Davey holding the cake and waited for him to put it in his mouth. He took a bite. She nodded and smiled.

'My Johnny had a terrible end, didn't he, lads?' she said, and Davey nodded with a mouth full of cake.

'If I had been a stronger woman I would have picked up a pillow and smothered him long before his last breath.'

'Jesus,' Davey said.

'Not physically, you understand, I mean emotionally. If I was emotionally stronger I'd have smothered him or drugged him or poisoned him or hired someone. I even read up on it. The internet's great for so many things. Hire a killer, buy a birdcage – you can do it all online these days.'

Davey threw Francie a searching look. *WTF.* Francie just smiled.

'I'd say your ma would have done what needed to be done, Davey.'

'Ah, I don't know,' Davey said, spitting crumbs.

'If she had witnessed what I witnessed, I think she would. She's a better woman than I am.'

'It's murder all the same, Mrs Faye,' Davey said.

'Ah, it is and it isn't. You've both smelled bedsores.' They nodded.

'I haven't been within fifty feet of a bedsore in twenty years and I can still smell it.' Her eyes brimmed and the tip of her nose reddened, but she smiled.

'To many my boy is just some sad story, but there were good times, great times, when there was so much promise and he was flying. Wasn't he, Francie?'

'Yeah, he was,' Francie said, placing his hands on her shoulders.

'Do you think they're together, Davey?'

'I don't know, Mrs Faye, but I'd like to think so.'

'I do. I believe. I think our Rabbit left this world early to be with him. Why else would they both die so young?'

Davey and Francie didn't have any answers.

'Take another bite, Davey,' she said, pointing to the cupcake.

'I'm grand.'

'One more.'

He bit into the cake.

'It's good, isn't it?' she said, and he nodded. 'The little retarded fellas make them and sell them on the stalls.'

Davey spluttered a little.

'What?' she said.

'I'm not sure you're supposed to say the word retarded anymore,' Davey said.

'Oh yeah? Since when?'

'I don't know, a while,' Davey said.

'Why's that, then?'

'I think it's hurtful.'

'God, I wouldn't want to do that. They're great fellas with their cupcakes, and always smiling. What should I say?' she asked.

'Mentally disabled,' Davey said.

'Right, and what if they're physically fucked as well?' she asked. Francie burst out laughing.

'Mentally and physically disabled,' Davey said.

'Jaysus, that's a mouthful,' she said.

'Don't mind him, Mrs F, you say what you want to say, you're hurting no one.'

'Ah no, Francie. I have to keep up with the times,' she said, and she grabbed what was left of the cupcake from him. 'Still, they're lovely cupcakes, aren't they?' she said.

'Excellent,' he said.

'Now, one more thing before you go – help me pull this bed back.'

Francie did as he was told. The wall was dusty; Mrs Faye took a moment to pull a dusting cloth from her pocket and clean the cobwebs away.

'Lean in,' she said, and Francie leaned in. Davey followed suit; behind the headboard there was another verse.

'He wrote this on his last day in this room. He didn't want it to be seen by anyone but Rabbit. I respected that, but being the day that's in it . . .'

123

They both read it. Davey looked from Mrs Faye to Francie and back to the wall.

'Read it for me, Francie,' Mrs Faye said, and she sat on her son's bed and closed her eyes and listened with a slight smile on her face.

*Dear God, she doesn't believe in you, in all you say and
   do and do not do.*
*There is no other life for her, no place to go, no love
   deferred.*
*But I believe, I conceive a world where I am Johnny
   Faye the singer and that boy on stage with her, my
   Rabbit by my side, making me laugh, making my life.*
*Dear God, if my end be suffering, open that door, let me
   fly in and when her time has come to land, dear God,
   allow me to grab her hand.*
Johnny Faye, 30 April 1989

'Holy fuck,' Davey said.

'The date,' Francie said to Davey.

'Yesterday's date!' he said.

'Give or take twenty-five years,' Mrs Faye said.

'Holy fuck,' Davey muttered.

'It's a mad old world,' Mrs Faye said, and she picked up her tray and moved to leave.

'You'll leave it as it was now, won't you, lads?' she said.

''Course, Mrs F.'

'Good on ya,' she said, and she left the room.

Francie helped Davey tidy the room, returning every-thing to where it had been before he'd touched it. Finally he smoothed down the bed. He looked around, satisfied the room was as they'd found it – a museum, and now not just to Johnny but to Rabbit, too. Davey sat on the edge of the bed and closed his eyes.

'You got your sign,' Francie said.

'I think I did.'

'Good, no more fucking around.'

As they were leaving Mrs Faye appeared with a plastic bag filled with cupcakes. 'Here, Davey, take these cupcakes from the mentally and physically disabled back to your mammy and tell her I'll see her at the funeral.'

He took them. 'Thanks, Mrs Faye.' He hugged her.

'A mad, mad world, isn't it, son?' she said, holding him tightly.

'It is,' he said, and when they let go he added, 'I loved him too, you know.'

'I do. Now go, we've all got a funeral to attend.'

Francie dropped Davey home. He could tell his mother was unhappy with him, as were Marjorie and Grace, but he didn't care. Juliet was subdued; he immediately noticed her black eye.

'What the . . .'

Molly put up her hands. 'I made a mistake, now let's move on.' When Vincent and Silent Ed arrived and parked outside, Juliet spied them through the sitting room window with her good eye.

'Is it time to say goodbye, Davey?' she said.

'It is, Bun— Juliet.'

'What then?'

'We'll go to the crematorium and play music and some people will tell stories about your mother. It will be nice.'

125

'Then they'll burn her.'

'Yes.'

'And then what will happen?'

'Well we'll go to a hotel with friends and family—'

'. . . to my ma?'

'Oh, well, they'll send us her ashes in a few weeks.'

'What will we do with them?'

'Whatever we want.'

'But what?'

'I don't know, Bunny.'

She gave him a dirty look.

'Let's just get through today.'

'OK,' she said. She took his hand in hers and Davey Hayes's thoughts turned from running away to making plans.

Chapter Twenty-One

Jack

JACK SLEPT ON AND off for five hours. Two of those hours were spent in the attic, surrounded by diaries, old boxes, spiderwebs and dust. When he'd showered and changed into his suit, he spent a few minutes alone in the dining room with his daughter. He dragged a chair over to where she was laid out and he sat on it and took out one of his old diaries and showed it to her.

'Look, Rabbit, it's an old diary from the fifties. I used to write, too, you know. Not like you, of course, but for a time there wasn't a day that went by that I didn't catalogue in some fashion.'

He opened it up and read aloud. '"Today I asked the woman of my dreams to dance. She took one look at me, told me to eff off, popped a hard-boiled sweet in her mouth and looked away. I'm not giving up that easily. When I look at her I see my future, a house, some kids, us against the world. She might not see that yet, but I do".' He closed the diary. 'Your mother made me work for it, Rabbit, I'll tell you that.' He looked around the room. 'But here we are, all these years later, and we were all so happy, weren't we, Rabbit? We had it all, really, even in the bad times, now that I realise there wasn't a day

127

without laughter – that's something to say, isn't it? Do you remember? I do. I remember. We were lucky, Rabbit, and I know that you had some terrible luck, love, but I also know you were born to make the best of things. That's what you always did, so that's what we'll try to do.' His face was wet. His collar was wet. His hands touching his face were wet. 'Oh, Rabbit,' he said, and he wept openly. *You're OK, Da, just breathe. I love ya, Da.*

Love ya, Rabbit.

Jack felt a hand on his shoulder and turned to see his wife.

'Where did she go, Molls?' he asked.

She shook her head. 'She didn't go anywhere, Jack. She's here – right here in our hearts and minds – and that's where she'll stay, with you and me, Davey, Grace, Juliet and anyone who ever knew and loved her.'

He grabbed his wife's hand. 'I love you, Molly.'

'Ah well, why wouldn't you, I'm a fucking ride,' she said, and she winked at him. He chuckled and kissed her hand but she didn't laugh or smile. Her eyes were dry and her touch was cold.

'How are you?' he asked.

'Don't ask,' she said, and she patted his shoulder and walked away.

When it was time Vincent and Silent Ed guided everyone into the dining room and they surrounded Rabbit. No one really knew what to say. They looked to Molly for a signal. She didn't give one. She just stood there, looking down on her child. Jack blessed himself. Davey held Juliet's hand and gave it a little kiss. Marjorie cried. Grace cried. Lenny couldn't look. He focused on his feet. Stephen put his hand on Grace's shoulder; she patted it and he let go. Ryan and Bernard just stood there, heads bowed. Jeffrey faced the opposite wall. Finally Molly looked around the room. 'Is everyone done?' They all nodded or mumbled the word 'yes'.

'Right, then,' she said. 'Vincent, if you wouldn't mind.' She left the room before the lid was closed over.

'Bye, Ma,' Juliet said as the coffin lid came down. They all filed out, leaving Jack standing alone with his daughter. He placed his hand on the hard wood. She was gone. The pain inside him raged, pulsed, and suddenly he was moving through the hallway, the kitchen and out into the back garden and he was screaming – a guttural scream from somewhere deep within. The neighbour over the wall, Tess Collins, waited till he was done before popping her head up.

'You're all right, Jack?' she said.

'Sorry, Tess, sorry for the noise,' he said. Tess could see Molly, Grace and Bernard lined up at the window, staring out at him, all with worried expressions.

'You just let it out.'

'I think I'm done,' he said, and he slumped onto the ground like a rag doll in his clean suit.

Molly was out of the house before Tess could say a word. She hugged her husband close to her. 'I think I let her down, Molly,' he said, and he bawled like a baby. Tess wasn't comfortable in the presence of a bawling man. She didn't know what to do so she ducked behind the wall, out of sight. She made her getaway on all fours, banging into a flower pot and mumbling the word 'shite'. She stood up as she got to her back door, brushed herself off and scurried inside. Molly held Jack close. 'You need to pick yourself up now, Jack, just for today, for Rabbit.'

Jack pulled himself together and Molly brushed him down with the tea towel she'd been wearing around her neck. As they walked inside, he stopped his wife. 'And after today, Molly, what happens then?'

His wife hunched her shoulders. 'Who knows?' she said sadly, and her despair traumatised him more than his own ever could.

Chapter Twenty-Two

Molly

T HE FUNERAL TOOK PLACE in Glasnevin Cemetery; the venue was a chapel, despite the non-religious service. Everyone helped, including Marjorie, and even Francie and Jay. Molly had asked the boys if they'd say a few words. Francie didn't hesitate but Jay was more cautious. 'I don't know, Mrs H, what can I say except what a fuckin' waste it is?'

'Exactly. Say that,' Molly said. Marjorie agreed to read the poem 'Do Not Stand at My Grave and Weep' by Mary Elizabeth Frye, if she could get through it once without crying.

'Think happy thoughts,' Davey said. It was his way of trying to help.

'Happy thoughts! My best friend is dead,' Marjorie said.

'Shut up, Davey,' Molly said. 'Cry if you want to, Marjorie.' She stroked Marjorie's back.

Rabbit's editor, Derek, agreed to prepare something when Molly rang him.

'It would be my pleasure.'

'Thank you, she'd like that.'

'And the book. I was thinking about approaching—'

'I don't care about the book, Derek. I just want to bury my daughter.'

'Yes, of course,' Derek said.

Molly read out the list of speakers: Marjorie, Francie, Jay and Derek.

'One of us will have to say something,' Molly said, and looked around at her family for volunteers.

Grace couldn't speak. Davey couldn't speak. Jack couldn't speak. Juliet couldn't speak.

'Fine, then,' Molly said, 'I'll do it.'

Davey took care of the music; he had spoken to Rabbit and he knew exactly what she wanted.

'I suppose there isn't a hint of a hymn in there?' Molly said.

'No, Ma.'

'Right, then,' she said. *It doesn't matter anyway.*

The chapel was full to the brim, with people standing outside listening to the service over a speaker.

'Jaysus, our Rabbit's like Princess Diana, they've come from all over,' Kev said as he sat into the pew behind Molly before leaning in. 'Sorry again, Mrs H. The missus couldn't make it. Looks like the youngest might have the measles.'

'Oh God, Kev, was the child not vaccinated?'

'Don't start me on vaccines, she's convinced they're shoving alien DNA into the kids. She's a mad yoke.'

'Well, she married you,' she said.

It was nice to see Kev, especially in proper clothes. When he was in the band, he wore a boiler suit for three years straight. It was his look. He sat back beside Francie, who was focused on reading his speech.

'What's up with you?'

'Just want to hit the right tone with me speech.'

'Yeah? What tone is that?'

'I don't know – sad but not depressing. Do you think I should tell a joke?' he asked.

'No,' Jay said.

'Sure?'

Molly turned in her seat and flicked Francie's ear. 'No jokes, I've had enough of bleedin' jokes.'

'Fair enough, Mrs H.'

Louis walked down the long aisle and shook all the mourners' hands. He hugged Davey.

'All right?' he said.

'You're handling the music,' Davey reminded him.

'All under control.'

'Nice one, Louis,' Francie said as he sat in next to him. Kev nodded 'hello'; he and Louis were never in the same band.

'All right, lads.' They saw each other rarely these days but that didn't matter. They were childhood mates, comfortable in each other's company no matter how long the passage of time. Molly liked that; those boys were her extended family. She loved them all. Each one of them carried a little piece of Rabbit inside them. That thought wasn't enough to lighten her heavy load, but it was something.

She'd contacted a civil celebrant through the people in Glasnevin. She seemed like a nice woman. She had a few kids, a husband and a dog. She had a kind voice on the phone and she asked lots of questions about her daughter. She'd talked about Rabbit to the woman for over an hour. She'd listened patiently and taken notes.

'Is that enough?' Molly asked at the end of their call.

'It's more than enough,' she said.

They all sat waiting in the chapel for the arrival of Rabbit. Vincent and Silent Ed were bringing her separately. Molly didn't know why. It was custom that the family would follow the hearse, but the hearse took a detour and the family car didn't follow it. Molly hadn't even noticed. She had spent the drive focused on her shoes for no reason other than she couldn't quite manage to hold her head up. When they arrived at the chapel, Grace had rushed them in before the hearse arrived. Molly just assumed it was how the non-religious do it, just to be bloody different. On the wave of Vincent's hand the bandmates, Jack and Lenny slipped away to the front door of the chapel. On the way Louis pressed play on the first song and the crowd stood and waited to see Jack lead Davey, Lenny, Francie, Jay, Louis and Kev as they carried Rabbit's basket down the aisle It was then that Molly realised Grace had well and truly stitched her up.

'A poxy basket,' she muttered under her breath.

'It's what she wanted, Ma.'

'Where did the coffin go?' Jack asked, confused by the change.

'It was a rental,' Grace said.

'I'll kill ya,' Molly said.

'I promised her, Ma.'

Molly just shook her head and sighed heavily. 'So be it, Grace.' She placed her hand on the basket holding her daughter and tapped it. 'She has your back, love,' she said to Rabbit.

The civil celebrant was called Caroline. She stood in front of the gathering dressed in a smart suit and wearing round glasses, her hair in a bun. She welcomed everyone and opened her speech about Rabbit with Molly's phone call. She talked about how it was obvious that Rabbit was loved and admired. Molly watched Juliet as Caroline spoke. She was drug-free and yet still so dazed. *Does she even know what's going on?* Davey held the child's hand in his. *Davey's her parent now. I don't even know what's going on.*

Caroline introduced a song.

'This was one of Rabbit's favourites,' she said, and she nodded to Louis, who gave her the thumbs up and pressed play. It was The Pogues' 'Rainy Night in Soho'. The familiar melody kicked in and without any nudge from Caroline or any discussion between parties, half the assembly sang along and the rest joined in for the chorus. All the voices singing in unison with Shane MacGowan was a thing to hear and see. Molly felt her heart ache as her husband nodded along.

'She'd have loved this,' Jack said, looking around to his wife perched on the end of the pew. All the while Molly's hand rested on the basket and tapped on it in time to the music.

Rabbit's editor, Derek, was the first to stand in front of the crowd. He introduced himself and explained to those who didn't know him that he and Rabbit had worked together for many years. He talked about how brilliant she was, how insightful and empathetic. He drew a picture of an employee who didn't take any shit from anyone. He mentioned a time when she was interviewing an actor and when he placed his hand on her knee and leaned in for a kiss, she grabbed him by the nose and gave him three seconds to move it. He moved it in one. Everyone laughed. He mentioned that he was currently editing her cancer blogs and a collection of memories she wrote in the last months and weeks of her life. He told everyone to 'watch this space'. He ended his short speech with the words:

'Rabbit may be dead, but she's not gone.' Everyone clapped and Caroline nodded to Louis, who cued the next song, 'Blowin' in the Wind' by Bob Dylan. Some were crying, some were smiling, some rocked, some tapped their feet, everyone sang.

Francie was up next. 'I'm Francie Byrne, I've known Rabbit since she was knee-high to a grasshopper. She went from being the baby sister of the drummer in my band to the annoying kid who followed us around, to our roadie, then our sound engineer. She was fourteen and she was on the road, standing her ground with hairy auld fellas and controlling a sound desk. She was old before her time, worldly-wise, not weary, and no one could talk to Johnny Faye the way she could. He was difficult long before he got sick with MS. He was a singer, after all.'

Everyone who knew Johnny, including his own mother, nodded vigorously. 'He could be an awful pain in the hole,' she said to the woman next to her, with a wide smile plastered across her face.

'Rabbit was honest, she said it like it was. She didn't dick around – she's like her ma that way. Nobody messed with Rabbit, but when you needed anything she'd be there, front and centre, sorting it all out.' He looked down at Molly, who nodded to him and smiled.

'She was a lot of things to a lot of people – daughter, sister, mother – but she was my friend. I'll miss her. Thanks.'

People clapped and he blew Rabbit's basket a kiss. Caroline cued Louis and the next song kicked off, Bruce Springsteen's 'I'm on Fire'.

Molly could hear the echo of a then-teenage Grace instructing Rabbit to *'rewind, play – no, too far, I don't want to hear the DJ, forward – no, go back.'*

'*Ah Grace, if I keep going it won't be just Bruce on fire, the tape will go up in flames, too.*'

Grace burst into tears; Lenny comforted her as best he could. 'Someone get your ma a fresh tissue,' he said to the boys when snot crept down Grace's face. Those assembled were not as familiar with all of the lyrics as they had been with the two previous anthems, but once the chorus kicked in everyone sang as if their own lives depended on it.

'This is mental,' Ryan said as he handed his father a tissue for his mother. Jay stood at the pulpit and spoke briefly. 'This is bullshit,' he said, and he moved to walk away but then, struck by a thought, he returned to the podium. 'Not the service, Rabbit being dead.'

Molly nodded and led a round of applause for him as he walked back to his seat.

'Well said, love,' she said as he passed. Marjorie was next up. She blubbered her way through the poem, losing her place twice, mumbling the word 'shite' three times, and snorted loudly.

'That was beautiful, love,' Molly said to poor Marjorie, who could barely breathe. 'Just breathe.'

'Can't.'

'You can. Davey, rub her back.'

Caroline nodded to Louis and he played another song. Britney Spears's 'Hit Me Baby One More Time'. Everyone burst out laughing and clapped as they sang along. Molly didn't laugh. She didn't clap. *Hit me what? God Almighty, Rabbit!* Juliet smiled and she even chuckled a little when she saw her cousins Ryan, Bernard and Stephen sing along. Jeffrey seemed a little bewildered.

It was Molly's turn to speak. She got up, brushed herself off and patted the basket. 'Here I go, love.' She stood in front of a full house; she knew so many faces but there were many present she didn't know at all. Her hand was sore from the sincere grip of mourner after mourner. It might even be a little swollen, she wasn't sure. It didn't matter.

'My name is Molly Hayes, I'm Rabbit's mother.' She stopped talking; no one moved, you could have heard a pin drop. She just stared out at everyone. Grace moved to rescue her mother but Jack laid his hand on her knee and shook his head. 'Give her a minute.' She stayed where she was. They watched and waited. Molly took out an envelope from her pocket and held it up. 'I have a letter here, it's from Johnny Faye to Rabbit.' She searched the crowd. 'Johnny's mammy's here, in the crowd. Where are ya, Karen?'

Karen Faye raised her hand.

'Do ya mind?' Molly said.

Mrs Faye stood up. 'I'd love it,' she said, then she waved and sat down.

Molly cleared her throat. 'I could talk to you about my memories of Rabbit all day. I could tell you how much I loved her and how she moved me. I could mention how lost I'll be without her, how nothing will ever be that good again. I could try to sum her up in a few lines, but I'm no poet and Rabbit deserves poetry. So this is one of many letters written to Rabbit from the love of her life while he lay dying.

Dear Rabbit,
*   I can feel myself slip away, inch by inch, and it's slow and torturous. My body is a bone bag but I'm still me,*

deep within. My bowels are tied; my bladder is attached to a catheter fastened to a dead leg with a Velcro strap. My sight faded so slowly that in the end it simply blurred to black but every now and then I see a flash of stars. Talking is difficult now, words no longer flow, my twisting tongue is a difficult hurdle to overcome. Dictating this letter takes a week. I get so tired and the nurses only have so much time, but although they don't know me they are kind to the fragile and frightened man deep inside, this stuttering, decaying bone bag. They say it's a young man's heart that keeps me in here but it's slowing; I can't feel much of anything these days, but I can feel that. I miss you, Rabbit, but not enough for you to return home and not enough to ask you to break your promise to never come here. Not yet but soon I know I will be in your presence once more when time is of the essence and I am granted a goodbye. There will be no real words spoken then, just small talk from you and salty tears from me, but those tears will be joyful. Till then know that you have been my world. Thank you for keeping a light on long after it became dark, for pushing and pulling and fighting the unknown. Thank you for being honest and true and for respecting me enough to argue, to call me out and for doing as I ask from deep inside this bone bag. Thank you for being you.

Molly stopped, took a breath. She didn't cry. She didn't even look like she was going to. She just needed a second to compose herself. She looked up from the letter and faced her daughter's basket. 'So now I'd like to say thank you, Rabbit, for being my world, for keeping the light on, for pushing and pulling and fighting the unknown. Thank you for being honest and true and arguing with us all till the very end, and I hope you're happy in your bloody basket.'

Sobbing turned to laughter in the crowd. It was a release – like a burst canister it came as a loud explosion and dissipated quickly. 'Thank you for being you.'

As she moved to walk back to her seat, the crowd stood on their feet and applauded her as though they were at some kind of show. She sat down beside her husband and he held her trembling hand. He was crying. Everyone was crying, but not Molly; she was comfortably numb, and despite being barbiturate- and alcohol-free, the rest of the service was a blank.

Chapter Twenty-Three

Juliet

WHEN SHE EMERGED FROM the chapel, Juliet felt small and lost amongst the enormous crowd. She let go of Davey's hand momentarily and became swept up in the moving tide of people. It was hard to find her way back. So she just stood amongst adults, mostly strangers, waiting for a gap to open so she could burrow her way to safety. That's when Kyle tapped her on the shoulder.

'Hiya,' he said.

She turned to face him. 'Hiya,' she said.

'Saw your gran yesterday, she nearly knocked me down,' he said.

'Yeah,' she said.

He showed her a cut to his elbow as proof.

'That looks sore.'

'Della's here,' he said. 'Do you want to say hi?'

She nodded. Della was Juliet's best friend. The last time she'd seen her was a few days previously when they'd sat together on the school's football field and Della broached the subject of Juliet moving in with her parents if she needed to. Juliet had not yet come to terms with her mother dying and as her entire family was lying to her about it, the offer came as a bolt from the blue. Overwhelmed, she jumped up and ran, leaving Kyle in her dust. Della had texted a few times as her mother lay dying but Juliet didn't reply. Now she couldn't think of anyone she wanted to see more than her except for maybe Kyle.

Kyle pulled her through the crowd of well-wishers; some people stopped them.

'So sorry about your ma,' one woman said as Juliet was dragged past her.

'Thanks very much.'

'She's in heaven now,' another older man said.

'She didn't believe in heaven,' she said as she moved on.

'Think of her as a bright white star,' an elderly lady said, and she grabbed for Juliet's hand.

'Ah no, that would be weird.'

Kyle pulled her away and towards a gap and fresh air. She stood on open ground and breathed in and out.

'OK?'

'Good,' she said. Della appeared from behind a car and hugged Juliet.

'Sorry I wasn't at the wake,' she said. 'Mam and Dad had a major row over a credit card bill and it was all a bit dramatic.'

'It's OK, I was drugged,' Juliet said.

'Shut up!' Della said.

'Seriously.'

'Where did you get the drugs?'

'Gran.'

'She is hardcore,' Della said.

'Yeah.'

'I heard you're going to live with Davey,' Della said, and tears sprang in her eyes.

'Please don't,' Kyle said.

Della gave him a thump. 'She can do what she wants. Is that what you want, Juliet? 'Cause my ma meant it when she said you could move in with us.'

'I can't,' Juliet said.

'Why?' Della asked.

'Me ma wanted me with Davey.'

'And what do you want?'

'I want me ma,' she said, and tears slipped from her eyes and ran down her face.

'I'm sorry.'

'America's cool,' Kyle said, pulling out a tissue from his pocket. It had clearly had been used to blow his nose. He tried to hand it to Juliet who refused it by waving it away.

'That's gross,' Della said.

Kyle looked abashed. 'Sorry.'

Juliet suddenly needed to sit down, so she did. She sat on the ground. Her friends followed her. One either side, shoulders touching.

'What if I hate it?' Juliet whispered.

'You couldn't, it's America,' Della said, and Kyle nodded and reiterated that America was cool.

'Besides, you can always come home,' he said, and Juliet's eyes leaked once more. *What is home?* she thought. *Home is where me ma is. I have no home, just like Davey*. After a lot more digging Kyle found a clean tissue and handed it to Juliet. She wiped away her tears. *I'm just like Davey*, she thought.

'You OK?' Della asked.

'No, but I'll be OK. I'll be with Davey.'

'I'll really miss you,' Della replied, 'but we'll Skype and WhatsApp and Viber all the time.'

'Yeah,' Juliet agreed, but already she felt distance creep between them.

Chapter Twenty-Four

Marjorie

FOLLOWING THE CHAPEL THE mourners were invited to gather in the Clontarf Castle for food and drink. Marjorie sat at the bar. Davey placed a glass of red wine in her hand.

'Hanging in there?' he asked.

'Suppose so,' she said.

'The poem was lovely.'

'Shut up, Davey.'

'I'm really getting sick of being told to shut up.'

She grinned a little. He sat on the stool next to her.

'Are you going to be OK tonight?' he asked.

'What does that mean?'

'It's just a question.'

'Right.'

'What do you think it means?'

'I don't know, Davey. I'm tired.'

She was staring over at her ex-husband and his new pregnant girlfriend, the effervescent Debbie.

'I see Neil came.'

'Yip.'

'That was nice of him, when all is said and done.'

'He was very fond of Rabbit,' she said, and she took a large slug from the glass of wine.

'So that's the girlfriend.'

'That's her.'

'Pretty.'

She took a moment to turn to him and give him a filthy look.

He smiled. 'Not a patch on you.'

'Why's she here, Davey?' she asked.

'Support.'

'What did they come to the hotel for?'

'I don't know.'

Neil looked over and smiled. He nudged Debbie and suddenly the two of them were heading their way. *Oh Christ.*

Davey jumped to his feet. The men faced off.

Neil put out his hand to shake Davey's. 'Sorry for your loss, Davey.'

Davey shook Neil's hand. 'That's very kind of you.' There was tension between the two men but ultimately Davey was a small cog in the wheel of the car crash that was his marriage, and Neil was a decent man and also clearly happy.

'So sorry,' Debbie said to Davey and shook his hand a little too vigorously.

She turned to Marjorie. 'Hello.' She put out her hand. It was their first time meeting.

'Hello,' Marjorie said, and shook her hand.

'I'm really sorry about your best friend.'

Marjorie burst into tears. Debbie tried to hug her and it was all a bit awkward – Debbie was tentative, Marjorie recoiled slightly and then there was that big belly between them. Marjorie tapped Debbie on the back and pulled away.

'Thank you,' she said, and she meant it. *Now please go away.*

'We're going to go,' Neil said.

Davey and Marjorie both nodded. He moved to walk away but turned at the last second.

'I wish you both luck,' he said and, putting his arm around his pregnant partner, they walked away. Davey turned to Marjorie and sat back down.

'Don't say anything,' she said.

He hunched his shoulders. 'I wasn't going to say anything.'

She drained the glass. 'Good.'

'I'm going out with the lads for a drink later, you want to come?'

'No.'

'They're your friends too, Marjorie.'

'No they're not. I was always outside of that world.'

'Not true.'

'It is true, Davey, and it's OK. I never really cared.'

'I don't want you to be alone.'

She stood up, leaned in and kissed him on the cheek. 'See ya, Davey.'

He grabbed her hand. 'Don't go.'

'Goodnight,' she said, and she walked away.

She met Molly in the hotel lobby. She was sitting alone on a chaise longue.

'You going home, love?' she said, and Marjorie nodded.

'Shit day,' Molly said.

'The worst.'

'You've lost Rabbit, Marjorie, and I know how close you were, but you have the rest of your life to live.'

'That's the word on the street.'

Molly smiled a little.

'Shit day,' Molly said again.

'The worst.'

The taxi came soon after. Marjorie hugged Molly.

'Do not be a stranger, Marjorie – you're one of us.'

Marjorie promised Molly she wouldn't be stranger, climbed into the taxi, gave the man her address and sobbed the whole way home.

Chapter Twenty-Five

Juliet

KYLE'S PARENTS LEFT THE hotel around three, leaving him behind.

When evening rolled in Lenny drove them home, Kyle and Juliet sharing the back seat. They weren't touching but she could sense how close he was. It felt weird and kind of electric. The hair was rising on her arms. *What's this?*

When they arrived at her house she asked Kyle if he wanted to come inside for a while. He looked to Lenny for his permission. He nodded.

'Till Davey gets home,' he said.

Lenny heated up some lasagna and left them in the kitchen to eat while he sat watching a match on the telly.

Juliet picked at her food. She hadn't really eaten in days; her stomach felt tight and sore and her throat felt narrower than before. Kyle devoured his.

'This is lovely, did Grace make it?'

'Someone dropped it over to me gran's. Her freezer is full.'

'I wish my ma cooked Italian. She only cooks Irish.'

'What's Irish?'

'Spuds, veg and meat.'

'Oh.'

'Yeah, it's either spuds, veg and lamb, pork chops or bacon, mincemeat, turkey, ham or if it's a special occasion a well-done steak.'

'That sounds terrible.'

'It's shite all right. Da says it's like living in the eighties.'

'What does that mean?'

'Dunno,' he said. 'I think life was just a little bit more shite back then.'

'My ma loved the eighties,' Juliet said.

'Yeah, but she was cool.'

Juliet smiled. 'Yeah, she was totally cool.'

After that Juliet and Kyle went into the sitting room and played a game on Juliet's Xbox. They didn't really talk, just made the odd comment on the game.

'You're tired. I should go,' he said.

She didn't argue. 'Thanks for being there.'

'That's OK.'

She walked him to the front door. She opened it and he stood close to her and then he moved in for a hug and her skin burned. She pulled away.

'Do you really have to go?' he said.

'Yeah.'

'Why?'

'Just 'cause.'

He looked like he was going to cry.

'I'll really miss ya.'

'I'll miss you too.'

He was crying. He was crying, and the only thing she could think to do to stop him was kiss his lips.

'Oh,' he said.

Juliet was shocked. She briefly wondered if she was still drugged. *What am I doing? What is wrong with me?*

'Sorry,' she said.

'Don't be. I think that's the best thing that's ever happened to me.'

She could feel the panic rising within her. 'You need to go.'

'I'll see ya tomorrow, then?'

She nodded yes. He skipped across the road to his house. She closed the door, feeling a little sick. *Ma's dead and I'm kissing a boy. Oh no. I'm so sorry, Ma. Oh no. Oh no.* She ran up the stairs, tore into her mother's room, ripped open the wardrobe and grabbed one of her mother's long-sleeve T-shirts and inhaled it, then she sat on the bed and hugged it as hard as she could. She fell asleep in her mother's bed, fully dressed except for her socks and shoes, pressing her mother's balled-up Blondie T-shirt to her face and sucking her thumb for the first time since she was five.

Chapter Twenty-Six

Marjorie

THE APARTMENT WAS COLD. Marjorie took off her high heels at the door and turned on the heating. She grabbed a bottle of wine, a glass and a blanket and sat on the sofa. She turned on the TV – *politics, no. Soap, definitely no. A rerun of a procedural crime drama – no, absolutely no.* She settled on a wildlife programme focusing on the mating habits of lions. *Christ, that's aggressive.* She was about to turn over when her phone rang. The number was unknown and she thought for a moment it could be Juliet – maybe she needed her. She answered with an urgent 'hello'.

'Marjorie, it's your father here.'

Marjorie's blood ran cold. The last time she'd heard that voice she was sixteen years old and he was telling her he had another family in the UK, a family that he wanted to be with full-time. He spoke about a woman he loved more than her mother and kids he loved more than Marjorie.

'You are old enough now to understand,' were his final words to her before he walked out into the night air never to return home. He left her alone with a mother who was hysterical and threatening suicide. Marjorie knew she wouldn't do it. She knew her mother was too religious to even consider risking hellfire. It didn't make it any easier. It was still terrifying. He left her to a woman who blamed her for destroying her life. A woman who could be vicious and mean, and said hateful, spiteful things. Just after he'd left and before he'd even made it to the end of the road, she'd screamed that she'd wished Marjorie had never been born. Afterwards she felt bad about wishing her mother would just fuck off and die. Every now and then, and for years after, she'd remind Marjorie that Daddy had left Mammy because Marjorie broke her and she couldn't give Daddy his son.

'Well that's not scarring at all,' Rabbit said the first time Marjorie confided in her, and it made Marjorie chuckle.

'Look, Marj, you got unlucky – your ma's a nutjob,' she said. Then she sat Marjorie down with Molly Hayes, who explained that her mother's broken fanny was not her fault but the fault of the doctor who botched up her birth.

'And to be honest, love, your mammy was a miserable bitch before you were ever born. I'm sorry to say it but it's true.' That made Marjorie smile.

'And Theresa Shea had one of those; she's in bits as well but she loves her kids, you know why?' she asked Marjorie when she was ten years old. Marjorie shook her head.

'Because Theresa Shea isn't a miserable bitch.'

Marjorie laughed again and then she cried, and Molly hugged her tight, and that was the first time she'd looked into Marjorie's face and said those words that meant the world. 'Who loves ya, Marjorie?'

'Molly does.'

Rabbit, Molly and the Hayes family saved Marjorie from a life of loneliness and pain both before and after her father ran out on her.

'Marjorie, did you hear me? It's your father here.'

'I heard you,' she said, and for a fleeting instant she wondered if he had heard of Rabbit's death and was reaching out to her, finally being her dad. Then she thought about it: how did he get this number? He must have read her thoughts.

'One of your bank colleagues gave me your number after I explained the circumstances,' he said.

'What circumstances?' she asked.

'Your mother had a stroke today.'

'Excuse me?'

'She had a stroke.'

'How do you know?'

'I'm still noted as her next of kin.'

Two thoughts crashed into Marjorie's head. *1. Oh shit, a stroke,* and *2. Of course he is, it's only been twenty-five bloody years.*

'Did you hear me, Marjorie?'

'I heard you,' she said dully, still processing what was happening.

'She's in the Mater Hospital.'

'How did you know I worked in the bank?' Marjorie asked.

'Does it matter?' he asked.

'Yes.'

'Your friend Rabbit tracked me down a few years ago and wrote to me, told me about you and how you were doing.'

'Why?'

'She said she wanted me to know what I was missing.'

'She didn't ask you to come and see me?' Marjorie asked, agog.

'No, she was very explicit about me staying away.'

Marjorie started to cry. He remained silent and waited for her to stop.

'Have you seen Mam?' The words were uttered before she had thought things through.

'I live in the UK, Marjorie,' he said in a tone that suggested he believed her to be dumb.

''Course you do.'

'I just wanted to let you know, so that she's not alone,' he said.

'That's big of you,' she said, finally mustering some sarcasm.

'Sorry.'

'Fine.'

'Really, I am sorry.'

'Dad?'

'Yes, Marjorie?'

'Go fuck yourself,' she said, loud and proud, Molly Hayes-style.

She hung up the phone. *Who loves ya, Marjorie?*

She polished off the bottle of wine alone. *Molly does.*

Chapter Twenty-Seven

Jack

JACK WAS TIRED BUT also wired. Molly sat staring at the TV, unfocused and unable or unwilling to talk. He knew where he wanted to be: up in the attic with his old diaries, back in a world before his youngest daughter was riddled with cancer and died an agonising death. Back to the start, that's where Jack needed to be. If Molly heard him pull down the attic ladder she didn't say. He made his way up into the darkness and flicked the small light on. Davey had replaced the beanbag with a spare chair that Molly kept in the hall for the purpose of standing on to change light bulbs. He sat down on it and picked a diary from 1962, the year he met Molly. He smiled to himself.

'We had it all to look forward to,' he said to himself, then he looked to the roof. 'You were only a glint in my eye, Rabbit. Oh but if you saw your mammy back then. She was something else, my girl, something out of this world. I'd never met anyone like her before – or even since, really, except for you and your sister.'

He opened up the diary and settled in. He started reading quietly, transported to a different time and place. He sat in silence, consumed by his own words, reminiscing as he read, then as if he'd just remembered she was there, he looked skywards again. 'Don't worry, Rabbit, I'll only read the good bits aloud,' he said. That's what he did. Every once in a while he'd read out a passage about life in 1960s Ireland before following up with an observation or two. 'Fields as far as the eye could see back then, Rabbit, and right on top of the city centre, too.'

'Did I ever tell you the deposit I paid for this house? A five-pound note. Five pounds! You wouldn't buy a packet of cigarettes for double that these days, but back then it was a fortune.'

The old man read and spoke to the ceiling on and off for much of that night, and when his eyes blurred with exhaustion and his back stiffened, and his neck and his legs had turned into jelly, he marked the page and placed it back in the box. He tried to stand up, cupping his knees in his hands. 'I have to go now, my girl, but I'll see you tomorrow.'

Night, Da.

Night, love.

He knew she wasn't really there, but alone in the highest point of the house with his old diaries, he felt close to her.

Chapter Twenty-Eight

Davey

IN THE PUB KEV got the first round in. Jay and Francie played a game of pool and Davey sat watching them with Louis.

'Do you ever think about Kitchen Sink now that you're in the big leagues?' Louis asked.

'All the time,' Davey said.

'Yeah, right, we were just stupid kids who thought we knew everything. Jesus, we knew nothing.'

'We knew enough.'

'I'm sorry I left when I did.'

'Why?' Davey asked.

'Feel like I abandoned the ship. Johnny was sick, we were going nowhere. I had a girlfriend and a kid on the way.'

'You don't need to explain,' Davey said. 'You did what you had to do.'

'Anyway, they got to trade up,' Kev replied, putting down the beers on the table.

'Yeah, right,' Louis said. 'As if they weren't handicapped enough with a disabled singer, they get a guy in a boiler suit on guitar.'

'Ah right, calm down, Captain Synth,' Kev said. 'I loved that boiler suit.'

Francie beat Jay two sets to one; they came over and picked up their pints. 'What are we talking about?'

'Louis is slagging Kev over his boiler suit, Kev's slagging Louis for playing the synthesiser,' Davey said.

'Don't mind them, Louis. It was good enough for Nik Kershaw, and look where he is now,' Francie said.

Kev looked up. 'Where is he?'

'Fucking nowhere,' Jay replied.

The lads laughed.

'Here, Louis, did I tell you about me balls?' Francie said.

Jay shook his head. 'Ah no, don't start about your bleedin' balls.'

'What happened your balls?' Louis asked.

Kev winced. 'He got the snip. The end.'

'The size of fuckin' turnips and the same fuckin' colour,' Francie said.

'You should sue,' Davey muttered. It was the second time in a week he'd heard the story.

'I should sue, I'm the one that has to listen to it all the bleedin' time,' Jay noted.

'Jaysus, maybe I should sue. Fuck, I knew I should have taken photos,' Francie said. 'The missus wouldn't let me, she said me balls would end up on the cloud and I'd be open to exploitation.'

Jay laughed. 'Who the fuck would exploit you and your balls?'

'Mad yokes,' Francie said. 'In case you hadn't noticed, they're everywhere.'

'Speaking of, no sign of Sheila B today?' Jay asked, and Francie nodded, grateful his ex-girlfriend from back in the day hadn't shown up and made a scene. 'Thank God for that, me nerves were gone.'

Later Davey joined Francie outside while he smoked. Francie offered him one.

'Better not,' Davey said. He liked a smoke every now and then when things got stressful, but seeing as his baby sister died of cancer . . .

'On a warning?' Francie said. Marjorie and Grace had threatened to kick him to death if they saw him smoking again.

'Yeah, something like that.' They meant it – they were vicious.

'Fair enough.'

They stood together looking out into a clear night sky.

'Nothing's ever going to be the same again,' Davey said.

'Nothing is ever the same, Davey. Change is our only constant.'

'Did you read that in the doctor's surgery?'

'A posh cracker.'

'So I'm a parent now.'

'Welcome to hell,' Francie said.

'I'm doing this.'

'Yes, you are.'

'It'll be fine.'

'Nope, it will break your fucking heart.'

'Jesus, Francie, I'm trying to stay positive.'

Francie exhaled and grey smoke curled through the fresh air.

'It will be worth it, Davey.'

Davey left after two pints. When he arrived back at Rabbit's Lenny was long gone and Juliet was asleep. He opened up his computer and booked two first-class tickets back to the States a week from the day. *If change is going to come, let it come.*

Chapter Twenty-Nine

Grace

GRACE WAS LOST IN her own thoughts as Lenny drove with the radio on. It was raining. The tarmac ahead shone under the street and car lights. The road appeared greasy, as though spotted with a purple vinyl film. Lenny cut through a large puddle, water parted and a wave curled and splashed. They were alone. Stephen was driving the boys home in a car he'd borrowed from a mate. They had lost sight of them in traffic a while back.

'What if he's not insured?' Grace said out of nowhere.

'Who?' Lenny asked.

'Stephen.'

'Ah, it's only a mile down the road.'

'We could lose the four of them in a fireball.'

'Ah Jaysus, Grace, that's not going to happen.'

'And I suppose insurance would be the least of our worries,' she said.

Lenny attempted to lighten the mood. 'Let's just hope they're stopped by the police and Stephen is charged, then.'

'Better than dying in flames,' she said.

They fell into silence once more. Grace focused on the rain dribbling down the windscreen and the busy and slightly scratchy swish-swash sound of the wipers. Ten minutes passed before Lenny turned off the radio.

'We need to talk about this morning.'

'I'm too tired.'

'Please, Grace.'

'What do you want me to say?'

'I want to know what's going through your mind.'

'I told you, at the moment I'm worried about the kids.'

'Grace!'

'Stephen is a shit driver, Lenny, we both know it.'

'Grace?'

'What?'

'Talk to me.'

'There's an operation I can have to remove my breasts and my ovaries.'

He paled; even in the dark she could see his colour fade.

'But you don't have cancer.'

'Not yet.'

'Maybe never.'

'But maybe tomorrow.'

'You can't do that.'

'I didn't say I would, but anyway, they're my breasts.'

'Oh but when it comes to snipping my balls we all get a vote—'

'I have the fucking gene, Lenny.'

He pulled the car into the side of the road, gripping onto the steering wheel.

'But that doesn't mean you'll get cancer, right? You can't just cut chunks out of yourself just in case – it's madness.' Lenny had seen the effect Rabbit's mastectomies had had on her. He was there for the post-surgical infections, the nerve damage and the mental toll and she had been a warrior. Grace came apart having a bloody blood test.

She turned to him. 'I just need to think,' she said. He stared at his wife.

'You need to think.'

'Yes. Me. I need to think.'

'Fine. You do that.'

He took the car out of gear and drove on. They didn't speak after that.

Lenny sat up that evening watching highlights of a football match. Grace lay in bed alone, eyes wide open, contemplating the last days of Knockers Hayes.

Chapter Thirty

Molly

MOLLY COULDN'T SLEEP THE night of her daughter's funeral, but she kept her eyes screwed shut. She lay there beside the hot heaving lump that was her comatose husband. She unwound jumbled thoughts and reduced them to a series of succinct and searching questions.

Q: Why did I ever believe in God?

A: Because I was told to.

Q: Why did I pray?

A. Because I was told to.

Q: Have I ever experienced anything that supported my faith?

A: No.

Q: Have I ever experienced anything that challenged my faith?

A: Yes.

Q: Do I still believe?

A: No.

Q: What does that mean?

A: I don't know.

Q: What do I know?

A: Life is unfair.

Q: What do I do about that?

A: I do what I always do. I fight.

Q: And then what?

A: I die.

Q: And then what?

A: Nothing.

I agree with you, Rabbit. Do you hear me, love? It's all bollocks . . . Please, love, talk to me like you talk to Grace. She told me you won't get out of her head. Talk to me. But Rabbit didn't talk to her mother. She was gone and she took God with her. *Sorry.*

The following morning, Molly opened her tired eyes to face the world as a slightly different version of herself; a little less hopeful, a little more fierce. The change would be imperceptible to acquaintances but to those who knew her, the shift was mighty.

Part Four

Year One

Chapter Thirty-One

Juliet

JULIET STOOD IN THE airport one week after her mother's funeral. She could feel the weight of her backpack on her shoulders rooting her to the dull tiled floor. She looked to those around her for cues as to how to react. Molly was stoic, refusing to show emotion. Grace looked like a ghost. Lenny seemed angry. Stephen wasn't there; he was at a study group, or something more pressing than saying goodbye to his cousin. Marjorie looked insane, with a large smile plastered on her face and her eyes wide open. Everyone was struggling in their own way. Bernard, Ryan and Jeffrey were subdued. They just hung around like puppets on broken strings. Jack sat in a chair with his head in his hands. It felt like the wake all over again, except this time there was no cake, booze or polite conversation; it was just people loitering in a large open space staring at one another, waiting for the inevitable and wishing for it all to end. Julie's brain was still fog-bound, and she remained comfortably numb.

'We have to go,' Davey said, and suddenly a tsunami of emotion engulfed her . . . Big fat warm wet tears cascaded, she shuddered and shook, her knees felt like jelly and her brain burned. *What am I doing? Where are ya, Ma? Please, Ma, come back. I don't want to go.* Davey clutched her hand and pulled her into his side. He held her tight but she could feel that he was shaking, too. Molly crouched down. 'I'm a phone call away. I'm a flight away. When you need me, I'll be there.'

Juliet hugged her granny tight until finally Molly prised them apart. 'It's OK, love,' she said, but it wasn't OK. They both knew it. Grace hugged Juliet and she cried and kissed her on the head, and then it was Lenny's turn. 'We're always here too, Juliet.'

'Thanks, Lenny.'

Then the kids said goodbye.

'See ya at Christmas,' Jeffrey said.

'It's not too far away,' Bernard said.

Ryan whispered into Juliet's ear. 'Don't let the bastards get you down.'

'OK.'

He made a fist with his hand and shook it as he nodded his head.

'OK,' she repeated. Then it was her turn to say goodbye to Marjorie. She was crying and holding a tissue against her runny nose and when she stumbled over the words 'I love you', Juliet pulled her in close and whispered in her ear, 'Don't be scared, Marjorie.' Because that's the kind of thing her ma would have said. Marjorie lost it and needed to hold onto Lenny while Grace helped her to a chair. *Shite. Sorry.* Finally she stood in front of her granda and he beckoned her to sit on his knee. She climbed aboard and within moments they were both sobbing and hugging.

'Right, that's it,' Molly said, and she took Juliet by the hand. 'That auld fella will drown you if you give him a chance. What's granda?'

'A sap,' Juliet said.

'A sap,' Molly repeated, and she winked and Juliet smiled. She turned to Davey.

'You know what I'm going to say.'

'Don't fuck this up.'

'Good man. I love you, son.'

'I love you too, Ma.'

'Go.' Molly choked the words out. 'Go now.' So they went.

Those first few months in America were a blur; one thing blended into another then into another. Places, things, people, sights, sounds, lights and even the weather were new and different to anything she'd ever experienced before. Everything seemed bigger and louder, brighter, bolder. It appeared to be an exaggerated world of excess in some parts and deprivation in others; the grime was grimier, the lonely just that little bit lonelier. Maybe it was just tiny Juliet from a small suburb in Dublin, Ireland that couldn't handle this new flashy world filled with music and soul, industry and passion, busy city streets and wide-open spaces, horses and limos, farmers and industrialists, world-class musicians and big business, or maybe she was just a little girl grieving for her mother and even the dimmest light burned a little too bright for her jaded eyes. Either way she knew by the end of the first week that she would never fit in. She wouldn't give in, though; she was stubborn like her mother and also scared of what waited for her back in Dublin. *Nothing*. Her mother was dead and her home was gone, rented to a couple with a two-year-old boy according to Kyle, when they spoke every Tuesday on Skype.

She lasted three months in school before she knocked out a girl in her class, the police were called and she was excluded.

'What did you do that for, love?' Molly said on Skype.

'She was horrible, Gran.'

'Ah but still—'

'She found Ma's blogs online and read them out in front of the whole class and made a joke of her,' Juliet said, and her eyes brimmed with tears. 'They were all laughing at me ma's words and worries.'

'Oh well, in that case I hope she has concussion,' Molly said.

Davey was touring a lot; so it made sense that he got her a tutor and brought her on the road. He hired a small six-berth sleeper coach, which had Wi-Fi, satellite TV, a galley kitchen and lounge and came with a driver named Bob. Davey slept in the first berth and Juliet in the last, with four berths between, creating the illusion of privacy. It wasn't perfect but they were making it work.

'And you don't miss kids your own age?' Grace asked over Skype.

'No one really talked to me in the school,' Juliet admitted.

'Did you really talk to anyone?' Grace asked.

'No.'

'Why not?'

'Me ma died.'

'Fair enough. Do you miss being with kids your own age?'

'Not really. Sometimes. I'm too busy,' Juliet said.

'Oh yeah, doing what?' Grace asked.

'Studying and hanging with Davey and the lads. Oh and his friend Trevor, the sound engineer, is helping me learn how to use a sound desk, like Ma.'

'And what age is Trevor?' Grace asked suspiciously.

'Seriously, Grace!' Juliet laughed.

'Are you happy?'

Juliet hunched her shoulders. 'My ma is dead.'

'Do you want to come home?'

'No.'

'OK. I love you.'

The truth was she didn't want to go home but she didn't want to live on a bus either. Driving from city to city was gruelling and often lonely but she would never leave Davey.

We were meant to be, weren't we, Ma? I mind Davey and he minds me. They spent a lot of time together, talking, reading, listening to music and eating shit food in shit diners. It was fun sometimes. It was Davey who'd thought she should find herself a hobby. He introduced her to Trevor. She was immediately drawn to the sound desk in every stadium they landed in. Davey noticed. Trevor was patient and kind to her, always open to her sitting with him during soundcheck and answering her many questions. He showed her photos of his wife and child. He knew what it was to miss the people you love. She could talk to him, and sitting at the desk listening to the sound ebb and flow from it she felt closer to her mam than she had in those last days lying beside her dying body. She told Kyle about Trevor over Skype.

'You know the way my ma used to do sound for Davey and the band when she was my age?'

'Yeah,' Kyle said.

'Well, Trevor the sound guy is really cool, he lets me watch him work, and during soundcheck he lets me mess around.

Sometimes he's teaching me things and the set-up is way bigger than Ma ever dealt with – she used a ten-channel desk. Trevor's is ninety-six.'

'Wow,' Kyle said, but it wasn't a believable wow.

'You don't care,' she said, and he grinned a little.

'I care,' he said, and she knew he meant it and it made her blush. He looked a little older on-screen. They talked a lot but she didn't talk to Della at all. Juliet missed her but she understood some friendships could only survive one on one and in the real world. Juliet didn't live there anymore.

She dreamed about her ma a lot. Weird, blurry, sad dreams that haunted her for days. A recurring dream involved her mother calling out for her help from the kitchen floor of their old rented house with blood flowing from her and pooling around her. She tried but she couldn't get to her. An invisible barrier kept them from one another.

'I'm here, Ma, can you see me, Ma? I'm coming.'

'Help me, Juliet.'

'I'm here.'

'Where are you, Juliet?'

'I'm right here.'

'BUNNY!!!!!'

'MA!'

Then she'd disappeared down through the floor, leaving only scorch marks.

That was deeply stressful, and for a while sleep became her enemy.

'Are you OK?' Davey asked her when he saw she was pale and moody from lack of sleep.

'What do you care?'

'I care a lot! What do you mean?' He was hurt. They were sitting together on the bus. It was the second hour into a six-hour journey.

'You disappeared for two days!' she shouted.

'I had to do some business in New York between shows.'

'You didn't even say goodbye!'

'You were on a different fucking bus. What was I supposed to do?'

'Phone me, Skype me, WhatsApp me, Viber, message me—'

'Right, right, you've made your point. Sorry,' he said.

'I thought we'd lost you.' She welled up and his face fell.

'Shite. Of course. Sorry.'

Davey wasn't a natural father but he was doing his best.

She spent a lot of her time with Gemma, her tutor. She was twenty-eight and married to a man in the military. He was in Afghanistan. Sometimes Juliet dreamed her mother was being held hostage in a cave, dressed in a burqa with the AC/DC *Highway to Hell* logo on the front of it. Gemma came and went. Davey flew her in for a day or two at a time, she'd teach and then leave assignments; she was always available on Skype. It was fine. Everything was fine.

On Juliet's thirteenth birthday she woke to the sound of her computer bleeping. She answered her Skype. Molly appeared on the screen.

'Hello, love,' she said, and she waved. 'Happy birthday.'

'Thanks, Gran.'

'And look who's here,' she said, and she moved the computer around to show Juliet a bunch of headless torsos. 'You have to raise it, Ma.'

'Raise what, Grace?'

175

'The computer – the child's looking at a bunch of stomachs.'

Grace leaned down. 'Hiya, Bunny . . . Sorry . . . Juliet . . . Happy birthday.'

'Thanks, Grace.' The computer moved and suddenly Juliet could see her gran, granda, Grace, Lenny, Stephen, Bernard, Ryan and Jeffrey. Jeffrey had lost more weight. 'Wow, Jeff,' she said, and gave him the thumbs up. They all sang 'Happy Birthday', even Ryan.

'Where's Davey?' Molly asked.

'In a band meeting on the other bus.'

'What are you doing to celebrate?'

'Oh, it's back-to-back shows so we'll probably just grab dinner.'

'That's it?'

'Casey has organised a cake and she sang to me at the concert.'

'A cake and a song from Davey's employer?' Molly said, and she sounded pissed off.

'She's Davey's best friend and she's kind to me.'

'What's Davey doing?'

'I'm only thirteen, it's no big deal.' Juliet suddenly felt teary.

'Your ma would be so proud,' Molly said.

Jack cried.

'Ah don't cry, Granda,' Juliet said, and she cried, too.

Molly elbowed him. 'Now look what you've done.'

'Ah Ma, mind me da,' Grace said, and after that the call pretty much descended into everyone shouting at one another and talking at once. It was brilliant. It ended with Molly telling her granddaughter she'd see her for Christmas. Juliet pretended to be excited by the prospect of going home but she wasn't. The idea scared her because back in Dublin her mother was really gone, more gone than she was anywhere in the States. Living away, Juliet could pretend that back home she was alive, surrounded by music and friends and family and all the things she loved. Juliet could pretend that one day soon she would see her again.

They didn't go home for Christmas; the tour dates just kept coming in, making it impossible, and Juliet was relieved. *Too soon.* Her gran planned to come and see them but her doctor didn't want her to travel after he diagnosed deep-vein thrombosis following her heart stent operation. It was fine. Juliet couldn't imagine Molly Hayes squeezing her larger than life personality on board a bus too small to withstand it.

Then came the shattering news that Grace had the gene. Davey told her over dinner as she sat silently playing with the food on her plate, stabbing it with her fork and then moving it around in circles and figures of eight. He spoke to her about getting checked when she was old enough. It was too much to think about, so she automatically tucked that piece of information tightly away in the deepest recess of her brain to be opened at another time when she could cope.

The days turned into weeks and the weeks into months, and in the blink of an eye it was coming up to the anniversary of Rabbit's death.

Two things happened on the day Davey broke the news to Juliet that they were going home to mark the occasion. The first was something small but it freaked her out. Trevor was showing her how to get an input level and then his hand brushed against her breast and he looked at her funny and carried on as though nothing had happened, and nothing really did happen except that it felt wrong. She found the input level and then Trevor's wife face-timed and she said a quick goodbye as he blew a kiss at Ashley, their four-year-old baby girl.

Davey broke the news that Grace was having her operation the week after Rabbit's first anniversary on a moving bus and over a ready meal.

'We're going,' he said.

'No.'

'It's time.'

'Grace is having her operation the week after my ma's anniversary?'

'It just worked out that way Bun . . . iet,' Davey said.

'Will you stop calling me Buniet?'

'Will you stop making me call you Juliet?'

'It's my name!' she shouted.

'Not to me it isn't,' he shouted.

They both wanted to storm off but there was nowhere to go.

'We're going home, Juliet,' he said.

'I hate you, Davey,' she shouted, and after that they ate in awkward silence.

Chapter Thirty-Two

Grace

IN THE YEAR AFTER Rabbit's death, Grace's life became a series of medical appointments and theoretical arguments around her options and the course of action she should or shouldn't take. She had appointments for mammograms, MRIs, counselling and psychotherapy, and appointments for an oncologist and then appointments for a second opinion, more mammograms, MRIs, psychotherapy, and it went on and on. Her life was reduced to a file of papers that was growing thicker each week and a schedule full of hospitals and doctors' offices, and all the while a bomb ticked away inside her. The mammograms were sore, the MRIs terrifying and the counselling painful, not just because Grace had to talk about how she felt, and listen to Lenny, who was wholly unsupportive of her doing anything other than monitoring the bomb and waiting for it to go off. The argument around that was repetitive and unproductive.

'You don't have cancer. You might never have cancer.' And 'You can't cut yourself into little pieces. It's insane.' And 'This is grief – it's guilt and grief.' That particular argument came after a pretty intense counselling session in which Grace admitted she felt guilty about Rabbit's death. She felt guilty because she hadn't been there for Rabbit when she needed her just after her diagnosis. Grace's fear of hospitals, blood and needles meant she was slow to jump on board, but she did and it was hard because Rabbit's life had become nothing but hospitals, blood and needles. She tried her best but she still felt guilty when she couldn't help dress a wound or when she turned her face having caught a glimpse of her sister's sick, twisted, raw, scarred, battered, bruised and bloody body. She felt guilty because she was alive and her younger sister was dead and she was glad that she was alive. She didn't want to die. 'You're not dying!' Lenny shouted in the car after the session, but the bomb was ticking so loudly it was hard to hear him. He couldn't hear it. Maybe he didn't want to. She felt petrified and so very, very sad. The best thing about having the test done was that she was in the system, they were watching her; there was a disposal team on standby. For some that would be good enough, but not for Grace – she couldn't sleep, think straight, laugh or even smile. *I have the gene.* Of course she was grieving, but more than missing her sister, worrying about her parents, Juliet and Davey, and more than the guilt she carried around like luggage, it was the ever-present inescapable loud tick-tock of the bomb that lay within that destroyed her confidence and stole her peace of mind. Of course she didn't want to cut pieces of herself away; she was terrified and horrified and sickened and, worse than all of that, she was utterly and completely alone.

Three words increased Grace's isolation tenfold: 'It's your decision.' The oncologist laid out all the facts and what could be done, but never what should be done. He began by explaining why she was high-risk and talking percentages that in that moment made no sense. Lenny took notes and nodded along; she just sat there as the consultant explained what was involved in an MRI. *A needle!* She heard him say that a dye would be injected into her arm and the rest was a blur. He recommended mammograms and MRIs twice a year to keep on top of things. Counselling was a must, especially if she was considering risk-reducing surgery. He talked at length about what was involved in a double mast- ectomy including various reconstruction options which all sounded barbaric and painful. Then he moved on to a bilat- eral salpingo-oophorectomy. Grace felt dazed. She found it hard to focus on anything but how heavy the air felt, but Lenny was on it.

'Oophorectomy – can you spell that?'

The consultant spelled out the word as Lenny wrote it in big letters.

'Now what is that?' he asked.

'It's the removal of a woman's ovaries and fallopian tubes.'

'But Rabbit had breast cancer – the only place she didn't have cancer was in her ovaries.'

'Rabbit?'

'My sister,' Grace heard herself say. 'In the end it was everywhere.'

'Grace's gene means that she is considered high-risk for both breast and ovarian cancer.'

'So you want to cut her breasts off and take her ovaries?' Lenny said.

'No, I don't want to do that.' Then came those three words. 'It's your decision,' he said, looking to Grace.

'But do you recommend that?' Lenny asked.

'All I can do is tell you what's available – it's your decision,' he repeated.

'I'm asking for your opinion.'

'Everyone's different. This is a choice. Some choose to have the operation, some prefer to increase their breast checks and rely on monitoring. It's your decision,' he said again, looking at Grace.

The psychotherapist, the consultant, the consultant's nurse, the radiologist, the counsellor, the surgeon they went to for a second opinion, even the girl on the helpline . . . Every single person within the system told her the gene could kill her, but when it came to deciding on risk-reducing surgery they all uttered those three same words. She wanted someone – anyone at all – just to tell her to do it. Have the surgery. Save your life. They didn't. 'It's your decision.'

'If it was necessary it wouldn't be up to you,' Lenny said. 'There would be no decision to make.'

She researched everything, spent hours online looking at protocols from country to country. *Tick-tock. It's your decision. Tick-tock . . .*

The MRI was Grace's first opportunity to confront her paralysing fear of needles. It was also a test of her strength and endurance. It did not go well. It took every ounce of mental and physical strength to get into the room. Lenny was there; he'd have carried her in on his back if he had to. She cried silently, she shook and her face was so pale that it became necessary to place her head between her legs for five minutes. *I'm being a baby. For God's sake, Grace, buck up. Rabbit did this on lunch breaks.* She finally held out her arm; she was looking away and crying more loudly and her nose was running and her legs felt so heavy that she worried the pressure would pop her knees right off. *Tick-tock. It's your decision. Tick-tock* . . . It became obvious in an instant that her veins were deep, narrow, fragile things. They were hard to reach, they couldn't withstand too much pressure and they collapsed easily. When the dye was finally inserted and she was lying on her front, still and crying, in a space age tunnel, she knew she couldn't do this twice or three times a year. It was just too much.

'That wasn't so bad,' Lenny had said afterwards when they were at lunch and she was just using a fork because the swelling from the damaged vein in her arm made it difficult to bend her elbow to use a knife.

He made little of her trauma. 'It was just an X-ray, Grace. If that's the drama we can look forward to for a simple MRI, can you imagine surgery?'

She could imagine surgery. It infected her every waking thought. It awakened her worst fears, gave them life and power over her. It was a nightmare. *Tick-tock. It's your decision. Tick-tock* . . .

It didn't feel like a decision; it felt like a burden. Lenny refused to engage. 'You don't have cancer.'

She asked to be put on the waiting list for surgery straight away because the list was long and it gave her time to think. She could always pull out. Better to be safe than sorry, but deep down inside and buried under layers of questions and fear she always knew what she was going to do. It took four months of tests, counselling, mammograms, an MRI and one Skype call with her niece before she finally made her decision.

'Please, please don't die, Grace.'

183

And that was it.

'I'm having the surgery,' she said, lying in bed beside Lenny. He was reading a Tom Clancy novel and she was staring at a spider crack in the ceiling. He dropped the book and took his spectacles off. She could hear them slam on the locker and worried he'd break them – those spectacles were varifocal and cost over five hundred quid. He didn't speak; instead he put the light out and turned away from her.

Grace broke the news to her parents over Sunday dinner. It was just the adults present. Molly had made a roast chicken and sent Lenny out for chipper chips when she realised she'd forgotten all the trimmings.

'Me head's up me hole,' Molly said by way of explanation. It didn't matter; Grace and Lenny weren't there to eat. They were at war and looking for allies.

'Ma, Da, I have some news.'

'Make it good, love,' Molly said.

'Sorry, Ma. Can't. I have the gene.'

'What gene is that, love?' Jack said.

'The one that gave Rabbit cancer.'

Jack dropped his fork. Molly sat rigid.

'You took the test,' Molly said.

'Yeah.'

'And you have the gene.'

'Yeah.'

'And now she wants to cut her breasts off and pull her ovaries out,' Lenny said, stealing her punchline.

'I don't want to,' she corrected her husband.

'But you're going to,' he said.

'I have no choice,' she screamed. She was so sick of repeating herself.

'You have a choice, you can just keep up with the checks. Tell her, Jack. Tell her, Molly, tell her not to fucking carve herself up for no reason.'

Jack's chair screeched as he pushed it back, stood up and walked out of the room.

'Da,' Grace called after him, and she was crying again, always crying, she was so fed up with crying.

'I can't,' he said, and the door closed behind him. Lenny and Grace both looked to Molly for support.

'Please, Molly,' Lenny said. 'Talk some sense into her.'

'Do it. Save yourself,' Molly said to Grace, and Grace was so relieved she sobbed into her hands. *Finally. Thank you.*

Molly stood up, gathered the plates and moved towards the sink. Lenny followed her.

'Do you know how serious these operations are? How many complications can occur? How open to infection she is? How dangerous anaesthetic is? What it can do to her overall health? Even without complications it's a life changing surgery. She'll become more fragile, she'll be sick and sore and mentally fucked, and that's just the mastectomy.' He was spewing his words, fighting for sense to prevail, fighting for his wife's life. The one she lived now. Not some shadowy figure carved to pieces just in case. Just in case wasn't good enough. Molly started washing the dishes as he ranted on and on. 'What about when they take her ovaries and her tubes, what about menopause? What will that do to her? Molly, please, I'm begging you.'

Molly stopped washing up. She dried her hands on her dress and placed them on his shoulders. 'Menopause is in Grace's near future anyway, love. As for the rest, you're right about everything – our Grace couldn't even get her fucking ears pierced without falling off the table and giving herself a concussion, and surgery is life-changing but cancer is life-ending. So you have to ask yourself one question. Are you really willing to take that risk?'

He slumped into a chair with his head in his hands and now he was sobbing like a baby.

'I'm sorry,' he cried.

'Don't be sorry, be supportive,' she said, and Grace was still at the table in tears. 'And for the love of Christ will yis all stop crying? I've a pain in my arse from crying.'

Canvassing for surgery was one thing; actually thinking about it and talking about it was quite another. Every time her mind went there her stomach lurched, her hands trembled and her legs felt as weak as a baby deer's. She had to be strong. *It has to be done.* Now Lenny was finally on board she couldn't give herself away. She didn't want to talk about it. *What is there to say, Rabbit?*

Nothing, Gracie, nothing at all.

To add to the pressure building, Lenny watched everything she drank and ate. If she even attempted to open a bottle of wine on a Friday she'd be met with her husband's wagging finger.

'Alcohol intake increases your risk of cancer.'

'Worth it.'

'Oh, so you're willing to give up your breasts, but not a glass of Merlot?'

'Fuck you, Lenny,' she'd say, and she'd down the entire bottle.

He was on at her about her diet and exercise. 'You need to stay fit if you want to recover properly.' Then he discovered antioxidants. If Grace was going in for surgery he was going to ensure that she'd train like an athlete for it. Grace joined Jeffrey in food and exercise jail, and it was no fun.

A month later they decided to tell the boys. *FUCK. Stephen will be fine. He's old enough to understand. Poor Bernard will be devastated. Jeffrey will be scared, but as long as I'm upbeat and I tell him everything will be fine, he'll believe me.* It was Ryan she worried about. *How will he take it?* She didn't know. He'd been doing so well since he started attending weekend classes for bright kids. They gave him enough homework to make life interesting and the other kids in his class actually challenged him. He was busy, way too busy to engage in criminal behaviour, although he was continuing to manage the stock portfolio he'd started with the proceeds of ill-gotten gains, which was performing so well his father had him invest on his behalf. This would be a blow. He'd pretend he was fine but it could derail him. All the good work of the past five months would be undone if he acted out. Jeffrey had been doing well. He'd lost weight, he looked good, he felt even better. He might slip backwards but she could manage that. Ryan was a different matter. *I'm sorry, Ryan. Please don't do anything stupid. Please don't hate me. Please don't wreck your life. It's only an operation. No big deal. I'm going to be fine.* Except it was a big deal, and Grace wasn't sure if she would ever be fine again.

Lenny made his famous vegetarian chilli, which wasn't famous at all. Grace and the kids sat around the kitchen table and he doled it out into bowls. The steam rose into the air and the boys were armed with their spoons.

'No meat again?' Ryan asked. 'You know I can pick it up cheap.'

'This family doesn't eat meat off the back of a truck, Ryan,' Lenny said.

'Are we vegetarians now?' Stephen asked.

'No, but it's good to have meat-free days,' Lenny said.

'Since when?' Ryan asked.

'Since now.'

'I like it,' Jeffrey said, lashing into the chilli with the gusto of a man deprived.

'So just because fatboy is a fat boy we have to live like tree huggers?' Ryan said.

'Don't call your brother fatboy, Ryan,' Grace said.

'Anyway I've lost two stone,' Jeffrey said. 'I'm not fat anymore.'

'Fair enough, pudge-boy,' Ryan said, and Stephen flicked some hot chilli at him. He screamed out. 'That hurt!'

Lenny served himself and sat. 'The reason we're eating less meat is for a number of reasons, one of which we want to talk about now. Mammy has the gene that gave Rabbit cancer.' The mood instantly changed in the room. 'It's not cancer. She doesn't have cancer, but her chances of getting cancer are increased.'

'By how much?' Ryan asked.

'Fifty-five per cent.'

'One in two people born after 1960 will be diagnosed with some form of cancer during their lifetime,' Ryan said.

'How do you know?' Stephen asked.

'*Stand Up to Cancer* on Channel 4.'

Bernard was already crying. 'What does it mean, Ma?'

'It means she's way more likely to get cancer than any-one else, and seeing as it's already one in two it means she's fucked,' Ryan said.

'Jesus,' Stephen said.

'Ah no,' Bernard said.

'It's OK, son,' Grace said. 'We have a plan.'

Jeffrey pushed his food away. 'What plan?'

'Your mammy is going to have surgery to remove her breasts and ovaries to reduce her chance of getting cancer.'

'By how much?' Ryan asked.

'By enough to make it worthwhile,' Lenny said, and he choked on the words a little.

'When?' Ryan asked.

'I'm on a list, so whenever I'm called,' Grace said.

'I think that's smart,' Stephen said. 'I think you're doing the right thing.'

'Thanks, son.'

She looked to Bernard who was sobbing and Jeffrey who was pulling on his ear, a thing he used to do when he was a baby and distressed. Ryan just looked straight ahead.

'Any questions?' Lenny said.

'Is my ma going to die?' Bernard said.

'No, son. Not anytime soon, anyway.'

'That's what you said about Rabbit.'

'Rabbit had cancer. Your mammy doesn't.'

'Yet,' Ryan said.

'Shut up, Ryan.' Lenny snapped.

'No, he's right,' Grace said. 'I don't have cancer yet, and if Rabbit had found the gene before she got cancer and had done the surgeries I'm about to do, maybe she'd be here today.'

'What about us?' Ryan asked. 'If Rabbit had the gene and Ma has it, what about us?'

Grace's heart stopped – of course Ryan would go there.

'You'll all be offered the chance to have the test when you're older,' Lenny said, and his voice broke a little. 'Stephen, you're old enough to have it if you wish.'

'But we don't have breasts,' Jeffrey said.

'Doesn't matter,' Ryan said. 'We're fucked, too.'

'Please stop saying that word, Ryan,' Lenny said.

Grace nodded. 'If you have the gene, it means you are more likely to get cancer.'

'Jesus,' Stephen sighed deeply. 'I just got a new girlfriend.'

'I'm so sorry, son.' The weight of everything came crashing down and Grace was in tears. Bernard jumped up and hugged his ma. 'I love ya, Ma.'

'I love you too, son.'

Jeffrey stood up and hugged his ma. Stephen walked over and kissed her on top of her head. 'It'll be fine, Ma. We'll all be fine.'

Ryan stayed in his chair and when his brothers finally broke away from his ma, he looked at her and hunched his shoulders. 'I just need to process, Ma,' he said, and he got up from the table and walked away.

Two weeks later Ryan walked up to his mammy holding on to a large brown padded envelope as she was taking the washing off the line.

'I know you're scared of needles and everything, so I got you something.' He handed her the envelope.

'What's this?' she said as she opened it and two cloth bags fell out. They had a picture of a rabbit on them and the names of Lenny and her four boys stitched into them.

190

'They're drain dollies,' he said. 'When you have the operation you'll have drains.' She felt her legs go; he caught her and steadied her. 'You won't have to look at them, Ma. They'll be hidden in these.'

He showed her. 'See, I got them to put a rabbit and our names on them to remind you why you're doing it.'

She burst into tears. 'That's the nicest thing anyone has ever done for me.'

He smiled. 'Cool,' he said. He began to walk away but before he did he turned to his ma. 'And don't worry about me – if any of us get the gene it will be Bernard or Jeff, it's got to be one or both of those two saps.' He winked and she burst out laughing.

'Thank you, son,' she said, and, five months after Rabbit's death, Grace finally exhaled.

The appointment letter came through the door on a Tuesday in late March. The date for surgery was 5 May. Nine days after the first anniversary of Rabbit's death. It was a lot to take in. It had been a year of heartache – a blur of medicine, pain, anguish, talking, listening and terror. Grace's war on her cancer gene was about to begin.

Chapter Thirty-Three

Davey

NOTHING IS EASY WHEN it comes to caring for a child. That's what Davey learned in the immediate aftermath of his sister's death, and it wasn't just Juliet's isolation, her expulsion and trying to find a new way to live and work on the road, it was the mundanity of parenthood. It's hard to be the fun, open-minded and open-hearted uncle 24/7. Harder still to be the confidant and to communicate freely when he was now the law, the governor, the dreaded parent. It was exhausting. He could feel sadness pull her away and it was to be expected, but the level of anger and bitterness often directed at him was an unwelcome surprise. It was hard to know how to handle his own pain and that of his niece, never mind keep her safe while doing so. He'd never been responsible for anything in his life except a cannabis plant, and he smoked that to death. He worried all the time; every waking moment was filled with thinking about what Juliet was eating, drinking, doing, thinking, saying, feeling. Her physical needs were one thing, her emotional needs quite another. When she wasn't angry and pushing him away, she was polite and tiptoeing around him. Their once-easy relationship became strained and difficult and he knew he was failing her. He just didn't know how to fix it.

Initially he tried to be all things to her and for her, but she didn't want him to. She wanted to be alone so he gave her space and tried to be respectful of her privacy. He didn't want to push, and every day she moved further away and he failed and then failed a little more. When she was turfed out of school and Juliet begged him to take her on tour he didn't put up much of a fight. Davey was always known for taking the easy way out. He hired a tutor and he convinced himself she was better off on the road.

At first she seemed better. Her spirits lifted. She got on well with all the crew and she seemed to enjoy moving from city to city, never staying in the same place, always on the go . . . Maybe she was like him and needed to keep moving, or maybe she was running away. He wasn't sure. She said she was 'fine'. He was doing his best.

Then Grace called. 'I have the gene. You could have it too and so could Juliet and mine, all of us.'

'Jesus.'

'Yeah.'

'Jesus Christ, Grace.'

'Yeah.'

'I'm sorry.'

'Don't be. Get checked.'

'I've been checked, Grace. I don't have it.'

'How?' she asked.

'When Rabbit was diagnosed I included it in my health check. Can't tour without that, do it every year.'

'Right,' she said. 'Good. Good for you.' She sounded disappointed.

'Would you rather I had the gene?' he asked, half joking.

'Don't be a dick.'

'I'll talk to Juliet,' he said. 'She's too young for all this now.'

'Agreed.'

'You should ring Ma, tell her you're fine.'

'You tell her.'

'For fuck's sake, Davey, she's up the walls, just call her.'

He attempted to finish the conversation with Grace by telling her he loved her.

'What do you think I should do?' she asked all of a sudden as he was about to hang up the phone.

'It's your decision,' he said.

'Davey?'

'Yeah?'

'Fuck off,' she said, and hung up. *Nothing changes on Walton's Mountain* he thought to himself.

He rang his mother straight after.

'I'm so relieved, son. I'm so relieved. Thank you. Thank you,' she said. She sounded broken.

'You all right, Ma?' he said.

'I'm like a shit on a swing-swong, love.'

'What does that mean, Ma?'

'I'm all over the place, love. She's going to be torn apart, Davey,' Molly said.

'I wish there was something I could do.'

'You've done it. At least I don't have to worry about you.'

He broached the subject of gene testing with Juliet. They agreed Juliet was too young. It was a horrible conversation. It made him feel physically unwell. *What if she has the gene?* It was unthinkable.

'You're doing a good job, son,' she said.

'You don't know that.'

'The child's still alive, isn't she? Right now that's good enough,' she said, and she hung up. Davey often missed his family, but then he talked to them.

As hard as parenting was, they did have some good times, days when Davey and Juliet would just hang in a new city and shop for pretty things and visit local sights. They'd talk and have ice cream or doughnuts or cronuts or steaks or cheeseburgers or whatever the state delicacy was. They both drew the line at cheese grits and spam. It felt like old times, two buddies just hanging. Sometimes during those rare moments she'd open the door just a crack. When they were sitting side by side on a rock in Central Park, or fishing in Lake Tahoe. When they were hammering into beef enchiladas on a busy side street in Colorado or standing on the Grand Canyon skywalk, she'd let him in, if only for a minute or two, before the door closed and the shutters slammed down.

'Do you think this is what heaven would be like if it existed, Davey?' she said, looking down four thousand feet into the canyon. Davey had lost the power in his legs and felt a little seasick. 'I hope not,' he said, eyes closed and battling the urge not to lie face down on the glass bridge and whimper. *Stay strong, Davey*. She sat down beside him, leaning her forehead on the glass and looking down. 'Everything looks so beautiful when it's far away.'

He'd volunteered to take her on a field trip to complement her home studies. He was really sorry he had. The tutor could have done it. He was paying her enough. *Jesus help me*.

'Yeah, it's lovely,' he mumbled.

'Like heaven, Davey.'

'Do you believe in heaven?' he said.

'No, but maybe there's somewhere else like heaven except without all the crazy God stuff.'

'Like where?'

'I dunno, maybe another world like this one, and the only difference is the people in that world know we exist and they remember us. Mostly they just go about their new lives, but every now and then they come to a place like this and it's a portal to see the people they love, just for a minute or two, just to check in. Do you think that's possible, Davey?'

'Anything's possible.'

'And maybe one day when I die I'll go to the new world my ma lives in, and when we want to visit with the people we love we'll come to a place like this together and look down.'

He opened his eyes and slowly moved his heavy arm around her shoulder. 'I think that would be lovely.'

She waved at the four-thousand-foot drop. 'I love ya, Ma. I miss ya. We wish you were here, don't we, Davey?'

'We do.' He kissed her head and she rested on his shoulder.

'Everything's OK, Ma,' she said. 'I'm studying really hard, one on one. I'm going to be a doctor before you know it. I'm going to cure cancer like I said I would.' She was high on possibility. It was a good day.

Juliet spent hours of her day studying. She passed every test with flying colours. Her tutor was really impressed, but Davey was worried that she was disappearing into her schoolwork in the absence of having friends her own age.

He didn't know what to do about that except support her, if she'd let him. After all nobody studied themselves to death or destruction and, as his mother had previously disclosed, the parental bar set for him was pretty low. *Just love her, Davey.*

What if it's not enough, Rabbit?

His sex life suffered irreparably, and not because he was now a full-time parent obsessed with real-world concerns, or touring city to city, state to state – that never stopped him before; instead he found that intimacy with strangers left him feeling unfulfilled, unsatisfied, cold and, worst of all, awkward. Marjorie laughed at his concerns when he moaned about his horrible sex life on Skype. 'Welcome to middle age, Davey.'

It was good to reconnect with Marjorie. They talked about a lot of things: the good old days when they were young and life seemed so much brighter, even though looking back Ireland was such a grey old place. They talked about the reality of their present. Marjorie complained bitterly about her terrible mother and her horrible job.

'Your mother doesn't deserve you. That bank doesn't deserve you.'

'Doesn't matter what they deserve, Davey, I am where I am.'

He talked about his concerns rearing a teenage girl on the road.

'It won't be forever, you'll be off the road next year.'

'Yeah, but for how long?' he said. It was good to talk, even if neither of them had the answer to life's problems. He looked forward to seeing her again. He thought about her a lot. He often fantasised about her. He tried to stop, telling himself it was nonsense. He warned himself to leave her alone; he'd done enough damage in her life. Then he found himself thinking of her breasts. *Oh God, she has lovely breasts.* Then he wondered why he hadn't fully appreciated that about her before.

What am I doing, Rabbit?

You're doing a Davey.

He promised his dead sister he would absolutely, positively not have sex with her best friend when he went home because that would be selfish and wrong and he'd grown up a lot since she died.

Liar, he heard her say.

Chapter Thirty-Four

Marjorie

MARJORIE FIRST VISITED HER mother two days after her stroke. She had been lucky, as it turned out. She'd felt unwell and phoned for an ambulance before she collapsed. The paramedics could see her on the floor from her large front window so they kicked down the door to gain access. She was a ten-minute drive from the Mater Hospital so she received treatment in what the consultant described as the golden hour. On finally meeting Marjorie he explained to her that Vera was eighty per cent back to herself within twenty-four hours, but weakness in her legs required time and physiotherapy.

'Can she walk?'

'Not without assistance.'

'You mean a stick? Or a frame?'

'She'll require a wheelchair for a time.'

'What kind of time?'

'It depends on the patient.'

'Well, are we talking a week, a month, a year?' Her voice was rising and panic was setting in. *What now? WHAT now? WHAT NOW????*

He put his hand on Marjorie's shoulder, attempting to comfort her. 'Don't worry, she'll be fine.'

'Oh I'm not worried about her, Doctor, I'm worried about me,' she said.

He pulled away, a look of distaste on his face.

'Judge all you want, but if she was your mother you'd probably put her down,' she said, and she walked away from a medical man with a gaping mouth. She wanted to run, just leg it, get out, go, never to return, like a man in the fifties just off to buy some cigarettes – in fact, very much like her own dad. *See ya*. She didn't, though; she made herself walk into the room where her mother lay. Her body felt heavy, as though she were wading through mud. *Why am I doing this? She's my mother, that's why. Shit mother, such a shit mother. If this were Molly I'd be here all day and all night. If it were Molly I'd buy a mini-fridge and move in, but Vera? Bloody Vera*. In that moment she really hated Vera more than she'd ever thought possible. *You get to live and Rabbit dies. How fucking dare you.*

Vera Shaw looked small in the bed. Marjorie hadn't seen her in a while, maybe a month or even two. In that time she seemed to have aged, but then again she wasn't wearing make-up. Marjorie couldn't recall a time before when she had seen her mother without make-up. It was her war paint, a carefully constructed facade, and she didn't leave her bedroom without it. There she was, clean-faced, haggard and vulnerable, staring up at Marjorie looking down. She didn't bend to kiss her. She just sat and placed a paper bag with three nightdresses on the floor by her feet.

'I bought you some clean nightdresses and some under-wear,' she said.

'Thanks.'

'How are you feeling?'

'Better.'

'Good.'

'I heard Rabbit died.'

Marjorie nodded.

'I'm sorry,' she said, and she looked like she actually meant it. 'I was going to go to the funeral but then I had a stroke, so . . .'

'As excuses go, it's a good one,' Marjorie said, and her mother sniffed.

'I suppose it is. I wanted to pay my respects. I was fond of Rabbit,' she said, and it hurt Marjorie because she knew her mother was not fond of her.

'So send a mass card.'

'Oh, I will. Once I get back up on my feet.' Silence followed. She'd need minding until that day and Marjorie had no intention of offering to help. *Find another sucker.*

She stayed for forty-five minutes. She was relieved when the nurse announced that visiting time had come to an end. As she moved to leave her mother grabbed for her hand.

'Thanks for coming,' she said. 'I really appreciate it.' *Here we go – emotional blackmail.*

'You're welcome,' Marjorie said, and she felt that first pang of guilt spark in her heart and dart to her stomach. *Bollocks.*

'Will I see you again?' she asked in a sweet voice Marjorie found hard to recognise.

'I'll be in tomorrow,' Marjorie said half-heartedly, and her mother smiled and patted her hand. *Bollocks. Fifteen–love to Vera.*

Marjorie headed for the door and was stopped by a little old dear who introduced herself as Janet followed by 'eighty-four'.

'Excuse me?'

'I'm Janet, eighty-four years old,' she said, and she took a bow.

'Good for you.'

'So you're Vera's girl, Marjorie,' she said, and Marjorie was taken aback. *How does she know?*

'Yes. I am.'

'Oh, she hasn't stopped talking about you, says you're very big in the bank.'

Did she? 'And you're as beautiful as she reported. God bless you. I was a looker myself back in the day.' *Big in the bank? Beautiful? The biggest compliment my mother's ever given me is that I was one of the few children who could be trusted to wear white. Thirty–love to Vera.*

'Thanks,' she said, trying to move past her, but Janet wasn't finished with her yet.

'She said you were away. I'm glad you managed to get back. She needs you now,' she said. *Forty–love to Vera – auld ones always stick together.* Janet had said what she wanted to say. She turned and walked away. *Game, set and match to Vera Shaw. BOLLOCKS.*

In the weeks after Vera Shaw's stroke, Marjorie was forced to engage with her mother on a more intimate level than either woman was prepared for. Everything was a struggle. The woman's legs weren't strong enough to hold her up and she needed to be lifted on and off the toilet. This was no fun at all, especially as Vera had endured a lifetime of complications following the symphysiotomy carried out during Marjorie's birth, complications which included bowel incontinence. Marjorie was forty years old and had never changed a dirty nappy or owned a dog, so cleaning or picking up shite was not a feature of her day-to-day life until her mother's stroke. It never occurred to her that visitors would be forced to endure cleaning of patients' legs, sheets, nightdresses, knickers and arses – that's what staff were for, surely? But it became quickly apparent that if you couldn't stand the smell of it or if you didn't want your mother sitting in her own dirt for longer than five minutes, the job became yours and yours alone. So with eyes watering and battling the urge to vomit, Marjorie wrestled with her mother to cleanse her of unholy muck, and it was hardcore.

'Get away from me.' Vera punched out at her daughter. 'Don't touch me.'

'She's only doing what's right,' Janet, the nosy auld one from bed three, said.

'Mind your own business,' Vera said.

'Your shite is my business when it's so potent I can't just smell it I can bleedin' taste it,' Janet said. *Too much.* Marjorie threw up a little in her mouth.

She lifted her mother out of the bed and onto a chair, then she pushed her into the bathroom.

'Get out, I'll do it myself.'

'OK, great, stand up and I'll get out.'

The woman couldn't stand up.

'Now can we just get on with it?' Marjorie asked. Vera nodded and allowed her daughter to clean her down and sit her on the toilet so she could attempt to evacuate whatever was left.

Marjorie wore gloves, but she still washed her hands in boiling water and used so much antibacterial soap that they became chapped. That first night she also stopped at an off-licence and bought a bottle of whiskey because wine just wouldn't cut it. After that it felt like her mother waited till she walked through the door to schedule a dump. While she cleaned and washed the woman's bits and bobs she'd shout at herself in her head. *She's doing it on purpose. What are you doing here anyway? She wouldn't do it for you. She wouldn't piss on you if you were on fire. But here you are. Not just eating her shit now, cleaning it as well. You're a fool, Marjorie.* She'd talk to herself because there was nobody else, nobody but Davey. He had finally kept a promise. He Skyped her once a week.

'I hate her, Davey.'

'Your ma?'

'Yeah, my ma.'

'It's hard to walk away, though,' he said.

'Suddenly she needs me. Where was she when I needed her?'

'She wasn't there,' he said.

'And now I'm supposed to be her slave?'

'No. Set boundaries. Stick to them.'

'She spent ten minutes today talking about Sodom and Gomorrah and how the world would soon end and we all deserved it. She's fucking looking forward to it, Davey. She only stopped when Janet told her to put a bloody sock in it.'

'Who's Janet?'

'A nosy auld one in bed three.'

'How long are they keeping her?'

'Until I get her house organised. I'm hiring a nurse for a while.'

'How much will that cost?'

'You don't want to know. It's all falling to shit, Davey.'

Once Marjorie had a husband, a best friend and a job she loved. Now she was single, friendless and in a job she loathed. Since the recession she spent most of her time killing people's dreams and dismantling their lives. It was not what she signed up for. She found it increasingly hard to sleep at night and then climb out of bed in the morning. She wanted out. She needed out, but her ungrateful mother's needs made escape impossible.

'Is it bad that I fantasise about swapping my mother for Rabbit?'

'Nah, the dead would love your mother, she's right up their street,' he said, and she chuckled.

'Depends on the dead,' she said.

'Those fellas in Dante's Seventh Circle.'

'She'd fit right in.'

'Do they play bridge in the Circle?' he asked.

'Eternally.'

'You don't owe your mother anything, don't throw away your future for hers,' Davey said, and tears stung Marjorie's eyes because as much as she wanted to, she couldn't just throw her mother away. *This must be what you felt about me, Mam,* she thought, and for the first time in her life she had insight into her own mother's twisted thoughts. She didn't want to talk anymore.

Months passed, and mostly she was kept busy tending to her mother's needs. Four months on, Vera was stronger and slowly getting back on her feet. Marjorie called to her mother's house most days; becoming a slave to the woman just crept up on her. She'd organised a bed downstairs and some home care, but her mother didn't like any of the 'foreigners' that walked through her door. So once or sometimes twice a day Marjorie received a call from her mother demanding her presence with the words, 'I'm an invalid, you know.' Marjorie the sucker hated her for it, and hated herself more for always eventually turning up. She'd arrive to be confronted by her angry mother humiliating a perfectly nice care assistant.

'I can't even understand her,' she said of a Croatian lady who spoke perfect English but mumbled the word *kuja* every now and then when Vera Shaw was particularly offensive. She didn't like a Thai lady because she was too small and Vera maintained she didn't feel safe, and when she spoke it was in a whisper. 'If I have to say "what" one more bloody time,' she complained. 'Speak up!' she roared into the ether. Neither woman was fired. They both left of their own accord. A Serbian woman lasted a day because she didn't come to Ireland 'to work for a dictator'.

Where had all the Irish gone? Vera lamented.

'Do you think any of them would put up with your bullshit?' Marjorie asked after a particularly stressful day.

'Of course they would, the Irish will put up with anything. That's what makes us special,' she said, and she believed it. *The lunatic.*

Marjorie missed Rabbit. She missed picking up the phone and hearing her voice. She missed her advice and her chuckle, the way she could turn everything around with a funny line or a piece of good advice. Marjorie really needed her friend's advice now. Her mother was running roughshod over her. Deep down she knew what Rabbit would say. *Don't let her get away with it, Marj, you're not a kid anymore. Call her on her shit and don't take any.*

Easy for you to say, dead woman.

As time passed, Vera's condition improved. Marjorie could see her mother gain strength in her legs and she could stand for longer. She could cross the living room floor with a stick. She maintained she still needed the wheelchair to go outside. She refused to even try. 'Do you want me to break a hip?' she asked.

'Of course not, if you're going to break something make it your neck,' Marjorie said, and Vera laughed. It was the first time Marjorie had seen her laugh in years. She laughed so much, she snorted and it was catching – Marjorie laughed, too.

'That was a good one,' Vera said when she finally stopped, then she squeezed her daughter's arm.

'Thank you,' she said, and Marjorie nearly had a stroke of her own.

Davey was worried about his mother; he asked Marjorie to go and visit her, so she did. Molly didn't look like herself: her hair was perfect, her nails painted and she looked healthy, but there was something off that Marjorie could not quite put her finger on. They sat together in the kitchen, drinking tea and sharing a doughnut. Molly admitted how sad she was.

'I miss her voice,' Molly said.

'I hear it all the time,' Marjorie said.

'She talks to you?'

'All the time.'

Molly looked like she might burst into tears. 'She talks to Grace, her da, Davey and Juliet, too, but not me. I try, Marjorie, but she won't talk to me.'

Marjorie didn't know what to do so she just hugged her tight. 'Who loves ya, Molly?' she said.

'Marjorie does,' Molly said, and she smiled a warm smile to let Marjorie know that that woman she knew was still there, behind all that pain. 'Now, tell me about that lunatic you have for a mother.'

Marjorie told her everything and Molly listened quietly, offering no words.

'Say something,' Marjorie said.

'Your mother is a narcissist, she'll bleed you dry if you let her,' Molly said. 'No home help no matter how experienced will be good enough for her as long as you pick up the slack when they're not there. I know from my own experience, love. Do what you have to. Cut the cord.'

'That's good advice.'

'Well, easier said than done. I hope the auld one doesn't take a gun to you,' Molly said.

The very next day Marjorie walked into her mother's home, and before the woman could even get a word out Marjorie laid down the law.

'The next care assistant that walks through this door, you'll be nice and polite and you will mind your manners. You will not be a bitch. You will be respectful and grateful and you will be glad of their help.'

'I don't need their help, I have you,' Vera said.

'No you don't,' Marjorie said. 'I'll visit twice a week, I'll do your shopping, but that's it.'

'So you're throwing me to the wolves?'

Marjorie didn't lose it. She kept her cool. 'I don't know if you are capable of real love, Mam . . .'

'Is that right?' Vera said.

'That's right.'

'You better go, then.'

'I will. See you on Saturday,' Marjorie said.

'Don't bother.'

'I will see you on Saturday, Mother, and when I do try to paste a smile on that miserable mug of yours,' Marjorie said, and she walked out of her mother's house with her head held high and the tightness in her chest slightly loosening.

Eight months after Rabbit died, Marjorie walked into the bank to be told that there was a voluntary redundancy package available to all. She jumped at it.

During that year, Davey Hayes became Marjorie's only real friend. She went for drinks with some of the girls she worked with in the bank, but she knew that as soon as she left, their relationship would end. It didn't matter to her. She had enough going on. Davey was excited for her when she told him of her impending redundancy.

'So what now?' he asked, and she didn't know. For the first time in Marjorie's life nothing was mapped out, but strangely, she'd never felt so in control.

Chapter Thirty-Five

Molly

MOLLY'S MOTHER USED TO say 'Get up or get out.' So in the immediate aftermath of Rabbit's death she did just that. Her house no longer felt like home. The urge was to keep moving, keep busy, fill the days with tasks, shopping, voluntary work with the homeless societies, collecting, cleaning, feeding soup to the disenfranchised, the alcoholics, the addicts, the poor souls with nowhere to go. BR – before Rabbit's loss – she visited the church once or twice a week and always brought a bit of polish and a duster to clean the place up as she prayed. Sometimes she sat but never for long. She knew where the brush was kept so often she grabbed it and swept the aisles.

It was while she was cleaning and contemplating that she'd chat with Father Frank; more often than not they'd take tea in the back kitchen next to the sacristy. Over the years they'd had many an existential conversation, argument and laugh in that back kitchen; they'd both even shed a few tears. He loved a gossip. He pretended he didn't but he was all ears whenever she filled him in on the goings-on between one fella and another. He'd feign shock despite being unshockable. The things he heard in confession must have curled toes. Still, he was a good sport and a good friend, as it turned out. She missed him but not enough to go back there. Not now. Not AR – after Rabbit, Molly was a different woman. The moment her child died marked her. She got through the funeral by not thinking and only doing. *Get up or get out.* But afterwards when people had left, the noise died down and her child was well and truly gone, Molly's thoughts roared back to life, dark thoughts exacerbated by Rabbit's silence. *Sorry.*

AR the church represented everything unjust and unfair, and so Molly looked elsewhere to attain some peace. Voluntary work kept her going: Monday and Wednesday mornings sorting clothes for the local charity shop; Tuesday and Thursday afternoons dropping meals on wheels to the local auld dears who couldn't cook for themselves; Friday nights she spent on the streets of Dublin doing a soup run. It was the only work that Jack had a problem with. 'It's night-time in Dublin city, Molly, and you'll be walking the streets handing soup and sandwiches out to God knows who.'

'I'm not alone, Jack, and anyway those poor creatures wouldn't hurt a fly.'

'It's not the poor creatures in doorways I'm worried about. It's all the other lunatics.'

'Ah now, who'd be interested in tangling with an old woman?' she asked.

'It's too dangerous, Molly,' he said.

AR Molly didn't care. Talking with the unfortunates took her mind off her own troubles. They seemed small by comparison to those of people ravaged by addiction or mental illness. She poured soup, and sooner or later she'd have them talking about the weather or politics or Kim Kardashian's arse. Some were trickier characters than others.

'Shove your sandwich, give us some drugs,' one auld one in a wheelchair said to her.

'Do I look like a dealer to you?' Molly asked.

'Me last one was about your age, although she made her grandkids do most of the work.'

'Well, that's not depressing at all,' Molly said flatly.

'Go on, will ya, give us some money, then, or I'll slash your tyres,' she said, eyeing up the car behind Molly, which wasn't Molly's car at all. Molly didn't even look back; instead she focused on the wheelchair. 'Not if I slash your tyres first,' she said, and the auld one laughed. 'Go on, give us some soup, then,' she said.

The volunteer work kept her going for a time, but she needed something more; she needed something to fight for or rage against, and her best friend Pauline knew just the answer. They had been inseparable ever since Pauline knocked on Molly's door one wild rainy night in the eighties with her face smashed in and two crying kids by her side. Molly was there for her when she threw her abusive husband out, and when the parish priest tried to talk her into taking him back it was Molly who sent him away with a flea in his ear. Molly gave her the strength to get rid of him and to stay rid of him. She had been there for Molly, too; throughout all of Rabbit's treatments, setbacks and disappointments Pauline stood by with a hot cup of tea, a slice of her famous coffee cake and a listening ear. She was head of the residents' committee and in charge of the local protest against the water charges, specifically the refusal to allow the installers to dig up their properties to install water meters. She was out of her depth and needed her pal. She invited Molly over on a Monday afternoon and offered to prepare lunch. She made a coffee cake specially. They sat together over a home-made tomato soup and smoked salmon on home-made brown bread.

'What have I done to deserve this?' Molly asked, knowing well the crème fraiche in the soup meant Pauline was looking to do a bit of business.

'I need help.'

'With wha'?'

'This protest, Molly. I've promised everyone we won't let those blackguards dig up our gardens and streets to put in those poxy meters, but sure what can I do?' she said, raising her arms. 'I'm four foot four and weigh less than a packet of crisps.'

'Well, no one is expecting you to fight the fuckers, Pauline,' Molly said.

'But what, then?'

'You organise a group, just like a strike, a few banners, an auld slogan, like loads of the other areas are doing.'

'Ah yeah, but people work, Molly, and there's a lot around here too old for that kind of thing.'

'Bollocks, too lazy more like. Get on the Facebook, tell them all what time these men are coming and get the names of those willing to stand up against them.'

'Will you, Molly?'

'Well, we'll see, I've a lot to do.'

'You see,' Pauline said, 'people are busy.'

'Yeah, but the difference is they care about this.'

'And you don't.'

'I don't know what I care about anymore, Pauline,' Molly said.

'Fair enough, good point. Sorry.' Pauline said, and she cut Molly an extra-large slice of coffee cake. 'Here you go,' she said, dolloping on the cream.

Five days later Pauline sent out a Facebook message to tell the residents the meters were being installed on a Tuesday morning. She asked for all those willing to participate in a blockade/ strike to contact her. Two people signed up, an eighty-four-year-old ex-librarian called Thomas Kelly who was on two walking sticks and had a hearing aid, and Nicole Donohoe, a retired shopkeeper in her sixties who was a little bored and very angry. Pauline's post received one hundred and twenty-one likes and two actual volunteers.

'We can't do it with three of us,' Pauline lamented, sitting on Molly's front wall while Molly used her free Thursday afternoon to cut the hedges.

'I'm in, then,' Molly said.

'Are ya sure?'

'Yeah, go on. Bleedin' cheek of them, coming in here and destroying our property. I read about an estate where they came, put in their meters and the bloody place sprung a leak as soon as they left. That was six weeks ago, and the council hasn't done a fuckin' thing about it.'

She was annoyed, Pauline could see it. 'There ya are, Molly.' Pauline said, enjoying her old pal's fighting spirit.

'Don't start,' Molly said, before mumbling, 'As if we don't pay for water already, in our taxes and VAT . . . bleedin' cheek of them.'

'It's not just about metering us, Molly. They've created Irish Water as a company so that down the road they can privatise it.'

Molly sighed and nodded to herself. 'Well then, Pauline,' she said, standing up from the wall, 'they can take our pensions but they'll never take our water.' Pauline clapped and stamped her feet. 'God bless you, Molly Hayes.' Before she knew it Molly was part of an Irish revolution.

She tried not to think about Rabbit a lot, what was the point? *Sorry.* Every now and then she opened her locker drawer and there was the metal heart-shaped box holding a sprinkling of her child's ashes, and pain coursed through her. *What in the name of God made me agree to my child's ashes being divided into one big box and four small silver boxes? Bloody Jack and his bloody ideas. My child divided, it's not right.* She stopped trying to talk to Rabbit, except to say sorry. She had let her daughter down and the guilt was slowly breaking her. She washed the dishes. *Sorry.* She served soup to a stranger. *Sorry.* She held a banner in the sky with the word 'Meter' placed between a drawing of the cheeks of an arse while chanting the slogan 'Shove your meters up your arse'. *Sorry.* She never used Rabbit's name. She just said sorry and then she got on with her business. She hid when Father Frank called to the door. She didn't want to speak to him. BR, he had a way of making her say things she didn't want to say. *Not today, Padre.* AR she did miss their chats, but she couldn't face him. *Sorry.*

She had a stent placed in her dodgy artery in September; she was in and out of hospital in three days. It was easy, no fuss. Jack was relieved when it was done and dusted.

'Onwards, Molly,' he said when she woke from the anaesthesia.

'Hmmm,' she said. 'I'm still alive, then.'

'Hurrah.'

'Can't kill a bad thing, Ma,' Grace said, leaning over her and kissing her on the forehead.

'No, love.' She grabbed her daughter's hand. 'So you and me will be fine.' She winked and Grace faltered a little. *Fucking gene.*

The gene was always on her mind; ever since Grace broke the news it became an obsession. She worried about Grace, Lenny and the kids, but she also worried about her granddaughter. Does she have it? Is she going to have to carve into herself, too? Will it get her before she does? She worried a lot about how Davey was choosing to raise Juliet but she tried to maintain a respectful distance. BR she wouldn't have cared – she'd have bulldozed her way into their lives and sorted it all out, Molly-style. AR she realised she didn't have all the answers and she was as helpless as anyone else. So she stayed out of it and hoped that she was doing the right thing, and every now and then she'd look up to the sky and whisper the word *sorry*.

When the meter installers came, Molly, Pauline, Thomas and Nicole parked their cars around the van, blocking it in before the lads even managed to get out of it. A round bald man, who introduced himself as Paul Preston, rolled down his window, a takeaway coffee in one hand and a doughnut in the other. A smaller, leaner fella was sitting in the front with half a bar of chocolate in his hand. A big heavyset fella leaned over Paul's shoulder from the back with a wrench in his hand.

'What are ya playing at?' he said to Molly, who rolled her window down; they would have been eye to eye except her car was tiny and low to the ground.

She looked up at him. 'What do you think?'

'You can't just trap us in the bloody van.'

'Well it looks like anyone can do what they like these days, so if ya can't beat 'em, join 'em.'

He rolled up his window. Half an hour passed with the man drinking coffee, eating a second doughnut and taking calls. The fella in the back was getting agitated. He opened the sliding back door, but Molly's car was lined up too close for him to squeeze out. He banged on her roof.

'Let me out,' he shouted. 'If I can't get past you I'll go through you,' he said, pulling on her locked back door. 'I'll pull this bleedin' door off.'

'You can try,' Molly said.

'We can do this the easy way or the hard way,' he said.

Molly grinned. 'We can.'

He kept wrenching at the locked door, and when she became worried that he might actually pull the door off its hinges, she unlocked it with the press of a button and he fell on his arse back into the van. The other fella in the front seat laughed. She grabbed the door again and locked it before he managed to get off his back. He was holding his ankle and crying out in pain. Paul sighed and shook his head.

'That's assault,' he said.

'Assault, my eye – you'd know if I assaulted you. I could break your back without breaking a sweat,' she said, and the big fella slunk back; he could see she had hate in her heart.

The smaller fella leaned across Paul. 'I really need the loo.'

'Tough shit.'

'When is this going to end?' Paul Preston said. His large work-mate was now trying to stand up in the back and was limping.

'I think I've turned me ankle.'

'When you agree to leave here and never return.'

'Or what?'

'Or the next time I burn this fucking van to the ground.'

'Do you hear all this?' he shouted to the other protesters. They all nodded. 'And you're all right with this, are yis?' he asked.

'Delighted,' Nicole said, and she blew smoke out the small crack of window she'd opened.

'And you?' He turned to Thomas, and Thomas thought for a moment. 'The true soldier fights not because he hates what's in front of him, but because he loves what's behind him,' he said with great authority before leading the others to chant 'Shove your meters up your arse'.

The police arrived two hours later; the lads had been corralled in their van for five hours. Two Garda stepped out of the car – a pretty girl in her twenties and an ugly fella in his early fifties. They surveyed the situation.

'I've seen it all now, Edel,' he said to his fellow Garda. She just shook her head. 'Who's in charge here?' he asked. Paul and Molly both said, 'I am.' He sniffed and made his way towards Molly. He didn't introduce himself; later she came to know him as Sergeant Kevin Fogarty.

'Molly Hayes.'

'You'll need to move this car, Molly.'

'And if I don't?'

'Then I'll have to arrest you under section 15, Non-Fatal Offences Against the Person Act.'

'For what?' Molly said.

'For false imprisonment.'

'They're not falsely imprisoned.'

'Are they free to leave?'

'No.'

'Well then, they are falsely imprisoned,' he said.

'They are vandalising private property.'

'They're doing their job and so am I, so it's time to go home.'

Molly called out to the others: 'Roll 'em up and lock 'em down,' rolling up her window so fast she nearly took the hands off the Garda.

Sergeant Kevin Fogarty shook his head. 'Molly Hayes and friends, I am arresting you under section 15, Non-Fatal Offences Against the Person Act.'

The station was quiet enough when Jack arrived, puffed up and pale-faced, with Molly's passport in hand. She had no choice but to call him; she wasn't allowed home until she had verified her identification.

'My God, Molly, what's going on in that head of yours?' he said.

At least I don't hide away in an attic, old man. She ignored him. Pauline jumped to her friend's defence. 'We all just got a bit carried away.'

A thundering Grace was hot on her father's heels. 'Carried away? Ma, you're being done for false imprisonment, and one of the lads is threatening to sue for assault,' Grace said in a very high-pitched voice.

'Sorry,' Molly said. *Sorry.*

Everyone was quiet on the car ride home. Molly and her cohorts would be forced to appear in court within thirty days. It was a big deal. *Sorry.*

'We'll need a solicitor,' Jack said.

'Just call Maurice.'

'Maurice is not a criminal solicitor,' Jack said.

'Good, because I'm not a criminal.'

'Well according to the fuckin' charge sheet you are,' Grace shouted. After that everyone was silent again.

In the kitchen Molly made herself a long-overdue cup of tea while Jack and Grace sat opposite one another at the table, both steaming. *Sorry*. She placed the pot between them and a few cups, milk and sugar. She sat.

After a while and with half a cup of tea inside him, Jack started to come round. 'I'm sure it can't be that bad,' he said, trying to lighten the mood. 'I mean, what exactly is false imprisonment?'

'It's when a mental auld one traps three men in a fuckin' van for five hours,' Grace said. She really wasn't taking it well at all.

'Ah but sure, I've been stuck in a lift longer, do you remember, Molly, in Blackpool?'

'Oh yeah, seven hours,' she said, 'we thought we'd never get him out.'

'I was lucky I was in it on me own, of bit a space and it was nice and warm. I just fell asleep, didn't I, Molls?'

'I was losing me mind, waiting for those doors to open, and there he was in the foetal position and snoring.'

'I could sleep anywhere back then,' he said.

'You can sleep anywhere now.'

It was the first pleasant conversation they'd had in weeks. BR they were two peas in a pod and the best of friends; AR they were either bumping heads or drifting apart.

'I think we're getting off the subject,' Grace said.

'I'll call Maurice in the morning,' Jack said.

'Are you ready for your surgery, love?' Molly said.

'No,' Grace said.

'You'll be grand, won't she, Jack?'

Jack excused himself. 'Maybe I'll try and ring him now or leave a message.' *Arsehole*. He refused to engage with anything related to the surgery. It was one of their many sticking points.

'He's just worried,' Molly said.

'I know,' Grace said, but her mother could tell that Jack's silence deeply hurt her. *I'll murder him.*

'Did I tell you how brave you are, Grace?' Molly said, and she smiled at her daughter and placed her hand gently on her face.

'You always say the only difference between bravery and stupidity is the outcome,' Grace said.

'In my case, not in yours. I think you're a hero.'

'Stop it, Ma.'

'I do. My hero.'

Grace grinned a little. 'Well I think you're a lunatic.'

'In the current climate, that's a fair assessment, love.'

'Love ya, Ma,' Grace said, hugging her mammy.

'Love ya, Gracie,' Molly said, holding her firstborn tightly. *Sorry.*

It was five days before the anniversary of Rabbit's death and thirteen days before Grace's operation, and Molly Hayes had no fucks left to give.

Chapter Thirty-Six

Jack

JACK SPENT MUCH OF the first year after his daughter's death alone. Initially he was holed up in the attic reading his old diaries, and that took him from May till August. When he emerged it was to an empty house – his wife was MIA most of the time. A woman who had once loved her home so much she had to be almost jimmied out of it, now seemed hell-bent on going anywhere and everywhere just to escape it. *Maybe Rabbit's corpse in the dining room wasn't the best idea in the world.* While Molly's world expanded, his contracted. She always seemed busy, with friends to see, posters and banners to write, meetings to attend. She'd somehow become political in his absence. She cared about things outside her family now, broader and bigger things like the right to keep the Irish water supply from the private sector. She was rallying, protesting, rebelling with the Irish masses. She had a cause, a reason to get up and get out. He stayed locked away with his memories. He missed his wife but at the same time he felt more content when alone. He wasn't able for the new world. The rain was too wet, the wind too wild, the sun too bright and the night was so very long and dark. It was easier to remain silent than to talk. It was better to sit than to walk. He'd rather read than watch TV. There was so much pain, inside and outside. Everywhere he turned, people were crying out for help, in despair. They were broke or broken, homeless or a few pay cheques away from it. They were lonely, lost, terrorised walking corpses, and the whole country was screaming *Help me*. They'd been calling out to the government to stop crippling them to pay the banks, but their voices had gone unheard. While Rabbit lay dying his countrymen's pain did not penetrate his mind and soul, but afterwards their mass suffering meshed with his own and it was so intolerable that he disengaged completely.

In September he received a call from Rabbit's editor. He had some news. 'We nearly have a deal,' he said. He'd been working on Rabbit's book since she died, and through an agent he had sent it to a number of publishing companies. Two had declined it, but two others had bid against one another.

'That's great,' Jack said.

'The company we're going for isn't offering the most up front, but my agent and I believe they have a better marketing plan and that's what we all want, isn't it, Jack?'

'My girl out in the world, absolutely.'

'Good stuff,' Derek said. Then he talked about figures. Derek had a share in the book – after all, he was Rabbit's voice after she'd gone. They had agreed all that formally beforehand. Jack didn't need to know. He really didn't care. Any monies earned from the book would go to Juliet, and whether it sold one copy or one million, she would want for nothing. It wasn't about money. It was about bringing Rabbit back to life.

'Any questions?' Derek asked after talking for a long time. Jack had zoned out; he was busy picturing the book with a photo of his beautiful daughter on the cover.

'No.'

'It's good news,' Derek said, and he sounded disappointed by Jack's despondency.

'Are you all right, Jack?'

Jack sighed heavily. 'I don't think I'll ever be all right again, Derek.'

'I'm so sorry.'

'Don't be, you and that book are the only chink of light in this dark world.'

'Christ Almighty,' Derek said, 'no pressure, then.'

Jack chuckled a little. 'Molly says I'm a dramatic effer, if you understand me.'

It was Derek's turn to chuckle. He did understand, except he knew she called him a dramatic fuck rather than effer, but poor Jack, even in his darkest hours, couldn't bring himself to repeat his wife's salty language.

'Do you want to read it, Jack?' Derek asked.

'I do but I'm scared.'

'Understandable.'

'Will it break my heart, Derek?' he asked.

'It will, but it will also raise you up.'

'She always raised me up, no matter what.'

'This book won't let you down,' Derek said with great confidence. 'When I'm working on it, it's as though she's in the room.'

'Send it on,' Jack said.

He received the book in late September, and he read a chapter a day for twenty days. The last four chapters he spaced

224

out, reading half a chapter every two days. He didn't want it to end. He wanted to stay with her in the moment, and it was such a beautiful and personal read, and so much better than his plain old diaries. Derek had brought his girl back to life even if it was only within the pages of a book. Molly would be an obstacle; they were once so unified but now they seemed to oppose one another when it mattered. Grace's operation and Rabbit's book were both major arguments. Molly wanted Rabbit's memory to remain private.

'The book wasn't finished, Jack.'

'Derek's finishing it.'

'And what would he know about our Rabbit?'

'He worked with her for over twenty years, Molls.'

'The dead should be left to rest, Jack.'

And she was happy for Grace to mutilate herself. 'It's not right, Molly!' he'd say over and over again. She wasn't sick. She might never be sick. *It's wrong.*

They shouted about Rabbit and Grace till their throats and heads hurt; there was no coming together, only drifting further and further apart.

Then there was the division of the ashes, which also caused an argument, the bulk in a box and the rest subdivided into four steel love-heart boxes. He'd decided to do that without really thinking it through. *Where do we put you, Rabbit? In your little silver box. Where's appropriate?*

I'm not going on the mantelpiece next to Ma's duck collection, I'll tell you that, Da, she said, and he listened.

Good call, love.

They both walked around the house arguing about his stupid bloody idea to divide Rabbit into small metal love hearts, never mind the large box carrying the bulk of her that was currently in their wardrobe. 'We should have just put her in the fucking wall,' Molly said, but Jack looked to the heavens and mouthed to his daughter, 'Not on my watch.'

He went back to mass once a week. He had been so non-committal for so long; all religious fervour in the house had been driven by his wife, and now that she had abandoned the Church in favour of revolution he took up the baton and repre-sented the house of Hayes. Father Frank noticed quickly that he was attending church alone. One Sunday he managed to grab him in the car park, still wearing his vestments and panting, having darted from the pulpit out the back of the sacristy.

'There you are,' he said as nonchalantly as he could between wheezing breaths.

Jack opened his car door, sat in and pointed to the seat beside him.

'It's good to see you in church,' Father Frank said.

'But you miss Molly,' Jack said.

'She said she's lost her faith, Jack.'

'And why wouldn't she?' Jack said.

'But here you are.'

'Well, maybe I'm just holding her place in line,' Jack said, and Father Frank smiled.

'You think she'll be back to us?' he said.

Jack shook his head. 'No guarantees with my Molly.'

'I see she's busy on the protests.'

'She's mad for it.'

'And what do you think?' Father Frank asked.

'If she's not fighting for something, who is she?' Jack replied, and Father Frank shook his head.

226

'At least this is something she has half a chance of winning. Tell her I was asking for her. The place isn't the same without her visits.'

'I will.'

Father Frank had called to the door many times in that first year but Molly refused to answer it if she was in, and if she was out Father Frank didn't disturb Jack for too long, but Jack could tell he missed his friend. *I miss her too, Frank.*

Part Five

The Operation

Chapter Thirty-Seven

Molly

MOLLY LAY WIDE AWAKE in bed, listening to Jack's gentle snores. She hadn't slept a wink that night. How could she? Her girl was going into hospital to have her breasts removed. It was the right thing to do. If Rabbit had known she'd had the gene, if she'd been given the opportunity to save herself, she would have. Molly knew that now. Sometimes it takes a death to put life into perspective. Even though she was on board she was worried. Medicine had progressed so much in so few years it was hard to wrap her mind around it. Her breasts would be gone but they would be replaced. She wouldn't be exactly the same woman ever again; she'd be battle-scarred but not broken, and most importantly she'd be alive.

Molly wished the day away. It was hard to be relegated to the sidelines; much easier for a woman like her to be in the thick of it, holding Grace's hand, putting on her gown, putting slippers on her feet, brushing her hair, whispering words of comfort and holding her hand right up until that moment when she disappeared through a door. She envisioned the trolley being wheeled into a sterile room and under lights, and Grace asleep while strangers cut into her and took pieces away. It would be better to be the one walking the hospital

231

floor with her phone on her hip and ready to respond to any nurse or doctor with news. She desperately wanted to be there when Grace opened her eyes to a new fuzzy world filled with pain and fear. She'd know what to say and what to do. She'd done it for Rabbit every time and she was Grace's mother, for God's sake, but Grace had Lenny and his place was by his wife's side. *Don't mess this up, Lenny.* It was going to be a long day, and she refused to spend it waiting for the phone to ring. The arrival of Davey and Juliet would be a great distraction later in the morning. Francie and Jay Byrne had organised a shindig in Rabbit's name for that very night, so all she had to do was get through the early part of the morning.

If there had been one day Molly considered going to church, that would have been it. She'd passed it three times while strolling around the area aimlessly, and maybe if Father Frank had been there and seen her pass by he could have enticed her in, but he wasn't and he didn't so she kept walking. It was five in the morning. *Sorry.*

Chapter Thirty-Eight

Grace

THE SURGERY WAS A bilateral risk-reducing mastectomy with dermal sling and implant. The consultant explained that Grace would have to lose her nipples. He'd make an anchor incision and, to create a natural shape, the muscle would be moved over the implants as opposed to under.

'Why do I have to lose my nipples?' she'd asked. He mentioned something about them going southwards or floating. She didn't understand even though she confirmed she did when he asked. He was hard to hear over the loud buzzing in her head. Later when calm and alone she researched it herself and she understood: her own nipples could end up facing the floor if she kept them – better to lose them and tattoo new ones on the right spot. They could even create nipple bobbles by pinching the skin, twisting then sewing, and once created they could tattoo around it. Nipple bobbling sounded pretty excruciating but maybe worth it. She'd think about that. It was something to be decided down the line.

It was six thirty in the morning. The sky was blue and at least two birds were chirping.

A big blue sky, your favourite – maybe that's a good sign, Rabbit.

Better than fine, Grace, you'll have the tits of a twenty-year-old, dead Rabbit said.

The hospital car park was empty save for the odd car scattered here and there. Grace sat in the passenger seat staring at the imposing grey building in front of her while Lenny was off getting a parking ticket. He came back and placed it in the window, mumbling something about being robbed. He slammed his door and waited for her to move but her legs were heavy weights and she couldn't take her eyes off the building. He moved round to the passenger door and opened it.

'Grace?'

'Yes, love?'

'It's time to go.'

'OK.'

She didn't move. He hunkered down and took her hands. 'We could wait,' he said, and tears sprang into her eyes. 'We could defer or something.'

She shook her head. 'No.'

'Grace, you can't even get out of the car,' he said.

'So help me,' she said through gritted teeth. He stood up and took a breath and nodded. He stretched out his hand and she grabbed it and he pulled and pulled and eventually she was standing and leaning on him. Her legs were like jelly but her spirit was determined.

The pre-op prep took place in a small clinic room. Grace was politely asked to undress, naked to the waist for the benefit of her consultant, anaesthesiologist, junior doctor, registrar and nurse. Only the nurse was female. She stood silently trying to steady her shaking knees while men measured and marked her breasts for removal and replacement. They discussed natural ptosis and alignment, and when they'd agreed on the right measurements, they were written in marker on her breasts. They agreed that they had good shape and volume to work with.

When they were done, Grace's consultant smiled at her. 'Don't worry, Grace, we'll have you sitting pretty.' She tried to speak but instead she just gurgled something that sounded like 'manks'. Rabbit would have made a joke, or maybe she'd have engaged with them on the matter of medicine; she would have been present, they would have been accountable to her. Grace might as well have been a piece of hanging meat. She couldn't connect; she was half naked and four men were colluding to lob her boobs off, so it wasn't the ideal setting to form new friendships.

The nurse, Lisa, was cool, calm and had a warm smile. She helped Grace dress herself and talked about the weather. 'Not too cold, although they said we should prepare for rain, as if that's something new.'

'No, not too cold.'

'Looking forward to the summer?'

'No, not really.'

Lisa sat Grace down. 'It's not going to be easy, but you'll get through it and you will be happy. OK?'

Grace nodded and cried a little.

'Time to go,' Lisa said, and Grace willed herself to stand. Her legs refused to cooperate.

'You wouldn't mind asking my husband to step in, would you?' Grace said.

'No problem,' Lisa said, and she was gone and back with Lenny within a minute. He used a similar hauling technique he'd employed at the car and she was up and out and skidding down the corridor on the backs of her heels. *Oh God, what am I doing?*

In the waiting area there was a moment when she was gowned up and looking around at men and women of all ages, sitting in chairs, signing forms, and she realised she was the only one in a gown. *Why? What are they here for? Why am I the only one with marker on my tits and my bum exposed?* She was wearing a light blue towelling dressing gown. The hospital was warm but she felt ice-cold. Lenny stood leaning against a wall while she sat on a padded chair. She wanted the loo.

'I need the loo. Where are my slippers?' she asked, realising her feet were bare.

'Don't freak out, I think I left them in the hall,' he said, and she wanted to murder him. The small suitcase hadn't been big enough for her slippers. She'd asked him to get the larger case down from the attic but he'd refused. 'For a pair of slippers? I'll take them in me hand,' he'd said.

'God Almighty, Lenny, I can't walk to surgery in bare feet.'

He retrieved the high-heeled shoes she'd insisted on wearing. He couldn't understand why she'd wear a pair of heels into a hospital. 'Because I fucking want to,' she said. Now, standing in a queue for the one toilet in the area, she felt stupid in her hospital gown, light blue towelling robe and red stilettos.

A woman with a hunch and a face like a chewed-up toffee looked from her stilettos to her face. 'Good look,' she said.

'Thanks.'

Lenny was holding her up, her knees were knocking and although she was freezing cold she was sweating.

'You all right, love?' the woman said.

'Grand.'

'You can go before me if you like,' she said kindly.

'No, honestly, I'm fine.'

'You don't look fine.'

'I am, healthy as a horse. Isn't that right, Lenny?'

'Nothing wrong with her.'

'If you say so,' she said.

When she returned to the room, her seat was taken so she leaned against the wall with Lenny, waiting. She wanted to slump to the floor, but if hospital staff found her there they'd probably object. *Germs or something.* A few more patients were gowned up now; they were speaking with their partners or friends in hushed tones. She felt sick. *Oh, God, what am I doing?*

When her name was called she stopped breathing just for a millisecond, long enough to ensure a small splutter followed by a ragged cough. *Oh, God.* Lisa was now standing in front of her, smiling. 'Time to go.'

'It's OK, I've got her, lead the way,' Lenny said, and Lisa nodded and turned and walked far enough ahead to allow Grace and Lenny a last few minutes together before surgery. He held onto her as she stumbled down the hall towards the door that swung open and closed behind Lisa. She slowed almost to a stop. *Oh God.* He pulled her along. *Oh God.* She dragged her feet. *Oh God.*

'You're all right, Gracie,' he said, but he sounded tearful.

'I'm fine,' she said, but then her knees buckled and she was crying. 'I have to. Please.'

'I know, love. I know,' he said, and he kissed her forehead and lifted her up in his arms and carried her the rest of the way down the hall. She hung onto him as though her very life depended on it, and then he placed her down in front of the theatre door. She found her feet in her red stilettos, stood and breathed in and out, and put her hand on the door. He placed his over hers and together they pushed it open. She turned to him. 'Thank you.'

'I love you,' he said.

'I love you too.'

The door closed behind her leaving her husband outside in the hallway.

In the anaesthetic room Lisa took her hand and together they walked to the bed.

'I like your style,' she said, pointing to the shoes.

She sat up on the bed and Lisa helped her remove and place them and her dressing gown on the tray under it. All the while Grace was breathing in and out, calming herself. *It's OK, you're OK. Are you there, Rabbit? Are you with me?*

I'm here, Gracie.

Lisa reintroduced her to the anaesthesiologist whom she'd met when her breasts were being marked. They went through a checklist for the third time that morning.

'What are you having done?'

'A bilateral risk-reducing mastectomy with dermal sling and implant.'

'Any metalwork?'

'No.'

'Allergies?'

'No.'

'Any anaesthetic in the past?'

'No.'

Lisa checked Grace's name band and gently pulled her gown down to reveal two large arrows on her chest. *Are the arrows really necessary?* When they were happy with their checklist, the anaesthesiologist inserted a cannula. He told Grace to close her eyes and breathe in and out.

'Nice and easy – slow down, we don't want you to hyper-ventilate,' he said. *Easy for you to say, motherfucker.*

'When's the last time you counted sheep?' he said.

'I was probably ten,' she said with her eyes screwed closed, and between mad breaths.

'Well, I was going to suggest you count them now, but no need, we're all done.'

She opened one eye to see a yellow port sticking out of her skin. *Son of a . . .*

'Trouper,' he said.

'Time to go to sleep, Grace,' Lisa said as the anaesthesiologist placed a needle into the cannula and Grace felt warm and weird and then her brain drowned and she was gone.

Chapter Thirty-Nine

Juliet

JULIET'S ANXIETY GREW DURING the flight. No movie or music could distract her. She could taste the bitter dread as it leached out of her bones and into her blood system. Her heart hurt and she spent the flight on the verge of tears. The Dublin skyline made her heart ache as it had ached those first few weeks after her mother's death. She didn't want to look, but as they approached that familiar coastline it became impossible to look away. The sky was a light blue, and as they plunged through a fluffy white cloud and the ground raced to meet them pain ripped through her. As she disembarked from the plane, she had to consciously move one leg in front of the other crossing the tarmac and into the airport. Familiar accents followed her on the travelator – people joking, laughing. Lads returning home from a stag party, following the stag, wearing T-shirts emblazoned with the words 'Decko's getting married – RIP little Decko', and singing 'There's only one Decko'.

A stranger walking in the opposite direction shouting, 'Sorry, lads, but I'm a Decko'.

'There's only two Deckos.'

'And so is me da,' he said, pointing to a little grinning auld fella.

'There's only three Deckos.'

Irish people mess around a lot, she thought. She had never realised it before. She forged on, following her uncle, who confidently led the way, an alien in her own country. At passport control the man took a look at her passport and then at her. 'Gone a while?'

'Yeah.'

'Welcome home, Juliet.' He pushed over a box of Roses. 'It's me birthday, have a sweet.'

'No thanks,' she said, but she could feel her spirits rise a little. Then it happened: she walked through customs and out through the frosted glass doors and she saw her granda. The pain in her heart subsided and she was running into his arms. Whether she liked it or not, Juliet Hayes was home.

Chapter Forty

Jack

JACK STOOD IN THE airport arrivals hall with his eyes glued to the frosted glass sliding doors, waiting for that first glimpse of his son and granddaughter. Davey appeared, pushing a trolley holding two cases. *He used to arrive with a rucksack on his back. How times change.* Seconds later, Juliet emerged. She looked taller, older. She wasn't smiling, she seemed grim, but then she saw him and her eyes lit up, a smile crept across her face and she bounced over to him like a playful puppy. 'Granda.'

'Ah, my Bunny.'

'Nobody calls me that anymore.'

'I do,' he said. 'I call you Bunny.'

'OK,' she said, and she hugged him tight. 'I missed you, Granda.'

'Oh, I missed you too, Bunny.'

Davey stood back and watched the scene unfold before holding out his hand to shake his dad's.

'We're being very formal, Davey,' Jack said, and he took his son in his arms.

'How are you, son?'

'Better for seeing you, Da.'

In the car Jack told them that Molly had spent the previous night making up the spare beds and that she had Davey's favourite Irish stew cooking slowly.

Davey had been informed of his mother's arrest a few days before when he called to confirm the details of their trip.

'What's happening with all that, Da?' he asked.

'She's appearing in court in three weeks' time. The solicitor will ask for disclosure. We'll see what they have and then decide on a plea.'

'Jesus.'

'I know. Your ma is going through a stage, Davey, like when she had the menopause except madder.'

'Is Gran going to be all right, Granda?' Juliet asked.

'She'll be fine, she's a pensioner, they're hardly going to put her in prison, are they?'

'Can you imagine Ma in prison,' Davey said, and everyone in the car laughed.

'She'd run the place within a week,' Jack said.

'How's Grace?' Juliet said.

'Yeah, Da, any word?'

'She went in this morning. Lenny will call when he has news.'

'When can we see her?' Davey said.

'Ah, I'd leave that till tomorrow. Of course your ma's going in this evening,' Jack said.

'What about you?' Davey said.

'Ah you know me, son. I don't do blood.'

'You did it with Ma!' Juliet said, and she pushed forward between her granda and Davey.

'There was no choice in that. I'll see Grace when she comes home.'

Davey and Juliet shared a look. No one spoke in the car after that.

Molly walked through the door with bags of shopping which she dropped as soon as she saw her granddaughter.

'There's my girl.' She opened out her arms and Juliet ran into them.

'Hi, Gran.'

'Hiya, love. Let me look at you,' she said, and she stood back and admired her granddaughter. 'Just like your mammy.' She hugged her again. 'It's good to have you home.'

She didn't say hello to her husband. He didn't say hello to her.

'Are you fighting?' Davey asked. 'Because if you are we're booking into a hotel. I'm not having that,' he said.

Molly looked at Jack. 'No fight,' she said.

'I'm fine,' Jack said, and sniffed and looked out the window.

'It looks like they are fighting,' Juliet said to Davey. Molly hugged Davey and kissed his cheek.

'Welcome home. Juliet, set the table. I'll serve up some of Davey's favourite stew,' Molly said.

Juliet set the table. Davey picked up one of Molly's banners and pointed to the bum cheek.

'Subtle,' he said, and Jack shook his head.

'Don't mention the war,' Molly warned.

Davey sat down opposite his father. Jack just looked out the window and up into the clouds.

'So what aren't you fighting about?' Davey said.

'Once again he's dragging his heels about visiting his daughter in hospital,' Molly said.

'What do you mean?' Jack asked, hurt. 'I was always there for Rabbit.'

'So why can't you be there for Grace?' Molly shouted.

'Because Grace is not sick!' he roared. He got up and stormed out.

'What about your stew?' Molly shouted.

'Shove it up your arse,' he roared, and he kicked her banner before he grabbed his jacket and keys.

'Did my da just curse?' Davey said, shocked.

'I think me granda's broken,' Juliet said, and Jack slammed the front door, headed outside and got into his car.

Something's broken, she thought as he drove away.

Chapter Forty-One

Davey

DAVEY RECEIVED A TEXT from Francie:

Call me when you've landed.

So he called him.

'You're home, brilliant. I thought you might be delayed by that storm in Atlanta.'

'Since when have you tracked my flights?'

'Since I set up a gig in aid of cancer and MS in Rabbit and Johnny's names.'

'Excuse me?'

'You heard, we're having a reunion – a Kitchen Sink and The Sound combo featuring Louis's nephew Jason on vocals.'

'No.'

'You have no choice.'

'Get someone else.'

'There is no one else. You are our drummer. Whether you like it or not.'

'Don't do this.'

'It's done and it's sold out.'

'Jesus Christ.'

'I prefer to be called God, but whatever.'

'When?'

'Tonight.'

'You're messing – you have to be messing because that's fuckin' insane.'

'Yeah, I'm not. A few reasons for that – tonight is Friday night, and that's when all the locals come out to play. The place is booked out for a self-help conference next Friday. You'll be gone the Friday after.'

'I haven't rehearsed.'

'You're a professional. You'll be grand.'

'I haven't played those songs in twenty years.'

'Listen, man, you were shite then, you'll be shite now. No one cares, it's a laugh for charity and it's in memory of Rabbit and Johnny, so put on your big boy pants and get down here. We have five hours rehearsal before soundcheck.'

'Who knows about this?'

'Everyone. Grace is fine with it. Your ma and da are coming.'

'Marjorie?'

'Sworn to secrecy. I know you two have been Skyping with a capital S,' he said.

'Don't start,' Davey warned.

'Don't have time to start. I'll see you at the back of The Escape in an hour.' Francie hung up.

Davey sat on his old bed in his old bedroom. It had fresh paint on the walls now, and a floral duvet. He stared out the window at a five-year-old kicking a ball while his mother sat on the wall speaking on the phone.

Shite, he thought, but he was smiling. *Playing again with the lads. Just like the old days. That would be something.* He also thought about Juliet. *She is going love this. This is what she needs.*

Nine days earlier, on Rabbit's first-year anniversary, he'd taken the day off and told her they could do anything she wanted. Her answer had been unexpected. 'I want to go to Hendersonville Memorial Gardens. It's not too far away. I can bring a picnic.'

'What's in Hendersonville Memorial Gardens?'

'Dead people.'

'Any particular dead people you want to visit?'

'Johnny and June Carter Cash.'

'Why?'

'Ma and I saw the film.'

'OK, and . . .?'

'We loved it, second only to *Thelma & Louise*.'

'And?'

'And I can't visit my own mother's grave, so I thought I'd take that tiny bit of dust they put in that stupid metal love-heart box and I'd bring my ma to visit people in actual graves.'

'Don't you think that will make her feel bad?' he said, and he was joking. She smiled.

'Dick,' she said. He grabbed his keys.

'Let's go.'

Juliet had a real problem with the fact that her mother didn't have a grave or even an inscription on a wall. 'It's like she was never here or we didn't care enough.'

All the family was doing was respecting Rabbit's wishes but it still hurt. He agreed to the Henderson trip because they needed to mark the day.

They arrived just after two in the afternoon. Davey was heading up to the main building.

'What are you doing?'

'Getting a map from reception.'

'I've got one,' she said, pulling it out of her pocket. 'Got it on Find A Grave.' She looked at it. 'We're in Garden of Matthew, latitude 36 . . .' She started keying it into her phone. Then the phone took over. 'Follow me,' she said.

The graves were side by side, large black marble slabs with gold edging around them and gold writing. There were vases on each slab with beautiful fresh flowers in them. 'Pretty,' she said. The date on Johnny's read 'Feb. 26, 1932' and 'Sept. 12, 2003' and under that was 'Psalm 19:14'. Juliet read aloud: 'Let the words of my mouth, and the meditation of my heart be acceptable in thy sight, O Lord, my strength and my redeemer.' She looked at her uncle.

'What do you think that means?'

'That he hopes God was happy with who he was, what he said – thoughts and deeds stuff, you know.'

'Not really, I've never done religion,' she said.

'Your mother was very clear about that.'

'Johnny Cash did a lot of shite things, drinking and drugs and stuff, but he seemed like a nice man, so fingers crossed,' she said.

'I'm sure he's been forgiven.'

'If he exists, God wouldn't be happy with Ma because she didn't believe in him.'

'I'm sure he'd forgive her,' he said.

'No way. I've read up on it, you can do loads of shite and get away with it as long as you say sorry and believe, but believing is number one, non-believers are . . .' – she mouthed the word – 'fucked.'

She looked at June Carter Cash's grave and read out: 'June 23, 1929 to May 15, 2003. Psalm 103:1: Bless the Lord, O my soul and all that is within me, bless his holy name.' She turned to Davey and pointed, 'See, there it is, "bless his holy name", that's sucking up, right there. All the Christians know that their God likes suck-ups.'

'To be fair I think all the gods like suck-ups,' he said, and he smiled a little to himself. The kid was right. *Our father in heaven, hallowed be your name . . .*

The gravestones were finished off with Johnny and June's signatures in gold. He watched her take in the two beautiful graves in which they lay, side by side, for eternity in their own plot. *Home.* Juliet placed the love-heart-shaped metal box with sprinkles of her ma in it between the gravestones. 'Ma, this is Johnny and June; Johnny and June, this is my ma, Rabbit Hayes. If there is an afterlife maybe you could have a word with God, you know, to let her in.' Juliet sat on the stone bench overlooking the graves.

A pain cut through Davey like a knife. *Oh, God how did I not see it?* He sat down beside her. 'Are you worried about your mother?' he asked gently.

Juliet hunched her shoulders. 'Would it be so bad to have a couple of holy rollers on her side, just in case?'

Davey hesitated. 'Do you believe in God? It's OK if you do.'

'Dunno. Ma was so sure that God didn't exist and Johnny and June were so sure he did. If Ma was right, well then it doesn't matter to Johnny and June because they just lie here forever. If Ma is wrong then they are with God and she's in hell.'

'What makes you think that?'

'I dream about it. She's in flames and darkness, begging to come home.'

Davey was at a loss for words; he didn't know if God existed or if he didn't exist. He didn't really care; he didn't bother God and God never bothered him. He didn't have an answer. He couldn't even pretend to have one. He just went with his gut.

'She's not suffering.'

She stood up and stared him down. 'How do you know?'

'I just do.'

'It's not an answer.'

'It's the only one I have.'

'It's not good enough,' she said.

'OK then, because of who she was, how she walked through the world, the people she touched, the kindness she showed, how funny and sweet, honest and loving she was.'

Juliet was crying now, silent tears, and nodding her head. 'Yes.'

'Your ma carried a whole world of love, joy and laughter inside of her; wherever she is, or isn't, that will never change.'

Juliet looked at the writing on June's grave. 'The meditation of her heart . . .'

'Exactly, and I don't know if that's acceptable to any god but it's acceptable to me,' Davey said. 'How about you?'

'More than acceptable.'

He stood up and took the crying child in his arms.

'It's time to stop worrying about her, Juliet.'

'I don't know if I can, Davey.'

'I know. Some habits are hard to break, kiddo.'

His jacket was wet and her eyes were swollen when she pulled away but she seemed lighter, a little brighter.

Davey had no idea how worried Juliet had been about her mother's soul. Of course she'd worry; she had grown up worrying, it was all she knew. *Grace would have seen it. She'd have understood. Jesus, a whole year. I'm such an asshole. I'm letting her down. What else am I missing?* While his eyes were wide open he realised something else that day as they were sitting on the back of the open truck and tucking into the picnic she'd carefully prepared with all his favourites. It was after she'd reminded him of his appointment with his barber and he asked her about his dry cleaning that it dawned on him – somehow over the past year he'd allowed her to slip into the role of caring for him, though obviously not in the same way as she'd cared for her mother. He didn't require bathing, lifting and washing, but when they weren't on the road, she ran the house, she cooked, she kept his schedules on the fridge, she woke him when he overslept, she made sure he ate – lots of little things that added up to her taking care of him when he was supposed to be taking care of her. *What the fuck is wrong with me? What else am I missing? How many times a day am I failing her? Failing Rabbit?*

But they were home now, with time for respite, and because of his best friends' efforts Juliet would glimpse her mother's past, when they were young and she had so much to live for. Davey and the boys were taking her back to a time when fear and failure wasn't an option. *Thanks, boys*, he smiled to himself, and then he thought about seeing Marjorie.

Chapter Forty-Two

Marjorie

MARJORIE SPENT HER MORNING in the hairdresser's getting her hair washed, cut and blow-dried. Gillian her hairdresser mentioned a few grey hairs and talked about touching them up with a little blonde the next time they saw one another. *Shite. That's the start of it, any day now ... menopause.* Next she went to her local beauty salon for a bikini wax and painted nails.

She told herself she was going to all this trouble because she was starting her new job on Monday. *Gotta look good.* The redundancy payout had allowed her the time and space to work out where she wanted to be and what she wanted to do. In the end, after weeks of research, she heard about the job through an old retired work colleague. The Irish Entrepreneurs Enterprise Group were looking for someone with a finance background to join their team. The aim of the group was to support start-ups with their business planning, getting them access to seed capital, introducing them to angel investors and generally making sure they were networked to the right people so that they had the best chance of succeeding. It wasn't the boutique that she'd once daydreamed of owning, but it felt perfect now.

When she got the interview she reached out to every contact she knew for information and guidance and studied the company set-up for two weeks solid. Marjorie walked into that company knowing more about it than the CEO interviewing her. She knew the job was hers even before she left.

'I'll be in touch,' the CEO said as he shook her hand, and she walked out onto the street by the canal.

Yeah, you will.

Twenty-four hours later she received the news. 'The job is yours.'

She had money in the bank, a new and exciting job; the country and the economy were finally turning a corner and, best of all, her mother was back on her feet with the aid of a walking stick. She hadn't cleaned shit in months. *It's a new dawn, a new day and a new life for me.* For the first time in a long time Marjorie Shaw was feeling good.

Over the year Marjorie had built a relationship with her mother based on searing honesty and mild aggression. When she arrived at her mother's house with news of her new job the woman almost seemed happy for her.

'The Irish Entrepreneurs Enterprise Group! That sounds like a made-up job,' Vera said.

'Every job is a made-up job.'

'Milking cows isn't a made-up job.'

'Fine, I'll milk cows, then.'

'It's better than being unemployed, I suppose,' Vera said, and that was as close to congratulations as Marjorie could hope for.

'Yes, Ma, it is,' she said happily. 'And if you're lucky I'll take you out to Sunday lunch.'

'Fine, then, but somewhere decent – the place we went to last time smelled of old people.'

'That was you, Ma.'

'My name is Mammy,' Vera said; she hated being called Ma, but she almost gave away a smile.

This new relationship wasn't ideal but it worked, and it was nice to have someone in her life even if it was her difficult mother.

She rang her from the salon. Vera insisted on answering her mobile phone with the words, 'The Shaw residence.'

'I won't have time to call in today but the supermarket is dropping off a shop between two and five.'

'Why don't you have time?'

'Because I have a life.'

'Since when?'

'Since today.'

'Oh well, good for you.'

'Thank you, Ma,' she said, and she hung up.

After the beautician had worked her magic she had shopping to do, all in preparation for her new job – at least that's what she told herself even as a chatty Cork woman yanked hair from her vagina.

'I'm seeing a few greys down there, so if you're thinking about laser it's now or never,' the girl said. *Jesus Christ, what the hell . . .*

After that she dropped a ton in the shops, mostly on workwear, but she also bought herself a new dress for the gig that night. She received a text from Davey in the afternoon:

I can't believe you didn't give me the heads-up. See you later. ☺

She was excited, like a child on Christmas morning. She told herself it was because of the gig. It would be a trip down memory lane. Seeing everyone, Juliet especially. She couldn't wait to see her little pal. She had often thought about flying over to see her but then with her mother's stroke and finishing up at work and her friendship with Davey . . . It seemed too complicated. Better to reunite on home ground. The lads would all be there, the old crowd, playing and bantering, and it would be a fitting tribute to Rabbit and Johnny. She'd been looking forward to it for weeks. She didn't allow herself to think about seeing Davey; the feelings that conjured up were too real. She had always loved him one way or another, but during the past year she'd fallen hard although she was in denial. *We are not meant to be. It's stupid. I'm just lonely and grieving. I've lost my best friend. He lives in the States. If it were real it would have happened by now.* There were so many arguments against her feeling what she was feeling, but she felt it anyway. *Ignore, deny, forget.* That was her motto. *We're friends, that's it,* she thought as she walked around the shops looking for the perfect shoes to match her perfect dress with a raw and sticky fanny. *I hope this new job is worth it.*

Chapter Forty-Three

Grace

GRACE WOKE WITH A cough and a splutter as the laryngeal mask airway was removed.

'Oh God, me chest, it's so tight, can't breathe.'

'You can breathe, Grace, it's just muscle tightness. The implants have been inserted under the pectoralis muscle – it's stretched, that's all. Just slow down, take gentle breaths and open your eyes slowly.'

Grace barely opened her eyes, saw a blurry face and screwed them shut again.

'My name is Alison, I'm your recovery nurse.'

'Alison, the pain, oh God the pain.'

'OK, all right, I'm going to give you some IV morphine for the pain. Do you feel sick, Grace?'

'No, no, just pain, real pain, oh God the pain.'

'Give it a second or two or three or four . . .' Alison said, and Grace felt a little relief like a small wave washing in some comfort.

'The good news is blood pressure, respiratory rate, pulse and oxygen saturation are exactly where we want them,' Alison said.

'What about my breasts?'

'You can look down if you like.'

Grace was afraid to move a muscle, any muscle; tears filled her screwed-up eyes. *Not ready.*

'Can't.'

'That's OK, there's no rush, they're looking good, though.'

'Still in pain, like, real pain. I had a wave of relief but I need a fuckin' tsunami,' Grace said.

Alice laughed. 'Stick with me, Grace, I'm giving you the maximum allowable. OK?'

'OK.'

'Do you feel sick?'

'No.'

Alison fixed a sticky dot on Grace's chest. 'One's trying to get away,' she said.

Grace looked up, alarmed. 'My tits?'

'No, your monitor sticker.'

'Oh, thank God. I thought it had fallen out, feels like they're falling out.'

'They're not falling out.'

'Has one ever fallen out?'

'No.'

'Sure.'

'Positive.'

Grace was still really out of it. The world around her was murky and surreal and only the pain felt real. Her thoughts ran away from her and were hard to pin down; in her head she was running around trying to catch them with a net.

'How's your pain?'

'Painful. Can I ask you something?'

'Ask me anything.'

'Could *Jurassic Park* really happen?'

'I'm going to say no.'

'Good, because that would be a worry.'

'Yeah?'

'I have four boys – I can't have them living in a world full of fuckin' dinosaurs.'

'That would be a problem. Any nausea?'

'Wha'?'

'Do you feel sick?'

'No. Ryan would be fine, he'd probably find a way to work with them. Bernard could probably outrun them, Stephen, he'd go underground – he was hide-and-seek champion two years in a row. Jeffrey'd get eaten on day one – even with the weight loss, he's slow on his feet.'

'I'm sure the other boys would help him. How's your pain?'

'Warm.'

'Your pain is warm?'

'Yeah.'

'Do you feel sick?'

'Nope.'

It was then the oxy sat probe attached to Grace's finger alerted Alison to a problem. The alarm went off. *Jingle bells, jingle bells . . .*

Alison checked to see if the probe had slipped from Grace's finger to give a false reading but it was firmly in place and her oxygen level was reading 86. Alison pressed the emergency bell and dropped the bed and Grace's head down. *Jingle bells, jingle bells . . .* The anaesthesiologist was there in a jiffy. Grace felt an oxygen mask on her face and when she opened her eye a crack she saw the fuzzy face of a man placing something into her cannula.

'I'm sorry, Grace,' he said, and the next thing she experienced was burning, infernal, excruciating pain. She couldn't open her eyes, they were so heavy, it was dark and she was screaming. *Oh no, I've died. I'm in hell. Stupid sex before marriage.*

'It's OK, calm down, Grace,' Alison said, and it was a relief to hear her voice because it meant she was still alive, unless Alison had died too. *No, that wouldn't happen. Would it?*

'Grace, you're safe. I'm here.'

'Fuckin' hell, Alison, what did he do to me?' *Oh God, oh God, oh God.*

'The morphine dropped your oxygen levels below 88, so we had to administer a reversal drug.'

'Oh no, I can't. I have to have morphine. Please. It's unbearable.'

'I know, I know, just breathe.'

'You just fucking breathe!'

'OK, we'll both fucking breathe. OK?' Alison said in a light tone.

'Not OK, not OK.' *Oh no, no, no, this is too familiar.* Tears rained down her face. 'This was Rabbit, when she was dying, I saw, I was there, I watched her beg for pain relief and nurses tell her it was all right.' Her breathing became rapid, her fists clenched; the pain was mind-numbing but at least she could catch and hold onto her thoughts. 'But it wasn't all right, she was dying.'

'You're not dying, Grace. You're a healthy woman.'

'She died.'

'You won't die.'

'But she died.' She could feel cool wet tears trickle from her eyes, down her neck and onto the bed.

'When did she die, Grace?'

'Just over a year ago.'

'I'm so sorry.'

'Me too,' Grace said. *Me too.*

After a few breathing exercises the anti-inflammatory and IV paracetamol started to kick in.

'Better?' Alison asked.

'Hmmm.'

'Pain scale one to ten?'

'Eleven.'

'You said it was better.'

'It *was* twenty-five.'

The consultant appeared to check on Grace and to consent to another form of painkiller.

'Twenty-five micrograms of fentanyl via a PCA with a five-minute lockout.'

'Will that get rid of the pain?'

'It will.'

'All of it?'

'I hope so.'

'Not more than me,' Grace said.

'No, Grace, not more than you, but you did well, really well. I know it doesn't feel like that now but you are looking good, lady. You can relax now. It's over.'

'It's over?' she said, and he was right – a year of stress, worry and fear was behind her, the decision was made and the deed now done. It was over. The ovariectomy was still looming but she'd worry about that another day. *It's over.*

She fell asleep after that.

Chapter Forty-Four

Jack

JACK DROVE AROUND FOR an hour before parking outside the home of his old friend Sean Murphy. He was still
steaming and also ashamed at his use of the word 'arse', especially as his grandchild had only just returned home after a
year in America. Ever polite, he phoned Sean from his car. He
answered on the third ring.

'I was only thinking of you,' Sean said.

'Were ya?' Jack said.

'I was, I was only saying to Flo that it must be Rabbit's
anniversary any day now.'

'Nine days ago.'

'Nine days ago? Jaysus, time flies, Jack.'

'It does and it doesn't.'

'How are you?'

'Not great, to be honest.'

'Ah . . . I wish I could say I was able for a pint but you
know the situation. Why don't you call round sometime?'

'How does now suit ya?'

'Today?'

'No, now – I'm outside.'

'Flo, put on the kettle, will you?' he said to his wife. 'See you
in two.'

Jack hung up the phone and walked up the driveway to be greeted by his pal's wife, Flo. She hugged him. 'Good to see you, he's inside.' She pointed to the sitting room door. 'Milk, sugar?'

'Milk, one sugar – thanks, Flo.'

He knocked as he entered. Sean was sitting on his armchair with his oxygen canister next to him and tubes coming from his nose.

'The grandkids call me The Walrus,' he said, and he nodded. Jack moved in to shake his hand, then sat on the sofa.

'How are you feeling?' Jack asked.

'Been better.'

Sean had been diagnosed with emphysema four years previously. He'd been a smoker all his life, and chose to continue smoking until the disease ravaged his lungs to the point that he was now housebound and had difficulty breathing. He couldn't smoke anymore; he couldn't do much of anything anymore. It was a high price to pay.

'And you, Jack, how are you?'

'Grace is having an operation today,' Jack said.

'What's wrong?'

'Nothing, she's as fit as a flea.'

'I'm not with ya, Jack.'

'She's having her breasts removed.'

'God Almighty,' Sean said, and he blessed himself. 'Why would she do that?'

'She has the gene – the same one that made Rabbit sick. It doesn't mean she'll get cancer, it just means it's more likely. So she's decided to cut everything out, first her breasts, next her ovaries.'

'God Almighty,' Sean repeated, and he took a shot of oxygen. 'I'm sorry to hear that.'

'Her mammy's all for it, thinks it's a great idea. Poor Lenny's been told what to think as far as I can see, but me, I can't believe she'd mutilate herself like that, after everything she saw Rabbit go through, after everything we've been through. It's not right,' he said, and he felt tearful but he didn't cry.

Sean sat back in his chair. 'Maybe she's doing it because of what Rabbit went through, because of what you all went through.'

'That's what Molly says, but Rabbit had cancer. Grace does not.'

'Did I ever tell ya my auld fella had COPD?'

'No.'

'He had it and it killed him. I smoked when I knew I shouldn't. I smoked long after I was diagnosed. Don't know why. I took my chances, I suppose.'

'Giving up cigarettes and disfiguring yourself is not the same thing.'

'Knowing what I know now, if someone came up to me and whispered in my ear, you have even a fifty per cent chance of getting COPD, not only would I stop smoking I'd cut out me lungs if they told me it would help.'

'That would kill ya,' Jack mumbled.

'You know what I'm trying to say.'

'I do.'

Flo arrived in with tea and buttered barmbrack. 'There you go, fellas, I'll leave you to it.' She left and Jack handed Sean his tea and held up the plate of barmbrack.

'No thanks,' he said.

Jack hugged his mug of tea. 'People die during operations or anaesthesia every day,' he said. 'Then there's the complications.

Rabbit had terrible complications, and nothing to do with the cancer.'

'Do you want my advice?' Sean asked.

'Will I like it?'

'No.'

'Go on, then.'

'Just be there for her.'

'How can I? I can't even look at her.'

'There's nothing I can do to help you with that,' Sean said.

'No,' Jack said. 'I suppose you can't, and there's something else – I think my marriage is in deep trouble.'

'Ah no. You and Molly, you're survivors.'

'We don't talk anymore. We shout but we never talk.'

'It's the grief, it has you upended,' Sean said. 'You'll find your way back.'

'Will I?' he mumbled.

Jack left his friend's house soon after that and drove around until he ran out of petrol. He parked up on the side of the road, asked a local where the nearest garage was and then he took himself off for a little walk.

Chapter Forty-Five

Molly

MOLLY SPENT THE AFTERNOON with her granddaughter. She'd asked her what she'd like to do and Juliet wanted to see her old house. So Molly grabbed the keys of her car.

'Let's go. You know other people live there now?'

'I do.'

'So we'll just sit outside?'

'That's good enough.'

'Oh Juliet, you're a stalker, just like your mother,' Molly said, referring to Rabbit's dogged pursuit of Johnny Faye.

That made her giggle. 'Yeah.' She bounced off to the car.

They pulled up two houses away. It looked exactly the same, except the new renter had planted a bush in the front garden.

'That's nice,' Juliet said.

'It's a rose bush. It's a little early for them to bloom – soon, though,' Molly said.

'Can I get out?'

'Whatever you like.'

Juliet walked slowly towards the wall that she used to think of as her own. She sat down and Molly joined her.

'I can see you on the road playing. I can see your ma calling you to come in for your dinner, standing in that porch, her long hair tied up in a ponytail, a rock and roll T-shirt on, tight jeans and flip-flops.'

Juliet smiled. 'Boots – she only put flip-flops on when it was hot.'

'Not now, Ma, I'm playing with Kyle,' Molly said in a high voice.

'I didn't sound like that.'

'I'm an alien, Ma, and he's my human friend,' Molly said, and laughed. At one point Juliet had genuinely thought she might be an alien because her father was a mystery and she was double-jointed.

Juliet laughed and playfully pushed her granny. 'It would have been cool to be an alien.'

'Definitely.'

'I wonder, do they die?'

'Everything dies.'

'Except hope – that's what Ma used to say.'

'Well she went and fuckin' took that with her,' Molly said, and Juliet chuckled a little. 'Yeah, I suppose she did.'

'Never mind, we always have tea and Pauline's coffee cake,' Molly said, and she winked. Juliet's unidentified Australian father never seemed to bother her, not while her mother was alive, but Molly wondered if her feelings had changed. *Now is as good as any time to ask*, she thought.

'Do you ever think about your dad?' Molly blurted out.

'No.' Juliet blushed red.

'Sure?'

'What's to think about?' she asked.

'I don't know, love. You have a dad out there somewhere.'

'Maybe not,' she said.

'Not this alien stuff again . . .'

'No, he could be dead, too.'

'Right,' Molly said. She couldn't really argue – after all, the child had a point. 'Do you miss him?'

'You can't miss someone you've never known.'

'That's a very grown-up answer.'

Juliet shrugged.

'If you ever want to talk about him you can talk to me,' Molly said.

'There's nothing to talk about, Gran,' Juliet said, and Molly had to accept her at her word.

'I'm always here.' Then, responding to her granddaughter's frown she added, 'until I'm dead, and on that day hell will freeze over.'

Juliet's face broke into a grin. Molly's talk of hell must have inspired Juliet's next question.

'Are you scared of going to jail, Gran?'

'I'm not going to jail. I might do a bit of community service, but I do that anyway.'

'Is Grace going to be OK?'

'She's going to be great.'

'I feel sorry for her. She hates needles.'

'Doesn't everyone?'

'Yeah, but not as bad as me granda and Grace.'

'Do you have any questions for me about the gene?' Molly asked.

'Davey and I talked about it. I'm going to get the test when I'm twenty-one.'

'Oh yeah?'

'Yeah. We think I'll be old enough to make the right decision by then.'

'Are you scared?' Molly asked.

'Nah, that's ages away – we could all be dead by then,' Juliet said, and Molly felt sad that, aged thirteen, her granddaughter was already so jaded.

'Or there could be a cure,' Juliet said, and Molly's spirits lifted.

That's right. Imagine that.

'If I'm not dead,' said Juliet, 'I'm going to find one.'

'Well, whether you do or you don't I'm really proud of you, Juliet.'

'Thanks, Gran.'

'Your mammy would be really proud too.'

The front door opened behind them. A woman in her forties with short hair and a pregnant belly stood in the porch. The little kid that Kyle said cried all the time was behind her legs. He wasn't crying but he had green snot hanging from his nose that was so long and dense it swung.

'Apologies,' Molly said, 'we're just leaving.'

'I used to live here,' Juliet said.

'You're Juliet?' the woman asked.

'That's right.'

'I'm Glenda, and this snot machine is James – forgive us, he has a nasty cold.' She took a tissue out of her pocket and cleaned the child's nose.

'Hi, Glenda,' Juliet said. Molly nodded. Glenda walked across the garden. 'You must be Rabbit's mother, Molly.'

That was a surprise. 'Oh, we've heard all about you. Come in, please.'

269

The place was the same but so very different. All of Rabbit's things were gone; Davey had had a bunch of movers take everything and paid for storage somewhere in Dublin. The old Hayes family photograph was now replaced by a framed poster of a dolphin. Molly followed Juliet, Glenda and James into the kitchen. She stood in a place once so familiar but now foreign; the walls, presses and countertop were the same, the table and chairs were different, bigger, maybe even a little too big for the room, the curtains on the windows had daisies on them. *Rabbit would have hated that.* No fridge magnets, different delph, a different smell – less bleach, more lemon zest. There was no sign of her daughter in this house; she was a stranger in a stranger's home.

Juliet looked out into the garden. 'Does James use the playhouse?' she asked, pointing to her old weathered playhouse.

'He loves it.' Glenda said.

'Good,' Juliet said. She walked to the doorframe where her mother had recorded her height. 'Still there,' she said, and Glenda nodded. 'I've started my own on James's bedroom door. I suppose that was your room,' she said, and Juliet nodded and bit into her lip. Molly couldn't work out what she was thinking.

'Would you like to see it?'

'No thanks,' Juliet said as she walked over to the wall and got down onto her belly to examine the skirting board. Glenda and Molly shared an uncomfortable look.

'Are you OK?' Glenda asked.

She got up, smiling. 'I'm fine.'

Molly put her hand on Juliet's shoulder. 'We should go.'

'Yeah, thanks for letting us look around,' Juliet said.

'I actually have some things belonging to your mother in the shed,' she said, reaching for a key. 'They were in the attic.'

'Oh, I'm sorry, I thought we'd taken everything.'

'Don't be silly, things get forgotten, and you should have this.'

Molly took ownership of a large box stuffed with old records and books, diaries and photos and knick-knacks collected over the years.

'Thank you,' she said. They left and got into the car. Juliet clawed through the box excitedly, 'Photos! Gran, photos of me ma when she was my age.'

'Ah, isn't that lovely,' Molly said. The child was glowing. It was as if she'd struck gold.

'And look at all this stuff – ticket stubs and old laminates, and what's that?' she said, pulling a weird furry doll out of the box.

'Ah no, you're joking.' Molly took it in her hand. 'That was her Monchhichi doll, she got it as her Christmas Day surprise when she was nine. She took that bleedin' thing everywhere with her.'

'Smells like it,' Juliet said, taking a sniff.

'We'll lash it in the wash,' Molly said.

'Gran, can I call into Kyle and say hello?' Juliet asked, now buoyed by the huge gift of her mother's stuff.

''Course ya can, love. One question, what were ya doing on your belly on the floor?'

'Ma's blood – it's still on the wall,' she said. 'I circled it in biro.'

'Why did you do that?'

'I knew they'd take away everything else.'

'Right,' Molly said. *Fucking weird. Mention that to Davey!*

'Do you think it would be OK if I asked Kyle to come to the gig?'

'I think that would lovely.'

'Brillo.'

She got out of the car and ran across the road. Molly watched Kyle open the door and her granddaughter disappear inside. She took out the old photographs of her daughter, Johnny, Davey and the boys back in the day, featuring clothes and hairstyles once considered high fashion, but now dated. She was entertained by the backgrounds of patterned wallpaper and brown, orange and yellow carpets, and what appeared to be a national obsession with wicker furniture – there was some kind of wicker furniture in nearly every shot. *God, we hadn't a clue.* The only person that could have been lifted out of that era into the current one was Rabbit, with her long sleek hair and her rocker T-shirt and jeans. 'You never changed, love,' she said, and then she picked up a shot of Rabbit when she was younger and donning an eyepatch, thick-framed spectacles and long ponytails either side of her head. 'Oh yeah, you did.'

Juliet arrived back at the car with Kyle.

'Hiya, Mrs Hayes,' he said, scrambling into the back seat. He'd grown at least a foot in the past year.

'The last time I saw you I was running you over,' Molly said.

'That's right, I still have a scar on me elbow.' He showed it to her.

'Where?'

'There,' he said, pointing to a small faded scar.

'That's not a scar,' she said, pulling out a photo of a beaming Rabbit showing off a long, stitched cut on her forearm. '*That*'s a scar.'

He put his elbow away.

'So are you staying over, or wha'?' Molly asked.

'If that's all right, Mrs Hayes.'

'That's fine, son. Well, strap in, kids, we're going to the northside.'

'Deadly,' Kyle said, and Molly looked into her mirror in time to catch her granddaughter's smile. *Sorry. I'm so sorry.*

Chapter Forty-Six

Juliet

JULIET TOOK KYLE ON a walk around her grandparents' local area. She pointed to the national school on their left. 'That's where Ma went to school.'

'Oh.'

She pointed to the church. 'That's where she made her Holy Communion.'

'I thought she was an atheist.'

'She was, but Gran and the school told her she had to do it, so she did. She was only seven.'

'Did she get confirmed?' Kyle asked.

'Yeah, but only because me gran threatened to never, ever speak to her again if she didn't.'

'So she was a Catholic, then.'

'When she turned eighteen she wrote the Church a letter.'

'Saying wha'?'

'I don't know, something like, you're a bunch of paedos, criminals and murderers and I'm out.'

'That would do it,' Kyle said, staring at the building. 'It's a cool church,' Kyle said.

'Ma saw Mother Teresa in there.'

'No way, she's famous.'

'Yeah.'

They crossed the street and walked up the steps of the church. It was locked, so they just sat on the steps looking down on the gardens, which led to the railings, the footpath and passing traffic.

'So why'd she go and see Mother Teresa if she didn't believe in God?'

'Because Johnny did.'

'Who's he?'

'The love of me ma's life.'

'Not your da?'

'No way, she didn't know him from a bar of soap.'

'Oh.'

'Johnny thought Mother Teresa could fix his legs.'

'What was wrong with them?'

'He had a disease called MS. He couldn't walk.'

'That's hard.'

'Yeah.'

'Did she fix him?'

'No.'

'Sorry.'

'Ma called her a talking walnut with a tea towel on her head, so they had a big fight.'

Kyle chuckled a little. 'Your ma was funny.'

'Thanks.'

'My ma has a blessed scapular,' he said.

'What's that?'

'It's a brown felt yoke on a string, you put it around your neck.'

'What does it do?'

'Saves you from hell.'

'Does she wear it?'

'No, it looks like shite so she keeps it in a drawer. I don't think she believes in hell. She likes signs though.'

'What signs?'

'Like if she sees a feather she thinks it belongs to her dead da.'

'Why?'

'It's supposed to be a thing – dead people leaving feathers.'

'Why?'

'Dunno, I never asked.'

'Oh.'

'Did you ever see any feathers?'

'No.'

'Or did a dove ever land on your windowsill? Ma says they're sent by dead people too.'

'That must be where the feathers come from.'

'Yeah, maybe.'

'I thought I saw a dove landing on me windowsill once – turned out to be a tufted titmouse.'

'A tufted titmouse?' he repeated, smiling.

'Yeah, it has a white belly and a grey Mohawk.'

'A tufted titmouse,' he repeated. 'Well, maybe there were no doves available so your ma sent a tufted titmouse with a grey Mohawk – that sounds more like her.'

Juliet laughed. 'Yeah, it does.'

They walked to the shops and Kyle insisted on stopping in a coffee shop and buying Juliet a hot chocolate. They sat down in the window, people-watching and sipping their drinks.

'I missed you,' he said.

'We speak all the time.'

'It's not the same.'

'No, I suppose not.'

'Do you like it there, Juliet?' he asked, and she didn't know how to answer.

'It's fine,' she said.

'Life should be better than fine.'

'Can't be, Kyle, me ma is dead.'

They drank their hot chocolates; Juliet stabbed at her marshmallows on the plate, Kyle dunked his in the chocolate liquid.

'I think whatever you believe happens when you die, happens,' he said.

Juliet frowned. 'I don't understand.'

'Well, your ma thought there was nothing, so maybe it's just over for her, and people that believe in heaven end up in some pleasant kind of bubble yoke, and people who believe they are going to hell end up tortured somehow.'

'What about people who blow up shopping centres full of people and think they'll be rewarded?'

'Oh yeah, not them.'

'So everyone else but not them?'

'Yeah, it's hard, I dunno.'

They walked on past the library Rabbit used to go to as a kid and past the swimming pool she used to swim in. Then they turned around and started on their way back home, past the credit union Rabbit saved her money in and past the first tree she fell out of.

'Is that how she got that big cut on her arm?'

'No, that tree is in my gran's back garden.' She touched the tree with her hand.

It was so strange that everything was still there – the church, school, library, credit union, swimming pool and even the trees – but her ma was gone. Everything reminded her of her mother. A year earlier it would have been too painful – but now it was nice to walk around and see the places Rabbit had been and touch the things she'd touched. She wrapped her arms around the tree. Kyle waited and waited.

'Juliet?'

'Yeah?'

'How long more are you going to hug that tree?'

'A minute or two.'

'OK.'

There was no one home when they got back to the house. They went up to the box room where Juliet was staying.

'Was this your ma's room?' Kyle asked.

'Yeah, she got the smallest room because she was the baby.'

'It doesn't look like her room.'

'Gran had the house redecorated after all her kids left home.'

They sat on the bed.

'Are you going out with anyone, Kyle?' Juliet asked. 'You never really talk about girls on Skype.'

Kyle blushed from red to purple.

'I've kissed one or two.'

'Yeah?'

'But they're not like you.'

He couldn't meet her eyes; now her face burned too.

'You?' he asked.

'Oh no, you're the only boy I know.'

He turned his head quickly and they both leaned forward at the same time, banging their heads together briefly.

'Ow,' Juliet said, rubbing her temple.

'Sorry,' Kyle said, and before she could say anything he kissed her. At first his tongue felt like a lizard's darting in and out of her mouth in quick succession. She didn't know whether to seal her mouth shut or grab onto his tongue during its next invasion. She pulled back and raised her hands. 'Stop.'

Kyle moved back. 'OK.'

'Feels weird,' she said.

'Sorry.'

'Can we just start again? Just, keep your tongue to yourself for a minute.'

'OK.'

They planted their lips on each other, moving a little bit; it was nicer but a little stiff.

'Now the tongue,' she said, and he went for it. She moved her tongue around a lot, trying to dodge his searching and insistent one. She pulled back. 'Still feels weird.'

'I'm really stressed,' he said.

'Me too. We should look it up on the internet.'

'OK.'

She grabbed her laptop out of her luggage and switched it on. He waited patiently for her to get into YouTube. She keyed in 'first kiss tutorial' and a list of videos opened up. Kyle moved towards the screen; they shared it on their laps. She pressed on a tutorial named 'How to kiss step by step for the first time'. They both watched intently.

One, before you begin kissing, you need to demonstrate that you want to.

They both agreed they could skip over that.

Two, if your desires are reciprocated, focus on the lips and move a little closer toward the mouth. Quick Tip: Just before you reach your partner's mouth, tilt your head slightly to avoid clashing noses.

They both smiled and acknowledged their earlier mistake.

Three, slowly and softly lock lips. Quick Tip: Do not shove your tongue in her mouth straight away. It can be offputting.

They both nodded to themselves.

'See?' she said.

He shrugged. 'I see.'

Quick Tip: All good kisses begin slowly and increase with passion.

Four, open the lips slightly and carefully caress your partner's lips. Gently holding hers in your mouth.

'Hold hers with your mouth?'

'Looks more like cupping,' Juliet said.

'Rewind that bit.'

'No, let's keep going – we'll watch it through again.'

Five, if your partner is enthusiastically engaging, you could now try to introduce your tongue. Start slowly and with the tip, caressing the lips then tongue. Not too vigorously, play calmly and with circular movements so as to entwine with your partner's tongue.

'Entwine?' Kyle said.

Quick tip: Do not stick your tongue down your partner's throat.

Juliet pointed at Kyle and he nodded and gave the thumbs up.

Six, remove your tongue and caress the lips before ending the kiss.

Kyle began practising, moving his mouth like a fish. He was not inspiring confidence.

There was a girl and boy kissing on the screen all through the tutorial. It was sexy – not at all like their experience.

They watched the video again; halfway through, during point number four, they started to kiss, caressing one another's lips. It was nice.

'Oh,' Juliet said.

They did that for the longest time before Kyle slowly introduced his tongue. They didn't hear the sound of the front door open, or the shopping hit the floor.

'Juliet, are you up there?' Molly shouted.

They pulled apart.

'Yes, Gran,' Juliet called back. 'We're just watching YouTube.'

'Right, then, well, you can do that in the sitting room!'

'OK, Gran,' she said, but she leaned in and kissed Kyle some more.

Chapter Forty-Seven

Davey

DAVEY WALKED INTO THE venue to be greeted by his mates standing on the stage rocking out. Kev and Louis had never played in a band together before, but the weeks of rehearsal had paid off and Kitchen Sink and The Sound melded into one band. The only person missing was Johnny. Kev spied Davey first. 'The man of the hour,' he said.

'You're not seriously thinking of wearing that boiler suit?' Davey said, pointing at Kev squeezed into a boiler suit two sizes too small.

'It's me look.'

'And it was shite back then, too,' Francie said, and he jumped down off the stage and took Davey into his big embrace. 'Welcome home.'

'Some homecoming.'

'As the kids say, it's gonna be epic.'

Jay nodded. 'You all right, DB?'

'Hanging in there, Jay. You?'

'I think me kids are plotting to kill me, but other than that it's all good.'

'All right, Davey?' Louis said, kneeling down on the stage and offering his hand. Davey reached up and they shook hands.

'Right, let's get this going,' Francie said, handing Davey the set list. 'We're doing half Kitchen Sink stuff, half The Sound's stuff.'

'Right,' Davey said, taking his jacket off and pulling out his sticks from his back pocket. He got behind the kit.

'This is the kit? Where are the cymbals and the rack toms?'

'You've got a snare, kick drums and some high hats – any more than that and you'd make a bollocks of it,' Francie said.

'Ah, for fu . . .' He sat behind the kit and knocked out a beat. 'You do realise this kit needs tuning?'

'Better get tuning, then,' Kev said.

Davey took a tuning key out of his pocket. 'This is going to be a slow-moving car crash.'

Jay laughed. 'Can't wait.'

When the kit was tuned and Davey got his head around playing half a kit, they practised the first song. It went OK – he messed up once or twice, but got into the groove quick enough.

'Nice,' Francie said when they'd finished.

'So, we're doing this without a singer?' Davey asked.

'Nah, Louis's nephew is gonna do the singing.'

'Before you freak out,' Louis said, 'he's good.'

'He's better than good,' Francie said. 'He'll do Johnny justice.'

'So where is he?'

'Working a shift in Tesco. He'll be here any minute.'

They were halfway through the second set when Jason walked through the door. He was in his mid-twenties, with tight short hair – a broad, body-beautiful gym nut, built like The Rock; he may have worked in Tesco but he looked like a rock star. He jumped up on the stage and immediately glided towards Davey – for a big dude, he was light on his feet.

He shook Davey's hand. 'I've heard so much about you, it's a real honour to meet you.'

'Honour me hole,' Francie said. 'Time to take your tongue out of his arse and start singing.'

Davey nodded to Jason, then he clicked his sticks – one, two, three – and the band kicked in. When Jason opened his mouth to sing, his uncle Louis was proved right – he was a real talent. *Holy shit.* He had a distinctive husky tone and he could reach every note, and then some. They rehearsed the set another two times, and by then Davey had it locked down. He struggled without a full kit, but he made it work.

They rehearsed until it was time to soundcheck; the burly sound guy with big hair and earplugs sat in behind the desk.

'Let's do this,' he said.

They soundchecked for an hour and then it was time to eat. The pub laid on a good meal. Davey was starving. They all sat around a large table, chowing down on fish and chips and drinking beers.

Francie raised a toast: 'To Johnny Faye, the best and fuckin' unluckiest man I ever knew.'

They all raised their glasses.

'And the mighty Rabbit Hayes,' Jay said, and everyone drank.

Davey was drunk long before he hit the stage.

Chapter Forty-Eight

Marjorie

WHILE SHOPPING, MARJORIE PICKED up a light cotton dressing gown for Grace. She also stopped off and bought a box of chocolates, lip balm and a light moisturiser. She had made up care packages for Rabbit all the time and now it was Grace's turn. She parked the car in the hospital car park and had intended dropping off the package at reception, before running smack bang into Lenny in the doorway.

'Marjorie, what are you doing here?'

'Oh, just dropping off a few bits.'

'You're very kind,' he said, and he took the bag from her. 'How is she?'

'She's in recovery. They'll be moving her to the ward soon.'

'Oh good. How are you?' she asked, and she briefly regretted the question when the man burst into tears. She took him by the arm and guided him to the café.

'Tea or coffee?'

'I'd murder a latte,' he said, wiping away his tears.

'Snack?'

'No, me stomach's in bits.'

She grabbed two coffees, handed him his latte and sat down opposite him.

'You're very kind,' he said.

285

'That's not what my mother says.'

'Your mother's lucky to have you,' he said, and he took a sip from his latte.

Marjorie and Grace had spoken on and off over the year. Marjorie was a big supporter of her doing what was necessary to avoid following Rabbit to the grave.

'You've been a huge help to Grace,' he said.

'She's strong. She'll be fine.'

'I had to reef her out of the car and carry her to the door of the anaesthetic room.'

'Rabbit and I used to nip out round the back of the hospital and take a couple of drags of a joint before hers – she used to float in, she called it her pre-op before her pre-op.'

'You're joking,' he said.

'Nope.'

'Well, wasn't she a dark horse?'

She grinned at the memory of Rabbit walking towards her operation humming the tune to Destiny's Child's 'Survivor'.

'You take courage where you find it.'

'Wasn't that dangerous?' he said.

'Probably, we never really looked it up.'

'Jaysus.'

'How are the kids?'

'They're fine. Jeff's a little quiet in himself but the others seem to have managed to get their heads around it, probably better than I have.'

'You and Grace should go on holiday as soon as she's fit enough,' Marjorie said.

'That will take a while. I keep wondering what it's going to be like.'

'I don't follow.'

'Being together . . . intimately. Is she going to be the same?'

'I thought the counsellor talked to you both about this.'

'I was mortified – couldn't take it in, didn't know what to say.'

'You're the same people,' she said.

'Did Rabbit feel the same, afterwards?'

'Rabbit was sick.'

'That's what everyone keeps saying, but was she the same after the operation?'

'No.'

Lenny's hands balled into fists; his eyes shone with tears. He nodded slowly. 'Thanks.'

'For what?'

'For being honest.'

'Rabbit isn't Grace, and she didn't have you.'

'No, but she always had you,' he said, and Marjorie took a moment to collect herself.

'Just take it slow. Be there. Mind her, and when she's well enough she'll mind you.'

'It's not just about sex,' he said.

'I know.'

'But she's my girl, you know.'

'She'll be your girl all over again – some men would love a new set of boobs.'

'I loved the old ones.'

'It will work out.'

'I used to believe that,' he said. 'Then Rabbit died.' He stood up and offered his hand. She shook it.

'Thank you, Marjorie.'

'Give her my love.'

'I will. Enjoy the gig. Give Davey a kiss from me.' He winked at her and was gone.

She sat in the hospital café finishing her coffee and fantasising about kissing Davey. *Get a grip, Marjorie, you're forty-fuckin'-one.*

Chapter Forty-Nine

Grace

GRACE SHIELDED HER EYES from the bright lights over-head and felt the pull on her chest as she raised her arm. She also felt the pull of wires. *Yuck.* The pain was manageable, though; she had a button in her hand, and she pressed it. *Hmmmm, better.* She pressed it again . . . *Nice . . . Good . . . OK . . . One for luck . . .* A new nurse, a Filipino man in his thirties, introduced himself.

'Melchor,' he said.

'I don't know what that is,' she said.

'It's my name, but you can call me Mel.'

'Oh. Thanks.'

'How's your pain?'

'Four.'

'Four is good.'

'Zero is better. I think I broke this,' she said, holding up the button.

He smiled. 'Give it some time. Sick?'

'No.'

'I spoke to your husband. He was very worried but I told him you are great.'

'Well then, you lied.'

He grinned. 'You are great, lady, doing very well.'

'Doesn't feel like it.'

'You want to sit up?'

She was sore lying on her back, but she was scared.

'Nice and gentle,' he said.

'Nice and gentle,' she repeated.

He raised the bed slowly and steadily, then leaned her forward. She cried out a little. He fluffed up her pillows and before she knew it she was sitting.

'Thank you.'

She was covered by her gown but nothing else; if she dared to, she could just pull it down and see herself.

Not yet.

She could no longer avoid the fact that she had wires coming from her body connecting her to machines and bags.

Just like Rabbit.

Except it wasn't like Rabbit. She didn't have cancer. *Not yet, and now, maybe, hopefully not ever. One operation down. One to go. Then freedom?*

She could see her hands, the yellow cannula. The IV drip feeding her fluids made her knees weak.

Maybe I do feel sick. Do I? No, just dizzy. Urgh. Don't look. Don't look.

She could feel the drains coming from each breast. *Definitely don't look. Do not look.*

She coughed. *Ouch. Ow. Ouch.* She pressed the button. One, two, three times. As she did it she could see the cannula move in her hand.

Bleuch.

'Ahhhh it's working again,' she said.

'I think you're very brave,' he said.

'I don't feel brave.'

'What do you feel?'

'Sensible.'

'Well, in this case it's brave to be sensible.'

'You sound like my ma,' Grace said.

'Well then, she must be very smart.'

'You've no fuckin' idea,' Grace said, and she chuckled a little. *Ouch. Oh. Aw* . . . 'No laughing, no laughing,' she said, pressing the shite out of the button. She fell asleep after that.

She woke to see Lenny sitting by her bedside, flicking through a magazine. The heavy blue paper curtain was pulled around the bed, creating a little cocoon and giving them privacy from the rest of the ward.

'Hello,' she said.

He kissed her forehead and rubbed her head. 'Howya?'

'I'm grand. You?'

'I've had shorter days,' he said.

'What did you do?'

'I walked the length and breadth of this hospital.'

'Pity you weren't wearing a Fitbit.'

'I definitely exceeded my ten thousand steps.'

'So you just walked for seven hours?'

'Marjorie came, she brought you some pretty things.'

'Really?' Grace's eyes leaked. 'How lovely of her.'

'We had a coffee and talked.'

'And what did you talk about?'

'You, and how lucky I am,' he said.

'We're both lucky, then,' she said. He moved to hold her hand, but she baulked. 'Ah, ah, ah . . .' She pulled it away. She couldn't have him touch the cannula. The thought of it made her sick.

'Sorry,' he said.

She took a deep breath. 'Lenny, I haven't looked.'

'No?'

'Can't.'

'OK.'

'Will you look?'

'Ah, Grace . . .'

'Please.'

'Fuck.'

'Please.'

'Right then, go on,' he said, and she closed her eyes and pulled down the front of the gown, revealing herself to Lenny. She heard him exhale.

'Tell me what you see.'

'Well the good news is they're sitting higher, you'll love that, and there's a straight-line scar with tan tape, a few layers of that. You've got some bruising and the two drains coming from under your armpits.'

'OK, but how are they?'

'I think you'll be pleased,' he said.

'Yeah?'

'They're fucking huge.'

'They're fucking swollen.'

He laughed. 'I think you'll be pleased.'

'Are you pleased?' she asked.

'You're my wife, the mother of my children and my best friend – I'm ecstatic.'

She took a deep breath. *Ouch, ow, fucking owww*. She pressed the button; a wave of serenity rolled in. She opened her eyes and looked down. 'Ohhh.'

'Well?'

'I can live with these,' she said, and then she caught sight of one of the drain bags Ryan had made for her with the bunny rabbit on it, and she cried with relief and grief, joy and sadness.

One op down and one to go. I love ya, Rabbit. I miss ya, Rabbit. Thank you.

Chapter Fifty

Juliet

MOLLY DROPPED JULIET AND Kyle off at the back of the venue.

'Just knock at the door and tell them you're with Davey.'

'I know what to do, Gran.'

''Course you do, love.' Molly waved, and then remembered something. 'I'll be back as soon as I can. Do you have money for drinks?'

'Yeah, Gran. I'm grand.'

'Good girl.' She spun off. They watched her go. They stood in front of the door.

Juliet was about to knock when Kyle asked, 'Do you want to kiss again?'

She nodded. She took him by the hand and crossed the venue car park towards some bushes and trees.

'This is as private as it gets around here,' she said, pointing to a gap in the bushes.

'Nice,' he said, and they made their way into the centre of the bush.

He started to kiss her slowly, using all the techniques they'd learned earlier. It was soft and gentle and nice and he was just about to reintroduce his tongue when she stopped. Suddenly she was crying.

'What did I do?' he asked.

'Nothing.'

'Why are you crying?'

'Don't know.'

'You're happy with Davey, aren't you?' he asked.

She swallowed deeply. 'Yeah.'

'I don't believe you.'

'He's good to me.'

Kyle took her hands in his. 'Come home.'

'Can't.'

'You sure about that?' he said, and she wasn't sure. Since she'd stepped off the plane she'd felt better than she had in over a year. *I'm home.* Her mother wasn't just a painful memory, she was alive somehow and present everywhere Juliet looked. *I'm home.* In one day Juliet had lived more than she had since she left. *I'm home.*

'I think we should go in,' she said, and he nodded.

'Sorry, Kyle,' she said, and he smacked his mouth on hers and kissed her as they walked towards the door.

'We're getting better at this, aren't we?' he said when he pulled away.

'We rock at this,' Juliet said.

Backstage the lads were a little worse for wear. Jay was sleeping upright on a hardback chair. They turned a corner to see Kev facing Davey and Francie, fixing his boiler suit. It was a little too snug, especially around the genital area.

'This has either shrunk or my mickey is huge,' he said, as Francie raised his hands in the air.

'Juliet Hayes!'

Kev turned to see her. 'Jaysus! Sorry, Juliet. Lovely to see ya. How are ya?'

'Comfortable in me clothes,' Juliet said, and the others laughed.

'It's like seeing a ghost,' Francie said with a little pride. Louis appeared with the set list in hand. He nodded Juliet's way, 'Howya?' and she gave a little wave.

'Where's Jay?'

'He's sleeping.'

'Wha'?' Louis said. 'Who let him sleep?'

'He always sleeps before a gig,' Davey said.

'He hasn't gigged in twenty years,' Louis said before mumbling, 'For fuck's sake,' and walking away.

'He has a point,' Davey said, but he really didn't care, he was too drunk.

'Are you OK, Davey?' Juliet asked.

Davey grinned and made the thumbs up sign. 'A-OK.'

'Oh no, who got him drunk? I'll kill yis!' She sounded cross.

Francie turned to Davey. 'Just like her mammy.' Then back to Juliet. 'We had to get him oiled up or else he'd moan all night about rack toms and cymbals and shite.'

'That's harsh,' Davey said. Jay rounded the corner with Louis.

'Juliet? Welcome home,' Jay said, and she tossed her hair. 'Who's this?'

'Kyle.'

'Hi Kyle. And what do you do?'

'Eh, dunno. I go to school?'

'Do ya?' Francie said. 'Are you sure? You don't sound sure.'

Juliet laughed. 'They're messing.'

'Oh, we're deadly serious,' Jay said. 'You all right with this kid, Davey?'

'He likes to eat worms,' Davey said.

Kyle's face blushed red and he stuttered a little. 'I don't – I didn't – maybe once. I was four.'

'He's a good kid,' he said, and winked at Kyle.

'Well, if you're all right by Davey, you're all right by us,' Francie said. The venue was getting busy. Juliet could feel the heat of the crowd and hear the noise increase; voices leaked through the walls, stamping feet vibrated on the ground. She knew enough to know it was going to be a full house. Jason turned the corner with a few litre bottles of water and threw them at the lads. 'Drink up, we're on in ten.'

'This is Jason,' Davey said to Juliet, 'he's singing for us.'

'Hiya, Jason,' Juliet said. 'I hope you don't mess this up – it's for me ma.'

He shook her hand. 'I will do my very best, Juliet.'

She heard Marjorie's voice before she saw her.

'Well, well, well . . .'

She turned. 'Marjorie!' she screeched, and Marjorie took her in her arms and hugged her tight.

'I missed you, little pal,' Marjorie said.

'Missed you too, Marj.'

Davey pushed forward. 'You knew about this and you didn't tell me?'

'I was sworn to secrecy,' she said, as they hugged.

'I'm going to kill you.'

'She's gone a year – we needed to mark it.'

'No better way,' he said.

'Five minutes,' Louis called.

'We should give them some room,' Marjorie said. 'Good luck, lads.'

'Cheers, Marj.'

Juliet walked out into the packed house between Marjorie and Kyle, and for the first time since her mother died she felt real happiness, without guilt. She felt at peace.

Oh no.

Chapter Fifty-One

Molly

GRACE WAS STARING INTO space when Molly walked onto the ward. Lenny was by her side reading a newspaper.

'She looks good,' Molly said, leaning down to hug Lenny. 'Good colour in her face.'

'She is good, Molly.'

'Hiya, Ma,' Grace said, refocusing.

'How are you feeling, love?'

'Like I've been put through a washing machine.'

'How's your pain?'

'Fine, if I don't move anything . . .' she said, urgently pressing her button. 'Where's Da?'

'He's minding Juliet,' Molly lied.

'Right.'

'He sends his love, though.'

'Right.'

'Have the kids been in?'

'They've just left,' Grace said.

'Were they all right?'

'They were fine – quiet, even Ryan.'

'Stephen's taken them off to the gig,' Lenny said.

'Ah good, that'll be a distraction. Have you been up on your feet yet, Grace?'

'No, Ma, tomorrow. I have a catheter.'

'Not for long, though,' Molly said. Lenny gave her his seat and buzzed off to find another one. The light was low and aside from the smell of antiseptic, it was a calm enough environment, not like when Rabbit was in hospital and everyone around her was deathly ill. There was a combination of smells, a terrible angst and lethargy in those wards, that made Molly feel nauseous.

Lenny reappeared with a chair and sat down.

Grace was coming in and out of it. 'I can't feel the catheter, Ma,' she said. 'It's like I have no bladder. Haven't wanted to go all day.'

'Oh, you've gone all right,' Lenny said.

'My mouth is dry.'

Lenny poured her water.

'And this button isn't working again.'

'It's not broken, Gracie,' he said. 'You've just reached your limit.'

'They're very scabby with the painkillers, Ma.'

'I'm sure they're doing their best, love,' Molly replied. It was hard to see Grace so diminished. She was pale, with flushed cheeks, the pain etched into her face. She hadn't moved anything but her button-pushing thumb since Molly had arrived. She was petrified in place.

'Are you going to the gig, Ma?'

'Ah yeah, I'll pop my head in through the door. It's for Rabbit and Johnny, after all.'

'If you're not careful, you'll miss it,' Lenny said.

'You're not going, Lenny?'

'Nah, Stephen took the kids, and he's going off with his girl-friend afterwards. I'm staying here as long as they'll let me.'

'You don't need to,' Grace said.

'I'm not leaving you alone, not if I don't have to.'

When Lenny left to get some tea, Molly moved closer to her daughter.

'Better, Gracie?'

'Better, Ma.'

'Good girl.'

'Do you want to see them?' Grace asked. 'I still can't look but Lenny says they're nice.'

'Well then, he wouldn't lie.'

'He fuckin' would.'

'What matters is you're here with us, I've got your hand in mine, I hear your voice, I see your mouth move as you speak. I feel your breath on my face—'

'Oh shite, sorry, giz a mint, will you?'

Molly took a mint out of a packet and tried to hand it to Grace but her arms refused to budge, so she popped it in her mouth. 'I was being poetic.'

'Well, you were trying . . .' Grace said, and she chuckled a little. 'Ow, ouch, ow, ow, ow . . . No laughing.'

'Well, that's OK,' Molly said. 'I'm not laughing.'

'My da's still angry with me, isn't he, Ma?'

'He just doesn't understand, Grace.'

'Why?'

'I don't know.'

'Does he hate me?'

'Of course not. You know what he's like. He'll come round.'

'He's hurting me, Ma,' she said, and she was suddenly weeping.

'I'm sorry, Grace.' In Molly's mind she was hitting Jack across the head with a bag of oranges.

Grace pressed the button urgently once more and the meds coursed through her veins and her face relaxed. 'Ahhh, it's working again, Ma,' she said, and she smiled a little, 'like warm waves. Do you remember when we were kids those summers in Blackpool – Davey, me and Rabbit all playing in the warm waves?'

'I remember Blackpool. I don't ever recall it being warm.'

'It was tropical, Ma. The three of us playing in the sea and you and me da watching from the beach.'

'Long time ago,' Molly said.

'It was magic, though, wasn't it, Ma?'

'Yeah, love. It was.'

'I'm tired, Ma.'

'Go to sleep, love.'

'I'm scared.'

'What are you scared of?'

'Tomorrow.'

'Don't be, Grace, don't be scared. I'm here, Lenny's here—'

'And me da, where will he be?'

I'll fuckin' kill him.

'Am I going to be me again?' she said, and her eyes brimmed over.

Molly leaned back in and was careful not to touch or brush against Grace's torso. She kept away from the hand with the cannula in it and was sure to avoid all the tubes and the drain dollies.

'Did I tell you what an ugly baby you were, Gracie?'

'Yes, Ma,' she said, and Molly took a tissue out of her pocket and cleaned the tears from her face.

'You had a face like an old man's arse and a head of spiky ginger hair, but you were something else.'

Grace smiled.

'Did I tell you how beautiful you are today, Gracie?'

'No, Ma.'

'You are and you always were, even when you were fuckin' ugly.'

Grace chuckled a little. 'Ow, ouch . . .' She pressed the button again. 'It's still working, Ma,' she said, and she drifted off to sleep.

Molly waited for Lenny to return before she left for the evening. 'You're a good man,' she said before walking away.

She drove through the city as daylight drifted into night and the street lights came on. She thought about Rabbit and holding her hand, hearing her voice, watching her mouth move as she spoke, feeling her breath on her face and that dry laugh of hers, her strong voice, her gentle soul, and if she'd had a weaker spirit she would have driven into a wall.

Sorry. I'm so sorry.

Chapter Fifty-Two

Davey

THE LADS WERE SOBERED by the buzz, and the atmosphere of a full house, friends, family and actual fans of the bands from back in the day was enough to propel them onto the stage. The crowd cheered, Marjorie, Juliet and Davey's nephews' roars amongst them. Lit up on the wall behind the stage were enlarged black and white photos of Johnny, Rabbit and the boys in Kitchen Sink and The Sound. The main photo was of Johnny sitting on the edge of a stage alone and singing into a mic and Rabbit on the sound desk, moving a dial, their eyes meeting. Davey didn't remember that photo ever being taken but it was perfect. Francie opened up the gig by shushing the crowd. The shouting, clapping and whistling stopped as soon as he raised his hand and everyone fell into silence.

'It's brilliant to see everyone, we appreciate you all coming out to celebrate the lives of our friends, our family. Johnny was twenty-six when he died and he left a world of love behind. He was a poet, a songwriter, a singer, a musician. He was a funny bastard.'

The crowd laughed.

'He knew what he wanted, and he wanted the world. That wasn't to be, but for a short time he had it all.'

The crowd cheered.

'Because he had us and he had you.'

The crowd stamped their feet.

'And he had Rabbit Hayes. What can I say about Rabbit? We loved her, she was our mascot, she was our sound engineer, our cheerleader, she broke up fights.'

'The crowd cheered.

'And then she started a few.'

They laughed.

'She kept us together for as long as possible, and for Johnny she was his muse, his best friend, his conscience, his passion and the love of his life.'

The crowd applauded and he raised his hand in the air to silence them once more.

'He used to think they'd be together again. She used to think death was the end. Who knows where they are or aren't, but either way . . .' – he looked back at the photograph of Johnny singing to her – 'they'll always be together, so let's get this show started.'

The crowd went wild. 'Thanks for your support – all the money goes to MS Ireland and the Irish Cancer Society, and this is a song about freedom . . .'

It was a venue that held two hundred, but the noise that filled the air sounded like two thousand. Davey clicked his sticks together – 'One, two, three' – and knocked out the beat. The band kicked in and as soon as Jason opened his mouth to sing the crowd joined in. The hackles rose at the back of Davey's neck, signalling this moment was special.

There were a lot of mistakes that night, but the twins had the audience in stitches, stopping songs and giving out yellow cards to anyone who made a mistake – mostly it was Davey as he hadn't been party to any rehearsals.

'Stop. Stop. Stop. The famous drummer's making a bollocks of things,' Francie said, taking a yellow card out of his pocket and throwing it at Davey.

'Well, if someone had told me I'd be playing here tonight . . .'

Francie threw a second yellow card his way. 'That's for whining – we have a no-whining policy.'

The drum kit seemed too small for Davey, or the seat was too low – either way his knees were in his mouth.

'Look at him, I've seen better legs hanging out of nests. Isn't that right, DB?' Francie said.

Davey hit the kit – *de-dum tish* – and the audience laughed.

The lads took turns to tell stories about the songs that Jason was singing.

'The next song is about unrequited love,' Jay said. 'It's a song Johnny wrote for Rabbit, a song I played her a couple of days before she died. I'm not going to tell you what she said or did that day, that's between us, but this is their song.'

Louis hit the piano keys, Jason's voice filled the room, and by the time the band kicked in Davey was sobbing behind the kit. *For fuck's sake* . . . The lads noticed but no one made a joke; it wasn't the time for that. The gig ended with thunderous applause; they played two encores. Davey had stepped back into the past for one night and it was a beautiful thing, playing with the boys, reliving their glory days, the banter, the laughter, the kinship.

Afterwards, as Davey waded through the crowd, shaking hands and high-fiving with familiar and strange faces, he bumped into Francie's mad ex-girlfriend, Sheila B. *Oh shite.*

His eyes darted around the room to check if Francie was a safe distance away.

'Don't worry, I'm not here to cause trouble,' she said.

'Ah no, Sheila, I wouldn't think that, it's good to see you.'

'I'm on me meds, you don't have to be scared. Francie's with his family. I won't go near him.'

Davey relaxed. 'How are you, Sheila?'

'I'm grand. Look, I just wanted to say that I was sorry about Rabbit. I should have gone to the funeral but I was just out of the nuthouse, everything was a bit raw, you know yourself.'

'Yeah,' he said. Once a beauty, she was ravaged by grim circumstance.

'Are your parents around? I'd love to give them my condolences.'

Davey looked around and saw his dad standing at the back of the room.

'My da's at the back there.'

'Right, then. Good luck to ya, Davey,' she said, and he felt sorrow as she moved to walk away. As unpredictable and scary as she was, Sheila B had been a big part of the history of Kitchen Sink – she was Francie's first real girlfriend, now she was a stranger.

'Sheila?'

'Yeah.'

'It was really nice to see ya,' he said. 'You deserve good things.'

'You were always a softy, Davey,' she said, and she moved on through the crowd.

Marjorie had been crying. She wiped her eyes and sniffed. 'Like old times,' she said, and they hugged. Juliet bounced up and down. 'That was brilliant. I loved the song for me ma, can we put that on my phone?'

''Course.'

'What's the news on Grace?'

'She's good, Davey. It's all good.'

Davey exhaled and sat down and put his head in his hands. 'Good,' he mumbled.

The place cleared out a little and Juliet, her cousins and Kyle scarpered off, leaving Marjorie and Davey to themselves. He took her in; she looked beautiful, glowing – a radiant being beamed down from the heavens. She was both sad and happy at the same time. He realised he was touching her before he fully decided to, cupping her face and rubbing his thumb along her cheek. She reacted by reaching up and holding his hand in place. He leaned in and kissed her, then and there in a room full of friends and family. He didn't think about it, mull it over, plan or bargain with himself; he just did it and she responded.

'Let's go,' he said, and he took her by the hand and they walked together towards the door.

'Are you going to say hello to your mother?' his ma said from behind him. He turned to face her. 'Hiya, Ma.'

'Great gig.'

'Thanks.'

'Rabbit would be proud,' she said.

'Will you take Juliet home?' he asked.

'You both off somewhere?'

'A hotel,' he said, and he looked to Marjorie, who nodded her agreement.

'Ah, Marjorie, what are you thinking?' Molly shouted after them as they sprinted through the door.

'You deserve better than a roll in the hay with that gobshite – sorry, son.'

'No problem, Ma.'

Davey didn't care, he just wanted to feel something other than failure, pressure and pain, and he wanted to feel it with Marjorie.

Chapter Fifty-Three

Jack

JACK STOPPED THE CAR outside Grace's house. The curtains were drawn and the place was in darkness. Lenny's car wasn't there. He was either still with Grace or in the pub, one or the other. Stephen's was parked on a verge across the road, so even if he was in bed sleeping at least there was an adult in the house. Bernard fished out his key from his pocket.

'You'll be OK, boys?' Jack asked.

'We'll be fine, Granda,' Jeff said as he bailed out of the back.

He watched the boys walk past the small rust bucket of a caravan that Grace and Stephen panic-bought when Rabbit was dying. Grace didn't have room for Juliet so she made room; it was crude but it was a solution, and had Davey not stepped in she would have made it work. He knew she kept it just in case. There was no other reason, and his Grace always prepared for worst-case scenarios.

Once the kids were inside, he watched the lights go on inside the house. He remained sitting in his car, not sure where to go next. He had no desire to go home, lacking the strength for an argument or, worse, enduring Molly's mighty cold shoulder. He was behaving badly. He knew it, deep down, but he felt helpless. Grace was tearing herself to pieces *just in case*, but mutilation and keeping a caravan in your driveway is not the same thing. He knew Grace had noticed how distant he'd become. When she walked into a room, her daddy walked out of it. When she smiled at him, he cast his eyes to the floor. *I don't feel like talking or smiling.* He was being stubborn and it was his worst trait. He knew it. He couldn't help it.

How did it all fall apart? He and his wife didn't really talk anymore. There was a Rabbit-shaped hole in their lives which seemed to grow with each passing day. Grace was self-inflicting torture. He'd been there for Rabbit, and it didn't matter that the scalpel was wielded by a man with a kindly face or that the care had been second to none; the pain and the drains, the infections, rashes, blown veins, bruising, swelling, constipation and bladder problems that were just surgery-related and nothing to do with the chemo and radiation to follow, were a form of torture. Rabbit had no choice – it was hell or death – but Grace . . . *How could she expect him to go through it all again?* The first time around nearly killed him.

Praying just didn't work for Jack, so instead he just kept his wife's seat warm in the church and listened to whatever it was Father Frank had to say, and even then he drifted sometimes. He'd watch the dust particles twirl and dance in the light shafts coming through the stained glass and creating mini-spotlights on the old tiled floor. When mass was over he'd leave immediately and via the side door to avoid another awkward encounter with the priest who missed his pal. How could he answer questions about Molly when he didn't know the answers himself? She was so caught up in her charity work and her political war cries, they were strangers. She'd murder him when she found out he'd registered to pay the water bill. That would be the fight to end all fights, but the law was the law and without it, chaos. Molly and her Band of Botherers were proof of that if nothing else. Of course he didn't say that to her, not that she'd listen. Jack felt the happy home they had built over forty years was slowly falling asunder. He could feel everything and everyone he ever loved slipping away. *It wasn't supposed to be like this, Rabbit. I was supposed to die a contented old man, leaving behind a happy, healthy family. I was supposed to go first.*

Sorry, Da.

It's not your fault, love.

An hour had passed and Jack was still sitting in the car outside Grace's house, staring at two cats scoping each other out. He knew the Noonans' ginger cat, it was about fifteen and had an ear missing; the other one was a white ball of fluff, younger, faster but not as streetwise, and despite feeling dreadfully sorry for himself, the feline stand-off was engaging enough. Suddenly he caught the caravan rocking slightly with the corner of his eye; he turned to look. *Yip,* the bricks beneath it were moving too – it was slight but there was definite rocking. *Earthquake? Not likely, but I'd welcome it.*

He watched for another minute or two, then he stepped out of the car. It was still rocking; he moved onto the path and surveyed it from there. *No, it's not me imagination or me eyesight, that thing is moving.* Then it stopped and he stopped dead in his daughter's driveway; now he was playing chicken with the caravan. *What am I doing?* Then it started to sway again, gently rocking, tilting, stopping . . . The bricks looked secure enough, there wasn't a puff of wind. There's someone in there! He picked up one of Bernard's stray hurley sticks leaning against the garden wall, raised it above his head and made a slow approach, so slow his grandson and his girlfriend had time to finish up, get dressed and open the small caravan door to be greeted by an old man shouting the word 'halt' and swinging a broken hurley.

'Granda?'

'Stephen?'

'Yeah, it's me, and this is Charlene,' he said about the girl hiding behind him.

'Oh now, I'm terribly sorry, I thought a vagrant had taken possession of the van.'

'It's all right, Granda, give us a minute,' he said to Charlene, who just nodded. It was hard to make out what she looked like, it being so dark and her being terrified and hiding. Stephen jumped out of the caravan, took the hurley and flung it aside, then put his arm around his Granda and escorted him back to his car.

'You'll give yourself a heart attack, Granda,' Stephen said.

'Not if you don't give me one first, and what's wrong with bringing the girl into the house?'

'Charlene likes the caravan.'

'Why on earth?'

'Our own private little place – I have a few fairy lights, a blow heater and some smelly candles.'

'Does your ma know?'

'She'd rather I did it in the caravan instead of in the house with the boys.'

313

Jack sat into the front seat of his car. Stephen sat into the passenger side.

'I saw the boys go inside over an hour ago. You been sitting here since?'

'Just thinking.'

'About what?'

'Everything and anything. There was a stand-off between the Noonans' ginger cat and a fluffy white fellow.'

'Who survived to tell the tale?'

'Dunno – the rocking caravan distracted me.'

'Ma missed you tonight.'

'How was she?'

'She's relieved it's over. She's in pain and out of it – you know, the way Rabbit used to be, all right one minute, talking shite the next. She asked Ryan if he had wings.'

Jack shook his head sadly. 'Why?' he mumbled.

'Granda, she did it so her kids wouldn't have to see her go through chemo and death. So forgive her, because if you don't she might never forgive you.'

Stephen got out of the car.

'Goodnight, Granda,' he said, and he headed back into the caravan. Jack took off down the road before it started to rock again. His grandson had given him a lot to think about. Grace didn't want to put the kids through cancer. Of course that made sense, but . . . He still didn't like it.

He parked outside his house and made his way inside. It was quiet, not a mouse was stirring. He looked in on Kyle sleeping soundly on the sofa and went into the kitchen to make a cup of tea before bed. He pulled his phone from his pocket and noticed a new message. He dialled his voicemail.

'Hello, Jack, it's Derek here. Good news – the contract's finally arrived, so if you have time this week, maybe we could meet in my office. The publishers tell me they plan to release the book within the year . . . Oh, and we have a name: *Never Let Go*. I'd love to hear your thoughts. Call me.'

Over the course of the year that had passed, Molly had made it clear she wanted nothing to do with the book. She especially didn't like the idea of Rabbit being opened up to criticism without being here to defend herself.

'But it's what she wanted,' Jack had argued.

'And if she's right about the afterlife, she wants nothing now,' she said. But Derek only required his signature on the contracts; Molly couldn't stop them unless she sued, and even the mighty Molly Hayes wouldn't do that. She knew deep down, whether she liked it or not, it was Rabbit's wish. *Why can't she just accept it and support us?* he thought.

And it was then the penny dropped. *Oh, God Almighty, I'm such an idiot. I'm so sorry, Grace.*

With no sofa to sleep on he headed upstairs, avoiding the creaking third step from the top. He looked in on Juliet, who was sound asleep with her computer opened on a YouTube channel with the video paused: Top Ten Best Kisses. *God Almighty, they're all at it.* He undressed in the hall and crept into the bedroom; thankfully Molly was asleep. He put on his pyjamas and slipped into bed, ever so gently. He resolved to visit Grace the very next day, with flowers and chocolates and the biggest card he could find. He needed to forgive and be forgiven, and he also needed allies; there was another much bigger fight brewing. Molly wanted to protect her daughter's memory and hold it close, and he wanted to share it with the world. In

315

all their years together Jack and Molly had fought many battles, but this would be their great war and he wasn't sure their marriage would survive it. It was a terrible thing to think at his age that his marriage could fail, that he could lose the love of his life entirely.

I'm so sorry, Molly. Are you?

Chapter Fifty-Four

Marjorie

THE HOTEL WAS BUSTLING with people; the bar was still open, a pianist played and people in expensive clothing lounged and drank expensive wines.

'Do you want a drink?' Davey asked.

'No.'

'Sure?'

'I would like sex, please,' Marjorie said.

'Great. Me too.'

The room was luxurious but small.

'It's all they had,' he said, apologising.

'The bed looks good,' she said.

He kissed her and she kissed him back, and it was slow and steamy and so much better than the night she lost her virginity to him in a park after a night spent in the pub and on hard, cold, wet ground, her only enduring memory a stabbing sensation in her vagina and a smell of shite in the air; or those other two times, the first in Rabbit's house, a rushed and frenzied encounter which ended abruptly when a six-year-old Juliet barged in on them and Davey told her they were playing leapfrog. Then there was that last time, in her marital bed, when she was so filled with guilt and self-loathing that it was hard to breathe, never mind feel anything. They started to undress and she had her dress off before it became apparent he had no condoms.

'Aren't you on the pill?'

'No. I'm single.'

'Exactly,' he said, and she pulled away. *For fuck's sake . . .* 'I'm not like you, Davey. I'm don't sleep with everyone I meet.'

'Oh come on.' He put his hands up. 'That's not fair.'

'You think I need an STD?'

'I don't have an STD.'

'Well with the skanks you screw, you probably do.'

'Oh that's nice, using our conversations against me. I have medicals all the time, it's part of my contract for insurance.'

Suddenly she was shaken awake. *What I am doing? I'm not a child. This isn't some fucking fantasy.*

'This was a bad idea.'

She picked up her dress and put it back on. He didn't stop her; he just perched on the side of the bed in his underwear.

'I'm sorry,' he said.

'It's fine.' She started to look for her shoe. 'It's my fault. I don't know what I was thinking.'

The beautiful night, filled with fond memories, warmth and love was all falling to shit, and suddenly she felt desperately sad. The tears came from a reserve inside her. They flowed openly and she tried to leave, even before she'd found her stupid shoe. *How hard can it be? The stupid room is the size of a postage stamp.* She limped towards the door.

It didn't take much manoeuvring from Davey to get from the bed to her. He put his arms around her and held her close, and it was only when she pulled back and looked at his face that she realised he was crying, too.

They lay facing one another on the bed, she in her unzipped dress, her make-up halfway down her face, with one shoe on and one shoe off, and Davey in his shorts and socks. The night had taken a turn, they both knew it, but lying there face to face, and for the first time stripped bare, was refreshing, comforting and real. They talked about old times, the band, the boys, Rabbit, Johnny and that epic love story that no ordinary mortal could compete with.

'They were star-crossed, and I ended up marrying a banker called Neil who lifted the cheek of his arse to fart and said "beggin' your pardon".'

He smiled at her and played with one of her blonde curls. 'I didn't even try.'

'Why?' she asked.

'Lots of reasons – I was scared, and I'm odd . . . so there's that.'

'There is that,' she agreed.

'Also, I loved Johnny, too, and what we had. I lost him to his illness and the lads in the band to their other lives. It seemed so easy for them to just pick up and move on, find a life outside of music, discard the dream, but not for me.'

'You were heartbroken,' she said.

'Just like you are now.'

'I am,' she said, 'and I'm lonely.'

'Me too.'

'You have Juliet,' she said.

'And she's opened the door to a life I didn't think was for me.'

'So now you want a wife and kids?' Her query came with an arched eyebrow.

'Now I want a real life with real love. I think Juliet deserves that, too.'

Marjorie was tired and emotional; her thoughts drifted to another time in her life, one when she and Neil were trying for the baby they hoped would fix them. It didn't work out; they had tests and they were inconclusive and their problem conceiving was described as unexplained infertility. It was after that diagnosis and two failed rounds of IVF that Marjorie had slept with Davey and got caught.

'What about you, Marj, do you want a husband and kids?'

'No,' she said.

'Why not?'

'Because I had a husband and I can't have kids.'

'What do you mean?'

'I mean we did it all and couldn't conceive – then Neil meets the lovely Debbie and now they have a baby girl.'

'That doesn't mean anything.'

'It does, and it's OK. I'd probably be a shit mother anyway.'

Davey wasn't buying that. 'Bullshit, you'd be the best mother in the world.'

'Stop, Davey. I'm not one of your girls who'll believe anything to stay in the bubble with you, as nice as the bubble is.'

'No, you're not one of my girls,' he said. He pulled her closer and she rested her head against his chest. 'The first time I saw you, you reminded me of Shirley Temple: blonde curls, a pink silk bow, a perfect little dress, patent leather shoes and socks with frills on them. You were the prettiest little thing I'd ever seen.'

'You looked like a dead bird in denim on denim.'

'You were there for me when the band broke up and I was drinking myself to oblivion.'

'I had a huge crush on you, and I knew if I hung around long enough and you were drunk enough you'd have sex with me.'

'Wow, slow down, Bill Cosby, I'm going to have to review our relationship.'

'Yeah, it was pretty shady.'

'I forgive you,' he said.

'Thanks.'

'Besides, you're the reason I ended up in New York, working in your uncle's bar. I met Casey and my whole life changed. You saved me.'

'Yeah, I'm a sexual predator slash hero,' she said. 'There *is* something between us, isn't there, Davey, it's not just me?'

'There's always been something between us, Marj.'

'Just a place and time thing, then.'

'Yeah,' he said.

'Are you ever coming home?'

'I don't know. What would I do here?'

'Everything, anything.'

'I don't know.'

'It's time I got myself a different life, Davey.'

'I know.'

They fell asleep in one another's arms.

Davey was in the shower when Marjorie woke. She sat up and checked herself in the mirror. *Holy shit!* She looked like the Joker. She grabbed some tissues out of the box by the bed and wiped off the heavy make-up. Her face was still dirty but she no longer resembled a comic book villain. The door was open; she walked into the bathroom and Davey turned to face her.

'Good morning,' he said.

'Good morning,' she said, and she realised she still had one shoe on and one off. She kicked it off.

'You coming in?' he asked.

'Do you want me to?'

'Yes.'

'We're still the same people we were last night.'

'I know.'

'OK.' She took off her dress and underwear and she joined him, and they pressed together and they didn't talk about protection and maybe that was because Davey had assured Marj he was STD-free and she had admitted she was infertile, or maybe it was because in that moment neither cared. Either way, the events in the bathroom led to the bedroom, and late checkout became an early dinner. They parted just before seven the next evening with promises to see one another again before he left for America six days later, but even after the best sex of her life and the renewed bond between them, she knew getting into her taxi that she wouldn't see him before he returned to the States. It was sad but it was OK; she had a new job to go to on Monday morning and a new life to find.

Part Six

Year Two

Chapter Fifty-Five

Jack

SAYING GOODBYE TO HIS granddaughter was difficult. He didn't want her to leave, and despite her protestations he was savvy enough to know that she didn't want to go either. Juliet was loyal to the man who had agreed to raise her and loyal to the memory of her mother, who had such high hopes for Juliet's substitute parent, but she was miserable.

The week flew in and it was filled with hospital visits to Grace and time with cousins and the neighbour boy Kyle. Jack took them to the cinema and sat between them. They didn't like that. *Tough.* Molly spent the week cooking Juliet and Davey's favourite foods and fussing over them both; it was nice to see her focused on something other than water meters. Of course she still didn't have time for him, and he kept his head down because the book contract signing was looming. *Armageddon.* Jack and Davey spent an evening down the pub drinking pints with Francie and Jay. It was a good night, full of laughter. There was always laughter with the twins. He admired that about them; their ability to joke their way through anything was a gift, one he didn't share. It was nice having his son home; he always regretted it when he left. He missed him. He missed his daughter. He missed his granddaughter. His missed his wife.

He finally visited Grace on the day after her operation; she was physically compromised by pain and mentally compromised by strong medication.

'Is that me da? I thought you didn't love me anymore?'

'Ah now, Grace, don't start that,' he said, holding his flowers, chocolates and big card.

'I don't think flowers are allowed in hospitals anymore,' Lenny said apologetically.

'Go on,' Jack said.

Grace giggled to herself. 'PC gone mad.'

'She's a bit stoned, is she Lenny?'

'Out of her box, Jack,' he replied.

Jack placed the flowers in the bin. Lenny gave him a seat.

'HOW ARE YOU, LOVE?' he said slowly and loudly.

'Better for seeing you, Da. Did Ma threaten you with a bag of oranges?'

'No, I came myself.'

'Aren't you a big boy . . .' she said, and Lenny nodded apologetically.

'I'm sorry, Grace.'

'For what, Da?'

'For not, well, um, for . . .'

'You're not sorry.'

'We have a difference of opinion, Gracie, but I love you and I want to be there for you.'

'Do you wanna see them, Da?'

'Ah, now!' He stood up and backed away.

'Sorry, Jack, she's been showing them to everyone.'

'Ah Grace, what are you doing?'

'They're not mine, Da, they're not real, they're an example of modern medicine.'

Lenny and Jack shared a concerned look. Grace hit the button and her eyes started to swim.

'The good news is, I love drugs.'

Jack visited his daughter while she was in hospital and every day for a month after she left; they never, ever referred to her mastectomies and implants again.

He met Derek in his office to sign the contracts. He had been to the office once before, when his daughter was excitedly showing him around the place.

'This is my cubicle, Da,' she said, and it was hard to miss: there were photographs of Juliet, her family, Johnny, the band and one with just him and her. It made him feel so proud – his daughter, the journalist. He passed her old cubicle; someone else was sitting in it, a young man with a checked shirt and a bun in his hair. No photos adorned his walls, but he kept body spray and hand cream on display. All traces of Rabbit were gone.

He sat at Derek's desk and he showed him the contracts he had already signed. 'You just have to sign here.'

He looked and picked up the pen; he hesitated. He had spent a year fighting with his wife about this and that. Everything, really. They seemed to agree on nothing anymore and now this, the thing that divided them most, Rabbit's book.

'Is everything all right, Jack?' Derek asked.

'It's fine,' he said, but it wasn't fine at all.

'You can take it home and think about it,' Derek said.

'You're a patient man, Derek. It's taken us over a year to get here.'

'What are your fears, Jack?' he asked.

'Me wife,' Jack said.

'She doesn't want this.'

'She thinks that by publishing Rabbit's last days we'll be exposing her to public scrutiny, and people can be so cruel. She doesn't want her girl to be ripped apart by strangers.'

'I understand that, but a lot of people will identify, they'll take comfort from her, they might even love her a little.'

'She wanted this, Derek.'

'She really did.'

'Did I ever tell you what she said to me on the day you published her first blog?'

'No.'

'She said, now Da, it's personal, difficult and sometimes it's ugly, so if you read it don't be sad or angry, just think about all the people who are going through the same thing, especially those who aren't surrounded by people like you.' He was crying. Derek handed him a tissue from a box he kept in the drawer of his desk.

'She was a brilliant journalist because she engaged, she connected and she cared . . . deeply,' Derek said, and he grabbed a tissue and blew his nose. 'She'd be laughing if she could see us both now.'

Jack sniffed and wiped his eyes. 'She'd say we were a pair of saps, but the truth is my Rabbit cried for others all the time.' The men disposed of their used tissues and Jack reclaimed the pen. 'She trusted me,' he said, and he signed the contracts, four sets.

'Molly will come round,' Derek said.

'Maybe, and maybe I've lost the will to care.'

Jack politely declined Derek's offer of lunch, and he walked through Rabbit's old office and out through the front doors into sunlight. It should have been a joyful day; it should have been a win. *We did it, love*, he said in his head as he looked up into the sky. *We did it*. He drove home, parked his car, walked to the local pub and for the first time in his life he got drunk alone.

Chapter Fifty-Six

Grace

GRACE COULDN'T RECALL MUCH of her first and second day after surgery, although that first shower remained imprinted. It was difficult to do anything with her arms planted by her sides; she couldn't raise them, it was too painful and it was also not recommended, moving out of the bed, arms by her sides, stepping onto the hard ground, shuffling, with drains hanging from her tender, screaming breasts. That was hard – hell, really – she was so fragile, so raw, her body didn't feel like her own, it felt like someone else's. She'd been patched together and sewn up. When she eventually made it to the bathroom holding the nurse's hand and crying softly to herself, she stepped behind the curtain. The drip and catheter were gone; the only things weighing her down were bottles of pus and blood hanging from her on long tubes sewn into the skin under her armpits. Ryan's cotton Rabbit bags held them up. She didn't want them to get wet so the nurse set about removing the bags. She couldn't look at the contents of the bottles. She couldn't touch them or hold them. They were too short to meet the floor and if she left them hanging they'd pull on her skin. The nurse brought a little stool into the area.

'We'll rest them on this, Grace,' she said, and Grace averted her gaze.

'Thanks,' she said. She turned the shower on and stood outside its scope, just watching the heavy water hit the tiled floor. She couldn't imagine standing under it, the pain of the water thumping on her tender breasts.

'You doing OK, Grace?'

'I'm fine,' she said. She washed her hands and then did her best to stretch out her arms. Everything hurt and strained and burned. She couldn't bring herself to stand under the water and she couldn't raise her arms; she was stranded and the nurse was waiting. No water touched her breasts or under her arms, her stomach, her vagina, her arms, hands or legs. She eventually leaned forward and wet her hair and face; she felt dizzy and was terrified she'd hit the deck. That was enough, maybe even too much. She cried all the way through. She tried not to look down, but her compression bandage was off and her patchwork breasts were hard to avoid. *No nipples*. She had never really loved her nipples, but now that they were gone, she missed them dearly. She nearly slipped on the way out; she automatically raised her hand and grabbed at the wall to stop her fall and the pain that went through her was truly spectacular. She screamed and the nurse was there to calm her down. She felt dizzy and nauseous; she needed to sit on the stool for a minute or two. 'You're OK, Grace, you're doing great. Next stop, home.' That's all she wanted, to leave that place and go home.

When she was finally discharged, she felt a combination of intense relief, abject fear and that old familiar creeping guilt. *She's dead. I'm alive.*

331

Fuck's sake, Grace, cop on. Grace tried not to pity herself; dead Rabbit in her head wouldn't allow it. At home, Grace's kids tiptoed around her, all but Ryan who referred to her as Frankentits. 'Do ya get it? Frankenstein, Frankentits. One of the lads in class came up with it.'

'Yeah, son, I get it. It's comforting to know you're spreading the word.'

'Didn't know it was a secret,' he said.

'It's not, Ryan, it's just personal.'

'Oh, OK.'

Stephen was on a mission to make his mother as comfortable as possible. 'Whatever you need, Ma.' When he wasn't in college he and his girlfriend Charlene, a quiet, tall, bright, preppy type, did the grocery shopping or they dropped Bernard to his various activities or Jeff to the gym. The mother of Jeff's mate Specs O'Leary (named for the oversized spectacles he wore) collected him from basketball and arrived with baked goods once a week. Ryan got the bus everywhere, stating he was his own man. The kids were taking care of each other and themselves. Lenny hired someone to clean the house and he took over cooking in the evenings when he came home from work. Her job was to get better. He bought her expensive creams and healing ointments; he bought her sexy silk pyjamas. One evening he'd arrive home with flowers, the next chocolates and the next a novel, and so on. He spoiled her. He also tended to her; he spread the creams and ointments when she couldn't raise her arms to do it herself. He knew her wounds and navigated around her ports better than she did. He never shied away, never made her feel less of a woman; he embraced their new reality and all the while she waited for the other shoe to drop.

She spent that first month propped up in bed or on the sofa or the big armchair with good back support, initially quite disabled without the use of her arms and definitely traumatised by the damage she'd sustained. She was fragile and weak and racked with pains. Another two weeks passed and she felt stronger, more capable; she could use her arms again. She was still sore but she felt more like herself. She was lucky in that her surgeon had been able to place a large volume of saline into her tissue expander during the surgery; she had been warned she could return from surgery with two empty sacs, but once the swelling went down it became obvious why she retained her ports under her arms – she needed to be filled again. She went to her doctor's clinic three times to have her breasts filled; each time, Lenny took the day off work and she tried her best to be brave as the needle went in and the pressure built under her skin. He took her to lunch afterwards if she felt able. He tried to make the best of it. She knew she was lucky but still waited for that bloody other shoe to drop.

Marjorie called once a week on a Saturday morning or a Sunday afternoon for the first six weeks. She'd always bring a little something, a plant or a scented candle, flowers or perfume. She knew Grace's brand. Marjorie was good at gifting. They'd talk about her new job. Marjorie was excited, buzzed even; she looked brighter and happier than she had since Rabbit got sick. It was nice to see. They talked about 'Davey and the hotel' once and it was brief, with Marjorie telling her it was nice but they were done and she was moving on.

'Good for you, Marjorie.'

Grace and Lenny didn't talk about sex for six weeks. It wasn't even an option; Grace could barely enjoy a cup of tea, never mind Lenny lovin'. Then eight weeks passed and she was feeling stronger and getting back to herself. Then twelve weeks passed and she was fit – not one hundred per cent, but eighty per cent. She had no desire, really, but Lenny had been brilliant and he deserved her to take the initiative, he deserved his wife back. It was a Friday night and Stephen was out with Charlene, Bernard and Jeffrey were playing sports and Ryan was God knows where, doing God knows what, and she trusted it wasn't illegal.

She bathed, and in her bubble bath she realised she was growing accustomed to her new breasts – nipples aside, they had a good shape and as soon as she'd removed the ports and tattooed on some nipples she was confident she'd feel almost whole again. Lenny's expensive creams and ointments had helped reduce the angry scars. She put on her favourite sexy bra, but it didn't fit. *Oh, yeah. I was told about this.* Still, for some reason it was a shock. She sat on the edge of her bed and cried for a few minutes before taking the bra off and putting it away. She didn't have the energy to go shopping, and she was still anxious about walking into a crowd; she needed to have the safety net of space around her at all times. She also couldn't face shopping *and* sex – it had to be one or the other. She put on a black silk robe and a pair of red silk knickers and she tried on the red stilettos, but they reminded her of being carried towards the operating theatre – *bollocks, there goes a good pair of shoes* – so she popped on a pair of black ones.

She heard the front door, and called Lenny upstairs. She counted the steps as his feet landed on the stairs and the third step from the top groaned. She was nervous, didn't know quite

334

where to put herself. *Jesus, I feel stupid.* She splayed herself on the bed. That didn't feel right. She sat at its edge, crossing her legs, with her chin resting on her index finger. *Not good.* She stood with her hands on her hips. *I look like fuckin' Wonder Woman.* When he came through the door she was between poses, so in a panic she curtsied. *God All-fucking-mighty.*

'What's this?' he said, taking in the sexy apparel and attempting to ignore the curtsy.

'It's time.'

'Are you sure?'

'Positive, but just don't touch them. No, that's not fair. You can, but really, really softly.'

'I don't know, Grace,' he said, taking off his suit jacket.

'Lenny, we are doing this.'

'And you're absolutely sure?'

'Look at me,' she said, and she was in the Wonder Woman stance again.

He sighed deeply, as though he was a condemned man. 'OK,' he said.

'OK.'

They walked towards one another and he stopped a small distance from her to give way for her new breasts and leaned in, and they kissed and it was tentative and fine but far from passionate. They kissed some more; now he was just buying time. Then they slowly moved over to the bed and she gently sat onto it and lay down and he kissed her some more as she thought *get the fuck on with it*, but he was careful to hover above her. They didn't touch from the chest to the crotch. He kissed her neck and, weirdly, her arm. She pulled off her knickers, hoping to make things more interesting. He pulled down his pants and sat on her, rocking a bit too, and after a few minutes it became apparent that he was as soft as butter on a warm day. *FUCK!*

'Sorry,' he said, climbing off her. 'I'm just tired. It's been a long week.'

'No problem,' she lied.

She took herself into the bathroom and cried.

It will get better; it's the first attempt. I'm still not completely right. It will be fine.

Seven more months passed and Grace and Lenny still did not have sex.

Chapter Fifty-Seven

Juliet

D URING THE WHOLE WEEK in Ireland, Juliet tried to tell
Davey how she felt and that she wanted to come home.
She rehearsed it in her head; she practised it in the mirror
and wrote it down. When it came to it she just couldn't do it.
Besides, what did she expect him to do, give up everything to
come back to Dublin? If not, how could she abandon him?
After everything he did for her, how could she leave him
now when he depended on her? Who would take care of
him? And where would she go? Into Grace's caravan? Or her
gran's box room? Gran and Granda were too old to care for
her and Grace had her own problems. She was being selfish
and cruel. Davey would be devastated. He had made a promise to her mother and she had made that same promise. She
couldn't break it. She had to suck it up. In four and a half
years she'd be in medical school. *Everything changes. Nothing stays the same.*

It wasn't hard transitioning back, she'd only been home
a week. She had improved at kissing Kyle and spent any
time that she wasn't with family with him. She cried saying
goodbye to him. He promised to Skype every other day. She
promised she would, too. She asked Davey if they could go

home for Christmas and he agreed, and even thought it was a good idea. Only six months to wait. Things were different; she could come home now, her ma wasn't dead in Ireland. She was more alive on the streets of Dublin than anywhere else in the world.

Back in Nashville, she slipped into her old routine quickly: study, taking care of the house, Davey's appointments and the laundry. He wanted her to stop, to be a kid, and told her it was his job to take care of her, but she liked doing those things, it gave her a reason to be there, she needed to feel useful. She argued her point; he nodded and told her that it wasn't expected. It was needed, though – Davey was a mess and she didn't really know how he ever managed without her. Maybe if he had a PA he'd be fine, but he didn't, and despite being a busy man who needed to be in different places at different times, he had no watch and no concept of dates or time. She was his watch and his calendar. She knew where he was supposed to be and with whom and for what meeting and she liked it. It wasn't as fun as being at home with Kyle, her cousins, her gran and granda, but it was something. It was a life.

They went back on the road in October, just when she'd settled in Nashville and her studies were going really well. She was acing exams and was well on her way towards academic excellence. Gemma her tutor wasn't available to travel. It was a blow. Her new tutor was a man called Zac. He was in his thirties, a hippy type who had been home-schooled all his life. He used the word 'man' more than most and he smelled strongly of sandalwood. He was a nice guy, but he wasn't Gemma. She could talk to Gemma about girly things, things she couldn't talk to Davey about. Gemma had been hers and hers alone.

They were on tour for two months, which took them right into the holidays, but Davey had promised her they'd go back to Dublin, so he bought two first-class tickets online and she dreamed about seeing her home and her boyfriend again.

'Do I need to worry about this boy?' he asked.

'I'm thirteen.'

'Going on fourteen.'

'That's still young, Davey.'

He nodded. 'If you ever want to talk about boy-girl stuff, you can come to me,' he said, choking the words out.

'Thanks.'

'Or your auntie Grace is always on the end of a telephone line.'

'OK. Thanks.'

'Or your gran.'

She looked at him.

'Maybe not her, she'd probably put down the phone and kill the young fella.'

'With a bag of oranges,' Juliet said.

'It is her weapon of choice.'

That was the conversation that made her want to tell Davey that Trevor the sound guy had been acting strangely. Since returning from Ireland she'd tried to stay away from him as much as possible. Every time he proposed a lesson, she made an excuse. Even then when they shared a lift or he stood behind her in the queue at a service station or canteen, he got too close. There was an atmopshere between them now. She didn't like it. He made her feel uncomfortable. She thought about what she'd say to Davey, how she'd approach it, but she didn't know how, or what was even happening – so she didn't. Maybe if Gemma had still been tutoring her, she might have said it to her.

They'd been touring six out of the eight weeks when Trevor knocked on her hotel room door with an old ten-channel sound desk in his hand. She'd just taken a bath, she was in her robe and she was tired. She told him she was going to bed and felt really awkward because she was naked under her bathrobe.

'Is Davey around?' he asked.

'No, they're rehearsing a new song for the set tonight,' she said, and she thought it was an odd question as she was sure he knew about it.

'I have something for you,' he said, pushing his way in and placing the desk on the bed. She thought about leaving the door open but then that would seem weird, so she didn't.

'It's like the one your mom used to work,' he said.

She stayed by the door.

'It's just like the one in the photographs.'

It was exactly like the one in the photographs. This enticed her to move forward. She touched the dials. 'It's so cool. You shouldn't have. Thank you,' she said, hoping he'd leave.

'You deserve it – we're friends, aren't we?'

She was instantly scared – she couldn't quite work out why. He was smiling but her stomach churned.

'I'll show you how to use it.'

'You don't have to.'

'I want to. It can be our project, something you can show off to Davey for Christmas.'

'It's OK, really.' She wanted him to go. *Get out. Please. Leave.*

'Juliet, it cost a lot of money.'

'Oh.'

'We're still friends, aren't we?'

'Yeah.' *No.*

'I'll give you a little lesson now,' he said.

'I'm tired,' she said, holding her bathrobe together tightly.

He didn't listen. He was busy pretending to give her a lesson on the desk; he leaned over her and stood too close to her, leaning into her, and she knew it was all going really wrong. *Oh no. Oh no.* She froze when he undid the belt of her dressing gown and suddenly her skin felt cold and then he grabbed her small breast and stood over her and she could feel him pulling himself off and felt him moving behind her. She didn't scream, she didn't move an inch; she just stood there hoping it would stop, terrified Davey would come into the room. *He'd kill him – he'd kill him, and then he'd go to prison and someone from a gang would kill him and it would be my fault.*

He finished himself off on the floor and then cleaned it up himself. She stood frozen to the spot, her heart beating wildly in her chest. Her fists were clenched so tightly her nails broke the skin on her palms.

'That was nice,' he said. 'I like spending time with you.'

Then he was gone and she felt so sick inside she tried her best to vomit but nothing came out. She didn't cry. She just put on her pyjamas and double-locked the door and curled up into the foetal position, hugging herself tight. She didn't answer Kyle's Skype call that night, and when her uncle knocked on the adjoining hotel room door and asked if she was all right she said she was fine, and goodnight, then she cried herself to sleep.

Chapter Fifty-Eight

Marjorie

MARJORIE LOVED HER NEW job. It was everything she had dreamed it would be. Friendly, fun, engaged staff and an easygoing atmosphere oftentimes tinged with excitement and adrenaline. Supporting new ideas, new ventures and new businesses gave her a buzz and she was good at it. She knew the banking business inside and out, she understood finance, she was good with people, she was energised and filled with a new hope: it wasn't all doom and gloom out there, people were finding their way through the fog of uncertainty and calamity. Some of the ideas were inspired and inspiring; it made her feel like anything was possible. That was a feeling she'd never really had before and she wasn't quite sure what to do with it. Client meetings were a daily occurrence and she fed off young minds and their energy and their possibility. Drinks happened every Thursday and Friday nights in hip bars by the glistening canal, or maybe the canal just glistened in her mind. Life had taken a turn for the better.

Her mother was doing better, too, and their relationship improved with every put-down and snide comment. There was an odd mother-daughter dynamic, but since she'd stopped being polite and internalising all her anguish and anger they'd really turned a corner. She celebrated a successful first month of her new job by taking her mother out to a posh restaurant for dinner. Vera was pretty handy on the stick at this point, so much so she deftly used it as a weapon in crowds.

'Please don't hit that child, Mam,' she said.

'It was a tap, not a hit, and he was clearly trying to trip me,' Vera said about the toddler in her way.

Once she tried to shove it into the spokes of a wheelchair when a disabled man bumped her elbow.

'God Almighty, I'm going to take it off you if you don't stop it,' Marjorie warned. Vera didn't really need the stick anymore; it was more of a mental crutch than a physical one, and it also served to remind her daughter she was an invalid now and not to be ignored. The restaurant was lovely and the food was divine, though naturally Vera had a problem with her main course, despite the fact that she practically licked the plate. When the waiter asked her if she'd enjoyed her meal she said, 'I'd have preferred if there was a little less garlic and a lot more spuds.'

They both ate ice cream for dessert.

'It's not like you to eat dessert,' Vera said.

'Well, I'm hungry.'

'You should watch your figure, it's around this time of life that women put on weight around the tummy.'

'This time of life?'

'Menopause.'

'I'm forty-two.'

'I was forty.'

'Ah fuck off, Ma.'

'Do not call me Ma. I am Mammy.'

They went home after that. Marjorie drove the car in silence.

'You're sulking.'

343

'Kids sulk – I'm just ignoring you.'

'You would rather not know what's facing you?'

'It's not facing me.'

'They say girls follow their mothers.'

'You had different issues.'

'The symphysiotomy can be blamed for most things that have gone wrong for me, but not that,' Vera said.

'I'm not menopausal,' Marjorie said.

'Any day now.'

'Can you please stop being a bitch?'

'I wasn't trying to be, I was trying to help you.'

'You've a funny way of helping.'

She walked her mother inside her home and told her she'd drop the shopping over on Wednesday evening and see her on Saturday for a walk.

'It's too cold to walk.'

'Tell that to your physiotherapist.'

'I'm not walking.'

'If I have to drag you out, you're walking.'

'I'm not the only bitch in this family,' Vera said.

'Now, now, Ma. I'm only trying to help.'

Other than Vera's talk of menopause and her slamming the door in her face, it hadn't been a bad evening.

'Why was the tomato blushing?' Vera said during their starters. Marjorie wasn't sure what to say; for a moment she feared the woman was having another stroke.

'Why was the tomato blushing?' Vera repeated.

'I don't know.'

'Because it saw the salad dressing,' she said, and nodded to herself and smiled.

Marjorie didn't know what to say. 'That was a joke, Ma?'

'I saw a young fella tell it on the telly,' she said, and then she laughed to herself and Marjorie laughed out of shock more than anything else, but a laugh is a laugh. Still, by the time she left the house all laughter was forgotten and she was awash with fresh concerns about the menopause.

Marjorie wasn't the type of person to keep records, and certainly not of her period. So it was only when she thought about it for a really long time that she realised she might be a little late. She'd had her last period while she was out of work, she'd now been in work a month, and when she really drilled down she remembered she'd been at a dinner party and run out of tampons. She had to ask her host for tampons but the woman only used panty pads, which felt like bricks in her pants and made for a very uncomfortable evening. She had the invite on her computer. She got home and opened up her email and she realised her period was nearly three weeks late. *Fucking menopause!* She looked up menopause and frightened ten kinds of shite out of herself. Period stops. *Check*. Mood swings. She'd called her mother a bitch at dinner. *Check*. Night sweats. *Not yet. Vaginal dryness. Oh, sweet suffering Jesus*. It was only the start, she wouldn't experience a lot of that until they'd stopped for a year. She had time to get her head around it. She had been feeling tired and reaching for more sweet things, which wasn't like her. She didn't feel like she was putting on weight, but having said that the new outfits she bought for work were feeling a tiny bit snug. She resolved to go to the doctor and get tested. She might as well know if she had any eggs left in the box, and there was always HRT. There's no way she was going through it alone.

She made the appointment for two weeks after that, hoping that she might have a period in the meantime. Nothing. Zip. *It's menopause. Shit.* She walked into the doctor's office and explained her symptoms, following up with, 'My mother's started at forty and I'm forty-two.'

'Right.'

'And there's no chance you could be pregnant?'

'Excuse me?'

'You haven't had unprotected sex in the recent past?'

'Um . . . eh . . . well . . . yeah, there was once, there a while ago.'

'How long ago?'

'About six weeks.'

'And your last period was eight weeks ago?'

'Thereabouts,' she said.

'And you haven't taken a pregnancy test?'

'No. I didn't even consider that. I tried to conceive for a long time. Didn't work.'

The doctor looked at her like she was an insane person.

She went to the bathroom and peed on a stick the doctor gave her. She returned to the room with the stick under her top.

'Keeping it warm?' the doctor said when she failed to remove it.

'No, just not sure I'm prepared for what it says.'

'I can take a look if you like?'

'OK.' She handed it to her.

She looked at it, nodded to herself. 'Well you're not menopausal,' she said, holding up a stick that read 'pregnant', and Marjorie burst into tears.

Chapter Fifty-Nine

Davey

JULIET HAD BECOME WITHDRAWN and clingy. She didn't want to be left alone; she became his shadow, unless he was on stage. She never came to shows anymore. She wanted to go home to Nashville. She didn't mind if he hired a live-in nanny, she just wanted to get off the road. He was confused: one minute she was stuck to him, the next she was demanding to be a thousand miles away.

Juliet all but had a breakdown at Christmas when they were snowed in and all the international flights were cancelled. She spent Christmas Day in bed, crying her eyes out, and even a Skype calls from Grace, Lenny and her cousins, her gran and granda and Kyle didn't help. She was inconsolable, and nothing he did seemed to make a difference. She was unfocused, and her ability to learn was suffering.

'What can I do?' he begged her, but she said she was fine and asked him to please leave her alone, so he did. She was deeply unhappy and there seemed to be nothing he could do. *I'm failing. I'm letting her down.*

'What do you think the best thing to do is?' Francie asked one night when they were talking on the phone.

'I don't know.'

'Bollocks,' he said.

'Don't be cryptic – I'm not able for cryptic.'

'Ask yourself: what does she need, and do it. That's what being a parent is.'

'It's not working here,' he said, and the words fell out of his mouth like lead plates.

'So sort it.'

'It's not that easy. I can't let Casey down.'

'Casey will find another drummer. All that little girl has is you,' Francie said.

That was it. The decision was made, the course of his life utterly changed during one conversation. But deep down he'd known it was inevitable; from the moment he asked his dying sister to consider him as Juliet's guardian his life had changed utterly. It just took him a year and a half to notice.

He knocked on Juliet's door, armed with his new plan.

She shouted at him: 'Go away.'

'I have news,' he said.

'Please, Davey, please go away.'

She sounded so terribly sad.

'I'm sorry, Bunny,' he said, and he was met with silence, 'but I was thinking, as soon as you finish your exams we could move back to Ireland. What do you think?' he asked, talking to Juliet's closed door. He heard a rustle and then footsteps on the floor, the door unlocking and creaking open. He was met with her puffy eyes and quivering lip.

'Seriously?' she asked.

'Seriously.'

'Oh thank you, Davey,' she said, and she was crying again – happy, grateful, relieved tears – and she wrapped her arms around his waist and hugged him tightly.

'I love you, Davey,' she said, and Davey exhaled. *It's done.*

Two hours later, he received a call from Marjorie.

'I was just thinking about you—'

'Davey, are you sitting down?'

'Why?'

'I'm pregnant.'

Davey sat down with a thud.

Part Seven

The Homecoming

Chapter Sixty

Molly

THE BIG FIGHT TO end all fights happened over Christmas dinner. It had been brewing since the court date.

The solicitor, who was a friend of their family solicitor and who agreed to act for all involved, was a man named Mark Mooney. He was in his fifties and a no-nonsense kind of man, with a low tolerance for waffle. He explained to all that they would not be pleading, he'd simply be asking for disclosure to gain insight into the evidence the Garda were using. Jack turned out for the hearing and sat down at the back.

The evidence was damning – mostly against Molly, the obvious ringleader. Mark explained that while the others might get off with a fine, she might be given community service.

'I do that anyway.'

'It's a conviction, Molly.'

'I'm in my seventies – what the fuck do I care?'

But Jack cared. He was horrified. 'It's not right.' Before court they didn't communicate much, and after that they stopped sharing a bed. Jack moved into Davey's old room. She stopped cooking and he stopped caring. He went to the pub for his lunch and visited Sean and some of the lads from bowls. She carried on as though her marriage and life wasn't imploding. *Sorry.*

Despite it all, she'd pulled out all the stops for Christmas Day. Grace, Lenny and the kids came, and it had been pleasant and polite enough until they reached dessert. Lenny asked Jack how the book was coming along.

'What's this?' she asked, and Grace groaned and Lenny's face fell.

'She doesn't know?' he asked.

'The book?' she said.

'Rabbit's book is coming out in March,' he said.

'You thundering cunt!' she shouted.

Lenny stood up. 'Kids, get your coats.'

'Calm down, Molly, you're getting snotty and there's no need for it,' Jack said.

She stood up. 'I told you not to put that book into the world.'

He stood up. 'And I told you that I would do as my daughter asked.'

The kids were mesmerised.

'Coats, now!' Lenny shouted. They didn't move.

Grace stood up. 'Ma, Da, let's just talk about this.'

'You're so desperate to be something special, aren't you, Jack?'

'It's not about me, you vicious old woman.'

'It's all about you, Jack.'

'She wanted this, she wrote it on her deathbed,' he shouted.

'She had cancer in her fuckin' brain. She didn't know what she wanted.' *Sorry.*

'That's not true, Ma,' Grace said.

'She gave her daughter to a man-child who lives on a bus. Rabbit was gone long before she died.' *Sorry.*

'No. That's not true, Molly,' Jack said.

'Kids, if you don't get your poxy coats and get into the car I'll murder you myself,' Lenny said. Stephen was having dinner at Charlene's; it was just Bernard, Ryan and Jeff.

'Is it all right if we take the chocolate log?' Ryan asked.

'Go on, son,' Molly said.

'Thanks, Gran,' he said, picking up the plate.

'Happy Christmas, Gran, Granda, love you,' Bernard said.

'Don't kill each other,' Jeff said.

'Hide the bleedin' oranges, Granda,' Ryan shouted as he closed the door behind him.

Grace and Lenny left them to it. 'I'll call you later, Ma,' she said, and Molly nodded.

'I want it stopped.'

'Can't. I signed a contract back in May.'

'You lying bastard.'

'I didn't lie. I told you it was happening. You just didn't believe me.'

'I'll sue you.'

'You can't.'

'I'll find a way.'

'I don't know why you're so afraid – if you read it, you'd see how beautiful it is,' he said.

'Beautiful, oh right . . . Yeah, it was all so beautiful. A young woman being mutilated and poisoned, pissing and shitting, bleeding and crying, and don't forget the begging. It was special, all right.'

'The book is much more than that. It's about love and joy and all that good stuff that you and I were a part of, don't you remember, Molly?'

'I want you out,' she said.

'No.'

'Get out, Jack.'

'And where am I supposed to go?'

'How about your new friend Derek's? I really don't care. You're not welcome here anymore.'

'You can't do that.'

'Get out,' she said, and he knew she meant it.

She received a call from Grace two hours later.

'So me da is on the sofa.'

'Fine.'

'How long is this going to last, Ma?'

'Forever, unless you kick him out. Maybe rent him that fucking caravan,' she said, and she hung up the phone and she cried her eyes out because if she couldn't protect her child in life the very least she should have done was protect her in death. *Sorry.*

Her marriage was in the toilet and the court case hung over her like a massive weight. She pretended she was fine about it – she was Molly Hayes, after all; she'd faced worse than this. This was nothing. Except it was something. She'd broken the law and now she would face the wrath of a court. She lost sleep over it. She'd never tell anyone. *Sorry.*

After a week spent in bed, avoiding calls from her daughter, the Fingal Four, the shelter, the clothes bank and the soup kitchen, Molly finally dragged herself up and went to her GP. Angus had been her GP for thirty years.

'You don't look like yourself,' he said.

'I don't feel like meself.'

'What's going on, Molly?'

'You know the way my mother suffered a bit with her nerves?'

'I do.'

'It used to terrify me that someday I'd end up like her.'

'How do you feel, Molly?'

'Like I'm dying inside, like I want to shut down and everything just needs to stop. It's too fast, you know?'

'It's OK to be depressed.'

'No, it isn't.'

'You've lost your daughter.'

'I have,' she said, and tears slid down her face. 'I have lost her.'

'I'm going to prescribe some antidepressants. Will you take them?'

'I don't want to be like my mother,' she said.

'You're not like her, Molly, you're just grieving and you need some help, that's all.'

'I don't know if I can find me way back.'

'You'll come back. You're Molly Hayes,' he said, and he chuckled to himself.

'Yeah, and what's so great about her?'

'Seeing is believing,' he said.

She left with a prescription. She filled it that day and started her first pill the same evening.

Marjorie called to the house three days later to tell her that she was pregnant. The news came as a shock; Marjorie was no spring chicken – forty-two and her first pregnancy.

'Christ on a bike. Jesus, Mary and Saint Joseph . . .' she said, immediately placing her hand on Marjorie's stomach.

'Is it Davey? Did he do this to you, love?' she asked.

'I wouldn't put it that way,' Marjorie said.

'So it's his?' Molly said, and Marjorie nodded. Molly inhaled and tears built in her eyes. She clapped her hands together and she smiled the brightest and biggest smile.

'Well now, isn't that something?' she said, and for a moment she looked around and she was about to call out to her husband. *Jack, did you hear that? Did you hear, our Marjorie and Davey are having a baby?* But she didn't because he wasn't there, so instead she took Marjorie in her arms and she held her tightly.

'Best news ever,' she said. 'Oh, our Rabbit would have loved this.'

Marjorie burst into tears. 'Thanks, I really needed that.'

'Have you spoken to Davey?'

'Two nights ago. He says he's coming home.'

'For you and the baby.'

'He says he was coming home anyway for Juliet, but yeah, I suppose. It's complicated – he's happy, though.'

It was everything Molly had dreamed of and hoped for, her son and granddaughter returning home, and still she felt so very numb.

'You'd think he'd tell his mother.'

'I asked him if I could.'

'Who loves ya, Marjorie?' Molly said.

'Molly does,' Marjorie answered.

Davey and Juliet arrived back three months later, and following a family meeting, Jack was installed back home in the box room. Molly didn't fight – she didn't have the energy – and Jack would have agreed to almost anything to get off his daughter's sofa. Juliet took Grace's old room and Davey took his. That first week home he got busy looking to buy a home for him and Juliet. She spent a lot of time alone or with a tutor he paid five hundred euro a week to. It was an interim solution while they decided on a home and school. During those early days Davey quickly admitted to his mother that he had failed to inform Juliet of Marjorie's pregnancy.

'You are joking?'

'Now Ma, don't go mental.'

'Marjorie is nearly thirty weeks pregnant, you big gobshite.'

'I know, but she'd been acting so strange, and then she was happy and I didn't want to ruin that by making her think I was doing this for me and not her.'

Molly sighed and shook her head. 'Well, you've just gone and made things worse.'

'So help me,' he said.

'I can't turn back time, son.'

'Tell her with me.'

'Fine. We'll tell her together.'

Molly served dinner to Davey, Juliet and Jack last. He didn't seem to notice – he was just glad to be fed and that she didn't throw the plate at him. She joined them at the table.

'This is great, Gran,' Juliet said.

'Ah, it's nothing, love.'

'I missed your casseroles,' Juliet said.

'That one is a chicken chasseur, your mammy loved it.'

'It's great, Ma,' Davey said. 'Isn't it, Da?'

Jack just nodded and Molly grunted. 'That auld fella wouldn't know a chasseur from a Kiev.'

Davey panicked; he couldn't afford the conversation to go sideways. 'Marjorie's coming for dessert. Isn't she, Ma?' He was attempting to remind his mother time was of the essence.

'Oh cool, can't wait to see her,' Juliet said between bites.

'Yeah, on that . . .' Molly said, and she cleared her throat. 'Did I tell you Marjorie was having a baby?'

'No way!' Juliet seemed genuinely pleased. 'Who's the fella?' she asked, and Davey held his breath.

'Funny story . . .' Molly said, and Davey buried his head. She could tell he was regretting asking for her help.

'Do you remember the night of the gig for your ma?'

'Yeah.'

'Well, Davey and Marjorie did some celebrating of their own.'

'What do you mean?'

Jack picked up his plate of chicken chasseur and left the room.

'The baby's mine, Juliet,' Davey said, and for some reason he raised his fork in the air to underscore the point.

'Yours?'

'Isn't that lovely?' Molly said, and she could see Juliet's eyes fill.

She pushed away her plate. 'Yeah, it's great,' she said, and she ran up the stairs.

Davey cursed. 'What was that, Ma?'

'I could have told her in the form of contemporary dance and it wouldn't have made any difference.'

Juliet refused to come downstairs when Marjorie arrived. Instead she remained in her room behind a fortified door. In the sitting room Jack watched TV with the sound on at a deafening level and Molly, Davey and Marjorie ate shop-bought pavlova in relative silence.

Jack and Molly lived as strangers under one roof, while Davey tried to placate his parents and Juliet and forge a new relationship with Marjorie. Molly watched from the periphery but she didn't engage. *What will be, will be.* It wasn't going to be easy, her with a baby on board and him the substitute parent of a teenager and with a lifetime of selfishness to overcome. She didn't know if it would work out but she hoped it would. She just kept taking her tablets and hoping she'd start to feel something again. *Sorry.*

Chapter Sixty-One

Marjorie

CHANGE WAS COMING AND it was coming hard and fast and Marjorie wasn't prepared.

We're family now, Rabbit.

We were always family, Marj.

What does Johnny think of this? she asked her dead friend one day.

Johnny doesn't think because Johnny's dead, Rabbit replied. She chuckled to herself.

She talked to Davey on the phone a lot during the three-month period when he was boxing up his life in America and preparing to ship out. Many of their conversations turned into negotiations on ways to move forward. He was all in.

'We don't need to pretend that anything will change between us,' Marjorie said.

'Not true,' he said. 'Coming home was the hardest decision I ever made. The only highlight was seeing you. I was about to call you to tell you that when you rang. I love you, Marj, always have, always will.'

It took a while for it to sink in and for her to believe it.

What do you think, Rabbit?

You love him, Marj, always have and always will.

Finally he arrived home and landed on her doorstep with a large bunch of flowers and a big grin. She burst into tears in his arms and they sat on the sofa and she cried and ate cake as he stared at her stomach and wrapped his hands around it. They laughed and she cried. They talked and she cried. They kissed and she cried. They had sex and she cried right through it, but she also smiled and moaned and yelled the words 'Oh thank you, sweet baby Jesus!' as she rode him like she was breaking a bucking bronco.

Her mother reacted to her pregnancy surprisingly well.

'Well, your life is over.'

'Can you please be happy for me?'

'I am, a new life is a wonderful thing and, let's face it, you've had a good run.'

'Thanks,' she said, knowing that was the best her mother could offer her. *Rabbit, behind all the misery, Vera's thrilled. I miss ya, Baldy.*

What started out as a house-hunt for two ended up being for four. Marjorie put her flat up for sale despite Davey's protestations. He could afford a house without her but if she was in she was all in. He understood. Juliet was not so amenable.

'So now she's living with us? Are you for real?' Juliet said, right in front of Marjorie's face.

'Whoa, who's this "she"? This is Marjorie we're talking about,' Davey said.

Juliet just walked out of the room. He couldn't work out what was wrong with her. 'I've explained everything, ten times over. She knows I love her more than life. She knows we're a family.' He tried and Marjorie tried; Molly tried; Grace tried;

Jack tried; even Francie and Jay had tried. She slammed her bedroom door on all of them.

The twins turned to Marjorie and the assembled Hayeses, who were hoping that if anyone could reach her it would be one of the Byrne brothers.

'She's a hard nut to crack,' Jay said.

'Just like her ma,' Francie said.

'She'll find her way back to us in her own time,' Molly said, and she patted Marjorie's shoulder. 'You've done nothing wrong.'

Marjorie understood. 'It's a lot of change, Davey, it's hard for me to keep up, never mind Juliet.'

She empathised with Juliet and was determined to get through to her, but the child that had once been her friend now seemed hell-bent on being enemies. *I don't know what to do, Rabbit. How do I fix it? What would you do?*

I'd hang in there, Marj.

Marjorie was tired all the time and doing her best to get through her workdays trying to keep up with enthusiastic millennials spitballing ideas while battling the urge to wee, vomit, fart or belch. Add to that her new boss's disgust with her condition. He tried his best to hide it, but maternity leave left him a staff member down for the six months she'd be out. She'd only come through the bloody door; she had not earned the right to leave them in the lurch. It was embarrassing and unprofessional and she found herself quite apologetic about her unexpected fertility. She did her best to compensate, working overtime to ensure she impressed, and she was impressive despite her swollen ankles and afternoon power naps. She didn't want to lose her perfect job. She didn't want to lose Davey or the baby or even Juliet, although she was being a bitchy teenager; finally Marjorie had something to lose. It was overwhelming, with the raging hormones and the fears of what if and the tests required to ensure this geriatric mother was giving birth to a healthy child. She aced every test, most of which Davey attended, and every time the result came back he did a little victory dance.

'A-OK, Marj, A-OK.'

Do you hear that, Rabbit? A-OK. A-OK.

Grace was really supportive; she gave solid advice and was always there to answer questions.

'I wanted to punch Davey in the face when he said good morning, am I losing it?'

'No, perfectly natural.'

'I want to cry all the time, is that normal?'

'Yip.'

'I want to have sex and cry and punch Davey in the face all at the same time, is that normal?'

'One hundred per cent.'

'Jesus, baking a baby is hard.'

'This is the easy bit. Wait till you have to hide the knives from yourself. Welcome to motherhood.'

Grace was always a little nuttier than you or me – right, Rabbit?

Oh yeah.

It was her last day at work. Marjorie was finishing up early and handing over to her colleagues before shopping with her mother and then meeting Davey to sign contracts for a large four-bed semi-detached house overlooking the sea in Clontarf. She was living the dream – someone else's dream, but still, it was a dream. She was way too pregnant to enjoy it, though; she was a tiny woman with a ginormous bump. Her stomach looked like a balloon about to burst, and she felt like she had burst, about two weeks to go. *I can't do this.* She pulled a wonky eyelash out and it felt like she was being stabbed in the eyelid and she screamed with pain. Everything hurt. And she was tired, so incredibly tired. She couldn't sleep, hadn't slept properly for weeks; the baby kicked and punched and played soccer with her bladder and did unforgivable things to her bowel. Her indigestion was off the charts. Food became her enemy. She'd always loved food. She missed it. Towards the end she lived on crackers and cake.

Her flat had sold within three weeks of going on the market and, after a bidding war, she made a nice profit. The recession was over. She'd bought the place at a rock-bottom price; the economy was on the rise. Davey had rented a place for the three of them. For the first few months she and he slept in the same room. That was weird but it was also nice; then she became so big that she needed all of the bed. The twisting and turning, the overheating and getting up every five minutes wasn't conducive to sharing space or intimacy of any kind. Davey moved into the spare room.

'Trouble already?' Juliet had said flatly the morning after the night he moved.

'Marjorie just needs her space.'

'This is a joke,' she said, and she ate her breakfast in her room.

'What's the difference between a snowman and a snow-woman? Snowballs. That's a joke,' he shouted after her.

'That's a joke?' Marjorie said. 'You're as bad as my mother.'

'I didn't say it was good.' He kissed her. 'She'll be OK – believe it or not, she seems happier than she was in the States.'

'That is not comforting,' Marjorie said.

'No.'

They held onto each other for a while. It was nice but also hot and sticky, and she battled an awareness of extraordinary pressure on a part of her body she'd never really taken any time to consider before – her perineum. If the baby didn't burst out she worried it would fall out.

Her co-workers celebrated Marjorie's maternity leave with cakes in the break room, and despite the fact that she'd only been working there eight months, everyone put in money to give her a card and a cute baby growbag. She was grateful and emotional and promised faithfully to be back within six months and raring to go. She cried in the car on the way to her mother's because she wasn't sure if she could keep that promise. *I'm so tired. I'm too old to be a new mother. This baby will kill me.* Her mother was waiting at the door. She had her shopping bag and her walking stick ready to go.

'How was your last day?' Vera said.

'Good, and it wasn't my last day.'

'That's what you think.'

'Please don't be negative,' she said.

'OK. You look lovely.'

'I look like an alien is about to burst out of me.'

'You're glowing.'

'I'm sweating.'

'You don't make being nice to you easy, Marjorie.'

'Sorry.'

'Can we stop for a coffee and a cake?' her mother asked.

'Go on, then.'

Vera smiled. 'Something with jam and cream.'

Vera Shaw had mellowed. It had been a slow and almost imperceptible process but she seemed less bitter, happier even; she received pleasure from little things that would never have pleased her before, and it was joyful.

'Whatever you want, Ma,' Marjorie said.

'Mammy,' Vera said.

'Mammy.'

'And I'd like to pick up something for the baby.'

'You don't have to do that.'

'I'd like to.'

Marjorie felt like crying again – happy tears. 'Thanks, Mammy.'

They spent an hour shopping in the centre, and by the time they'd picked up all of Vera's shopping and something nice for the baby, Marjorie needed to sit down and eat. She couldn't touch coffee or tea, the heartburn was ridiculous, so she drank a glass of cold milk and tucked into a slice of double-chocolate cheesecake while her mother enjoyed a Victoria sponge with extra cream. Marjorie was halfway through her cake when her mother brought up the subject of her father.

'Would you like your father to know about the baby?' she said.

Marjorie nearly choked. 'No.'

'I understand, but are you sure?'

'I'm positive. He doesn't care about me – why would he care about the baby?'

'I don't know,' she said. 'It just seems like news you pass on.'

'Well it isn't.'

'OK.'

Marjorie went off her food. She drank the milk she would not have touched before she was baking a baby.

Vera played with her food. 'No one's perfect,' she said.

'I know that.'

'Some of us are far from it. I wasn't a good mother. I know that.'

'You were fine, Mammy.'

'In my experience, fine is not good.'

'I don't know what you want me to say.'

'Nothing. I'm just apologising – you deserved better, that's all.'

Marjorie cried openly. Vera finished her cake.

In the car ride home they talked about Grace's looming oophorectomy and Molly's court case, which was scheduled for the next day. Vera wasn't judgmental about Grace removing her ovaries, or mean about Molly's war on the law. She wanted to be, Marjorie could see her internal struggle written all over her face, but she kept quiet and it was appreciated. They talked about the new house and how nice it would be to be beside the sea. As they parted Marjorie took the opportunity to apologise to her mother.

'I'm sorry.'

Vera turned to her. 'For what?'

'For the state of your fanny.'

Vera chuckled. 'That wasn't you,' she said, cupping Marjorie's face, 'that was them,' and she raised her finger to the sky, her voice quivering a little.

'I'm sorry anyway,' Marjorie said, and she meant it. Her mother gave birth to her and it destroyed her – finally she empathised.

Vera smiled and said, 'You'll be a good mother,' before getting out of the car.

Marjorie couldn't speak so she just waved and drove off, but she cried so hard she had to pull in by the side of the road because she couldn't see straight. A copper leaned in. 'You all right, love?'

'My mother just told me she loved me, well, not in those words but . . . yeah . . . she loves me,' she said.

He was staring at her mighty bump. 'Due any day, are ya?'

'Two weeks.'

'Brain fried?'

'Yeah.'

'Do you want an escort?'

'Ah, no.'

'Sure?'

'I'll just cry for a bit longer, if that's OK.'

'There's a car park just in behind the bar on the corner, lash in there and you cry as much as you want to.'

'Thanks,' she said, and she pulled into a spot behind the bar and bawled like a baby. *If you could see me now, Rabbit.*

Chapter Sixty-Two

Davey

DAVEY HAD TO RECONSIDER what he would do for a living. He still loved music and wanted to work in music, but just not schlepping around playing drums every night. He wanted a home life with Juliet, Marj and the baby. He looked online at college courses; there was a music degree he could apply for. He researched it and he knew it was for him. He'd get his degree, he'd even do a masters. He could teach. He'd like that. It felt right. He was scared of course, but he didn't miss his old life. Before Juliet he had been so lonely. He just hadn't really noticed.

She became my world, Rabbit.

I know.

She's still my world.

Tell her.

I'm trying.

Marjorie and the baby felt right, too. After everything they had been through, they just fit. They understood one another. She saw the best in him and was patient with the worst in him. *Like Rabbit.* He had no fear and concern when it came to their relationship. But Juliet worried him. *What am I missing here, Rabbit?*

Just keep pushing, Davey.

It kept him awake. He tried to talk to her but she shut him out. He worried about his mother, too. She wasn't the same woman. She was diminished. His dad was heartbroken and both of them were so angry. He worried for them, worried for everyone, but yet he was happier than he'd ever been and he dared to hope everything would work out.

Chapter Sixty-Three

Grace

Sex is a habit and, as it turned out, an easy one to break. After the first attempt, when Lenny could not achieve erection, both Grace and Lenny pretended it wasn't a big deal and that they could move on quickly. They didn't, though; instead one or both of them used any and every possible excuse to get out of intimacy. Grace had her aches and her pains, Lenny his long hours and work stresses. One month turned into two, then three into four and so on until they were nine months down the line and they had barely touched one another. They didn't talk about it, due to an unspoken agreement. They got on well together, still loved one another, made each other laugh and were there for each other, but it was a big problem, and as much as they pretended everything was fine, it was far from it. Another time bomb was just waiting to explode. *Fucking great.*

Marjorie's pregnancy had brought Grace and Marjorie even closer together. Grace would even go as far as calling Marjorie a real friend. She wondered if Rabbit would mind. *She's always going to be your best friend, Rabbit. I'm just a stand-in.* Grace had friends of her own, of course, but they were all busy bringing up children, and if she was honest she let them slide. The girls met once or twice a year for a celebration or Christmas drinks and then it was small talk and laughing about the past – no one brought their troubles to those nights. Marjorie was there for Grace in a way her own friendship circle couldn't be. Marjorie understood. She'd been through it with Rabbit. Still, she kept most of her concerns to herself most of the time. Marjorie provided much-needed hope. Rabbit was gone, her own breasts gone, her ovaries soon to be gone, but now, amidst all this loss, a brand-new Hayes was being born. *Who would have thought it?*

They'd lunched together two days earlier, when Marjorie didn't have long because she was trying to finish up a funding proposal before she began her maternity leave. They ate in a little café near Marjorie's office.

Grace had been tinkering with the idea of talking through her uneventful sex life with Marjorie for a while, and Marjorie was sitting in front of her and she was so desperate for a ride it actually hurt her . . .

'Marj?'

'Yeah?'

'Can I ask you something?'

'Absolutely.'

'How do I get my husband to fancy me again?'

Marjorie nearly choked on a piece of cake.

'Oh.'

'Yeah.'

'Have you had sex since . . .?'

'No.'

'Because . . .'

'We tried once. He couldn't get it up.'

'And that was?'

'Two months after surgery.'

Marjorie pushed the cake away and drank from her glass of milk.

'I'm desperate, and my ma is MIA, so . . .'

'Have you spoken about it?'

'Speaking about sex makes it worse, doesn't it? It should be natural.'

'Have you done the sexy underwear thing?'

'Yes, I have a drawer full of it.'

'Have you just grabbed him by the collar and had your way?'

'No, that's rape.'

'You know what I mean.'

'What if he's disgusted by me?'

'He's not – he couldn't be, you look amazing.'

'You've haven't seen me.'

'I'm looking at you right now.'

'He couldn't have sex with me, first time ever, and he watched me give birth to four big babies.'

'He also took care of you after surgery, he bathed you, he plastered you in all those expensive creams, he took care of that infection around your port, he was there for the filling of your expanders, he saw the pain you endured and how delicate you were.'

'You think he associates my breasts with pain?'

'I think you have undergone something incredibly traumatic, both of you.'

'You're not as thick as you look, Marj,' Grace said.

Marjorie smiled. 'Coming from you, that's a huge compliment.'

Grace needed a day or two to think about what Marjorie had said. She had a point. Lenny had basically nursed her back to health single-handed, because of her fear of blood; she'd refused to take any responsibility for her own care. It made sense. Of course Marjorie might be wrong, and in that case her marriage would slowly implode, but if there was a chance she was right, she needed to show her husband that she was fine, better than fine: she was healthy, robust and her new breasts were healed and perfect and pain-free. They got a little cold in winter, but other than that she was good to go. It was timely in that Lenny had the morning off as he was flying out to a conference in London that afternoon. She took a shower, plastered herself in cream and perfume and put on her newest and sexiest piece of lingerie. She fixed the girls, positioned them just right. She looked in the mirror, cupping them. 'We can do this.'

The kids were in school, Stephen was in college and Lenny was downstairs reading the newspaper at the kitchen table. She walked into the room in her black one-piece lingerie and a pair of thigh-high boots, which she'd bought in an online sale when drunk and emotional. He had his back to her, so it didn't have the impact she was hoping for. She walked towards him and put her hand on his shoulder.

'You all right, love?' he said without glancing her way.

'No, but I will be,' she said, and she grabbed his face and turned it her way. She was holding him a little too firmly and it was all a little awkward, so she let go and stood back and put her hand on her hip like the kids do on Instagram.

'What's this?' he asked.

'You know what it is,' she said.

'Ah Grace . . .'

'No,' she said, and she straddled him on the kitchen chair and kissed him and put his hands on her boobs and held them there. 'This is happening,' she said, and suddenly she was on her back on the table and her husband was between her legs and before either could say boo to a goose they were moving together, his hands all over her, and it wasn't exactly the same as before. For a start it was their first time having sex on the table her children ate their breakfast on, and she wasn't sure but she thought she could feel a wet teabag on her back – it was different and nice and, above all, sexy as hell. There was life after mastectomy and dermal implants, and there would be life after an oophorectomy.

They took themselves into the shower and had sex again – this time less intense, more intimate, both of them naked, stripped bare. Lenny touched her new breasts in a way that wasn't medical, and the more she encouraged him the less tentative he became.

'You won't break them.'

'Any pain?'

'None.'

'Any sensation?'

'Yes,' she said, and he sighed and he looked like he was going to cry, so she kissed him. She was surprised she had some feeling, not just tingling, and the sharp nerve pain was totally gone. It was pleasant, it was comforting, and she felt like she was home.

Afterwards they lay in bed together for an hour, just staring at each other's facial expressions and tracing each other's body contours. They were like kids, rediscovering themselves and each other. They talked easily and laughed at silly things; they were like a young couple, new to one another and excited.

'Why did this take so long?' he asked.

'I think we were both suffering a little PTSD,' she said.

'I wish we'd done it sooner, me balls have been bursting.'

'I had a little lady-bursting of my own going on.'

'You're having the oophorectomy in a month's time.'

'We're not going to let this happen again,' she said.

'You're going to experience the change.'

'It will be managed. I will manage it. We know what we're doing now, right?'

'Your ma was mental.'

'My ma is mental.'

'You're kind of mental, too.'

She laughed. 'It's going to be fine.'

'Yeah,' he said, and they had sex for a third time. She was exhausted, and poor Lenny felt so depleted he considered missing his flight. He left in a taxi and she passed out into a blissful sleep, but before she did she counted her blessings.

Chapter Sixty-Four

Jack

JACK FOUND MOLLY'S ANTIDEPRESSANTS one day while she was out making soup or sorting clothes or God knows what. He rifled through her room trying to find evidence of the woman he still loved. The tablets were a shock. *This is not you, Molly. Where did you go?* He didn't tell anyone about it. He didn't say anything to Molly; he just watched out for her as much as he could and he tried his best to be as considerate and kind as she'd let him. Davey tried to talk to both of them but he didn't get very far – they weren't fighting, there was no shouting or cross talk, and his mother's lethargy was insurmountable.

He was worried about the court case. He wasn't sure how it was going to go. He'd never been to court before in his life. It was daunting. He wasn't even sure if his wife wanted her family there, but they all planned to go – the Hayeses in court en masse. *Oh God.* He hadn't mentioned the fact that he'd signed up for a water bill. He didn't see the point in aggravating his wife further, but now, with the case only one day away, he was afraid that it would come up in court. It would be a shock for her to be told her husband had betrayed everything she fought for while she was on the stand defending herself; it definitely wouldn't end well. She might even kill him.

The doorbell rang after eleven. Molly was out and Jack had been snoozing in the chair. He woke with a start and composed himself, calling out to the insistent man or woman with their thumb jammed against the bell, 'I'll be right there.'

He opened the door to a delivery man holding a large cardboard box.

'Jack Hayes?'

'Yes.'

'Sign here,' he said, and he pointed. Jack signed. He handed him the box. It was heavy. He dropped it as soon as he closed the door. It didn't occur to him what it could be. He grabbed a knife from the kitchen and sliced through the thick tape holding the box together. He opened it and found tissue paper and pulled it away and his heart threatened to stop – it was Rabbit's book, maybe thirty of them piled up on top of one another. He pulled one out and held it in his hands. *Never Let Go* by Rabbit Hayes. The cover was white with a sketch of Rabbit on the front. It was beautiful. He hugged it and cried.

He'd pulled himself together by the time his wife came home. She walked in weighed down by shopping and he took it from her and placed it on the kitchen table.

'I have something for you, and you're not going to like it,' he said. Then he handed her the book and it took her breath away. She sat.

'I'm sorry,' he said. 'But it's what she wanted.'

Molly turned it over and saw a small postage-stamp photo of Rabbit on the back. She held it close to her heart and closed her eyes and smiled. It seemed to be going well, so Jack took the opportunity to inform her he'd signed them up for a water bill. She then took careful aim and threw the book at him.

Chapter Sixty-Five

Molly

JACK WENT RUNNING AND Molly collected herself and picked the book off the floor. She held it and cried. *What will they say about you, Rabbit? What cruel things will some stranger throw your way? How will they justify their spite? How can I bear it without taking up arms and going to war with every single one of them? #AllDressedUpNowhereToGo.*

Things had been getting slightly better; the medication had kicked in and she didn't feel the same level of lethargy and despair, but she still fought to recover her old self. Davey and Juliet's return was a big boost, and of course the baby was a blessing, a miracle even, but it was also another huge source of concern. *What if it's sick? What if it dies? What if it kills poor Marjorie?* How could she be happy about it until she knew the baby and Marjorie were safe and sound? She couldn't take more sickness and death. She'd rather her heart just stopped and she died than suffer another loss. She held her breath and she waited for something good or bad to happen, and in the meantime she had to face a judge and she wasn't going to enjoy it, because in a court of law the judge had all the power and she had none; this as a dynamic that did not suit her. She missed her husband, too. She missed his tenderness and their

381

long talks about everyday things; they used to be such a great team and she'd sidelined him, and she knew he'd try to fix it if he could. Although signing up to Irish Water really was the last straw. *What the hell were you thinking, old man?*

She made a cup of tea and she was still holding the book. She sliced off a piece of cake and she was still holding the book. She drank her tea and ate the cake and she was still holding onto the book. She looked at the photo of her beautiful girl; she traced her fingers around the raised lettering that spelled Rabbit's name. *What did you want to let the whole world know, Rabbit? What did you need to say so badly? How can this text exist without me reading it? How can I survive even one page now that you're gone?*

Pauline knocked on the window.

'There you are, Molly.'

Molly opened the door still holding the book close to her chest and under her cardigan.

'Did I catch you reading?' Pauline said, pushing into the kitchen.

'Something like that.'

Pauline put the kettle on. 'I'm walking the walls over there, Molly. I keep having nightmares that I'm going to end up in a shell suit with arrows all over it and locked into a birdcage.'

'You were always as odd as fuck, Pauline.'

'True,' she said. Pauline made tea for herself and for Molly. 'Do you think they'll go easy on us, Molly?' she asked.

'They'll go easy on you, Pauline.'

'No, no, if you go down, I'll go down too,' Pauline said, and it made Molly smile. Pauline would have done anything for the Molly who had saved her all those years ago, but that was the old Molly. *This Molly isn't worth fighting for, Pauline.* She told her friend not to be so silly. 'We're old women, Pauline – what can they do to us that hasn't already been done?'

She left soon after, and Molly took the book she'd been hugging into the sitting room and she closed the door, sat down and opened it, and she read.

My name is Rabbit Hayes. I died aged forty on 28 May 2014. It was a cold but sunny day. I can't tell you exactly how it ended because, well, I'm dead, but I know that one thing's for sure, I wasn't alone. My family and friends remained no matter how long, uncomfortable, sad or terrible the whole sorry business was. That's the thing about a terminal disease: in the end it's just a waiting game. I can see it all now, Ma by my side, cursing the whole world and dodgy-dealing with God . . .

Heavy tears coursed down her face. *Sorry, love. I'm so sorry.*

Chapter Sixty-Six

Juliet

JULIET'S RELATIONSHIP WITH KYLE was strained since she'd come home. After the assault she had pulled away from him and everybody, cocooning herself from the world, living life in the smallest bubble she could find. She ran and hid from her attacker. She discovered after a month of avoiding the gig venues and the hotel restaurants and bars, double-locking her hotel doors and sometimes resting a chair against them, that he was not interested in a repeat performance, he was one and done. It didn't help – not really – she was still scared and traumatised and felt so utterly alone. Back in the States she'd wanted to tell Davey but she didn't have the language for it. She just couldn't bring herself to say it, and what would happen if she did say anything? Everything would kick off and maybe she'd have to face him again. She felt sick inside every time she thought about that. She'd rather just bury it deep and try her very hardest to move on.

When Davey announced the move home, relief washed through with the force of a burst dam, and the invisible weight pinning her down slowly dissipated and finally lifted and floated away. Juliet Hayes, although still acutely traumatised, felt lighter and brighter than she had in years.

Davey saw her pain. He was moving home for her and leaving his old life behind because he loved her and because she was enough. With Davey by her side, she could leave Trevor behind and bury the memory of his terrible act in a foreign land. She believed that they could start again surrounded by family and friends who would never hurt her. When Davey's secret was revealed and she was face to face with Marjorie's bloated belly, she realised Davey didn't see her pain. He hadn't moved home for her. He had left his old life because he loved Marjorie and the baby. She wasn't enough. She was nothing. Trevor saw that she was nothing and had no one; that's why he did what he did.

She avoided Kyle more than she saw him and he tried to understand what had changed, but how could he? She didn't have it in her to explain that she'd never really fancied him; he had been a nice distraction from grief and a link to home, but after her encounter with Trevor she'd rather be alone.

One afternoon she met Kyle in a coffee shop on Wicklow Street. He was sitting by the window.

'How come you're off school?' she asked.

'Teachers' meeting.'

'Oh.'

'Thanks for meeting me,' he said.

'I was in town anyway.'

'Oh.'

'I think we should break up,' he said, and he couldn't look at her – he just stared out the window at a busker singing and clacking his knees together, playing a tambourine . . . badly.

'Were we really even going out?' she said, and that really hurt him. He flashed her an angry look.

'Sorry, didn't mean it,' she said, and she was relieved it was over.

'You don't care, do you?'

'Sorry,' she said.

I'm a user, Ma.

Everybody needs somebody, Bunny.

Don't call me Bunny.

I'm dead, I'll call you what I want.

He got up to leave. 'I did like kissing you,' she said, but he didn't turn to face her, he just pushed his way out through the crowded coffee shop; but she could see as he walked down the street he was wiping his eyes. She felt nothing at all.

Maybe I'll never fall in love, Ma.

She got the bus to Francie's house. She knocked on the door and one of his kids answered, she wasn't sure which one, a handsome boy with cool hair and brilliant eyes. He looked her up and down.

'Yeah?'

'Hi, I'm Juliet. Is your da in?'

'How old are you?' he said.

'Nearly fifteen. How old are you?'

'Seventeen and a bit.' He grinned before turning away from her.

'Da!' he roared down the hall. 'There's a girl at the door, says her name is Juliet.'

Francie appeared on the stairs. 'Juliet Hayes,' he said. 'What can I do you for?' he said.

'I need to talk to you about a grave,' she said. His son, whom he introduced as Darren, looked at him. 'So she's not an illegit, then?'

Francie laughed. 'She's too attractive to be mine, clearly – fuckin' state of you.' He ruffled his son's hair.

'Charming,' Darren said.

'Get in here and have some pancakes with us.'

They made their way into the kitchen. Darren dished out the pancakes. The longer Juliet stared Darren's way, the more handsome he became, so handsome she blushed every time he looked back at her.

'Syrup or chocolate?' he asked.

'Syrup,' she said, and she watched him pour the syrup. He had really strong arms.

'Say when, or he's going to drown you in it,' Francie said.

'Sorry, when,' Juliet said, and Darren handed her a plate of syrup with a pancake on the side. Once she had the pancake in her she refocused on the task at hand.

'You know Johnny Faye's ma, don't you?'

'Like me own,' Francie said.

'Will you talk to her for me?'

'About what?'

'About putting me ma's ashes in the grave with Johnny.'

Francie grimaced. 'Ah.'

'Where are they now?' Darren asked, sitting down beside her. His leg touched hers and she nearly peed her pants.

'Most are in a big urn in a wardrobe, and then the rest are in silver hearts all over the place.'

'Jaysus,' he said, 'that's mad.' He offered her another pancake.

She blushed. 'No thanks.'

'Lash it over here,' Francie said, and Darren threw the pancake on his plate. 'The thing is, we can't just pop Rabbit's ashes into the grave, we have to pay for the plot and make it official.'

'That's what I want, all official, me ma's name on the gravestone. I have the money,' she said.

'Right,' he said, and he wasn't smiling or as assured as he usually was.

'What's wrong?' she asked.

'It's just that I think that's a family plot for the Fayes.'

'Can't they shove me Ma in there too? She's only little now that she's ashes.'

'Let me talk to Karen,' he said, and she grinned. 'I'm not promising anything.'

'I know.'

'So stop grinning like that.'

'Can't.'

'Why not?' Darren asked.

'Because if anyone can talk someone into doing anything it's your da,' Juliet said, her face now the colour of a tomato. Darren was getting even better-looking with every passing second. The room felt hot.

'Are you OK?' he asked.

'I think I'm coming down with something,' she said, and Francie got up and put his arm around her and walked her to the door. 'I've seen that look before – on your ma's face when she looked at Johnny Faye.'

She looked back at Darren. 'See ya, Darren,' she said, and he nodded, smiled and waved.

'Hope you feel better soon,' Darren said.

Juliet grinned at Francie.

'Don't start stalking that fella,' he said.

'As if,' she said.

'Yeah, right – if you're anything like your mother, you'll be in a building across the road with night vision glasses and a pair of fuckin' handcuffs.'

Juliet giggled to herself. He opened the front door and she walked outside into the cool air.

'Do you think Mrs Faye will say yes?'

'I don't know but I'll talk to her, and Davey too.'

'Do you think it's weird?'

'Just about weird enough.'

'Thanks, Francie,' she said, and she skipped down the road.

Ma, guess what: I think I'm in love with Darren Byrne.

Chapter Sixty-Seven

Davey

THE SOLICITOR, MAX MURPHY, called Davey and Marjorie into his office. They all shook hands and he observed that the bump was coming along and then they moved quickly to business. He talked about the sale, what they were buying and the legals around it. They were in the enviable position of being able to buy the house outright and without a mortgage. Davey was putting the majority of the money in. Max went through the division of the monies, and that's when Marjorie asked to be excused and ran out of the room.

'Everything all right?' Max asked.

'Doesn't look like it,' Davey said, and he followed her out and to the bathroom she'd locked herself in. He knocked on the door.

'Marjorie?'

'Hi.'

'Any chance you'd open the door?'

She opened the door and he squeezed in. She was sitting on the toilet but thankfully the lid was down.

'What are we doing, Davey?'

'We're buying a house, Marj.'

'No, you're buying a house, I'm throwing in a few quid for a sofa.'

'We're buying a house, Marj.'

'Why?'

'Because we're together.'

'Why?'

'Because you're having my baby.'

'People have babies all the time, it doesn't mean they move in together.'

'Are you happy, Marjorie?'

'That's not the point.'

'I think it is,' he said.

'I think we're rushing into things, Davey,' she said, and tears poured from her eyes.

'If I hadn't got pregnant—'

But you did get pregnant, against all odds.'

'You're not going to start talking about miracles – Rabbit would turn in her grave.'

'How do you feel?' he asked, and he felt nervous of the answer because if it was the wrong one it could shatter him.

'I've never been happier,' she admitted.

'What's so bad about that?'

'Rabbit's gone, and I've never been happier.' She was crying again. He held her and he felt the same way. Then he reached into his pocket.

'I was waiting for the right moment,' he said, and he showed her the box in his hand, then flipped it open to reveal a diamond ring.

'I know you're fussy. We'll exchange it for whatever you want. I just wanted to have something when I asked you to marry me.'

She looked at the ring and then at Davey. He could see she was starting to panic again.

'We can be engaged for as long as you like if you'll marry me. Will you? Marry me?'

She smiled and nodded. 'It will be at least two years, the kid will be walking or maybe in school.'

'That sounds good to me,' he said.

'This is insane,' she replied.

'It's perfectly normal,' he said. 'We're having a kid, buying a house and getting married. No big deal.'

'You have changed, haven't you, Davey?'

'Had to,' he said, and he took the ring out of the box and placed it on her finger.

She looked at it and smiled and they kissed. Then she took it off and put it back in the box.

'Don't want to damage it before it goes back,' she said. He placed the ring back in his pocket and reached for her hand to pull her upright. 'What about Juliet?' she asked.

'We'll keep this to ourselves, and when she comes round – and she will – we'll tell her and she'll be happy.'

'You sound so sure of yourself.'

'Well, someone has to be sure of me,' he said, and he winked at her. *I've been king of the gobshites long enough.*

They went back into the room and they signed the documents for their new home and the old Davey would have felt burdened and beleaguered by the prospect of marriage, a house and a baby, but this new Davey felt free as a bird.

Chapter Sixty-Eight

Molly

MOLLY SAT ON HER sofa for four hours solid reading her daughter's book; her legs were numb, her back was sore, her arse felt like it was on fire and she had a bladder that was threatening to burst, but she couldn't put it down. She inhaled every word. *There ya are, love. There ya are.* It was astounding to be so close to her daughter once again. She was dead to the world, but inside those pages she was vibrant and very much alive. *My girl.* Jack was right. She had nothing to fear; it didn't matter what naysayers said. Haters gonna hate and fuck them, her girl was going to soar. *Sorry.*

The door opened behind her and Grace appeared.

'Hiya, Ma.'

'Hiya, love.'

'What are you doing?'

'Reading Rabbit's book.'

'No way,' Grace said, and her mother lifted the book and showed her the front cover.

'Happy?' Grace asked.

'It's like she's here and still with us, Grace.'

'It's beautiful,' Grace said, and took it in her hands and turned it over and read the back. 'It's really happening.'

'No thanks to me.'

'Ah, Ma, you were just trying to protect her. I get it.'

'I'm an old fool.'

'You are no fool,' Grace said.

They went into the kitchen and Molly made tea and they opened the book onto a page she'd highlighted. Grace read the passages out loud and they reminisced and laughed together. It was lovely – going back in time to the eighties when Rabbit talked about her childhood, the band and Johnny, *Swap Shop* on the TV, climbing trees, falling from trees, hanging out with Grace, stalking poor Davey, big hair, batwing jumpers, long leather coats, having nothing, having everything, and that old avocado bathroom.

'That avocado bathroom – you thought you were the bee's knees, Ma.'

'Jaysus, Grace, it was ugly, and poor Pauline saved up for ten years to buy a putrid pink one, just as everyone else was getting a clue and changing back to white – she still has it, the poor cow.'

She read out another part of the book: Rabbit talking about mighty Molly's famous temper.

'God Almighty, am I that bad, Gracie?' she said.

'Nah, Ma, you're better.'

Molly laughed to herself; she felt more at ease than she had in nearly two years and still she was sorry, so very sorry.

'It's like she's in the room, Ma,' Grace said.

'Yes. Yes it is, love.' *Sorry.*

Molly's family didn't know what she had done, how she had let Rabbit down. *Sorry.* She had kept it to herself for one year and nine months. *Sorry.* How could they know? *Sorry.*

Everyone around Molly believed the change in her was down to grief but it was guilt, and a mother's guilt is so much worse. *Sorry. Oh Rabbit, I'm so, so sorry.* Her dad hadn't let her down, though. He'd fought for her. Molly wanted to see him, to tell him what a good man he was. He was playing bowls but she couldn't wait. She wanted to forgive him even if she couldn't forgive herself.

Chapter Sixty-Nine

Grace

Grace parked her car outside the clubhouse and they both got out and walked up the steps, through the clubhouse and out the other side to the viewing area. Jack and his bowls friends were engaged in a serious game. They watched for a minute or two before the rain started to fall and Molly got bored.

'Jack,' she shouted. 'Jack Hayes.' He looked up and she waved. His face went pale and he started running.

'Oh God, Ma, he thinks something's wrong,' Grace said, and she ran to meet him to let him know all was well before he had a heart attack. He was halfway up the steps and gasping when she reached him. 'Everything's fine, Da,' she said.

'Are you sure?' he said.

'She's sure,' Molly said, and Grace stepped back.

'Molly?'

'I've been reading the book.' She hugged him tight. 'You were right and I was wrong.'

'About everything?'

'Don't push your luck.'

He hugged her back and Grace watched her mother tell her father she'd missed him.

'I missed you too, Molly.'

'I said some things in anger, Jack, and I didn't mean them – you're a good man, a good father, and I'm sorry.'

'I've had a lot of good days in my life, Molly, but this is right up there with the best.'

Jack left his game of bowls behind and he and Molly took off in his car for a drive and a bit of late lunch. They had a lot of catching up to do. Grace watched them drive away together. Jack was as happy as a man could be and it was nice to see. Their relationship had been slightly strained since the operation. He tried his best, and it was mostly business as usual, but there was a silence on the subject that just sat between them, a large elephant in the room that wouldn't go away – not until the next operation was done and dusted and maybe not even then. It didn't matter, though; they still loved one another and there was no point dwelling on the subject. She agreed with him on one thing: she'd had some good days in her life, but seeing them take off together put this one up there with the best of them.

Part Eight

The Court Case

Chapter Seventy

Grace

LENNY MADE THE KIDS sandwiches and Grace ran around trying to tidy the place, dress herself, fix her hair and apply make-up for her mother's court appearance. Stephen wanted to talk about whether or not it was time he moved out.

'There's a room for rent in a house near the university.'

'A room in the house that your girlfriend lives in,' Lenny said.

'Yeah.'

'Is it her room?' Grace said.

'Yeah.'

'You're not even twenty and you want to move in with a girl?' Lenny asked.

'There's five other people in the house,' Stephen said.

'Your father and I are not paying for it.'

'I earn enough for rent, working in the bar.'

'And what about food and bills?' Lenny asked.

'I'll take an extra shift if I have to and I'll make shitloads in the summer.'

'Lenny?' Grace said, walking around the kitchen looking for something, but she couldn't quite remember what, with Stephen following. 'What do you think?'

'I think it's time, but don't get her pregnant,' Lenny said.

'OK, Da, thanks for the tip.'

'Are you sure?' Grace said to Lenny.

'He can always come back,' he said. 'Best thing I ever did was leave home and stand on my own two feet.'

'Can I move out?' Ryan asked.

'No.' Lenny and Grace said together.

'I can afford it more than him,' he said, and he was probably right. He was also only sixteen.

'NO.'

'I'm never moving out, I'm living with me ma forever,' Bernard said, as if it was a badge of honour.

'Sap,' Jeffrey said, before announcing he'd be moving in with Ryan.

'My bollocks.'

'Ryan, none of that language, please,' Lenny said.

'I know all your secrets,' Jeffrey said, and he touched his nose with his index finger.

'Fuck off, cyber-nerd!' Ryan said, unnerved.

'Ryan!'

'Sorry, Da,' he said. Jeffrey had replaced his love of food with computer coding. He told his mother he wanted to be a hacker when he grew up. Maybe he already was one. *That's all we need, another bloody criminal in the family . . .*

Lenny broke Grace's train of thought with a kiss and a large stack of sandwiches in tinfoil. 'Just in case you're there through lunch.'

'Thanks.' She kissed him. He kissed her back and it went on a bit, much to the disgust of Bernard and Jeffrey.

'Ah, Ma, please,' Bernard said.

'Gross,' Jeffrey said.

Grace was sure they would be in and out, no need for a packed lunch, but she was grateful. Ryan demanded he go with her.

'Go to school.'

'I'm way ahead of those morons and you know it,' he said. He was but she didn't want him anywhere near the courthouse.

'Juliet's going,' he said.

'Yeah well, you are not Juliet.'

'It would be good for me to experience a courtroom setting,' Ryan said.

'No.'

'Might put me off a life of crime.'

'No.'

'For fu—'

'Do not push me, Ryan.'

'Fine,' he said, and he handed her a small book. 'Give this to me gran.'

She took it and looked at it. '*The Little Book of Prison, a Beginners Guide?*'

'Just in case.'

'Jesus.' She put it in her handbag, *just in case.*

She walked out to the car with Lenny following. She looked at the caravan parked in her front garden as she passed it. 'It's time to get rid of that.' She knew it was no longer required. Juliet was safe. Her eldest was moving out. Life was moving on.

Chapter Seventy-One

Molly

MOLLY WOKE TO THE smell of a fry. She emerged down-stairs in her dressing gown to find Jack frying bacon and enough sausages to feed an army.

'Sit down there, Molls,' he said, pointing to the place setting, and he handed her a cup of tea. 'Won't be long now.'

'I'm not really hungry.'

'Ah, no, feed yourself, you'll need the sustenance.'

She picked at her breakfast as a mark of respect for the man who'd cooked it.

Grace arrived with Davey and Juliet in tow. Jack served them sausages while Molly got showered and dressed. She was worried about her friends, how they were and the toll her behaviour had taken on them, especially Thomas, a man in his eighties who shouldn't have to face a criminal proceeding. *Sorry.* She applied make-up and checked her hair and walked downstairs to Juliet, who was holding up her mother's book.

'Have you read it yet, Gran?' she asked.

'I have,' she said.

'And?'

'And it's very special.'

'I can't make myself open it,' Juliet said.

'She wouldn't mind at all, love, you do it in your own time.'

'Do you think I'm weak, Gran?'

'God no, you're fierce.'

'We'll never forget her, Gran.'

'Absolutely not.'

Juliet kissed the book and walked into the kitchen. Molly's smile faded; she sat on the stairs for a minute, collecting her jumbled thoughts.

Jack appeared in the doorway, with Grace, Davey and Juliet behind him.

'You ready, love?' he asked.

'As I'll ever be,' she said, and they were off.

The courthouse was small with a big wide tiled reception filled with people preparing to fight their cases. There were three doors: one led to the district court, the other to the circuit and in the middle there was a door to a marble staircase that led somewhere the plebs were uninvited.

Molly and her cronies were lucky; the director of public prosecutions considered their particular form of false imprisonment to be mild in nature and scheduled it for summary disposal in the district court. Mark, their solicitor, explained that as a result the maximum sentence would be one year in prison and the maximum fine would be five thousand euro. Of course he was hoping they would face neither, and instead their good standing in the community, their ages and the fact that they had never been in trouble with the law before would ensure a small, more manageable fine and no jail time. Thomas was equal parts nervous and ebullient. 'My nerves are gone but sure it's better than bingo,' he said when asked if he was all right or if he needed a chair. They were standing in the centre of the reception, huddled around Mark, who instructed them on where to sit and how to answer the judge. Given no choice they were pleading 'guilty', and he would assure the judge that the four had learned their lesson and would seek the court's leniency on the matter.

Pauline grabbed Molly by the hand. 'We've been through worse.'

It was true. They had both been through a lot worse than a stupid court case. Despite her words of comfort she could see Pauline was nervous. Nicole was terrified, Thomas up one moment and down the next. Molly didn't feel fear. She felt anger, and it increased when she spotted her accusers. *Arseholes.*

The courtroom was small. Molly and the three other defendants sat on a bench to the left-hand side. The solicitors for each side were in the middle of the room, the family and friends of the defendants on the left, and those of the prosecution on the right. A woman in uniform yelled the words 'All rise,' and Judge Diarmuid Ryan appeared through a wooden door at the top of the room and sat in his seat, looking down at the solicitors, with their stacks of paper and unnecessarily thick folders, flapping his arms. 'Sit, sit, sit. We haven't got all day.' Molly watched as the main door opened and Sergeant Kevin Fogarty and his partner Edel Flynn entered and sat in the front row. He nodded at Molly as he sat and she nodded back. Despite the room being small, it was hard to hear the solicitors as they outlined their case.

'Can you hear them?' Pauline asked.

'A word here and there,' Molly said.

'I don't know what's going on,' Thomas said.

'My feet are in bits,' Nicole said.

'I'm sorry, are we disturbing you?' the judge said.

'You would be if we could hear anything that's going on,' Molly said.

Mark sighed and shook his head.

'Speak up, for God's sake.'

It was all fuss about nothing. Mark pleaded guilty on behalf of them all.

'And you understand what a guilty plea means?' the judge said.

'We're not stupid,' Molly mumbled.

Pauline squeezed Molly's hand.

'Can I just beg the court's indulgence for a moment?' Mark asked.

'You wouldn't be earning your money if you didn't,' the judge said.

Mark went on to talk about what good characters the four were, and mentioned their ages and ailments. It should have been straightforward, but then the judge spoke to Molly.

'Impeding men doing their jobs should be a crime, non-payment of water charges and leaching off the state should also be a crime, but happily false imprisonment is a crime, and a serious one at that. You're elderly and your solicitor is using your age as a reason for this court to treat this matter lightly, but I believe your age should have better informed you as to the meaning of right and wrong. One year's suspended sentence and a five hundred-euro fine each. And I hope that, even in your twilight years, it is not too late to learn a valuable lesson.'

That's what did it. Molly stood up, and before anyone could do anything she opened her mouth. 'Oh, lessons have been learned, all right: the likes of you can get away with stealing from the likes of me, but you will never get away with speaking down to me, you cheeky fucking pup. Water is a human right, and in the absence of laws protecting the people of Ireland from ruling-class corruption, I will do whatever is necessary to have my say and win the day and you, Judge Whatever-your-name-is, can go fuck yourself.'

The intake of breath was audible. The ripple of 'Oh sweet Jesus' was palpable. Jack made a low whining noise; Grace put her arm around him to hold him up. Davey covered his face with his hand, Juliet smiled so wide Molly wondered if her cheeks would explode, and Molly herself, she just felt bone-tired. *Sorry.*

Of course the judge sent her down for contempt of court. She would be held in the women's prison known as the Dóchas Centre until she returned to the court to apologise.

Pauline wasn't quite clear on what was happening. 'I don't understand,' she said when Sergeant Kevin Fogarty stood up and reached out to take Molly's arm.

'Where are you going?' Pauline asked.

'Prison,' Nicole said.

'Ah no.'

'To be fair, you can't go around telling judges to you-know-what,' Thomas said.

'Ah no,' Pauline said again, and tears burned her eyelids.

'I'll be fine,' Molly said.

'Let's go,' Sergeant Fogarty said. He turned to Jack, Grace, Davey and Juliet. 'Give us a few minutes – wait outside, I'll find you,' he said, and Jack nodded.

'Molly?' Jack asked.

'Don't start, Jack, please don't start.'

Not fully appreciating the implications, Jack found himself caught up in the moment. 'You're standing up for what you believe in, just like you always have. I'm proud of you,' he said. 'And . . . well . . . fuck them.'

She grabbed him and kissed his face. 'Love ya, Jack.'

'Love ya, Molls.'

She walked with Sergeant Fogarty to the holding cells at the back of the courthouse.

'What now?' she said.

'Now I try to talk some sense into you. You can apologise before the day is out.'

'No way.'

'It's prison, Molly, not a day at the flipping zoo.'

She patted his arm. 'I'll be fine,' she said, but she wasn't fine – she was determined to suffer. *Sorry.*

Chapter Seventy-Two

Jack

ONCE THE REALITY OF their situation was in sharp focus, Jack needed to sit down for a minute or two. The thought of his wife doing time in a prison cell was as unbelievable as it was unbearable.

'What did you go and support her for?' Grace asked Jack.

'Sure what else could I do?' he said. 'The damage is done, Gracie.'

'I'll kill her,' Grace said.

Jack was scared and vulnerable and wondering what in the world his wife was thinking.

'I don't understand how we got here,' he said to Davey, and Davey told him everything would be all right even though he looked unsure.

'I've heard that before, son,' he said.

'This time, Da. This time it will be fine,' Davey promised, while banging his hand off his head.

Mark appeared, harassed-looking. 'Well, they've taken her to a holding cell at the back of the prison. She has the opportunity to apologise to the judge before the day is out, but if she refuses she's going to be transported to the Dóchas Centre later this afternoon.'

Pauline was in an awful way. 'It's my fault, I should have stood on her toe or covered her mouth, kicked her in the shin or knocked her out.'

Davey explained to a weeping Pauline that the god of thunder couldn't have stopped her. 'You know what she's like, Pauline.'

'But this, Davey? She's not able for this. Not on top of everything else.'

Thomas and Nicole paid their fine and got out of there quickly. 'I'm sorry, Jack, but everyone knows that part of probation is not fraternising with fellow criminals,' Thomas said as he practically ran out the door.

Jack just nodded. He was in no mood to fraternise with criminals either. Grace helped him to his feet. They followed Mark to a quiet corner in the reception area of the courthouse.

'You have to talk to her and get her to apologise, it's the only way.'

'Can we see her?' Grace asked.

'Follow the Garda,' Mark said.

'Aren't you coming?' Jack said.

'I can't, Jack, I've got another matter to attend to this afternoon, and frankly there's nothing else I can do here today. It's up to you.'

Mark gestured to Sergeant Fogarty, who approached.

'He's taking us to her?' Jack pointed to the enemy.

'Sergeant Kevin Fogarty,' he said, offering his hand to Jack, who shook it before he could gather his thoughts. *The enemy!*

'Now let's try to talk some sense into your wife,' Sergeant Fogarty said.

'She's a very sensible woman,' Jack argued, despite his current feelings and the situation at hand.

'I'm sure normally she is, but the wheel has come off the wagon here, Mr Hayes, and we need to get it back on because no one here wants to see that lady incarcerated,' the sergeant said.

Juliet grabbed her granda's hand. 'It's going to be fine, Granda.'

Despite Jack's attempt at solidarity with his wife he hoped that his granddaughter was right. Deep down he knew that this act of madness wasn't just a result of his wife going off the rails. There was something eating at her soul, robbing her of all joy and peace. Something inside her agitated and aggravated and sought to destroy her. He knew it; he just couldn't put his finger on what. *We lost our girl, Molly, but why all this?*

Chapter Seventy-Three

Grace

THE HOLDING CELL WAS located down a long narrow corridor at the back of the courthouse. Molly sat on a bench attached to a wall. She was pale, and despite her crossed arms Grace could see that her mother was trembling. Sergeant Fogarty felt it would be best if the family entered the cell one by one, as opposed to overwhelming the woman.

'She's in a fraught state. Best course is one on one,' he said.

Grace put her hand up. 'Me first, Sergeant Fogarty.'

'Call me Kevin.'

'Me first, Kevin,' she said.

'That all right with you, Mr Hayes?'

Jack nodded. 'Call me Jack.'

He let Grace into the cell and she sat on the bench beside her mother.

'They frisked me, coming in here,' she said, taking her sandwiches in tinfoil out of her bag. 'I thought they'd take these.' She unwrapped them and handed one to her mother. Then she took one out for herself and took a bite.

'Tuna,' she said. 'Lenny's mad for tuna.'

Molly put hers down on the bench and scratched her head.

'You're going to apologise, Ma,' Grace said.

'No, I'm not.'

'Ma, this is serious.'

'Grace, I know how serious this is.'

'You're not achieving anything. You're just being stubborn.'

'Sometimes you have to stick by your guns, no matter what,' Molly said.

'You can't win here.'

'It's not about winning, it's about staying the course, right to the end.'

'BOLLOCKS,' Grace said. 'You're just being a stubborn old goat and you know it.'

Molly sighed, picked up the sandwich, opened it and rubbed the tuna in Grace's hair.

'Oh, very mature,' Grace said, pulling the bread off her head.

'You have my answer, Grace,' Molly said.

'Unbelievable.' Grace put her tinfoil sandwiches back in her bag. 'You've lost it, Ma. I hope you know that.'

'I do,' Molly said.

Grace took out *The Little Book of Prison* and handed it to her mother. 'This is from your grandson.'

Grace emerged from the cell, with tuna chunks in her hair.

'Who's next?' Kevin said.

'Me,' Davey said, fixing his shirt and stretching his neck.

Grace sat down on a chair alongside her father, niece and poor distraught Pauline.

'Is that tuna in your hair, love?' she said.

'Yep.'

'You don't have any more in your bag?'

'Yep.'

'I always get hungry when I'm anxious,' she said, and Grace handed Pauline the tinfoil-wrapped sandwiches and watched her munch through five of them.

Chapter Seventy-Four

Davey

'MA, SAY SORRY AND COME home, this is fucking ridiculous,' Davey said.

'Thanks, Davey, but I'm grand here.'

'Ma, I have a heavily pregnant woman at home, can you please stop this?'

'No.'

'Ma, I've been an asshole over the years, so I can recognise the behaviour when I see it – you're being an asshole and we all know how much you hate them.'

'Sorry you feel that way, son.'

'Oh for the love of . . .' he said, and he left the cell, hands in the air.

'She won't listen, it's like she's determined to drag herself down . . .' he said to the others, then he shouted for his mother's benefit . . . 'AND US ALONG WITH HER.'

He sat down next to Pauline, who apologised when she burped tuna.

'Can I go in, Davey?' Juliet asked.

Davey looked to Sergeant Kevin Fogarty for the go-ahead.

'She might as well, the rest of you are striking out.'

'Do you know what you want to say?'

'Yeah.'

'Do you want me to go with you?'

'No.'

'Sure?'

'Positive.'

'I'm here.'

'I'm fine on my own.' It was a pointed statement. He let it pass.

Kevin opened the door to the cell and Juliet entered. Davey looked to Pauline. 'Any of those sandwiches left?'

She handed him the last of them.

'You all right, Da?' he said, before tucking in. Jack looked right through him and nodded.

'You know your mother,' he said, and Davey sat eating a tuna sandwich wondering what in the world would come next.

Chapter Seventy-Five

Juliet

JULIET WALKED INTO THE cell and stood opposite her gran.
'Gran,' she said, holding her arms by her sides, the way her gran did when she meant business.

'Yes, love,' Molly said, her face and eyes soft.

'I've been reading a lot about grief and they say it's all right to be happy,' Juliet said.

'I know.'

'Do ya?'

'I do, love,' Molly said, brushing invisible dirt from her skirt.

'Ma said you always brushed invisible dirt from your skirt or massaged your hands when you lie.'

'Did she?'

'Yeah.'

'Well, thanks for the tip.'

'Ryan put a tenner on you going down.'

'He knows me well,' Molly said, holding up the book.

'Gran.'

'Yes, love.'

'It's all right to be happy,' Juliet said.

'Tell that to yourself,' Molly said, and Juliet walked out of the cell before her gran could say anything else.

Chapter Seventy-Six

Jack

JACK WAS LAST IN.

'It all rests with you,' Sergeant Fogarty said to him.

'Then we're done for, I'm afraid,' Jack said, before entering the cell.

Molly looked up and smiled at him and held out her hand. He took it in his and sat beside her on the bench.

'You're standing up for what you believe in,' Jack said.

'Telling a judge to fuck off isn't going to change society, I know that,' she said.

'What can I do, Molly?'

'Bear with me.'

'I don't want you going to prison, Molly, but we've been together long enough for me to know that you'll do what you feel you have to.'

'I'm not sure I know what I'm doing, Jack.'

'So come home, Molls.'

'I will, just not today.'

He kissed her cheek. 'When you're done, come back to us, Molly. All the way.' He stood up.

'I'll do my best,' she said. 'Now leave me.'

He emerged from the holding cell. 'No go, I'm afraid, Kevin.'

419

'I'm sorry for that,' Kevin said, leading the family and Pauline away.

'Is me gran going to prison now?'

'Yes, love,' Jack said.

'Why?'

'Because it's something she needs to do,' he said, and he mustered the strength not to cry.

Chapter Seventy-Seven

Molly

SERGEANT FOGARTY OPENED THE passenger door of his car and Molly sat into it.

'You didn't have to bring me,' she said as he closed the door.

'I'm not having you in a van with God knows who,' he said, sitting into the driver's seat and belting up.

'You don't owe me anything.'

'I know that, put your belt on.'

'So why are you being so kind to me?' she asked, belting up.

'You remind me of my mother, she was a nutcase, too.'

Molly smiled. 'But you loved her anyway.'

'I did,' he said.

Sorry.

They drove through the suburbs of Dublin. It was after four and a large yellow 'M' sign loomed ahead.

'I'm starving,' he said. 'Wanna stop for some McDonald's?'

'As opposed to going straight into prison?'

'A Big Mac it is,' he said, pulling into the left lane so that he could veer off. There was a drive-through, but he insisted on going inside. He demanded she sit in a corner booth near the window; it was a warmer spot, away from the door.

421

'What are you having?' he asked. She remembered she didn't have her purse. 'Don't be silly, it's on me.'

Sorry.

'I'll have what you're having,' she said, and he rubbed his hands together. 'A feast for two.' She sat in the window looking around at all the people eating burgers and talking amongst themselves. *Are any of them heading to prison?* she thought. *Probably just me.* It seemed so surreal. *What are you doing, Molly?* she asked herself, and she didn't have the answer. She just wanted the pain and anguish to go away. Sergeant Fogarty arrived back to the table with a tray laden with food: two Big Macs, two fries, two six-piece chicken nuggets, two curry sauces and two chocolate milkshakes.

'You'll die in your sixties if you keep eating like this,' she said.

'Then I'll die happy,' he said, sharing out the food.

She was hungry; she only realised it when she was biting into a burger. It tasted good, like dessert dressed up as a main meal. 'I haven't eaten McDonald's since the early nineties,' she said.

'Why's that?'

'No idea, it just didn't occur to me.'

'Do you want me to talk you through the procedure inside the jail?'

'No,' she said.

'It can be invasive.'

'Bringing three kids into the world is invasive.'

Sorry.

'Molly—' he said seriously, and she knew another lecture was forthcoming so she cut him off at the pass.

'Chocolate milkshakes are my new favourite thing,' she said, and he nodded. He didn't try to intervene again. Instead they ate their way through a ton of food and she watched him finish his milkshake, while watching the clock. It was approaching five.

He drove her to the jail and parked up outside the reception door.

'Tomorrow you'll get into the van and go back to court and you'll say that you're sorry,' he said.

'Do you think?'

'I do.'

'Why's that?'

'Because whatever's going on in your head, it's not just about you. You've a family and friends waiting to get you home.'

'I'm a stubborn old fool,' she said.

'So was my ma.'

'But you loved her anyway.'

'I did,' he said, and he put on his hat and got out of the car. 'Now let's see about getting you locked up.'

Sorry.

Molly followed him through the reception doors and through the scanners and into the door on the right. There was a female prison officer waiting for her.

'This is where I say goodbye,' he said.

'Thank you,' Molly said.

'Thank me by apologising to that haughty fuck on the bench tomorrow,' he said, tipping his hat.

He left her alone with the woman, who introduced herself as Martina. 'Now I'm sorry but I'm going to have to ask you to strip,' she said, and Molly may have delivered three children, but she realised she was not prepared for this at all.

So sorry.

Chapter Seventy-Eight

Jack

JACK HAD NEVER BEEN to a priest's home before, at least not that he could remember. The hallway was dark save for a lamp on a sideboard. Light emanated from a crack in the door leading to what Jack presumed to be the kitchen. Father Frank stood in front of him; without his collar he didn't look like himself. He was wearing a tracksuit.

'I was just about to head to the gym,' he said, patting his stomach. 'Have to get rid of the pounds before they get rid of me.'

'Sorry to disturb.'

'Don't be silly,' he said, and Jack followed him into the bright kitchen, with floor-to-ceiling glass looking out on to a wild garden filled with colourful flowers, trees, climbers, plants and three bird feeders. It seemed like it was dinnertime for an entire flock.

'Did you do the garden yourself?' Jack asked.

'It's my secret pleasure,' Father Frank said.

It was beautiful, a real haven. 'You're full of surprises.'

'You should taste my Baked Alaska.' Frank grinned. 'Tea?'

'Go on then,' Jack said.

He was tired; it had been another very long day. He sat at the table while Father Frank made tea and plated up some custard creams. 'I know they're old-fashioned but there's something special about a custard cream,' he said as he sat down.

Jack agreed. 'You can shove your fancy biscuits, right enough.'

They both drank from their mugs. Father Frank placed his down.

'Now, what can I do for you, Jack?'

'I don't know,' Jack said.

'Molly?'

Jack nodded.

'You know I haven't seen her since the funeral,' Father Frank said, and he seemed saddened by that. Nearly two years had passed and he still missed his buddy.

'She hasn't been the same since,' Jack said, by way of apology.

'No, I suppose she wouldn't be.'

'Could you talk to her?'

'Lord knows I've tried,' Father Frank said. 'She keeps running off on me.'

'Well, she's not in a position to run off anymore,' Jack said.

Father Frank didn't follow.

'She's in jail.'

Father Frank was drinking tea and the intake of breath sent it into his windpipe. He coughed and spluttered, and Jack found himself on his feet and patting Father Frank's back.

'Sorry,' he said.

'God Almighty, Jack, why is she in prison?' Father Frank asked between coughs.

'She told a judge to fuck off.'

'Well at least she didn't kill him,' Father Frank said when he'd collected himself.

'That's the silver lining all right,' Jack agreed. He then explained where she was, and Father Frank wasn't sure what he could do, although he did know the chaplain in the Dóchas Centre.

'I could talk to Sylvia,' he said, but he made no promises.

'I can't get through, no one can,' Jack said.

'I'll talk to Sylvia and I'll see what I can do,' Father Frank promised.

'I'm desperate.'

'I know, Jack.'

'Thanks, Father.'

'Don't thank me yet,' Father Frank advised as they made their way down through the dark hallway. 'If I do manage to get to her, she might kill a man yet,' he said, pointing to himself.

'I'll pray for you, Father,' Jack said.

Jack left the priest pulling a stray weed in his front garden. He got into his car and drove home to his empty house, hoping and praying that even though Rabbit's beautiful book or a new grandchild on the way didn't ease his wife's troubled mind, sense could still prevail and she would find her way all the way back to him.

Chapter Seventy-Nine

Grace

LENNY CAME HOME FROM work to find his wife in bed. He took off his jacket and shoes and he climbed in beside her. She was on her side, facing the wall, so he spooned her.

'Ma's in jail,' she said.

'The kids told me.'

'It's like a bad joke.'

'Things will work out,' Lenny said

She turned to face him. 'I'm sick of hearing that.'

'Things are working out, Grace.'

'I got my appointment for the oophorectomy this morning. It's in six weeks.'

'Good,' he said. 'Then I'll book us on a holiday for six weeks after that.'

'What about the kids?'

'Fuck the kids,' he said, and she laughed.

'What about me ma?'

'Fu—'

'Don't you dare.'

'I've spoken to Stephen – he'll help out with the younger ones, and so will your parents.' He leaned over and pulled out a brochure for a tropical island and handed it to her.

'That's where we're going?'

'Ten days, just you and me.'

'What if I'm menopausal?'

'We'll deal with it.'

'What if I don't want to have sex?'

'Not an option,' he said. 'Besides, who could deny all this?' he said, pointing to himself.

'What if my ma is still in prison?'

'She won't be.'

'You're so sure about everything.'

'Yip,' he said.

'Lenny.'

'Yeah.'

'Lock the door.'

'Seriously?' he said. They could hear the kids moving around downstairs and at least one of them was in their bedroom down the hall.

'Yeah.'

He jumped out of the bed and locked the door; on the way back he had his trousers and jocks off before he hit the bed.

'Sexy,' she said, looking at his shirt, tie, stiff cock, bulging balls and black socks.

They sank into one another, giggling like kids, and Grace felt like a teenager in her own house and it didn't matter that she had another operation due or that her ma was in prison – she was in love. After twenty-six years together and everything she and Lenny had been through that was worth celebrating, even if only for eight minutes.

Chapter Eighty

Marjorie

MARJORIE SPENT HER DAY in bed. She was too big and too uncomfortable to move. Davey kept her apprised of Molly's jailing over the phone.

'Seriously?'

'Deadly.'

'God Almighty, Davey!'

'I'll see you soon, Marj. Love you,' he said, and he hung up. *Molly Hayes is in jail!* She needed the loo so she stood and waddled to the en suite. It was there she felt a severe cramp. *What's this? I've two weeks to go. Shit.*

She went to the loo and struggled back to the bed where she experienced a second stabbing cramp sensation. *Oh no . . .* Then she waited for another cramp, looking at her watch. An hour passed and nothing. *Maybe it was wind.*

She heard Juliet enter through the front door.

'Juliet? Is that you?'

She heard her feet trample on the stairs before she came to the door.

'What?'

'You OK?'

'I'm fine.'

'Where's Davey?'

'He's picking up the pram.'

'Oh yeah. Wanna sit with me and talk?'

'No.'

'Just for a few minutes.'

'I have to go.'

Juliet left and bounced down the stairs and Marjorie sighed and looked to the ceiling. *I'm doing my best here, Rabbit.*

She called after her. 'Don't forget we're shopping for your bedroom furniture tomorrow morning.'

'No,' Juliet shouted up the stairs.

'No is not acceptable. You will come with me if I have to drag you there myself.'

'That's assault.'

'Yes it is.'

The front door slammed. Marjorie looked to the ceiling. *Don't judge me.*

Chapter Eighty-One

Juliet

JULIET CYCLED PAST FRANCIE'S house eight times before Francie caught her; he was getting out of his van when he spied her wheeling past.

'Juliet Hayes! Are you stalking my Darren already?' he shouted, and she stopped her bike and blushed a ruby red.

'I am not!' she said, pretending to be horrified by the very idea. 'I was looking for you, actually.'

'Really?' he said, leaning on his van.

'Have you spoken to Mrs Faye yet?'

'Give me a chance.'

'I know, but time is of the essence.'

'Why's that?'

'It's three months to Ma's anniversary; it would be nice to do it then.'

'I'll talk to her tomorrow.'

'OK,' she said, and she started to cycle away.

'Hold on, what's happening with your Mrs H?'

'She's in jail.'

'Well, that was always going to happen. What did she do?'

'She told the judge to go fuck himself.'

''Course she did.'

'If she doesn't apologise they won't let her out.'

'How's Davey?'

She shrugged her shoulders.

'You need to forgive him, Juliet.'

She cycled off.

'And Juliet . . .'

She turned to face him. 'Darren's too old for you.'

She gave him the thumbs up for some reason unknown to both of them.

'Darren hasn't a fucking hope,' he shouted as she cycled away. 'You're just like your ma!'

Chapter Eighty-Two

Molly

D URING AN EXCRUCIATING HALF-HOUR, Molly had to get naked and was internally X-rayed. The examination had not been as invasive as childbirth but it was far more traumatising, even though the officer who introduced herself as Fiona was a pleasant young girl from Cork who apologised every time she asked Molly to degrade herself.

'Strip off for me. Sorry now. And turn around, sorry now, and sit on the Boss, that's our body orifice scanner, sorry, so sorry, nearly there, sorry.'

Molly wanted to cry but she didn't; instead she made jokes about auditioning for *Sports Illustrated* and whether or not Hugh Hefner would be man enough for this bunny. Fiona laughed politely. She wasn't really amused; it wasn't an amusing situation – it was a strip search in a prison, not amateur hour at a local comedy club. *Sorry.*

Following that fresh hell, she was moved to a holding cell in the committal unit. She followed the nice Cork girl down the cream hallway lined with light brown doors. 'If you're here with us beyond tomorrow morning you'll be assessed by the governor, to see where we'll put you,' Fiona said.

Molly didn't speak. She couldn't find the words. *Sorry.* Fiona called out before she opened the door and with a rattle of heavy keys the door swung open and Molly was confronted by a bedraggled woman in a mottled velour tracksuit, sitting on a bed with her head in her hands.

'All right, Sheila?' the prison officer said.

'Sick as a pig, nurse.'

'I'm not a nurse, I'm a prison officer.'

'Oh yeah.'

'This is Molly, she'll be sharing the cell with you tonight before we get you both settled.'

The woman looked up, dazed and confused, and Molly recognised her instantly.

'Sheila B?' The girl who was the best Irish dancer on the northside of Dublin, Francie's first love, a certified lunatic but with a heart of gold. *God love ya, Sheila B.*

'Mrs H?'

'Sheila, what in the name of Jesus are you doing here?'

'I could ask you the same thing.'

'Friends or foes, ladies?' Fiona asked.

'Friends – she was always very kind to me, nurse,' Sheila said.

'We'll be just fine,' Molly said. The door closed behind them and Molly sat on the bed opposite Sheila.

'What's happening, Sheila?'

'I'm coming off the booze; it's going to be a long night Mrs H, sorry,' she said, lifting up a large bucket. On the floor beside her were towels, wet wipes and a bottle of water.

'I didn't know you were an alcoholic.'

'For a long time neither did I, that's the problem,' Sheila B said.

'What did you do, Sheila?' Molly said.

Sheila lay down on the bed, shivering. 'It's fucking freezing in here.'

'Sheila?'

'Shoplifting.'

'You were never a shoplifter.'

'Yeah well, times change,' she said, and she grabbed the bucket and puked.

'You were doing so well when I saw you at Rabbit's anniversary,' Molly said.

'Was I? Don't remember it, I was locked.'

'You didn't seem locked.'

'That's me secret weapon,' Sheila said, and she threw up again.

'Why shoplifting?'

'I knew if I got caught enough it would get me in here.'

'I don't understand,' Molly said.

'You know the way they said I was bipolar when I was younger?'

'Yeah.'

'Well I've got a personality disorder too.'

'Oh no, I'm sorry to hear that.'

'Can't manage it, Mrs H. I try but I can't do it. I know a girl who came in here for six months and they sorted her right out: good meds, made sure she took them, got her act together. It's not so bad, you know, there's apartments and everything in the big yard. I have to do something. I couldn't think of anything else.'

'God Almighty, Sheila, isn't that what the mental health services are for?'

'They just talk at me, take me in when I've totally lost it, fuck me out as soon as they can. I need help, Mrs H, I know I do, but then sometimes I don't want it and I just want to burn everything down. In here I don't have that choice.'

'You're very brave,' Molly said.

'Nah, I'm just desperate.' Sheila threw her guts up again. After Molly cleaned her up, Sheila B told Molly that her daughter Sandra was marrying The Claw.

'The fella that lost his hand to a samurai sword?' Molly said.

Sheila began to cry. She was shaking now and scratching her skin. 'They stitched it back on. She doesn't want me at the wedding,' she said, and shrugged. 'Don't blame her, I made a show of her at the engagement do.'

'When is the wedding on?'

'Early next year,' Sheila said.

'Well then, you'll be on your meds and booze-free and fine by then, won't ya?' Molly said, and Sheila wiped the tears from her eyes.

'Yeah,' she said, 'that or dead, so either way it's a winner.'

Molly was about to scold her for such negativity when the keys rattled at the door. It opened and another female guard with a tight ponytail stood in front of them.

'Molly Hayes?'

'Yeah?'

'You requested to see the chaplain.'

'No.'

'It says here you did.'

'Go on, give us a few minutes of privacy – think I'm about to have the shits,' Sheila B said.

'OK,' Molly said. 'Sip on that water.'

436

She walked down a series of hallways, the guard locking and unlocking doors as they continued towards their destination.

'How are you finding us?' she said. She didn't give her name, or if she did Molly was too distracted by Sheila B's insides coming out.

'A real palace, all that's missing are the scented candles,' Molly said, and the ponytailed woman chuckled.

'We aim to please.'

'Sheila's very sick.'

'We're monitoring her. She'll see the doctor first thing, so will you.'

'There's nothing wrong with me.'

'It's standard procedure.'

One more door to open and close and they were outside the chapel. 'I'll be back for you,' she said, walking away and leaving Molly standing outside. She pushed on the door and revealed a small, dimly lit room with scattered chairs, a table with a cross on it and some artwork and handwritten signage on the wall. Sitting on a chair in front of the makeshift altar was a man in black.

'Hello?' Molly said, and Father Frank stood up and turned to face her. He waved.

'Frank?'

'Hi, Molly.'

'You're doing the rounds,' she said.

'I know the chaplain here, we did a course together. Sit down.'

She sat. 'Jack?'

'He called to me this afternoon.'

'Sorry for wasting your time,' she said.

'Am I?' he asked.

'I don't know what you want from me, Frank.'

'How about a bit of honesty?' he said.

'I'm an open book.'

'Bollocks,' he said, and it was the first time she'd ever heard the man curse.

'Fine. What do you want to know?'

'What happened, Molly?'

'You know what happened – my daughter died.'

'But what happened?'

'I don't know what you're talking about,' she said, and she stood up to leave. He grabbed her hand and refused to let go. She sat.

'What happened?'

The prison walls fell away and Molly was back in another small room, the hospice, sitting on that hard chair, watching her daughter die. Outside the birds were singing. Inside the small, overcrowded, slightly pungent hospice bedroom Molly Hayes was holding her daughter's hand in hers. Light streamed through the window opposite, warming Molly's face and hurting her tired eyes. Despite exhaustion she remained awake, eyes wide open and staring at her once-beautiful child, so unrecognisable and battling to breathe. Scattered around her and sleeping on chairs were the rest of Molly's family and Marjorie. Their breathing in contrast to their dying baby sister's, slow and steady. *I love ya, Rabbit. I love ya. I love ya so much. Your mammy loves ya.* Then she thought something, something she found difficult to recall and something she was deeply ashamed of: *go on, Rabbit, just let go.* She mumbled it: 'Just let go.' She wanted her daughter to let go, she needed her to because her back was sore, her hips and knees were stiff; she had a headache and a gnawing in her stomach. It had been hours of sitting, watching and waiting. Her head was fried. Her eyes were strained, every muscle screamed. She needed to get out of that room, to roam around, to stretch, to walk, to drink tea, to sleep, to live, to breathe, anything but sit there a moment longer. *Just let go*, she ordered her dying child. *Just let go*. And Rabbit obliged and gripped Molly's hand, frightening the living shite out of her. She levitated off the chair. 'Frigging fuckersticks,' she mumbled under her breath and held her heart. When it resumed normal rhythm she steadied herself and leaned in towards her dying daughter.

'Rabbit?' she whispered. 'Are you still with me, love?'

'Have to catch the van, Ma,' Rabbit said.

This is it. Her eyes filled, nose blocked, ears buzzed, throat burned. 'Safe trip, Rabbit,' she said, and she wanted her to go. She wanted her to get into that invisible van and go because she couldn't stand waiting one more second. One moment later, her child's grip loosened and she was gone. *Oh God, what have I done? Oh no.* She didn't move, the urge suddenly left her and she couldn't feel anything now. She was numb. *Just let go.* Outside on the windowsill a bird twittered. Inside and just underneath that window, the heater hummed. A spider tootled across the window before jumping onto the wall. Molly sat up straight, her head and spine perfectly aligned, caressing her daughter's head. In her final moments she'd abandoned her own flesh and blood. She deserved to be alone, adrift and hopeless. She was unwholesome, unworthy, unforgivable. She had willed Rabbit dead;

439

she valued a cup of tea over the life of her child. 'Just let go.' In that moment Molly had lost her child and her God. A woman of faith who'd lost all faith in a just or forgiving God. She lost faith in herself. No one had ever asked her about those last moments before; everyone sleeping in that room presumed Rabbit died in that coma. She didn't correct them. How could she admit what she did, how she felt in that moment? Relief. Gratitude. *Oh God.* She decided that there was no God in her life, not because she didn't still feel his presence but because they were unworthy of one another – we are not friends, you and I. She missed him, though, not as much as her child but the loss tore away at her; she had to stop herself from calling out to him, from talking to him, from seeking and gaining small comforts. She lost her girl and she lost her God and she deserved to be alone. Finally admitting what she had willed her child to do in those last moments of her life and how her child had responded was both a terrifying and liberating experience.

'Just let go.'

'People say and think that all the time. It was a mercy, Molly,' Father Frank said.

'I had a pain in my arse, Father,' she said, 'It had fuck all to do with mercy.'

'God loves you.'

'I hate him.'

'No, you don't.'

'I do.'

'You miss him and he misses you.'

'Bullshit.'

'Is it?'

'I want to hurt him,' she said, and tears burned her eyes. 'I want to be hurt.'

'That's OK.'

'It's not OK. We let her down.'

'No you didn't. You did your very best and that girl needed to go, and you were there to see her off, just as you were to see her in. You had a pain in your arse – you're human, Molly. You're one of the best and most caring people I know.'

'Fuck off.'

'You've also got the foulest tongue, and I've been around some charmers in my day,' he said, and she smiled through cascading tears.

'The truth is, God's not omnipotent, and neither are you, but I like to think you both try,' Father Frank said. 'Take comfort in that, Molly.'

She hugged her priest and squeezed him tight. 'Be careful of the ribs there, Molly.'

She cried on his shoulder, and when she was exhausted from tears, she lay with her head on his shoulder, spent from emotion, and for the first time since that fateful morning, grateful to be alive. Before she knew it he had started to sing, and to be fair to Frank he had a lovely tone to his voice. 'Amazing Grace! How sweet the sound . . .'

'Ah, will ya stop?'

'Sing it with me, Molly.'

'That saved a wretch like me . . . Come on, Molly, sing it with me . . . I once was lost, but now I'm found, was blind but now I see.'

Molly joined in. It was one of her favourites, and seeing as she had just bared her soul in a prison chapel, she thought . . .

what the hell . . . 'Through many dangers, toils and snares, I have already come. 'Tis grace has brought me safe thus far, and grace will lead me home.'

When they were done singing, like two drunks at a party, Molly sat quietly, and then she heard it – the most beautiful sound in the world, Rabbit's voice inside her head. *Well, I've fucking seen it all now, Ma. #Mortified.*

Molly was laughing. 'Oh Rabbit, there you are, love. There you are, my girl. Your ma loves ya – you know that, don't ya?'

Of course I do, you big sap. I was here all along, Ma, you just couldn't hear me.

I'm so sorry, love. I hear you now.

Father Frank looked around, not quite sure what to do as Molly raised her hands to heaven and cried happy tears. 'She's come back to me, Frank.'

'You're not seeing things are you, Molly?' he asked, concerned.

'No, you big eejit, I'm hearing things,' she said, as if that was any better.

'Like what?'

She listened. 'Rabbit is calling us a pair of saps and saying religion is bollocks.'

'That does sound like her.'

Before they parted Father Frank confirmed that Molly was going to apologise to the judge in the morning.

She nodded and she laughed. 'It will be a pleasure.'

'Now, Molly,' he warned, 'don't start.'

'As if I would.'

Neck of him, she heard Rabbit say, and she laughed a little.

'I've too much to live for to hang around here, Frank,' she said.

The ponytailed guard returned for Molly just after 8 p.m. She spent the rest of the night tending to a very sick and sorry Sheila B. She rubbed her and soothed her, she gave her water and brushed her hair. She wrapped her in blankets when she was too cold and stripped them off her when she was too warm. She cried with her, she spoke to her, told stories of the past and even made her laugh between vomiting and hallucinations.

'There's a man caught in the curtains.'

'There's no man and no curtains.'

'Sure?'

'I wouldn't lie to you, Sheila.'

'So sorry for all this, Mrs H.'

'It's my privilege, love.'

Molly spent the night cradling the vulnerable and desperate Sheila B and cleaning up her vomit and shite. It was the most content she had been since her youngest child drew her last breath.

Part Nine

The Birth

Chapter Eighty-Three

Davey

Davey sat in Francie's back garden drinking coffee while Francie enjoyed a cigarette. He had called Davey and asked him over so that he could talk to him about Juliet's request before he discussed it with Karen Faye.

'She wants to bury her ma's ashes in with Johnny?' Davey said.

'In a nutshell, yeah.'

Johnny fuckin' Cash,' Davey mumbled to himself.

'Jaysus, that's harsh,' Francie said. 'So am I talking to her or what?'

'Talk to her. Tell her I'll pay her whatever she needs. I'll buy her a new plot if I have to.'

'Sure?'

'Our Bunny wants her ma to rest in peace with the boy she loved. It's the least I can do.'

'I'll get on it,' Francie said.

'You're a good friend, Francie.'

'I'm the best friend,' Francie replied. 'The cheek of you.'

Davey was still smiling when his phone rang. It was his da.

'Good news, Davey, your ma's seen sense – she's saying sorry to the judge this morning.'

'Oh that's great, Da,' Davey said, and put him on speaker.

'Great news, Jack,' Francie said.

'Ah, hello, boys. You'll never believe who she was inside with . . .'

'Who, Da?'

'Sheila B.'

'Fuck off, Jack.'

'I won't. I'm serious.'

Francie started laughing again. 'You couldn't make it up.'

'Ah, God love her. Molly said she was in an awful way and she was such a lovely Irish dancer in her day. I better go and pack up some fresh clothes for your mammy,' he said, and he hung up before Davey could say goodbye.

'Poor old Sheila B,' Francie said, and Davey just nodded and drank his coffee.

Chapter Eighty-Four

Marjorie

JULIET WAS SULKING AS they walked around the furniture shop. There were ten beds lined up and each one looked more comfortable than the next. Marjorie just wanted to fall into one of them and stay there. Her ankles, stomach, vagina and arse screamed, all saying the same thing: *get this kid out of me!* She was used to everything hurting but the pain was sharper and more intense. She'd experienced Braxton Hicks contractions on and off the previous day, so she didn't panic – she had looked them up, she was fine, they just made her shit state a little shitier. She was experiencing an escalation of Braxton Hicks at that very moment. She sat on the bed. Jane, the young, tall shop assistant with an attitude like she was God's gift to the universe, approached her for the third time in ten minutes.

'Still OK?'

'I'm fine. I promise I won't give birth on the bed.'

'I hope not – that's our most expensive one.'

'Good to know. Any chance of a glass of water?' Marjorie said.

'This is a furniture shop.'

'There's a water dispenser just by the counter.'

Jane mumbled something as she walked away. Marjorie moved to the next bed and waited for her water. A sullen Juliet appeared and sat next to her.

'Well?'

'Whatever.'

'Oh great, there's a Peppa Pig bunk in the sale.'

'LOL,' Juliet said.

'I'm doing my best, Juliet.'

'Me too.'

'Well, that's a lie.'

'No it's not.'

'You've been a bitch to me since you got back. We used to be best pals.'

'We were never best pals – you were my mother's pal and she's dead.'

'I was your pal and well you know it. I'm still your pal.'

The woman appeared with a glass of water. 'Anything else I can do, your majesty?'

'You've a really bad attitude,' Marjorie said.

'I'm not the pregnant lady who's been sitting on show-room furniture for an hour with no intention of buying anything.'

'How wrong you are, Jane, and please check and see if the white sleigh bed, double, is available with the matching dressers.'

'No problem,' she said, and she walked away.

'The sleigh bed never dates, it's a classic,' Marjorie said, and Juliet nodded.

'I miss you,' Marjorie said. 'I'm having this baby and your mother's not here and you are being mean to me.'

'I'm not being mean to you,' Juliet said.

'You won't talk to me, you sulk and give me shit every time I try to talk to you. What did I do?'

'You took Davey away,' Juliet said.

Jane appeared with a set of forms in her hand. 'Yes, that's fine, we have everything in stock.'

'Go away, Jane.'

Jane thought about it and walked away and sat at a desk. Marjorie faced Juliet. 'I have not taken Davey away. I couldn't do that even if I wanted to, and I don't.'

'That's just words. This baby will come and you'll be a family.'

'You are my family.'

'Bullshit.'

'You think he just came home for me and this baby? You're wrong. He came home because you were miserable in America.'

'That's not true.'

'It is true. There was a change in you after your last visit: you were unhappy, unsettled, you couldn't focus on your schoolwork, you were moody and sad and no matter what he did he couldn't help you. He didn't know I was pregnant when he made that decision. He moved home for you, Juliet.'

Something changed in the child. Marjorie saw the change happen before her eyes. She softened; the anger ebbed away. Juliet wiped away a tear. 'And now he's landed me on you.'

'I wanted to raise you as my own but I was living in a one-bed flat after the divorce.'

'As if.'

'Ask your gran or your granda or Grace or Davey, who I gave shit to because I was jealous and I didn't think he was good enough for you.'

Juliet smiled a little. 'Poor Davey, everyone gives him shit all the time.'

'I want us to be a family, and I think if your ma is looking down – and I know she's not but *if* she is – she'd be over the moon.'

Juliet nodded. 'You really wanted me?'

'Really I did.'

'Marjorie?'

'Yes, love.'

'Something terrible happened in America.'

Jane returned with the forms. 'Are you buying anything or not?'

'Go away.'

'I work here.'

'Not for long if I have anything to say about it,' Marjorie said. Jane was gone.

There and then, while sitting on the second-dearest bed in a furniture shop in the city of Dublin, Juliet told Marjorie the story of Trevor and what he did to her and how scared and isolated, guilty, dirty and ashamed it made her feel. Marjorie could feel her temperature rising and her temper kick in. *Oh, Rabbit.*

Be cool, Marjorie, be cool.

Her insides ached and her baby kicked and her mind flooded with memories she'd locked away since she was eight years old. The anger rose inside her, raising her core temperature so much she could feel her head sweating.

'I'll track him down, torture him, kill him and bury him in lime.'

'That's very specific,' Juliet said. She couldn't look at Marjorie; her eyes were cast down towards the floor, her cheeks were flushed, she was on the verge of tears.

I know this, I understand this, I was you. Marjorie took her into her arms. 'It's not your fault. He's a scumbag and he will be dealt with. Your uncle Davey . . .'

But Juliet panicked; she didn't want Davey to know, she couldn't face it. 'Juliet, he needs to know, Casey needs to know. We can't have him anywhere near children, can we?'

'No,' she said, and she was shaking.

'It's going to be fine. You're going to get through it. Do you know why?' Marjorie said, and Juliet shook her head; she wasn't so sure she would.

'I had an uncle and he did things to me and he hurt me.' The words sounded strange coming out of her mouth. She had never uttered them, not in thirty-seven years. They echoed in her head; she felt a little dizzy.

'Did you talk to someone?'

'I'm talking to someone now,' she said, and tears coursed down her cheeks. 'I'm telling you.'

Juliet hugged Marjorie tightly. Jane stared over at the woman and child crying all over her expensive duvet set.

'Did you get over it, Marjorie?'

'I thought I had but I think I made some bad decisions just 'cause I was scared, do you know what I mean?'

Juliet nodded.

'I locked myself away for a long time, Bunny. I don't want that for you.'

'What happened to him?' Juliet asked.

'He got stomach cancer and died.'

'I'm glad,' Juliet said.

'Me too,' Marjorie said. 'Now we know each other's secrets and we'll both be OK.' Marjorie took Juliet into her arms and when they stood up, Jane approached again, clipboard in hand.

'Right, that's it, buy something or get out,' she said in an aggressive tone which suggested she wouldn't be taking no for an answer this time.

'We'll buy,' Marjorie confirmed, and her waters broke right there on the carpeted floor.

Jane stood back. 'For the love of . . . I'll call a taxi.'

So Marjorie sat on a hard, wipeable plastic chair near the door of the shop experiencing excruciating contractions five minutes apart and, after confirming that Juliet did in fact love the white sleigh bed and lockers, she filled out the endless forms, paid in full and set a delivery date.

Juliet held her hand and she phoned Davey as the pain cut through her and she thought she was going to faint and she could hear Juliet telling her to breathe.

'I'm in labour!'

'It's happening. It's happening!' Davey shouted, and she could hear the Byrne boys roaring and hollering.

It's happening. Oh Jesus, Rabbit, it's happening.

Chapter Eighty-Five

Juliet

THE TAXI MAN GROANED when he saw Marjorie. 'I have a towel in the back, sit on that,' he said. He wasn't excited at the prospect of bringing a labouring woman to hospital. 'The Rotunda at this time of day . . .' he said, trailing off. Traffic was busy. Marjorie sat in the front seat, Juliet sat in the back. The taxi driver insisted that Juliet stay belted up, so she couldn't lean forward as much as she'd like but she could still talk to Marjorie and say supportive things.

'Still five minutes apart, Marj, doing great.' Juliet was an avid fan of medical dramas and documentaries about giving birth. She was so confident, she'd have taken an exam. Marjorie on the other hand avoided medical dramas and documentaries about giving birth like the plague.

'Thanks,' Marjorie said, banging the side of the taxi with her fist.

'Please don't do that,' the driver said.

'Sorry.'

'Fine, but this isn't just my car, it's my workplace, and I've three kids of my own to feed.'

'Sorry,' Marjorie said again. Juliet felt aggrieved. She leaned forward and took a photo of the driver's ID.

'What are you doing?' he asked.

'I'm reporting you.'

'For what?'

'For being a prick.'

Marjorie laughed.

At the Rotunda, the man almost dragged Marjorie out of the car, and, after taking his fare, he drove off at the speed of light, leaving Marjorie leaning on Juliet at the hospital entrance. Juliet told her to stay where she was and she ran inside and got a wheelchair, then she pushed Marjorie inside to reception where a receptionist took her details and called a nurse. Marjorie's contractions were now three to five minutes apart and lasting forty-five to sixty seconds. It felt urgent but the receptionist and the nurse were entirely blasé. Juliet's mother's emergencies were never treated so calmly. It was hard to mentally adjust.

'I'm Denise, let's get you onto the labour ward,' the nurse said to Marjorie.

'The baby's coming,' Juliet said. Denise looked at the chart. 'How long have you been experiencing contractions, Marjorie?'

'Her waters broke at 3.05, she immediately began contracting, it started at five minutes apart, moved to between three and five minutes apart, and each contraction lasts between forty-five and sixty seconds.' She looked at her watch. 'That's been happening for just over forty minutes.'

'Well now, ever think of being a midwife?' Denise asked.

'No, I'm going to be a doctor,' Juliet said.

Marjorie squeezed Juliet's hand. 'She's going to cure cancer.'

'Good for you, Juliet,' Denise said.

She waited outside while Denise settled Marjorie in a bed and examined her. She heard her scream out a little. A lot had happened since she'd entered the furniture store. She realised that Davey and Marjorie loved her and she knew things were going to change. She knew she'd never have to see Trevor again and Davey was too far away to kill him, but he'd be found out and he'd lose his job and maybe even his wife and his kids and she was glad. *Screw you, Trevor*, she thought. *You messed with the wrong girl.*

Juliet wouldn't be Davey's whole world anymore, but that was OK because he wouldn't be hers either; she would have Marjorie and a kind of half-sister or brother slash cousin. She'd have school, and maybe even friends. In truth, even with the best of intentions, they weren't enough for one another. Her mother would have wanted this for her. Marjorie wanted her! She understood her. She wasn't alone.

'You can go in,' Denise said as she walked out of the room.

'Where are you going?' Juliet said.

'Don't worry, I'll be back.'

'But the baby's coming!'

'Don't worry, plenty of time yet,' she said.

Juliet walked into the room. 'I don't think she's taking this seriously,' she said, and Marjorie laughed.

'I'm fine, Juliet. Everything's fine.'

Juliet poured Marjorie a glass of water. 'You should stay hydrated.'

Marjorie took a sip and handed it back. 'I was going to get my hair and nails done and a wax.'

'You look lovely.'

'I look like I've been dragged through a hedge backwards.'

'Still lovely.'

Davey rang from the road. 'Still in traffic, how's everything going?'

'We've landed safely, she's been seen, they say there's plenty of time so don't die on the way,' Juliet said, and handed the phone to Marjorie.

'I'm having the baby, Davey. Can you believe it?' she said, and she was crying.

Juliet couldn't hear what Davey said but Marjorie was beaming. She hung up the phone and handed it to Juliet.

'Are you scared?' Juliet said.

'I'm terrified,' Marjorie said, and she took Juliet's hand in hers. 'But I've got you and Davey on my side.'

'And me gran, granda, Grace, Lenny, the boys and your ma . . .' Juliet said. It was overwhelming; poor Marjorie was in tears. She bit her lip. 'And my ma. Even though she's dead, you still have her.'

'Are you scared, Juliet?'

'Nah, I've been through way worse than this,' she said. 'This is the good stuff, Marj.'

Marjorie reached for a hug. Juliet snuggled in. Marjorie grabbed her by the hair and pulled. 'HOLY SAINT JESUS . . .'

Juliet calmed her down. 'Let go, Marjorie.'

She let go and Juliet disentangled herself.

'Now breathe,' she said, taking four steps backwards away from the crazy lady exploding in the bed.

Can you see me helping, Ma?

She'd be lost without you, Bunny.

Chapter Eighty-Six

Molly

MOLLY SAID GOODBYE TO Sheila B before she got into a van that would take her back to court.

'You're strong, Sheila, and you will get there.'

'How are you so sure?'

'Because you want to.'

'I hope so,' she said. 'I'm sick of being a joke.'

'You're not, love, and I'm always there if you need me.'

'Thanks, Mrs H,' she said, and Molly kissed her gently on the forehead.

Two other women shared the van with her but she didn't talk with them. She was busy talking to Rabbit.

And I'll tell you something else, love, the food's not bad either . . . All in all I've stayed in worse places. Do you remember that kip in Blackpool?

Yeah, Ma, Davey got food poisoning and shat everywhere.

That's right.

She waited her turn and stood up in front of the judge. He was determined to humiliate her, but it's hard to humiliate a woman who doesn't care, so after a lengthy lecture, which she smiled through, he told her she was free to go.

'Thank you, thank you so much, it did me the world of good,' she said, and as her thanks were genuine she left the man very confused.

'You're welcome,' he stammered as she walked to her husband on air.

She hugged him tight once they were outside the court.

'I'm back, Jack.'

'A hundred per cent?' he said.

'A hundred and fifty per cent,' she said.

'Well, thank eff for that.' He grabbed her hand. 'Good news, Molls, Marj is having the baby.'

'Now?'

'Right now.'

'A new baby,' she said, and suddenly she was tearful.

'A new Hayes,' he said, putting his arm around her shoulder.

Isn't that something, Rabbit?

It sure is, Ma.

Chapter Eighty-Seven

Marjorie

THE CONTRACTIONS WERE EXCRUCIATING. Marjorie had never suffered from illness. She'd never broken anything or really even cut herself before. Up to now waxing was the most pain she'd ever experienced. She had mentioned it to Molly when they first discussed her pregnancy. She explained how nervous she was because she hadn't really known physical pain. She asked if she could prepare somehow, and Molly thought about that for a moment before sighing and wiping her hands on her apron.

'You could shove a grenade up your fanny but it's not advisable,' she said, and she made tea and put out some biscuits. Marjorie panicked a little and Molly placed her hands on her shoulders.

'Or you could be lucky and you could fire it out, not a bother.'

'Do you really believe that?'

'At your age, not a chance,' she said, and Marjorie felt like crying. 'But no matter what, we'll all be there for you, you'll be taken good care of and it will be worth it. Believe me on that.'

Marjorie nodded her head and burst into tears. 'OK, Molly. I will.'

'Who loves ya, Marjorie?'

'Molly does.'

'That's right,' she said, and she kissed her on the forehead.

Marjorie didn't discuss her fears around pain and labour again, and although they didn't go away, she comforted herself with the thought that no matter what, it would be worth it. Then as the due date fast approached, her fears grew. *What if the baby dies? It could die. Babies die all the time.* Then the nightmares came; every time she closed her eyes a baby died. She woke up screaming and Davey ran into the room. 'Is it now? Are we a go?' He held up two pre-packed hospital bags for mother and baby. She cried and told him she had dreamed the baby died; he sat on the bed and held her close. Despite all her fears, the baby was doing well, she was being monitored closely, everything was as it should be but still that fear crawled inside her and spread out. *What if the baby died?* She wasn't sure she could live. That would be the final straw. *I barely survived you, Rabbit; I definitely won't survive that.*

She had found herself worrying more about things that were mostly out of her control: climate change, famine and earthquakes; for the first time in her life living on a small island really preyed on her mind. 'One tsunami and Ireland's gone. That's all it would take.' She cried all the time: at cute dogs, homeless dogs and dead dogs. She couldn't watch anything with human pain and suffering, especially children – the news was out, dramas were out, even some comedies made her cry. She deleted her social media. 'There's so much sadness.' One more 'my granny/son/mother/daughter/father died' post and she'd have lost it. One more 'save this animal from horrible torture

462

in a remote village in God knows where by simply sharing a post' request or signing a petition for a woman who'd been gang-raped and now faced a lashing for being indecent, one more terrible war story or photo of the face of a hopeless child. She cried for all of them; they took up residence in her head and broke her heart.

She had turned off her computer; instead she took to her bath with candles and a light-hearted book, pre-approved by a lovely lady in her local bookshop. She felt great anxiety and did all she could to battle it because she knew it was bad for the baby. She went to yoga twice a week, she meditated, she banished all negativity . . . well, not all, she still saw her mother. It wasn't easy. Davey was kind and loving, and she needed to be calm.

Just relax, Marj, one day at a time, dead Rabbit said all the time.

Easy for you to say, Baldy. I'm trying my best, but as Gwen Stefani puts it, this shit is bananas.

Juliet was doing her best to help Marjorie calm down and use her breath. She was very good with the breath – she'd helped her own mother breathe through pain a lot.

'Slow and steady, in and out, unclench, unclench, unclench . . .' Juliet said, screeching slightly towards the end of the sentence. Marjorie realised she was squeezing the child's hands to mush.

'So sorry,' she said, letting go.

'That's fine, now breathe in and out.' Juliet flexed her fingers.

'I am.'

'No, you're just inhaling, you're not exhaling. You keep inhaling, you'll end up having a panic attack or faint or something.'

'Oh God,' she said, and she inhaled a little more.

'Exhale, exhale – out, get it out, breathe it out.'

Marjorie tried hard to exhale; it was as though she'd forgotten how. She was sitting at the edge of the bed with her hands now resting on Juliet's shoulders.

'Think of your favourite things,' Juliet said, trying something new to distract or divert Marjorie from having a full-on panic attack.

'What?' Marjorie was steadying herself. The pain had passed and Juliet was using her stopwatch to count down to the next attack.

'When Ma was really bad and we were waiting for her drugs to kick in, we'd talk about her favourite things, places and people. We talked about you a lot,' Juliet said, and Marjorie smiled.

'Yeah?'

'Yeah.'

'OK, one of my favourite things is a vintage handbag I bought in a market in Paris when was I was twenty-one,' she said, and suddenly she was in the throes of agony once more. It felt like the kid inside had a Swiss army knife and was hacking its way out. 'Oh God, kill me.'

'Focus on the breath, focus on the good. Give me a place.'

'Easy,' Marjorie said, and then she squeezed her eyes shut and stuck her fingers deep into Juliet's shoulders. 'Oh holy Saint Jesus.'

'A place?' Juliet suggested, before screaming for Marjorie to let go. She did so and stared into Juliet's face.

'The Hayes family kitchen table, Sunday roasts, laughter and mayhem, your gran and granda, Grace, Davey, Johnny, all the band and your ma. Everyone scrambling for roast spuds and talking all at once, throwing shapes, bantering, making big plans and arguing over the last piece of beef or who was first for dessert.' The kid must have been made of flames, because her insides burned but she talked right through the fiery contraction and remembered to breathe right through it. A tear rolled down her face. Juliet used a tissue to dab it, then she patted Marjorie's damp forehead.

'And person?'

'Well, the obvious of course is your ma.'

'Or Davey,' Juliet said.

'Or the mighty Molly.'

Juliet grinned and nodded. 'Yeah,' she said.

'But I'm going to say you . . .' Marjorie said, cupping the back of Juliet's head and guiding her head gently towards her so that their foreheads touched. 'You are my favourite person.' And she reached up and kissed Juliet's forehead. 'That first smile, when you reached for my hand, your little stories, when you were convinced you were an alien, your bravery, your big heart and how capable you are, the way you took care of your mam. When she died and you were leaving everyone you loved and you saw me. Don't be scared, Marjorie, you said. You break my heart, kiddo. We've always been family one way or another, you and I.'

'I love you, Marj,' Juliet said, and she grinned that little imp grin that melted Marjorie's insides, 'now breathe – your face is going purple.'

Marjorie did as she was told. She inhaled and exhaled.

'Davey asked me to marry him,' Marjorie said. 'I said yes. He said we should tell you when you were happy. So I'm telling you now.'

'We're going to be the Hayes family,' Juliet said.

'Yeah,' Marjorie said.

'Sunday roasts.' Juliet chuckled, and Marjorie nodded with a smile.

She couldn't speak because the little bastard was trying to take her stomach with him or her, she wasn't sure which. She'd refused to find out the sex. She'd wanted a surprise. She was surprised, this kind of pain was profoundly surprising. She had an image of a baby wearing her stomach and/or bowel as a rucksack. *Holy Saint Jesus.* Juliet was rubbing her back, down low, good pressure. *Oh that's good. That's really good.* 'We're going to deal with Trevor, you and I,' she said, and Juliet stopped rubbing. *Oh God, don't stop.*

'OK,' Juliet said. 'I never have to see him again.'

'Never.' *Please, please rub my back.*

'I never have to speak about him.'

'Except to a therapist.'

'I will if you will,' Juliet said, and Marjorie sighed and nodded. It was time to face that very old demon. An inconvenient time, but time it was.

'Deal,' she said. 'Now for fuck's sake, start rubbing.'

Juliet laughed. 'That's what Ma used to say.'

'Who loves you, Juliet?' she said, and Juliet grinned.

'Marjorie does,' she said.

Davey hit the room like a tornado, swinging both bags high in the air. 'I knew I'd be killed if I arrived without them.'

He knew her so well, despite all their years apart. He was here, they were a family and with the next violent contraction she faced her fears and let go.

466

Chapter Eighty-Eight

Jack

THE CAR RAN OUT of petrol on the James Larkin Road. The petrol dial had been broken for a while; Jack kept telling himself he'd have it fixed, but then he'd forget until the next time he ran out of petrol. He usually kept a can in the boot but he'd used that the previous Friday, when he ran out on the way back from a game of bowls in Greystones and he'd forgotten to replace it.

'I'll kill you,' Molly said.

'Ah now, Molls, calm down, we're grand.'

'We're in the middle of the bleedin' road,' she said, pointing out the obvious. He was busy opening the boot and pulling apart a cardboard box he kept an array of dry clothing in: woolly hats, gloves, extra-warm jumpers, a cardigan and some long johns. They all went flying, some landing on the ground. Molly picked up the long johns. 'What are ya doing?' she said.

'Have you a pen?' he asked.

'No,' she said, following him round to the front passenger side of the car. She watched as he riffled through the glove box.

'Lipstick?' he said, coming up empty. She checked her handbag and pulled out a red lipstick.

'That will do nicely,' he said, and he placed the cardboard on the bonnet of the car and started writing in red lipstick.

So very sorry, the car ran out of petrol and we are having a baby. We are on the run. Please forgive us for any inconvenience.
Jack Hayes

He added his phone number and placed the sign in the windscreen. Molly looked at it and shook her head.

'We're having a baby?'

'We are, Molls,' he said, and he giggled to himself before launching himself onto the road and screaming 'Taxi!' at a man in a black cab.

They were in the car when Davey rang Jack's phone. He answered it with the words 'Jack Hayes', expecting a policeman or a clamper to be calling.

'I know who you are, Da,' Davey said, and Jack clicked his fingers at Molly. 'It's Davey. Hello, Davey, how goes it?'

'She's in bits, Da.'

'Ah yeah, that's the way of it, son, your mammy kicked me in the face when I delivered Rabbit.'

Davey had heard the story many times. 'Vera refuses to get a taxi, she's nervous on her own.'

'No problem, son, we'll swing by on our way.'

'They don't really like everyone being here,' Davey said, and Molly grabbed the phone. 'Tough shit, they can't stop us from grabbing a bite in the canteen.'

'She could be a while, Ma,' Davey said.

'I know, son, and we'll be there.'

468

'I won't stop you,' he said, and she could hear the smile in his voice. 'Juliet can't stay in the room when she's pushing and I don't want her on her own.'

'Never,' Molly said, and Davey hung up. 'What's Vera Shaw going there for?' she said to Jack.

'She's Marjorie's mother,' Jack said.

'Oh is she? Has anyone told her that?'

'Ah now, Molls, don't start,' he said, and he gave the driver the woman's address before grabbing her hand and squeezing it.

'We're having a baby, Molls,' he said, and his wife nodded and closed her eyes. 'This time one year, nine months and eight days ago, who would have thought that?'

She raised her arms and stamped her feet. 'Amen.'

Chapter Eighty-Nine

Molly

JACK BANGED ON VERA'S front door while Molly waited in the taxi with the driver who tapped his fingers on his steering wheel. Music was playing faintly in the background; he tapped in time. He had rhythm. No sign of Vera. Jack looked in the window and pounded again before walking back to the car.

'She won't open the door. I know she's there, I hear her tapping that stick of hers,' he said.

'I'll shove that stick up her—'

'Ah now, Molly.'

'Excuse me, love,' she said to the taxi driver. 'I won't be long.' She got out of the car and Jack got back in.

'Better leave the ladies to it,' he said to the taxi driver, who was craning his neck to see what would come next. Molly marched up to the door and opened the letterbox.

'Vera Shaw, open this door or I will pick up that stupid-looking oversized garden gnome of yours and I will fuck it through your front window.' She waited for a second or two before hearing Vera's heavy steps and the clicking of her stick on the tiled hall floor. She opened the door a crack.

'You were always very aggressive,' she said.

'And you were always unreliable,' Molly said.

'She doesn't need me there,' Vera said.

'You're right, she doesn't, but she asked for you,' Molly said, pushing her way past Vera. She moved towards the coat rack, picked out a coat and threw it at Vera. 'Put that on, it's freezing out there.'

'I can't,' Vera said.

'What is wrong with you?' Molly said.

Tears rolled down Vera's face. 'What if it goes wrong?'

'Then we'll be there,' Molly said.

'I couldn't go through that, not again,' Vera said.

Molly calmed herself and spoke in a gentle tone. 'It's not like it was – they won't do to her what they did to you, Vera.'

Vera nodded. 'You're a good mother, Molly.'

'Thank you.'

'A terrible person, but a good mother,' Vera said.

'Not as terrible as you, Vera, surely.'

Vera nodded to herself. 'At least I'm not a criminal,' she said as she put on her coat.

Molly smiled. 'Ready to become a grandmother?' she asked, and tears flowed from Vera's eyes.

'I am.'

Molly opened the door and followed Vera outside.

'Try and make a better go of things this time round, Vera.'

Vera nodded. 'Noted,' she said, before getting into the front seat of the taxi. Molly sat in the back alongside Jack.

'Onwards, driver.'

The driver saluted her. 'Will do,' he said, and once more they were off.

Chapter Ninety

Grace

RYAN, BERNARD AND JEFF refused to allow Grace to leave the house without them. 'We're coming too,' Bernard said.

'I'm not even supposed to be there,' Grace said.

'Yeah well, we were there for all the shite stuff when Rabbit was dying, we want to be there for the good stuff,' Ryan said.

'And there's no food in the house,' Jeff pointed out.

'Right, text your brother where we are and get in the car,' Grace said, and Jeff pulled out his phone and had the text sent before she'd finished the sentence.

She rang Lenny from the car. He was on the golf course so she left a message. 'Marj is in labour.' Then she remembered he never listened to messages, so she had Jeffrey text him the same message including that she and the kids were in the hospital and asking him to ensure he ate at the golf club.

They were initially denied entry to the hospital, but Grace was well used to security people in hospitals telling her what to do.

'We've business in the canteen.'

'Excuse me?'

'Is the canteen out of bounds?'

'No.'

'Well, then.'

'You're not allowed on the ward.'

'It's a good thing we're going to the canteen,' she said before he let her pass, and then she turned back. 'Where is the canteen?' she asked. He pointed the way and she thanked him and marched on, her boys following closely. Jack, Molly and Vera were already there, and so was Juliet. She jumped up and down as soon as she saw Grace and the boys.

'The baby's coming – I was there when the waters broke.'

'No way?' Bernard said.

'All over the carpet in the furniture shop,' she said.

'Mad,' Jeff said.

'Who are you?' Bernard asked Vera.

'I'm Marjorie's mother.'

'Marjorie has a mother?' Ryan said, and Grace kicked him. 'She can see you kicking me,' Ryan said.

'Force of habit,' Grace mumbled.

'It's all right,' Vera said.

'Hiya, Mrs Shaw,' Grace said.

'Hello, Grace, I'm sorry for all your troubles.'

Grace suddenly felt a little overwhelmed. 'Thank you.'

'If you are half as strong-willed as your mammy, you'll sail through.'

'I know,' she said. 'Thanks.' She handed Bernard some money. 'Go feed yourselves. Juliet, eat something.'

Juliet nodded. 'I'm starving.'

'That's right. Good girl, you eat with the boys,' Molly said. Everyone noticed the change in her, like the curtains had been drawn and finally daylight had streamed in.

'Funny old world,' Molly said, watching her grandchildren queue up at the counter, chatting together and laughing easily.

Grace turned to her dad. 'All right, Da?' she said, and he smiled her way.

'Better than all right, Gracie.'

'I hope she doesn't take too long – they won't keep this place open all night,' Grace said, looking around.

'Then we'll wait in the hotel around the corner till it's done,' Molly said.

Vera was feeling uncomfortable around so many Hayeses. 'I'll stay for an hour, maybe. I'll find my own way home.'

'Not a chance,' Jack said.

'Excuse me?'

'We'll be going home together when the child is delivered,' Molly said decisively.

'That's the Hayes way,' Jack said. 'We did it for all of Grace's.'

'I'm not a Hayes,' Vera said.

'Maybe not, but you're family now,' Molly said, and Grace watched poor Vera wilt a little as she absorbed that sobering information. Ryan and Bernard wrestled for the fifty-euro note, with Juliet on Ryan's back and Jeff on Bernard's, much to the annoyance of the adults in the queue. Grace grabbed a chair and sat down.

'I'm betting a tenner it's a girl – who's in?' she said, and took some bets.

Chapter Ninety-One

Davey

THE MIDWIFE, ANNETTE, A woman in her mid-fifties, was yelling 'Push!' Marjorie was pushing and squeezing Davey's hand so tight he thought his fingers might break. She was really scared, and she was trying so hard to be brave, he could tell. Annette, a tiny woman with big hands for catching babies – at least that was how she introduced herself – was at the business end.

'Any minute now, Marjorie, just wait for that next contraction,' she said, and Marjorie waited and panted and finally let go of his fingers and she looked at him, wild eyed and fearful.

'It's going to be OK, isn't it, Davey?'

'It's going to be great.'

'You're not going to leave us, are you?'

'Of course not.'

'I mean, you can leave me if you want, I'll understand, but you won't leave the baby, will you?'

He leaned down to her and placed his hand on his forehead.

'I will never abandon my child and I would never abandon you.'

'You can't go back to America, Davey.'

'I'm going nowhere. We've just bought a house, we're getting married.'

'My parents bought a house, they got married.'

'I'm not your dad.'

'I know.'

'I'll never be like him, me ma would kill me.'

'She would.' Marjorie cried and laughed a little, her nose ran and she wiped it with her arm.

'Friends first,' she said, and she held out her hand and he twisted his little finger around hers.

'Friends always.' Then a contraction came and she nearly ripped his little finger off. 'Holy fuck!' he shouted.

'Holy Saint Jesus!' she cried, and she looked over at Annette. 'We're having a baby,' she said, and Annette nodded.

'I see that,' she said, looking at the head crowning Marjorie's nethers. 'We're having it now.'

Davey watched as Marjorie's eyes bulged in her head and her face reddened and large veins popped in her neck.

'Push, Marjorie, push,' Annette said.

If she pushes any more she'll fucking explode.

'PUSH.'

'Holy Saint Jesus,' Marjorie roared as the baby tunnelled through her and into the world. Annette raised the child up in her large hands, covered in blood and vernix, with a long white-and-purple blood vein attaching it to its mother. It wasn't pretty, but it was spectacular. She rubbed the baby and the baby cried and Davey didn't know it then but he was crying too, just like the baby, tears and snot and sobs, real unadulterated sobs.

'It's a boy,' Annette said, and he turned bleary-eyed towards Marjorie, who seemed to be in shock.

'It's a boy,' he said.

'A boy? We have a boy?' she said.

'A boy,' he repeated, and then they were hugging and he could feel his heart rip but it wasn't breaking, it was expanding. Annette cleaned down their boy and cut the cord. She wrapped him in one of the blankets that came from the hospital bag and handed him to Davey. 'Take your son to his mother,' she said.

He looked at his little face, his tiny button nose, his soft, full cheeks, his rosebud lips, his dark curly hair, and when he opened his dark blue eyes he stared right up at his da and he struggled against the cotton wrap to stretch his arms.

'Wow,' he said. 'Oh, wow.'

Annette helped Marjorie to sit up. Davey placed the baby in her arms. They both just stared. Marjorie still had the placenta to deliver and was too blissed out or drugged up to pay attention to the small woman tugging on the placenta dangling between her legs.

Davey and Marjorie had discussed names for the child, both boys and girls. They liked Amber for a girl; they'd discussed Mia, too. It was Rabbit's given name and, although beautiful, it went unused for most of her life. They decided against it. Rabbit was Rabbit, she was never Mia and there was only one Rabbit. They liked Jack for a boy, after Davey's father. It was a strong name. He was a good man. Davey liked the name Cody but Marjorie explained it was a shit name and he'd spent too much time in the States. They went into hospital undecided. Marjorie looked from her little boy to Davey.

'What's his name?'

'After seeing what I've just seen, it's your call,' he said, and she nodded.

'Johnny it is, then.'

'Really?' he said, and he was blubbing again. 'Sorry, so sorry, don't know what's going on here.'

The placenta was ready to deliver and Johnny needed to be checked.

'Why don't you go and tell your family so they can give us back our canteen?' Annette said.

He kissed Marjorie on the forehead. 'You did good, Marj,' he said, and he skipped out of the room like a leprechaun on crack. He danced into the canteen and his family were all waiting, along with Francie and Jay. Francie was holding cigars, Jay had a bottle of Jack Daniel's.

Molly stood. 'Well?'

'It's a little boy,' he said.

'All fine?' Molly asked.

'Perfect,' he said.

Molly bent over and slapped her thigh. 'Well now. Isn't that something?'

Everyone gathered round and he was hugging them and kissing them and he felt like he might just be the happiest man in the world. Jack was crying, Grace was crying, the kids were all high-fiving.

Vera sat still and alone amongst the Hayes throng. Davey moved towards her.

'Thanks for coming, Vera.'

'What's his name?' she asked, and everyone was suddenly quiet.

'We're calling him Johnny,' Davey said.

'That's a lovely name,' Vera said, and he heard an explosion of sound – happy, clapping sounds.

'Johnny Hayes,' Jack said. 'Well now, if that isn't a rock star, I don't know what is.'

'I hope not, Da.'

'So you named the child after the unluckiest man in the world,' Molly said, and the room fell silent as she sighed deeply and then held her son by his ears. 'Time for Johnny's luck to change then, isn't it, son?' She beamed and nodded to herself. Everyone else sighed with relief.

Francie grabbed him into a headlock. 'She's right, ya mad fuck.'

'Johnny'd love that,' Jay said. 'He'd fucking love it.'

Francie kissed the top of Davey's head before letting him go. 'Nice one, DB, nicely done.'

Davey found Juliet standing beside Ryan. 'Johnny?' she said.

'What do you think?'

'I think it's cool.'

'We want you to meet him first.'

'Yeah?'

'It's not just you and me anymore, kiddo.'

'Good,' she said, and her eyes were damp but she was determined to smile through. He took her by the hand and brought her into the room where Marjorie was holding her little boy in her arms. She looked up and grinned at Juliet.

'Juliet, meet Johnny.'

'Call me Bunny. Johnny and Bunny,' Juliet said.

Davey nodded. 'Bunny and Johnny.'

She grinned.

I wish you were here, Rabbit.

I'm here.

Chapter Ninety-Two

Juliet

'BABIES ARE BRILLIANT, AREN'T they, Gran?' Juliet said to her gran, who was holding Johnny and gazing at him.

'They are,' she said, touching his little button nose with her finger. 'I can see your ma in him.'

'Me too,' Marjorie said.

'His jawline,' Molly said.

'That stare.'

Molly grinned. 'She could freeze balls with that stare.'

'Ma!' Davey said, and everyone laughed.

Vera cried when she held him. 'Perfect, just perfect.'

Grace, Lenny and the boys only stayed long enough to say hello and see the baby. The nurse was quite insistent that there were to be only two in the room at any given time. At one point there were eleven.

'He's a little wonder,' Grace said, and she sobbed all over the beautiful baby. When it was time for them to go Ryan pulled Juliet aside.

'You want to hang with me and some of the nerd squad on Saturday afternoon?'

'Is it all boys?'

'Girls too, one is Chinese but she has a thick Dublin accent.'

'OK.'

'I'll text you.'

'Ryan.'

'What.'

'Thanks.'

'For what?'

'Being my friend.'

'Sap,' he said, and he followed his family to the car.

It's going to be OK, Ma, it's finally going to be OK.

Epilogue

IT WAS THE SECOND anniversary of Rabbit's death and, below a big blue sky the whole family, the lads from the bands, Vera Shaw and Karen Faye stood around Johnny Faye and Rabbit Hayes's brand-new gravestone. The gravediggers had dug a small hole and covered it over with a piece of fake grass; Jack lifted it and placed the urn now filled with all of Rabbit's ashes into the freshly dug earth. The family had come together the previous night to pour the contents of their heart-shaped boxes into the urn. Juliet wanted her mother kept together and all in one place. Father Frank stood with the family, Francie, Jay, Kev and Louis and they said a prayer for Johnny the believer and played a song on Davey's phone for Rabbit the atheist. It was the song Johnny had written for her, and his voice rang out over their new joint gravestone, heralding their eternal love. On the gravestone was the black and white photo of Johnny sitting on the edge of the stage and Rabbit staring up at him from the sound desk below, eyes locked, slightly smiling, lost in their own time and world. It was a beautiful photograph, which encapsulated them and their story. Underneath the photo were Johnny's words:

> Dear God, if my end be suffering, open that door, let me fly in and when her time has come to land, dear God, allow me to grab her hand.

Followed by the words:

'By Johnny Faye, written for the love of his life, Rabbit Hayes.'

Their birth and death dates lay underneath Johnny's poem. Juliet was charmed. Rabbit was exactly where she was supposed to be, and when the deed was done, before anyone made a move to leave for the pub, Marjorie whispered, 'Who loves ya, Rabbit Hayes?'

Molly squeezed her shoulder and said, 'We do.'

If you enjoyed *Below the Big Blue Sky* – and I hope you did – if you are an Instagram user you can find me there, too.

This is me, @mcpartlin.anna

I can't promise my posts will change or enhance your life in any way, but I'll do my best to make you smile once in a while. #Trying

Yours,

A McP. X

Acknowledgements

This book could not have been written without the help of Lisa Kirsch, Nurse Rebecca Canny, Detective Joe Griffin and Dr Nikki Sweeney. Thank you, Lisa, for your bravery and raw honesty. Thank you, Rebecca, for your work in the NHS and for giving me so much time and technical information. Thanks, Garda Joe Griffin, for walking me through an arrest and court case and finally, to Dr Nikki Sweeney, for talking to me about medicine and addiction services in prison.

A very special thanks and big love to my agent, Sheila Crowley. Thank you for your unwavering support, brilliant advice, patience and light. To all in Bonnier, Kate Parkin, Jane Harris, Georgia Murray and especially to my editor Margaret Stead, who added phenomenal value to this book: THANK YOU. It's an absolute joy working with you all.

Thanks to my friends and family for putting up with me.

Thanks to my husband for your kindness.

I love you all.